The Highest House

Become our fan on Facebook **facebook.com/idwpublishing**
Follow us on Twitter **@idwpublishing**
Subscribe to us on YouTube **youtube.com/idwpublishing**
See what's new on Tumblr **tumblr.idwpublishing.com**
Check us out on Instagram **instagram.com/idwpublishing**

COVER ART BY
YUKO SHIMIZU

PRODUCTION & DESIGN BY
ROBBIE ROBBINS

SERIES EDITORIAL ASSISTANT
ELIZABETH BREI

SERIES EDITOR
DENTON J. TIPTON

COLLECTION EDITORS
JUSTIN EISINGER AND
ALONZO SIMON

PUBLISHED BY
GREG GOLDSTEIN

ISBN: 978-1-68405-354-4
21 20 19 18   1 2 3 4

Originally published as THE HIGHEST HOUSE issues #1–6.

Greg Goldstein, President & Publisher
John Barber, Editor-in-Chief
Robbie Robbins, EVP/Sr. Art Director
Cara Morrison, Chief Financial Officer
Matthew Ruzicka, Chief Accounting Officer
Anita Frazier, SVP of Sales and Marketing
David Hedgecock, Associate Publisher
Jerry Bennington, VP of New Product Development
Lorelei Bunjes, VP of Digital Services
Justin Eisinger, Editorial Director, Graphic Novels & Collections
Eric Moss, Sr. Director, Licensing & Business Development

Ted Adams, IDW Founder

For international rights, please contact
licensing@idwpublishing.com

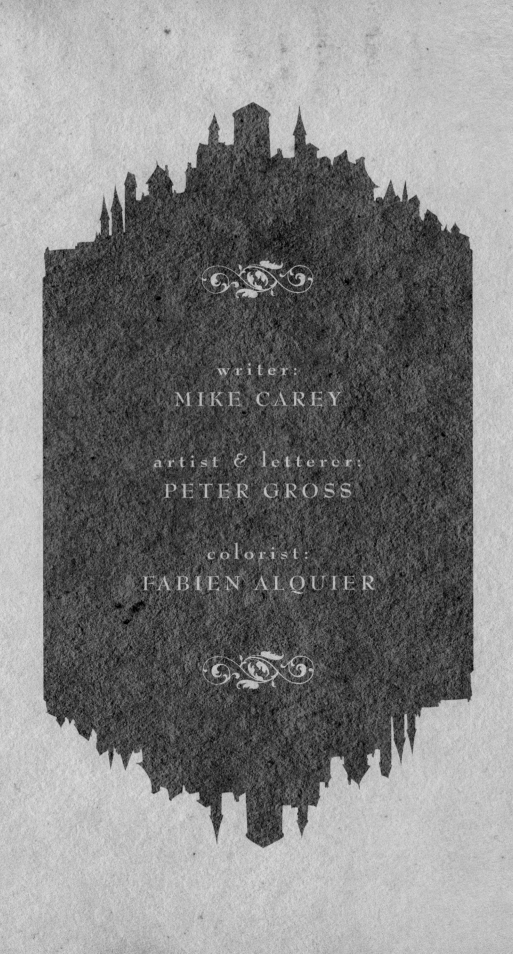

writer:
MIKE CAREY

artist & letterer:
PETER GROSS

colorist:
FABIEN ALQUIER

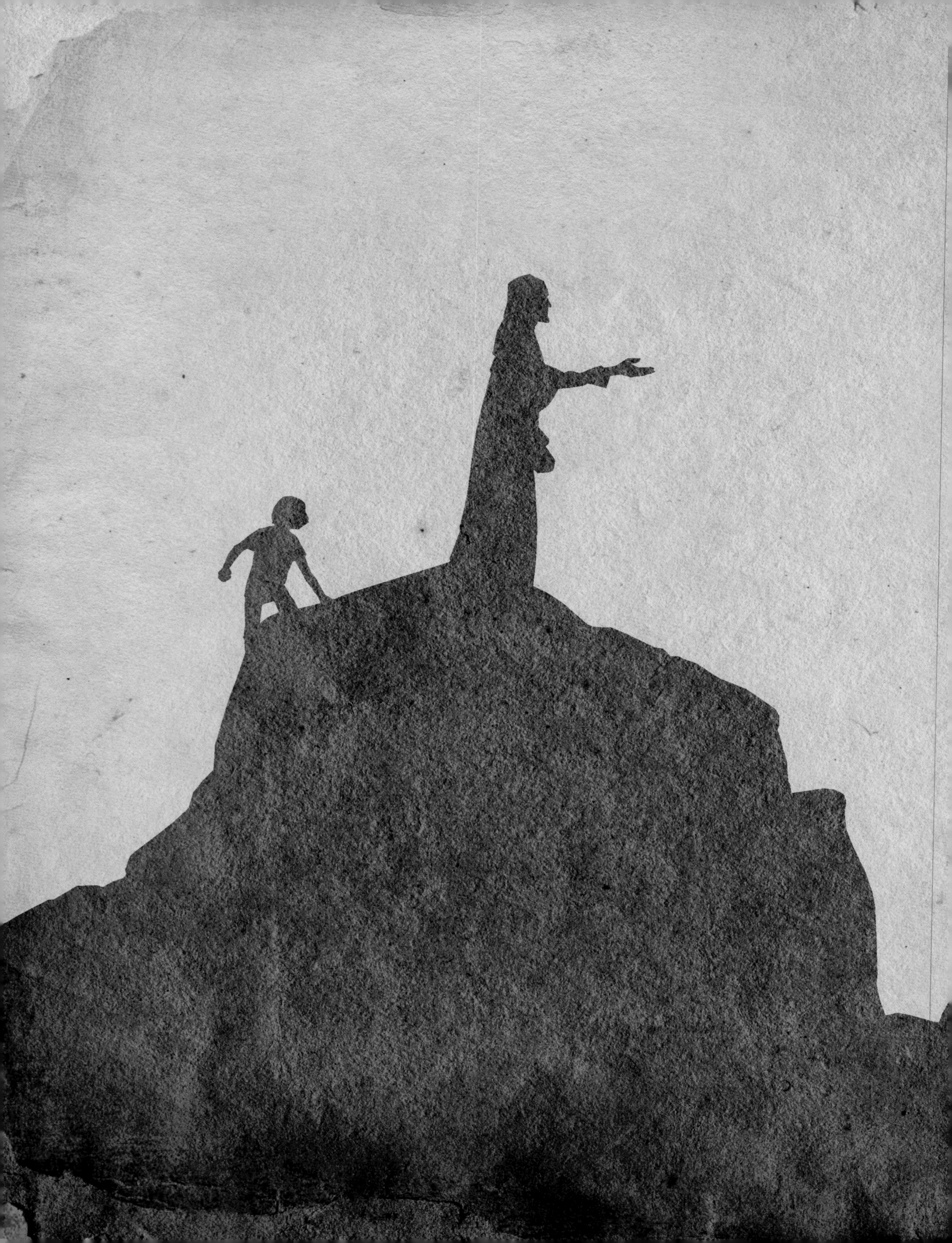

Chapter One

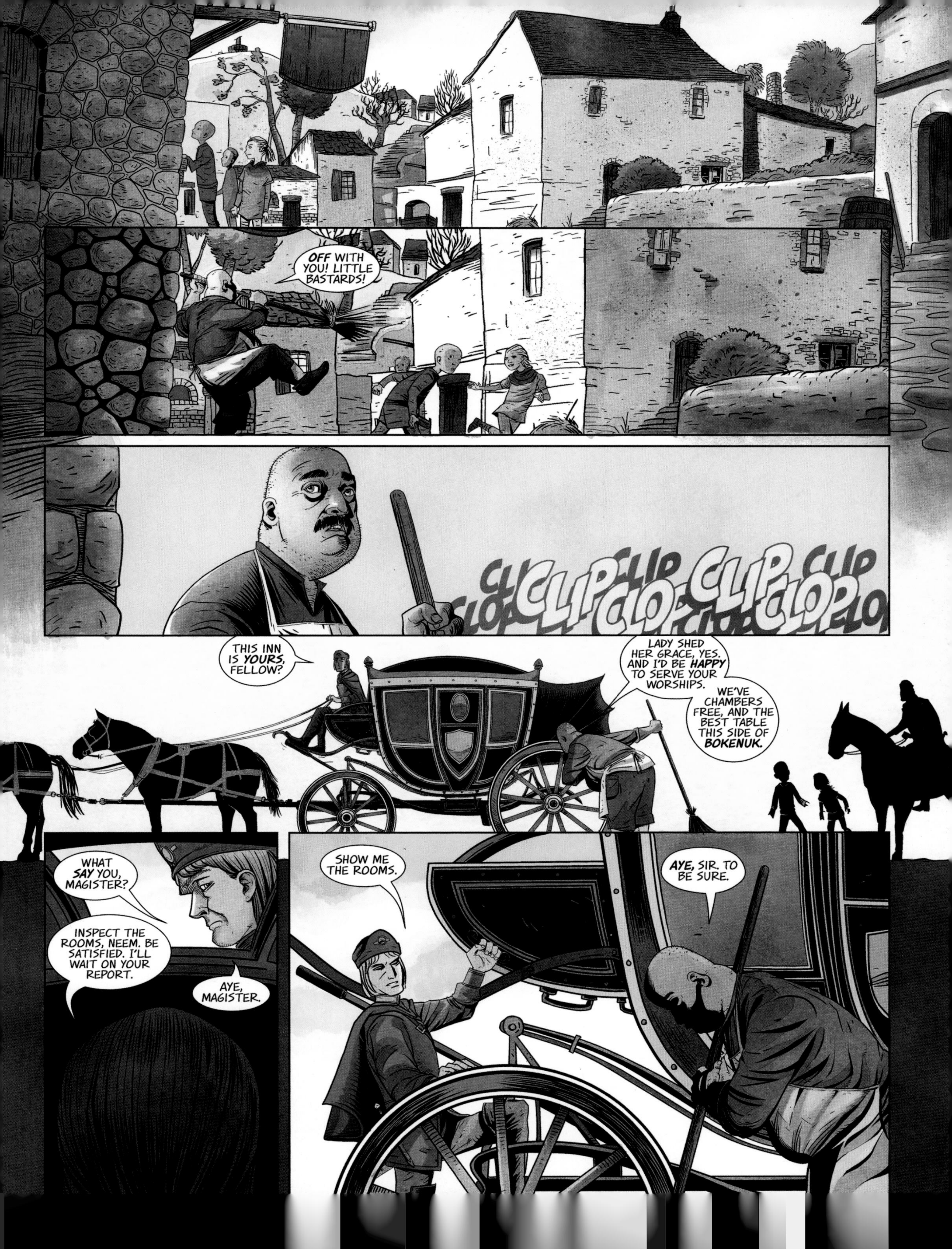
OFF WITH YOU! LITTLE BASTARDS!
CLIP CLOP CLIP CLOP CLIP CLOP CLIP CLOP
THIS INN IS YOURS, FELLOW?
LADY SHED HER GRACE, YES. AND I'D BE HAPPY TO SERVE YOUR WORSHIPS.
WE'VE CHAMBERS FREE, AND THE BEST TABLE THIS SIDE OF BOKENUK.
WHAT SAY YOU, MAGISTER?
INSPECT THE ROOMS, NEEM. BE SATISFIED. I'LL WAIT ON YOUR REPORT.
AYE, MAGISTER.
SHOW ME THE ROOMS.
AYE, SIR. TO BE SURE.

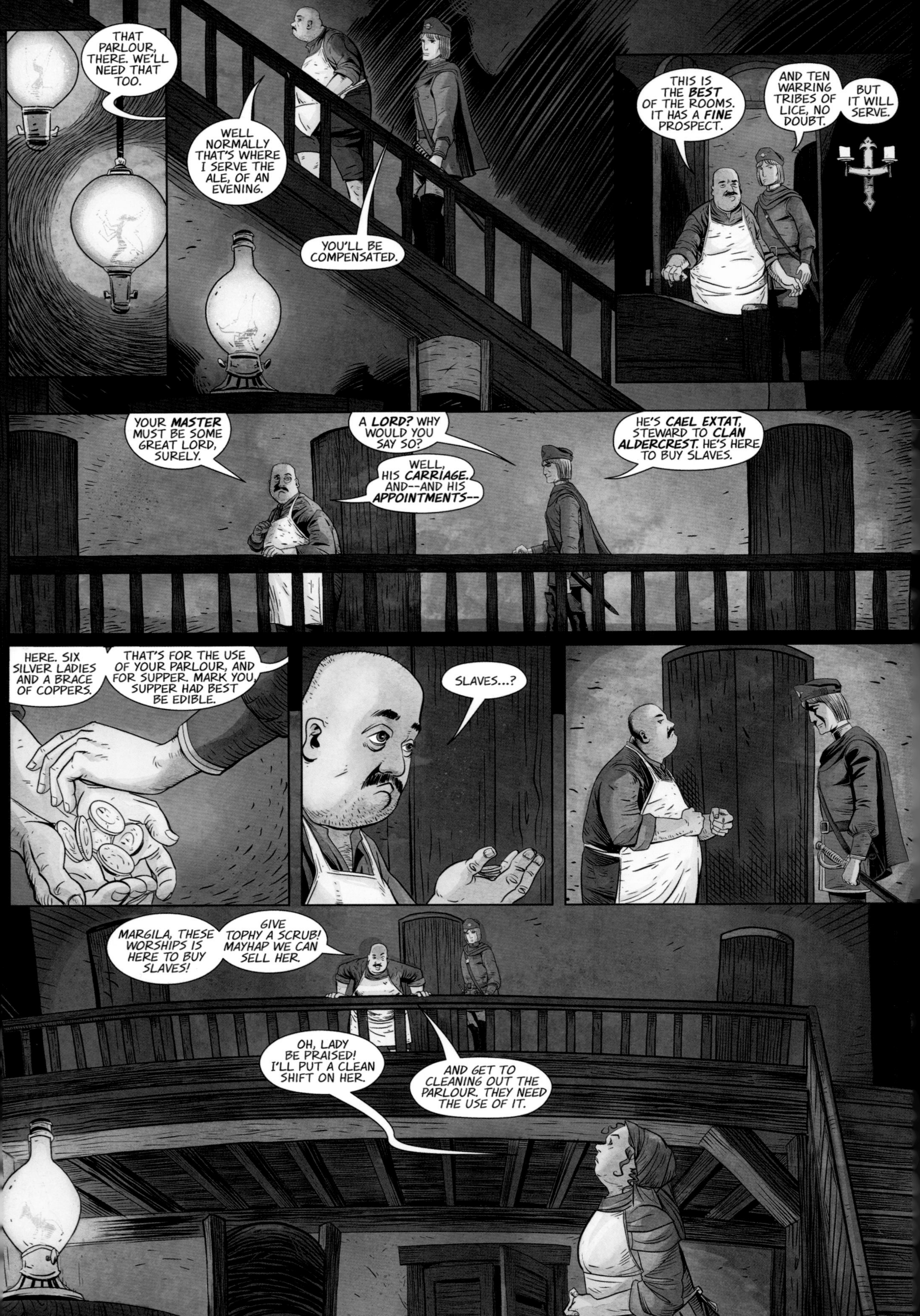
THAT PARLOUR, THERE. WE'LL NEED THAT TOO.
WELL NORMALLY THAT'S WHERE I SERVE THE ALE, OF AN EVENING.
YOU'LL BE COMPENSATED.
THIS IS THE BEST OF THE ROOMS. IT HAS A FINE PROSPECT.
AND TEN WARRING TRIBES OF LICE, NO DOUBT.
BUT IT WILL SERVE.
YOUR MASTER MUST BE SOME GREAT LORD, SURELY.
A LORD? WHY WOULD YOU SAY SO?
WELL, HIS CARRIAGE. AND--AND HIS APPOINTMENTS--
HE'S CAEL EXTAT, STEWARD TO CLAN ALDERCREST. HE'S HERE TO BUY SLAVES.
HERE. SIX SILVER LADIES AND A BRACE OF COPPERS.
THAT'S FOR THE USE OF YOUR PARLOUR, AND FOR SUPPER. MARK YOU, SUPPER HAD BEST BE EDIBLE.
SLAVES...?
MARGILA, THESE WORSHIPS IS HERE TO BUY SLAVES!
GIVE TOPHY A SCRUB! MAYHAP WE CAN SELL HER.
OH, LADY BE PRAISED! I'LL PUT A CLEAN SHIFT ON HER.
AND GET TO CLEANING OUT THE PARLOUR. THEY NEED THE USE OF IT.

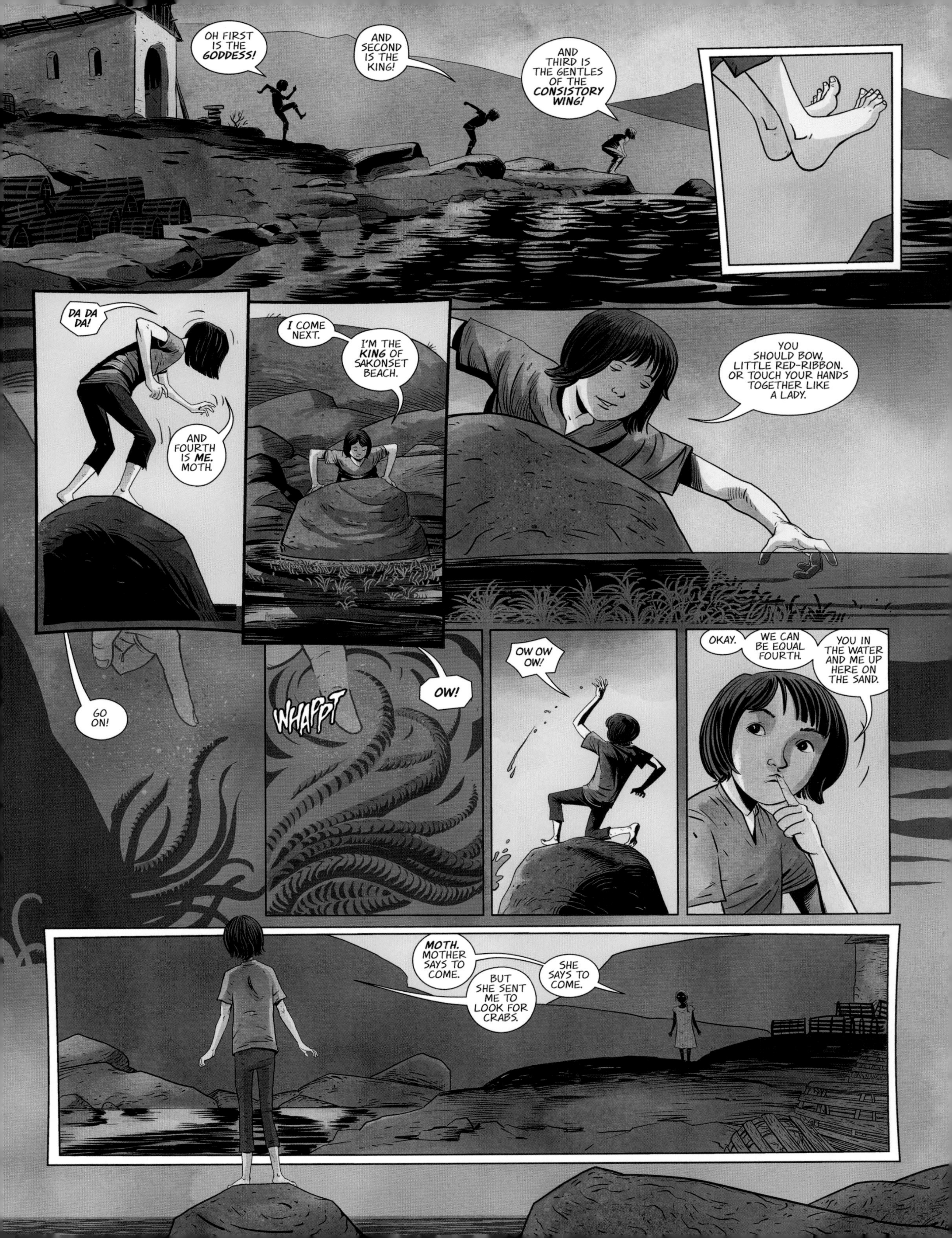

OH FIRST IS THE GODDESS!
AND SECOND IS THE KING!
AND THIRD IS THE GENTLES OF THE CONSISTORY WING!
DA DA DA!
AND FOURTH IS ME. MOTH.
I COME NEXT.
I'M THE KING OF SAKONSET BEACH.
YOU SHOULD BOW, LITTLE RED-RIBBON. OR TOUCH YOUR HANDS TOGETHER LIKE A LADY.
GO ON!
WHAPPT
OW!
OW OW OW!
OKAY.
WE CAN BE EQUAL FOURTH.
YOU IN THE WATER AND ME UP HERE ON THE SAND.
MOTH. MOTHER SAYS TO COME.
SHE SAYS TO COME.
BUT SHE SENT ME TO LOOK FOR CRABS.

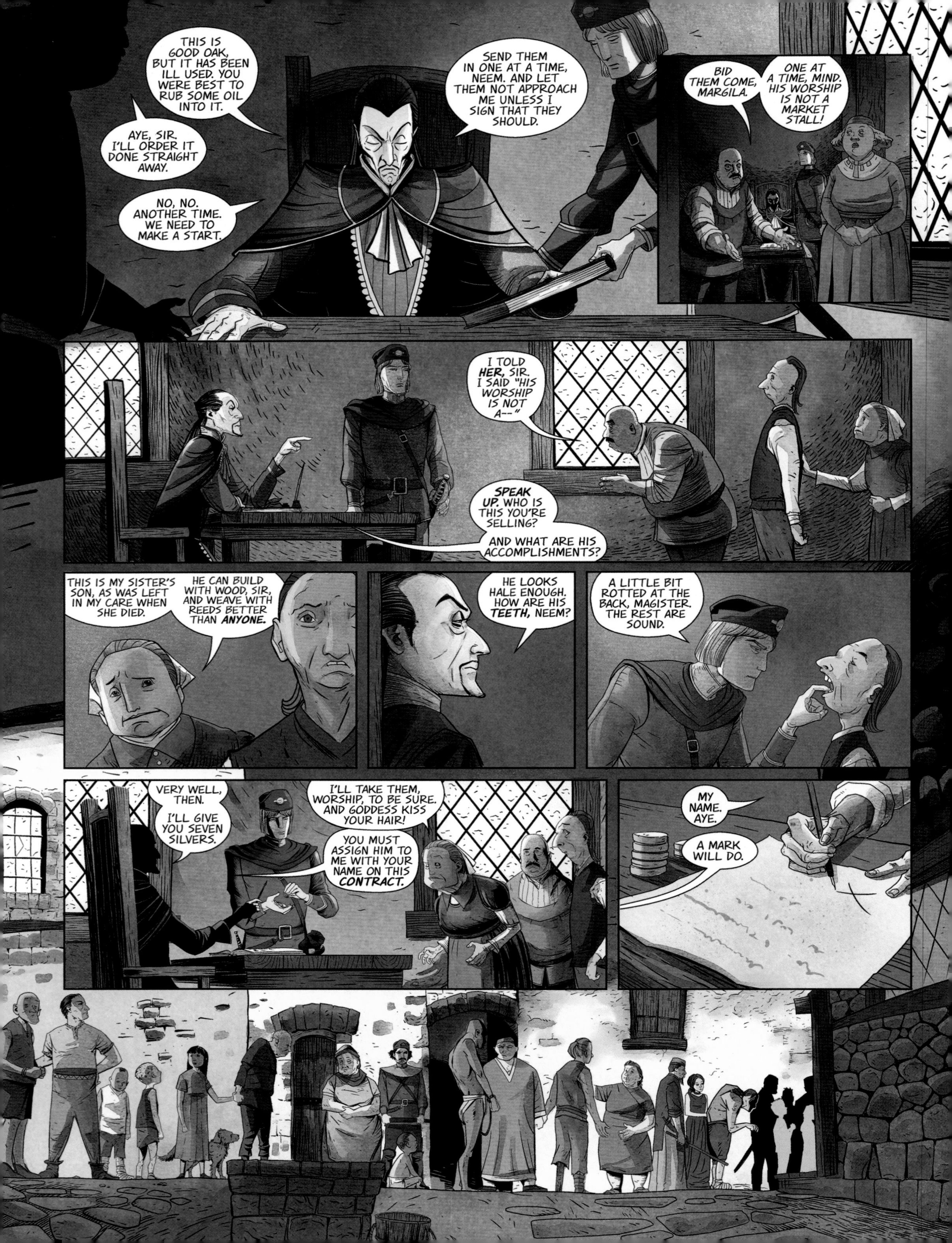
THIS IS GOOD OAK, BUT IT HAS BEEN ILL USED. YOU WERE BEST TO RUB SOME OIL INTO IT.
AYE, SIR. I'LL ORDER IT DONE STRAIGHT AWAY.
NO, NO. ANOTHER TIME. WE NEED TO MAKE A START.
SEND THEM IN ONE AT A TIME, NEEM. AND LET THEM NOT APPROACH ME UNLESS I SIGN THAT THEY SHOULD.
BID THEM COME, MARGILA.
ONE AT A TIME, MIND. HIS WORSHIP IS NOT A MARKET STALL!
I TOLD HER, SIR. I SAID "HIS WORSHIP IS NOT A--"
SPEAK UP. WHO IS THIS YOU'RE SELLING?
AND WHAT ARE HIS ACCOMPLISHMENTS?
THIS IS MY SISTER'S SON, AS WAS LEFT IN MY CARE WHEN SHE DIED.
HE CAN BUILD WITH WOOD, SIR, AND WEAVE WITH REEDS BETTER THAN ANYONE.
HE LOOKS HALE ENOUGH. HOW ARE HIS TEETH, NEEM?
A LITTLE BIT ROTTED AT THE BACK, MAGISTER. THE REST ARE SOUND.
VERY WELL, THEN.
I'LL GIVE YOU SEVEN SILVERS.
I'LL TAKE THEM, WORSHIP, TO BE SURE. AND GODDESS KISS YOUR HAIR!
YOU MUST ASSIGN HIM TO ME WITH YOUR NAME ON THIS CONTRACT.
MY NAME. AYE.
A MARK WILL DO.

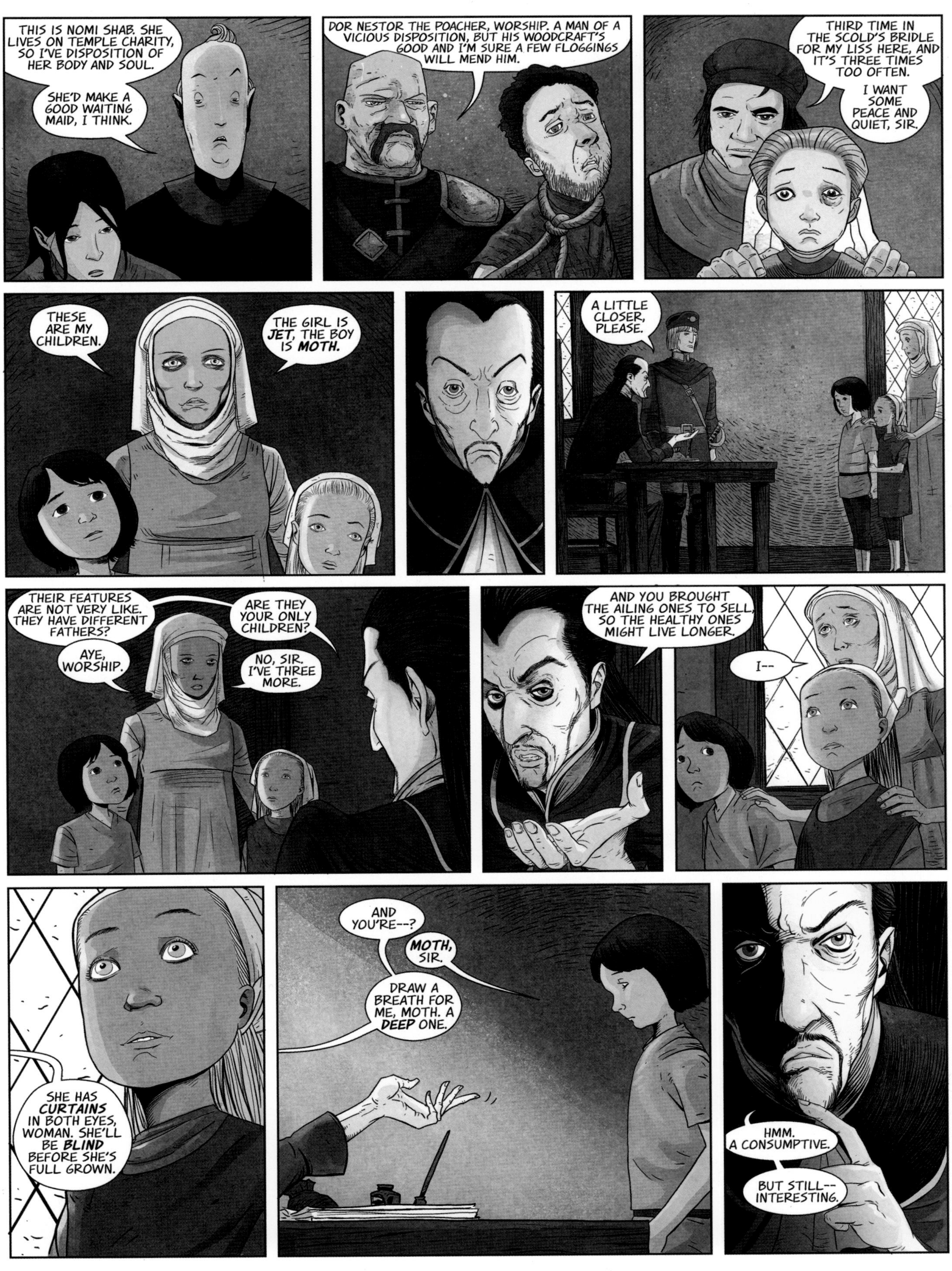
THIS IS NOMI SHAB. SHE LIVES ON TEMPLE CHARITY, SO I'VE DISPOSITION OF HER BODY AND SOUL.
SHE'D MAKE A GOOD WAITING MAID, I THINK.
DOR NESTOR THE POACHER, WORSHIP. A MAN OF A VICIOUS DISPOSITION, BUT HIS WOODCRAFT'S GOOD AND I'M SURE A FEW FLOGGINGS WILL MEND HIM.
THIRD TIME IN THE SCOLD'S BRIDLE FOR MY LISS HERE, AND IT'S THREE TIMES TOO OFTEN.
I WANT SOME PEACE AND QUIET, SIR.
THESE ARE MY CHILDREN.
THE GIRL IS JET, THE BOY IS MOTH.
A LITTLE CLOSER, PLEASE.
THEIR FEATURES ARE NOT VERY LIKE. THEY HAVE DIFFERENT FATHERS?
AYE, WORSHIP.
ARE THEY YOUR ONLY CHILDREN?
NO, SIR. I'VE THREE MORE.
AND YOU BROUGHT THE AILING ONES TO SELL, SO THE HEALTHY ONES MIGHT LIVE LONGER.
I--
SHE HAS CURTAINS IN BOTH EYES, WOMAN. SHE'LL BE BLIND BEFORE SHE'S FULL GROWN.
AND YOU'RE--?
MOTH, SIR.
DRAW A BREATH FOR ME, MOTH. A DEEP ONE.
HMM. A CONSUMPTIVE.
BUT STILL-- INTERESTING.

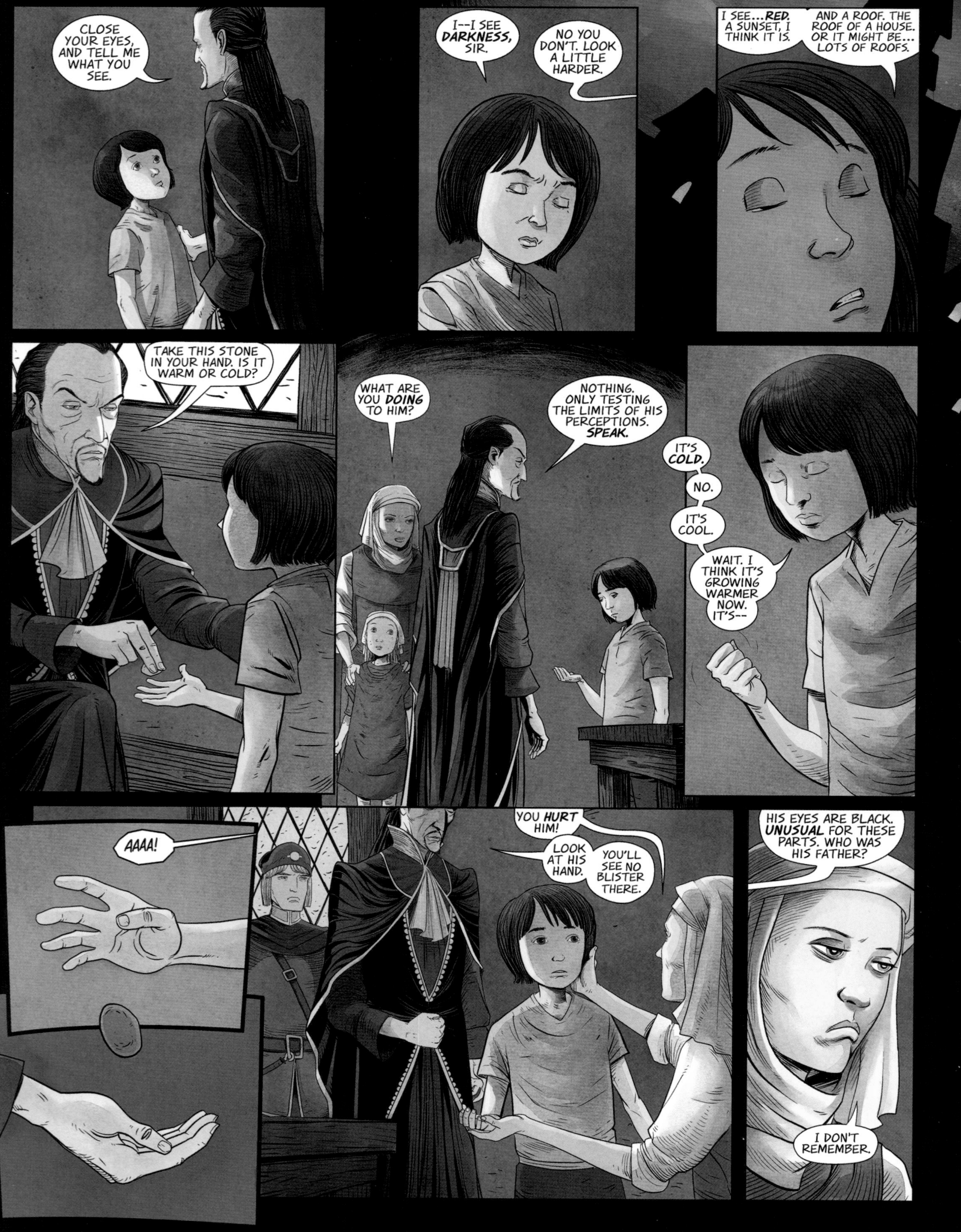
CLOSE YOUR EYES, AND TELL ME WHAT YOU SEE.
I--I SEE **DARKNESS,** SIR.
NO YOU DON'T. LOOK A LITTLE HARDER.
I SEE...**RED.** A SUNSET, I THINK IT IS.
AND A ROOF. THE ROOF OF A HOUSE. OR IT MIGHT BE... LOTS OF ROOFS.
TAKE THIS STONE IN YOUR HAND. IS IT WARM OR COLD?
WHAT ARE YOU **DOING** TO HIM?
NOTHING. ONLY TESTING THE LIMITS OF HIS PERCEPTIONS. **SPEAK.**
IT'S **COLD.**
NO.
IT'S COOL.
WAIT. I THINK IT'S GROWING WARMER NOW. IT'S--
AAAA!
YOU **HURT** HIM!
LOOK AT HIS HAND.
YOU'LL SEE NO BLISTER THERE.
HIS EYES ARE BLACK. **UNUSUAL** FOR THESE PARTS. WHO WAS HIS FATHER?
I DON'T REMEMBER.

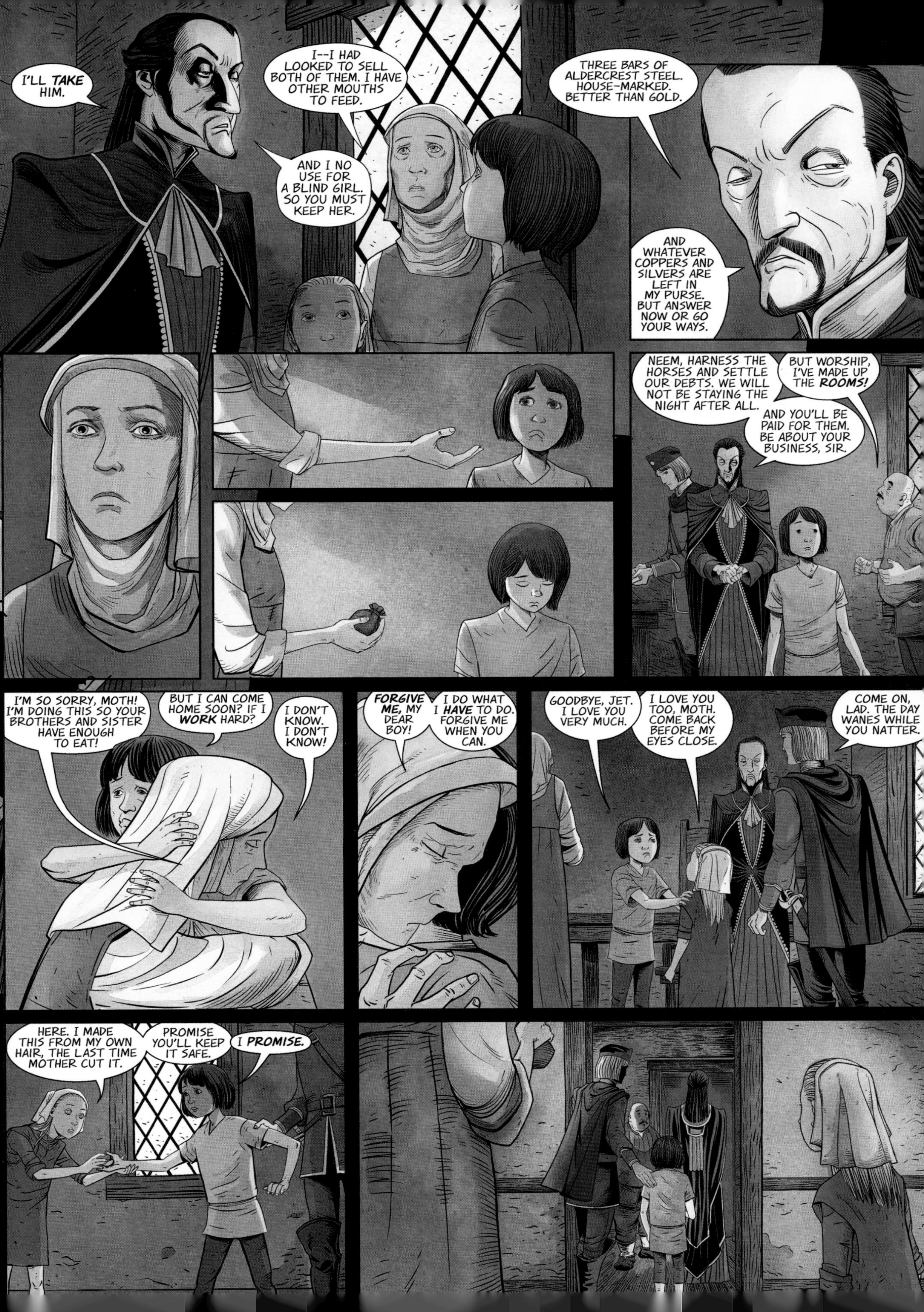
I'LL TAKE HIM.
I--I HAD LOOKED TO SELL BOTH OF THEM. I HAVE OTHER MOUTHS TO FEED.
AND I NO USE FOR A BLIND GIRL. SO YOU MUST KEEP HER.
THREE BARS OF ALDERCREST STEEL. HOUSE-MARKED. BETTER THAN GOLD.
AND WHATEVER COPPERS AND SILVERS ARE LEFT IN MY PURSE. BUT ANSWER NOW OR GO YOUR WAYS.
NEEM, HARNESS THE HORSES AND SETTLE OUR DEBTS. WE WILL NOT BE STAYING THE NIGHT AFTER ALL.
BUT WORSHIP, I'VE MADE UP THE ROOMS!
AND YOU'LL BE PAID FOR THEM. BE ABOUT YOUR BUSINESS, SIR.
I'M SO SORRY, MOTH! I'M DOING THIS SO YOUR BROTHERS AND SISTER HAVE ENOUGH TO EAT!
BUT I CAN COME HOME SOON? IF I WORK HARD?
I DON'T KNOW. I DON'T KNOW!
FORGIVE ME, MY DEAR BOY!
I DO WHAT I HAVE TO DO. FORGIVE ME WHEN YOU CAN.
GOODBYE, JET. I LOVE YOU VERY MUCH.
I LOVE YOU TOO, MOTH. COME BACK BEFORE MY EYES CLOSE.
COME ON, LAD. THE DAY WANES WHILE YOU NATTER.
HERE. I MADE THIS FROM MY OWN HAIR, THE LAST TIME MOTHER CUT IT.
PROMISE YOU'LL KEEP IT SAFE.
I PROMISE.

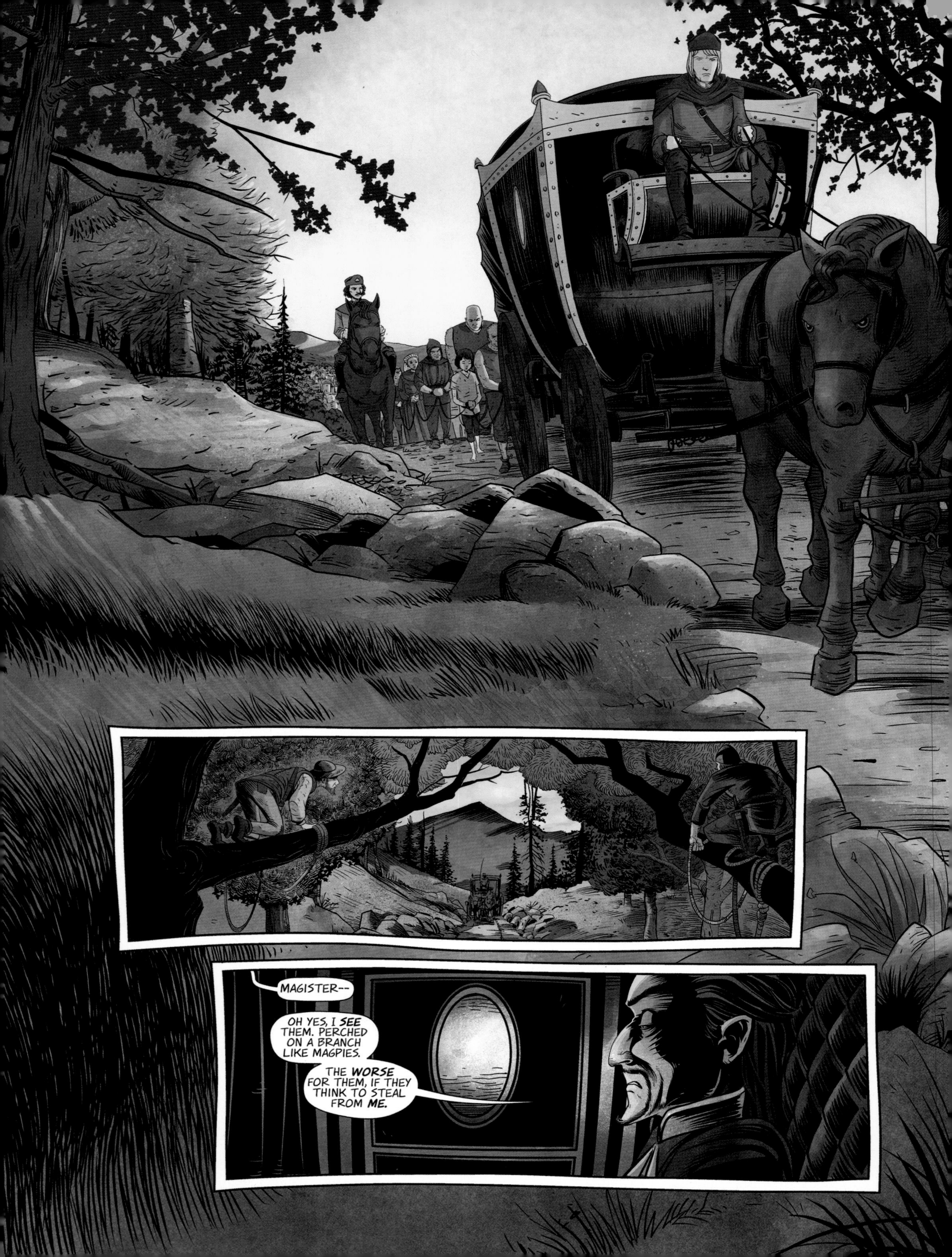
MAGISTER--
OH YES, I SEE THEM. PERCHED ON A BRANCH LIKE MAGPIES.
THE WORSE FOR THEM, IF THEY THINK TO STEAL FROM ME.

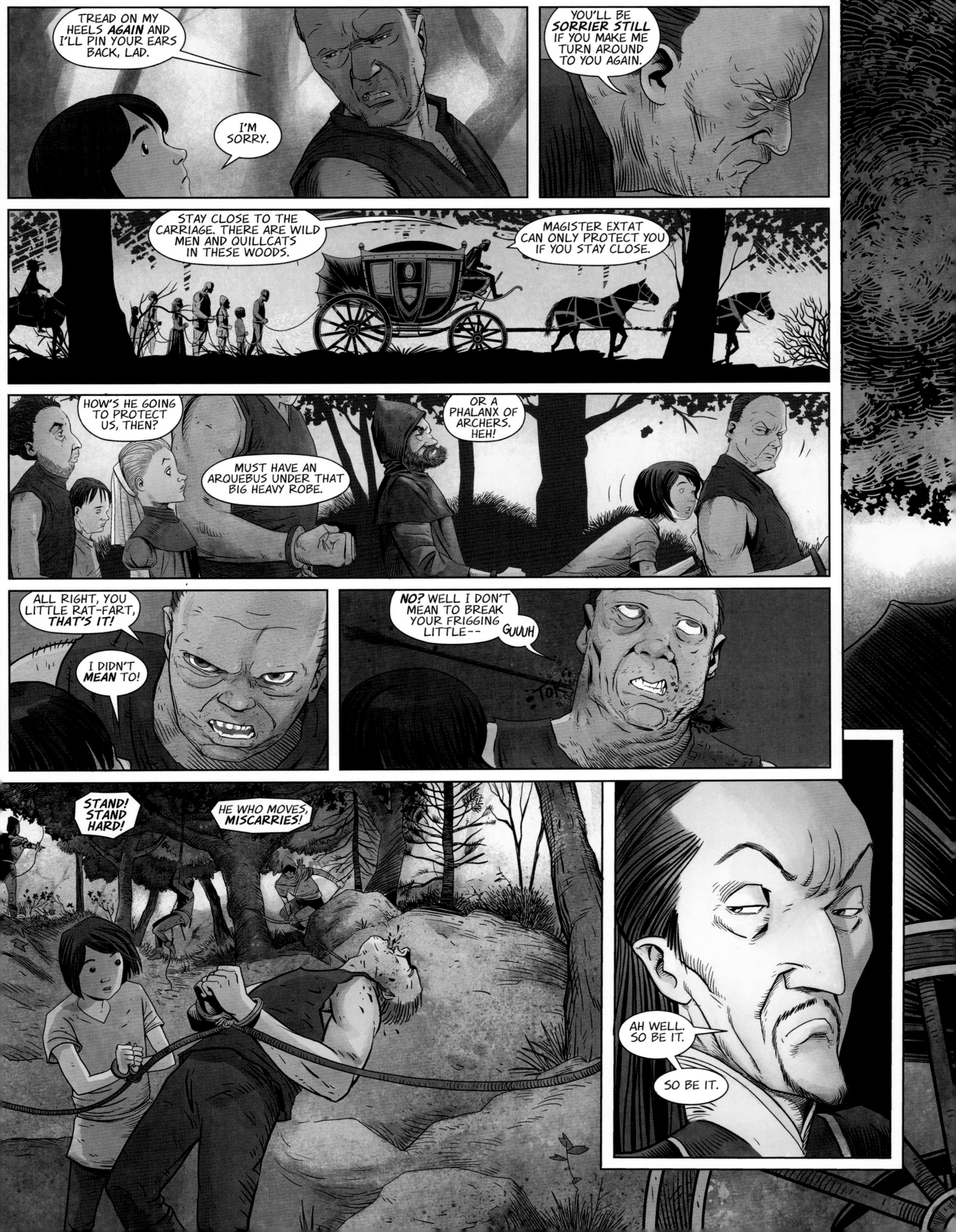
TREAD ON MY HEELS AGAIN AND I'LL PIN YOUR EARS BACK, LAD.
I'M SORRY.
YOU'LL BE SORRIER STILL IF YOU MAKE ME TURN AROUND TO YOU AGAIN.
STAY CLOSE TO THE CARRIAGE. THERE ARE WILD MEN AND QUILLCATS IN THESE WOODS.
MAGISTER EXTAT CAN ONLY PROTECT YOU IF YOU STAY CLOSE.
HOW'S HE GOING TO PROTECT US, THEN?
MUST HAVE AN ARQUEBUS UNDER THAT BIG HEAVY ROBE.
OR A PHALANX OF ARCHERS. HEH!
ALL RIGHT, YOU LITTLE RAT-FART, THAT'S IT!
I DIDN'T MEAN TO!
NO? WELL I DON'T MEAN TO BREAK YOUR FRIGGING LITTLE--
GUUUH
STAND! STAND HARD!
HE WHO MOVES, MISCARRIES!
AH WELL. SO BE IT.
SO BE IT.

HAND IT OVER, OR WE'LL GUT YOU.
LET US GO BY. WE'RE SIMPLE TRAVELLERS.
TRAVELLERS WITH BARS OF ALDERCREST IN YOUR PURSE.
THIS IS UNSEEMLY.
AND IT WILL STOP. NOW.
ORKRAM'S NAME! WHAT'S THIS?
I DON'T CARE WHAT IT IS. IT SHUTS ITS HOLE OR IT EATS MY BLADE.
THIS BLADE?
THIS BLADE IS A TOY.
A TOY?
LOOK AT IT. WORK-HARDENED IRON, NOT EVEN FIRED. HOW DO YOU KEEP IT STRAIGHT?
IT DOES ITS JOB, CULLY.
PROVE IT.
WHAT?
I SAID PROVE IT, YOU GRUNTING OAF.
ARE YOU DEAF AS WELL AS DULL-WITTED?
BY THE GODDESS'S CUNNY--
AHHRRR
SHRAKKT

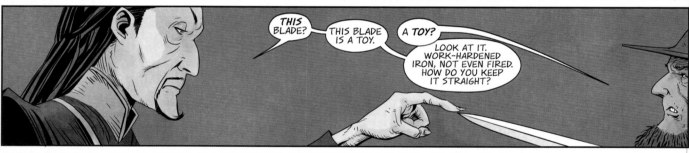

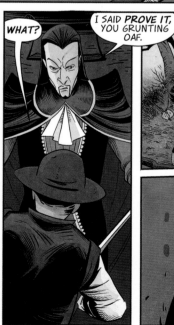

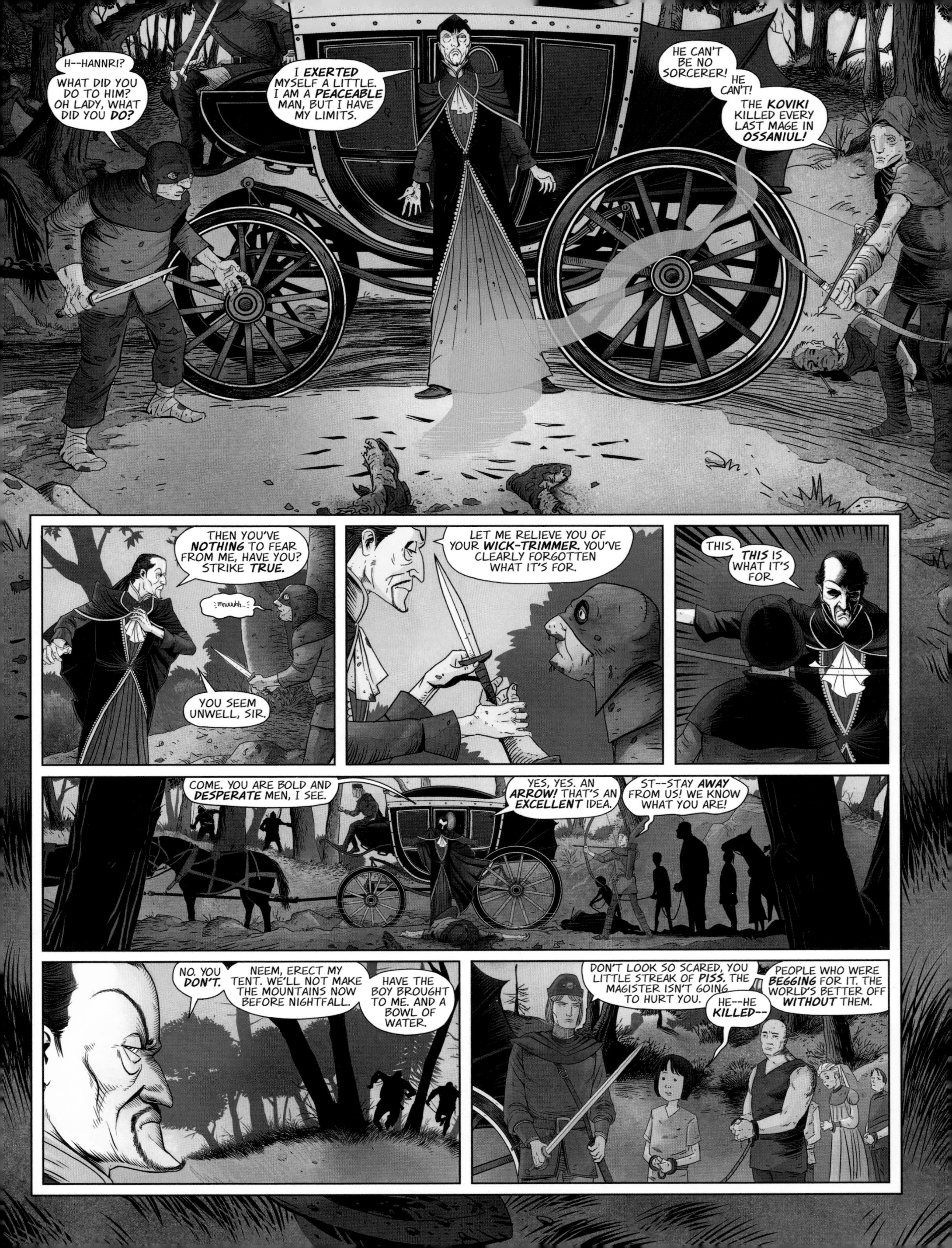

H--HANNRI?
WHAT DID YOU DO TO HIM? OH LADY, WHAT DID YOU DO?
I EXERTED MYSELF A LITTLE. I AM A PEACEABLE MAN, BUT I HAVE MY LIMITS.
HE CAN'T BE NO SORCERER!
HE CAN'T!
THE KOVIKI KILLED EVERY LAST MAGE IN OSSANIUL!
THEN YOU'VE NOTHING TO FEAR FROM ME, HAVE YOU? STRIKE TRUE.
mnuuuhh...
YOU SEEM UNWELL, SIR.
LET ME RELIEVE YOU OF YOUR WICK-TRIMMER. YOU'VE CLEARLY FORGOTTEN WHAT IT'S FOR.
THIS.
THIS IS WHAT IT'S FOR.
COME. YOU ARE BOLD AND DESPERATE MEN, I SEE.
YES, YES. AN ARROW! THAT'S AN EXCELLENT IDEA.
ST--STAY AWAY FROM US! WE KNOW WHAT YOU ARE!
NO. YOU DON'T.
NEEM, ERECT MY TENT. WE'LL NOT MAKE THE MOUNTAINS NOW BEFORE NIGHTFALL.
HAVE THE BOY BROUGHT TO ME. AND A BOWL OF WATER.
DON'T LOOK SO SCARED, YOU LITTLE STREAK OF PISS. THE MAGISTER ISN'T GOING TO HURT YOU.
HE--HE KILLED--
PEOPLE WHO WERE BEGGING FOR IT. THE WORLD'S BETTER OFF WITHOUT THEM.

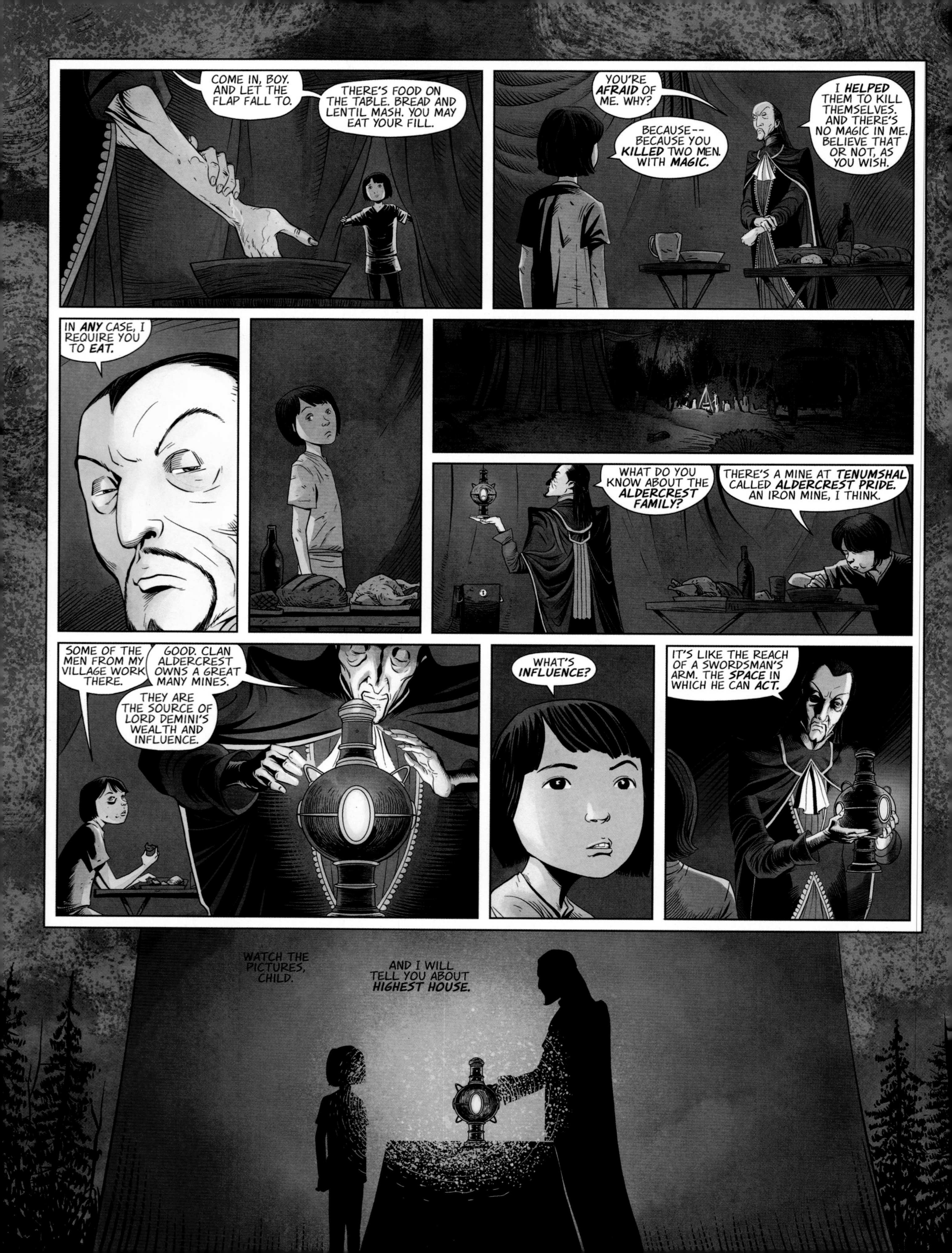

COME IN, BOY. AND LET THE FLAP FALL TO.
THERE'S FOOD ON THE TABLE. BREAD AND LENTIL MASH. YOU MAY EAT YOUR FILL.
YOU'RE AFRAID OF ME. WHY?
BECAUSE-- BECAUSE YOU KILLED TWO MEN. WITH MAGIC.
I HELPED THEM TO KILL THEMSELVES. AND THERE'S NO MAGIC IN ME. BELIEVE THAT OR NOT, AS YOU WISH.
IN ANY CASE, I REQUIRE YOU TO EAT.
WHAT DO YOU KNOW ABOUT THE ALDERCREST FAMILY?
THERE'S A MINE AT TENUMSHAL CALLED ALDERCREST PRIDE. AN IRON MINE, I THINK.
SOME OF THE MEN FROM MY VILLAGE WORK THERE.
GOOD. CLAN ALDERCREST OWNS A GREAT MANY MINES.
THEY ARE THE SOURCE OF LORD DEMINI'S WEALTH AND INFLUENCE.
WHAT'S INFLUENCE?
IT'S LIKE THE REACH OF A SWORDSMAN'S ARM. THE SPACE IN WHICH HE CAN ACT.
WATCH THE PICTURES, CHILD.
AND I WILL TELL YOU ABOUT HIGHEST HOUSE.

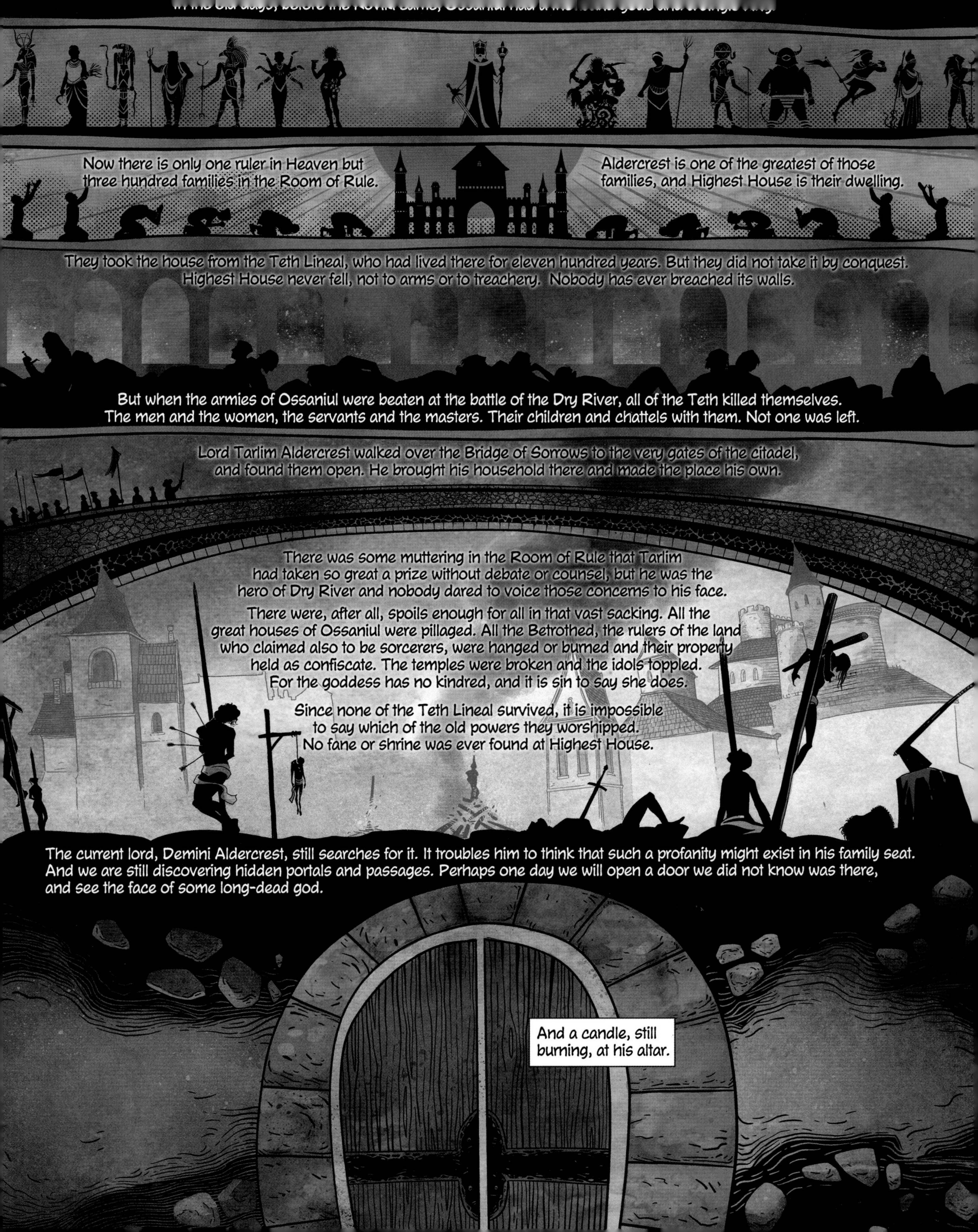

Now there is only one ruler in Heaven but three hundred families in the Room of Rule.
Aldercrest is one of the greatest of those families, and Highest House is their dwelling.
They took the house from the Teth Lineal, who had lived there for eleven hundred years. But they did not take it by conquest. Highest House never fell, not to arms or to treachery. Nobody has ever breached its walls.
But when the armies of Ossaniul were beaten at the battle of the Dry River, all of the Teth killed themselves. The men and the women, the servants and the masters. Their children and chattels with them. Not one was left.
Lord Tarlim Aldercrest walked over the Bridge of Sorrows to the very gates of the citadel, and found them open. He brought his household there and made the place his own.
There was some muttering in the Room of Rule that Tarlim had taken so great a prize without debate or counsel, but he was the hero of Dry River and nobody dared to voice those concerns to his face.
There were, after all, spoils enough for all in that vast sacking. All the great houses of Ossaniul were pillaged. All the Betrothed, the rulers of the land who claimed also to be sorcerers, were hanged or burned and their property held as confiscate. The temples were broken and the idols toppled. For the goddess has no kindred, and it is sin to say she does.
Since none of the Teth Lineal survived, it is impossible to say which of the old powers they worshipped. No fane or shrine was ever found at Highest House.
The current lord, Demini Aldercrest, still searches for it. It troubles him to think that such a profanity might exist in his family seat. And we are still discovering hidden portals and passages. Perhaps one day we will open a door we did not know was there, and see the face of some long-dead god.
And a candle, still burning, at his altar.

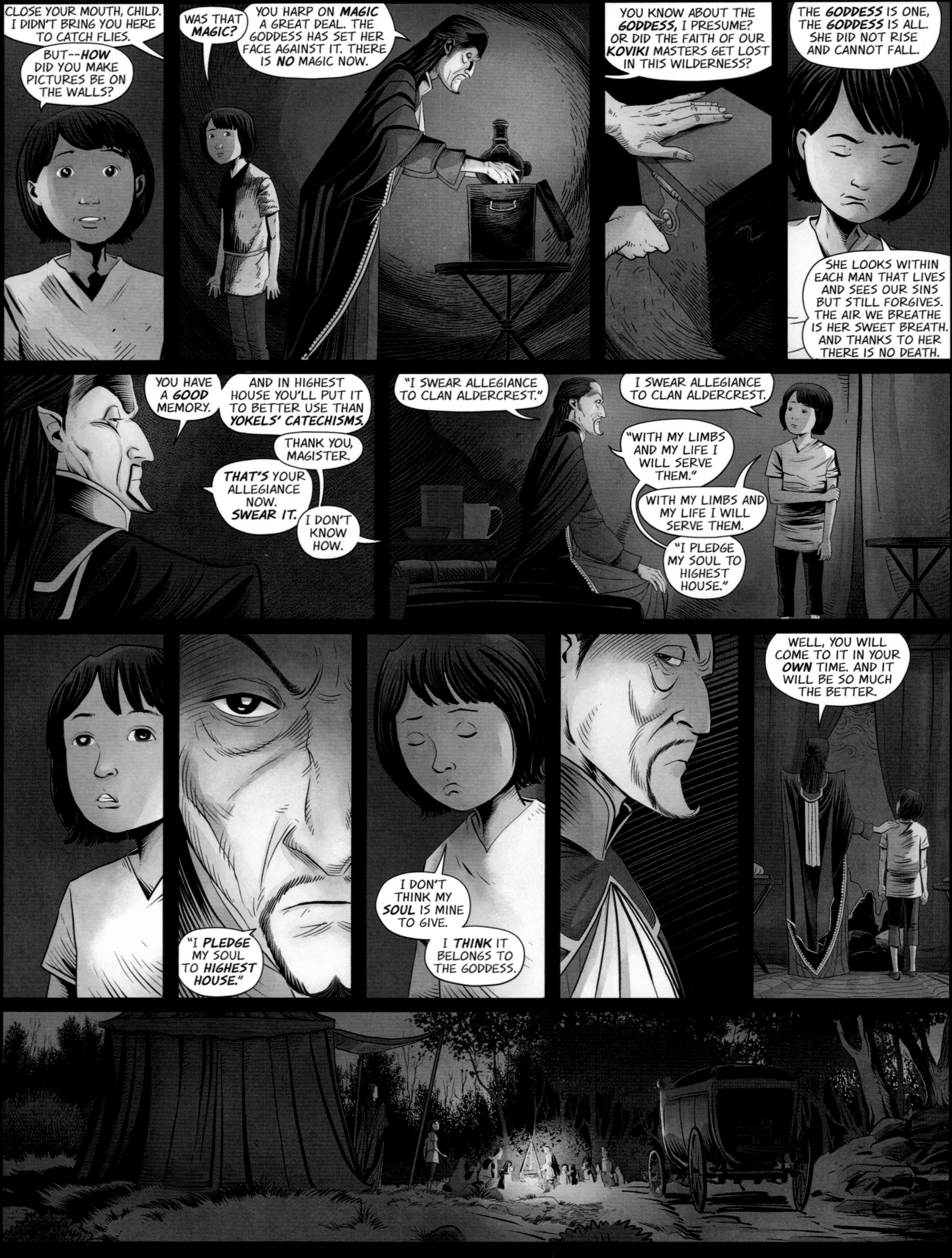
CLOSE YOUR MOUTH, CHILD. I DIDN'T BRING YOU HERE TO CATCH FLIES.
BUT--HOW DID YOU MAKE PICTURES BE ON THE WALLS?
WAS THAT MAGIC?
YOU HARP ON MAGIC A GREAT DEAL. THE GODDESS HAS SET HER FACE AGAINST IT. THERE IS NO MAGIC NOW.
YOU KNOW ABOUT THE GODDESS, I PRESUME? OR DID THE FAITH OF OUR KOVIKI MASTERS GET LOST IN THIS WILDERNESS?
THE GODDESS IS ONE, THE GODDESS IS ALL. SHE DID NOT RISE AND CANNOT FALL.
SHE LOOKS WITHIN EACH MAN THAT LIVES AND SEES OUR SINS BUT STILL FORGIVES. THE AIR WE BREATHE IS HER SWEET BREATH. AND THANKS TO HER THERE IS NO DEATH.
YOU HAVE A GOOD MEMORY.
AND IN HIGHEST HOUSE YOU'LL PUT IT TO BETTER USE THAN YOKELS' CATECHISMS.
THANK YOU, MAGISTER.
THAT'S YOUR ALLEGIANCE NOW. SWEAR IT.
I DON'T KNOW HOW.
"I SWEAR ALLEGIANCE TO CLAN ALDERCREST."
I SWEAR ALLEGIANCE TO CLAN ALDERCREST.
"WITH MY LIMBS AND MY LIFE I WILL SERVE THEM."
WITH MY LIMBS AND MY LIFE I WILL SERVE THEM.
"I PLEDGE MY SOUL TO HIGHEST HOUSE."
"I PLEDGE MY SOUL TO HIGHEST HOUSE."
I DON'T THINK MY SOUL IS MINE TO GIVE.
I THINK IT BELONGS TO THE GODDESS.
WELL, YOU WILL COME TO IT IN YOUR OWN TIME. AND IT WILL BE SO MUCH THE BETTER.

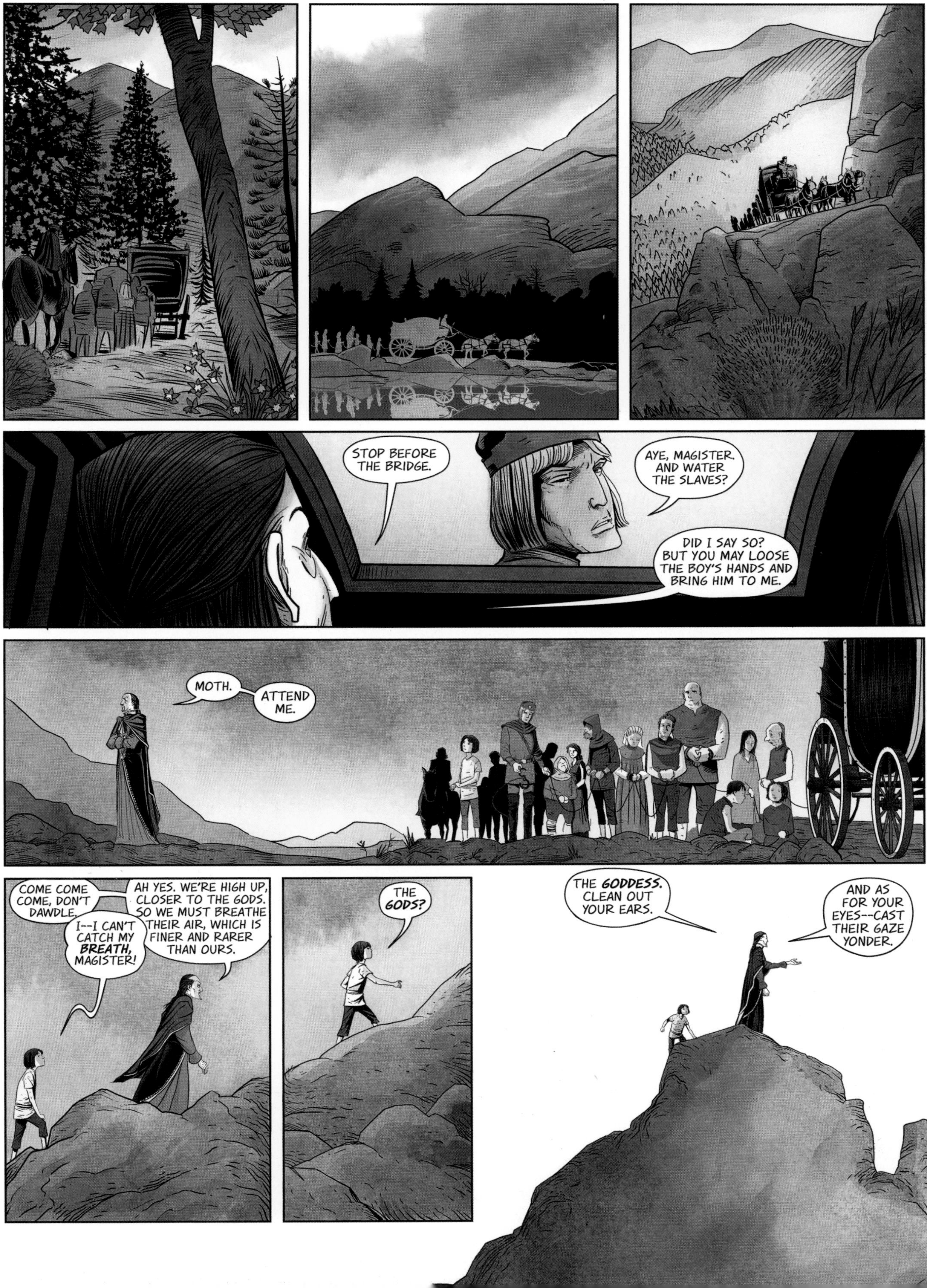
STOP BEFORE THE BRIDGE.
AYE, MAGISTER. AND WATER THE SLAVES?
DID I SAY SO? BUT YOU MAY LOOSE THE BOY'S HANDS AND BRING HIM TO ME.
MOTH.
ATTEND ME.
COME COME COME, DON'T DAWDLE.
I--I CAN'T CATCH MY BREATH, MAGISTER!
AH YES. WE'RE HIGH UP, CLOSER TO THE GODS. SO WE MUST BREATHE THEIR AIR, WHICH IS FINER AND RARER THAN OURS.
THE GODS?
THE GODDESS. CLEAN OUT YOUR EARS.
AND AS FOR YOUR EYES--CAST THEIR GAZE YONDER.

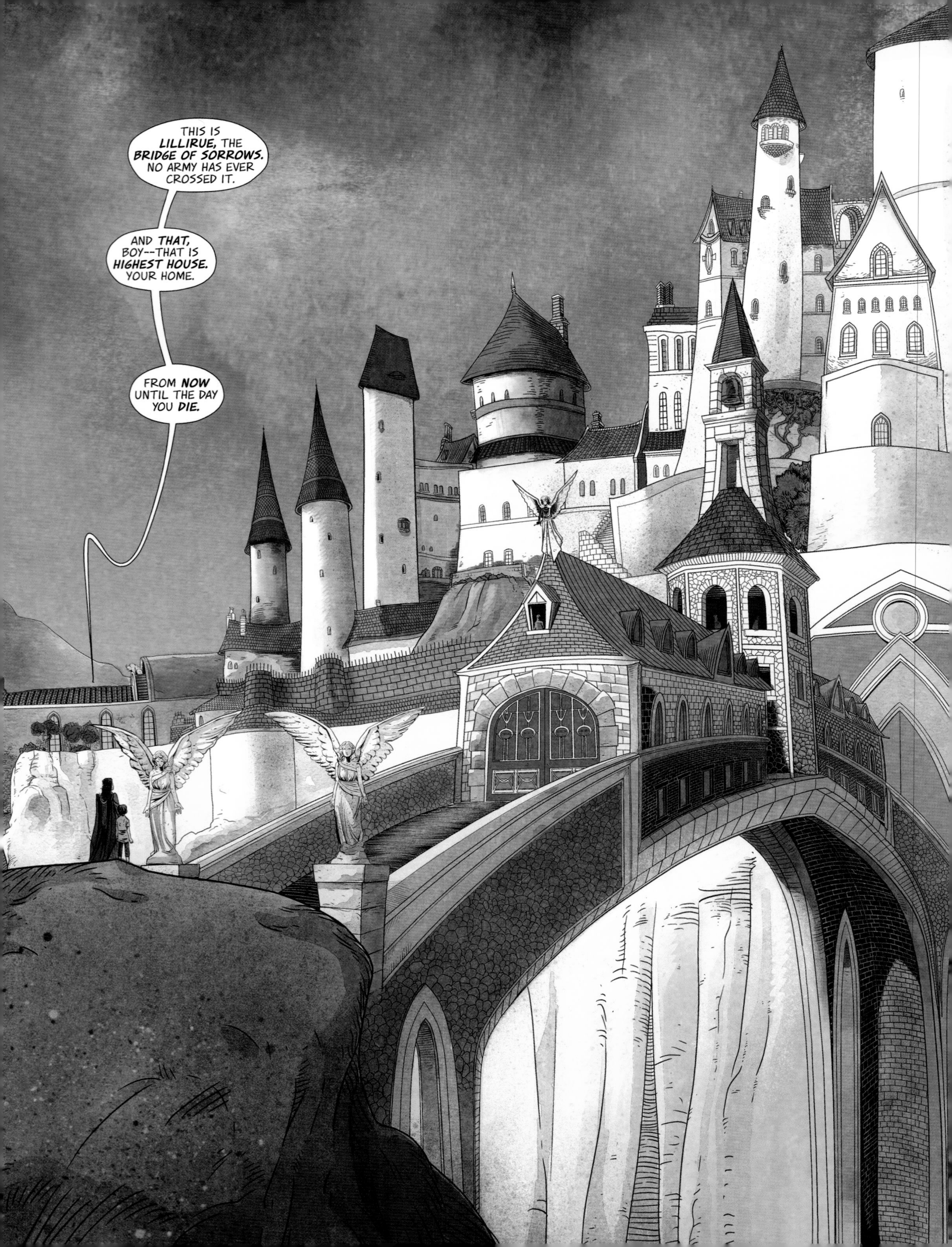

THIS IS **LILLIRUE,** THE **BRIDGE OF SORROWS.** NO ARMY HAS EVER CROSSED IT.
AND **THAT,** BOY--THAT IS **HIGHEST HOUSE.** YOUR HOME.
FROM **NOW** UNTIL THE DAY YOU **DIE.**

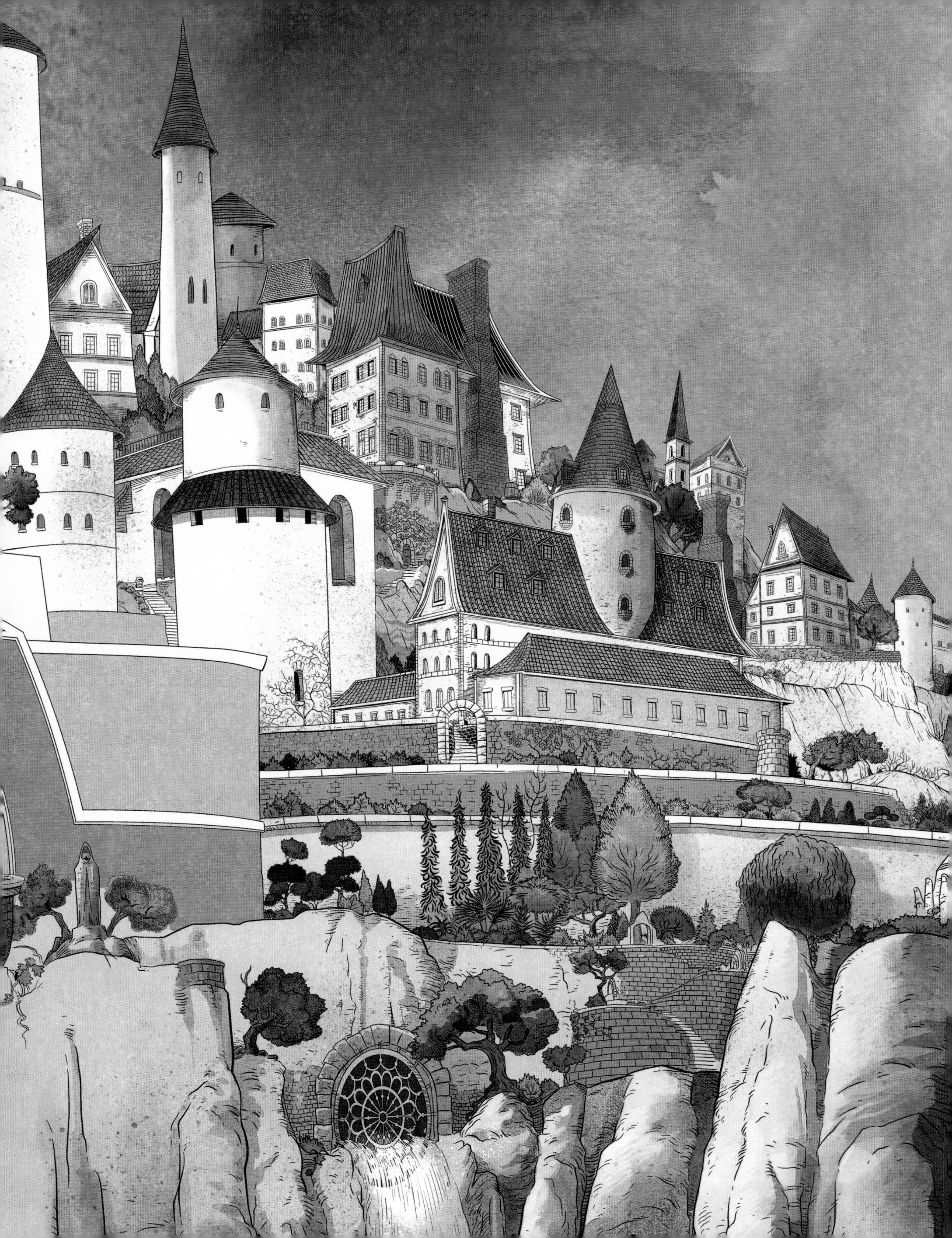

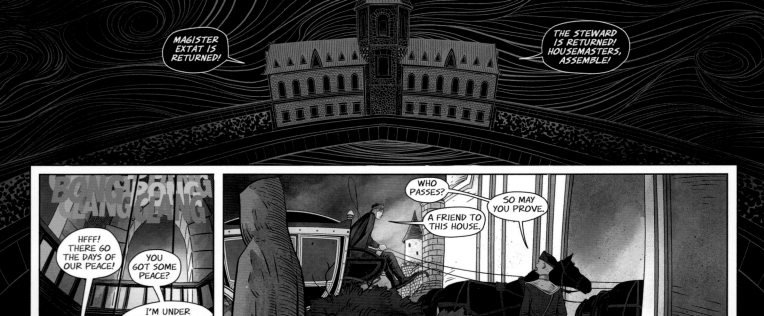

MAGISTER EXTAT IS RETURNED!

THE STEWARD IS RETURNED! HOUSEMASTERS, ASSEMBLE!

WHO PASSES?

A FRIEND TO THIS HOUSE.

SO MAY YOU PROVE.

BONG BONG CLANG CLANG

HFFF! THERE GO THE DAYS OF OUR PEACE!

YOU GOT SOME PEACE?

I'M UNDER MASTER TEMTOLLER SO YOU KNOW FULL WELL WHAT I GOT.

IT'S A JOY TO SEE YOU SAFE HOME, SIR.

THANK YOU, THILIUS. IS MY LORD IN RESIDENCE?

HE'S STILL IN SHAU KILL, MAGISTER. AND THE FAMILY WITH HIM.

THE HOUSEMASTERS AWAIT YOU, MASTER. THEY WISH TO OFFER THEIR RESPECTS.

AND NO DOUBT TO HAVE FIRST PICK OF THE NEW SLAVES.

OUR SERVICE TO YOU, MAGISTER.

AND THE HOUSE ACCOUNTS ARE READY FOR YOUR INSPECTION WHENEVER YOU--

YES YES YES. LATER FOR THAT

WELCOME HOME, MAGISTER.

LINE UP THE SLAVES. YOU MAY CHOOSE IN ORDER OF PRECEDENCE.

CHAMBERMASTERS FIRST. THEN PARLOUR, YARD AND WALLS.

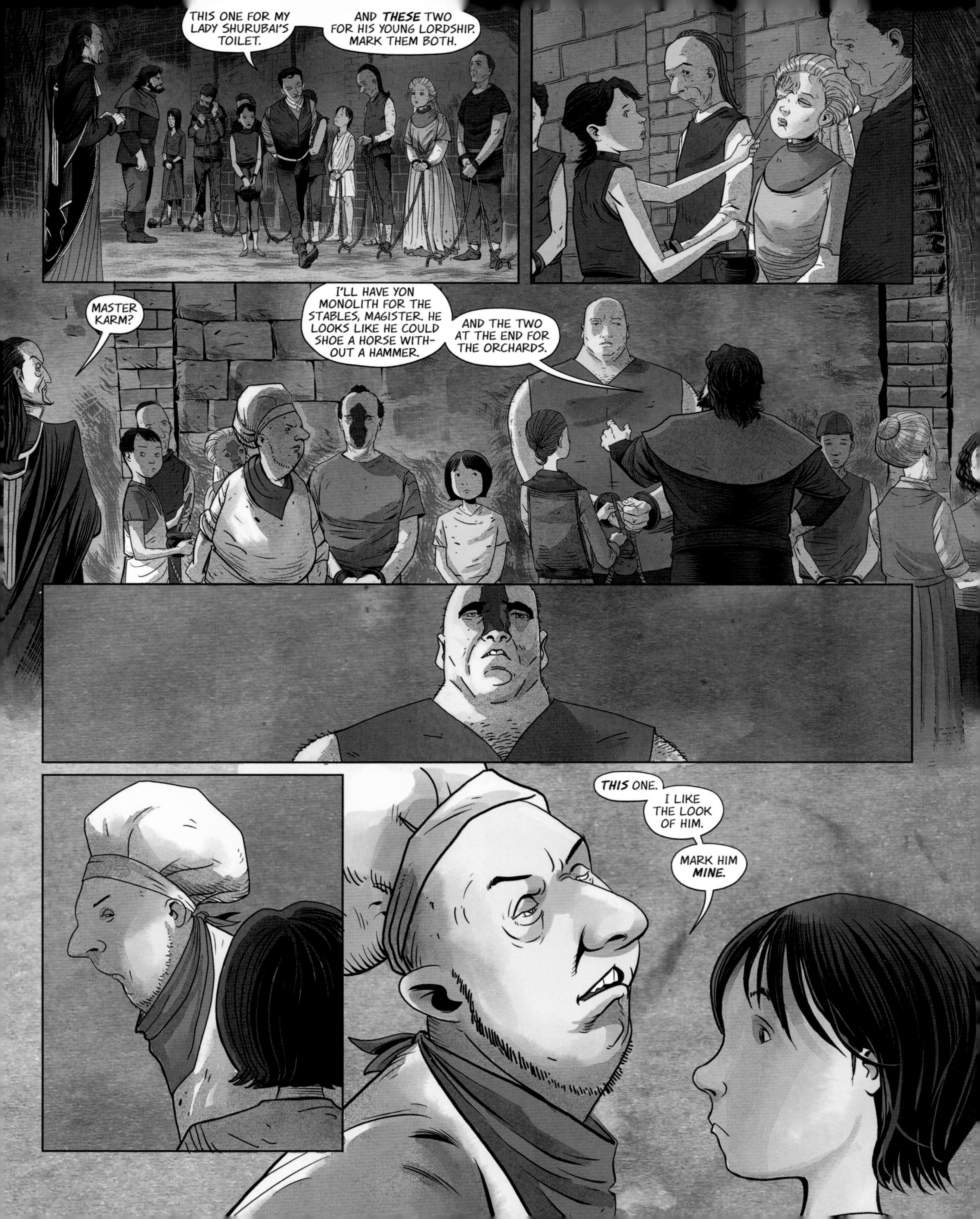
THIS ONE FOR MY LADY SHURUBAI'S TOILET.
AND THESE TWO FOR HIS YOUNG LORDSHIP. MARK THEM BOTH.
MASTER KARM?
I'LL HAVE YON MONOLITH FOR THE STABLES, MAGISTER. HE LOOKS LIKE HE COULD SHOE A HORSE WITH-OUT A HAMMER.
AND THE TWO AT THE END FOR THE ORCHARDS.
THIS ONE.
I LIKE THE LOOK OF HIM.
MARK HIM MINE.

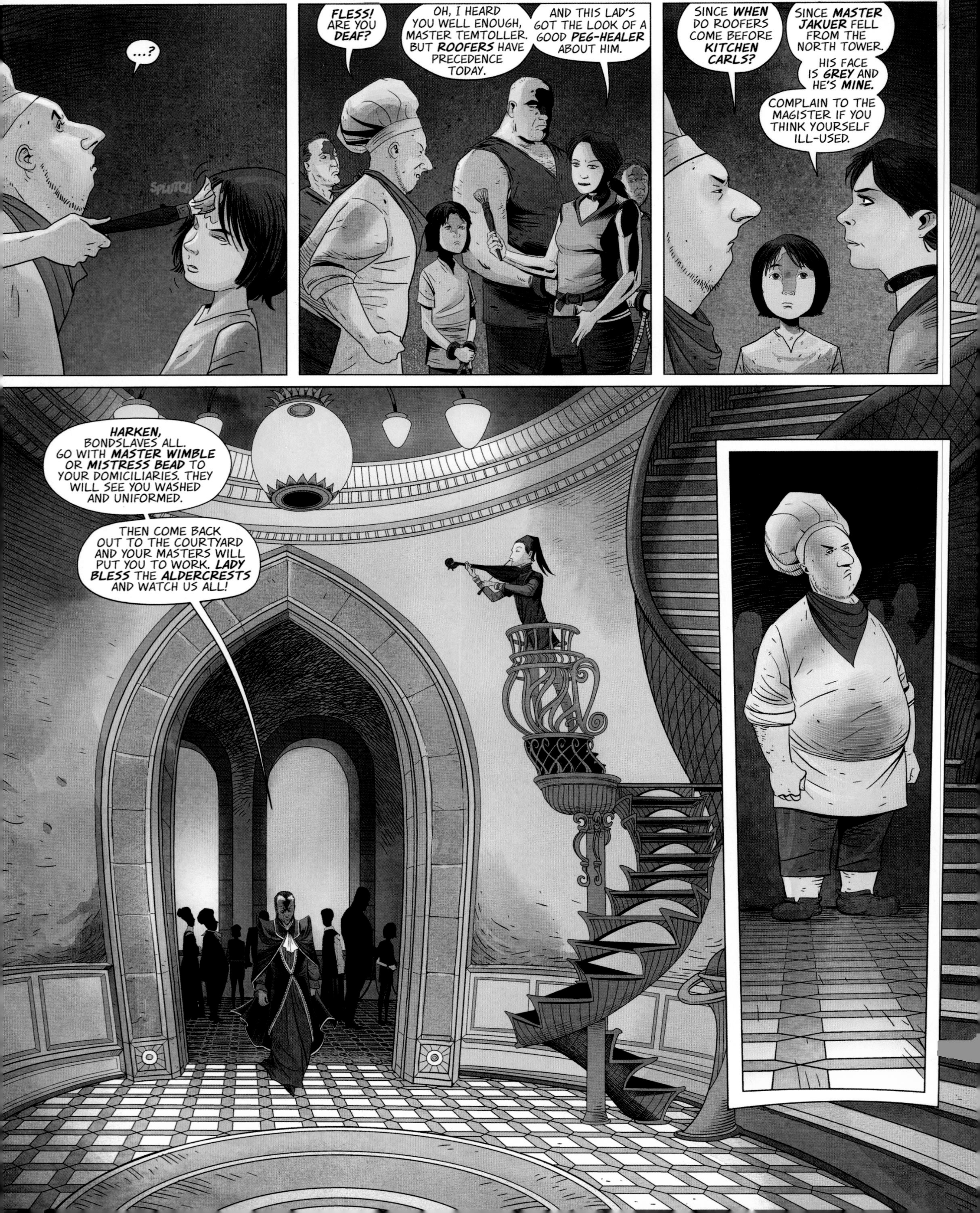
...?
SPLUTCH
FLESS! ARE YOU DEAF?
OH, I HEARD YOU WELL ENOUGH, MASTER TEMTOLLER. BUT ROOFERS HAVE PRECEDENCE TODAY.
AND THIS LAD'S GOT THE LOOK OF A GOOD PEG-HEALER ABOUT HIM.
SINCE WHEN DO ROOFERS COME BEFORE KITCHEN CARLS?
SINCE MASTER JAKUER FELL FROM THE NORTH TOWER.
HIS FACE IS GREY AND HE'S MINE.
COMPLAIN TO THE MAGISTER IF YOU THINK YOURSELF ILL-USED.
HARKEN, BONDSLAVES ALL. GO WITH MASTER WIMBLE OR MISTRESS BEAD TO YOUR DOMICILIARIES. THEY WILL SEE YOU WASHED AND UNIFORMED.
THEN COME BACK OUT TO THE COURTYARD AND YOUR MASTERS WILL PUT YOU TO WORK. LADY BLESS THE ALDERCRESTS AND WATCH US ALL!

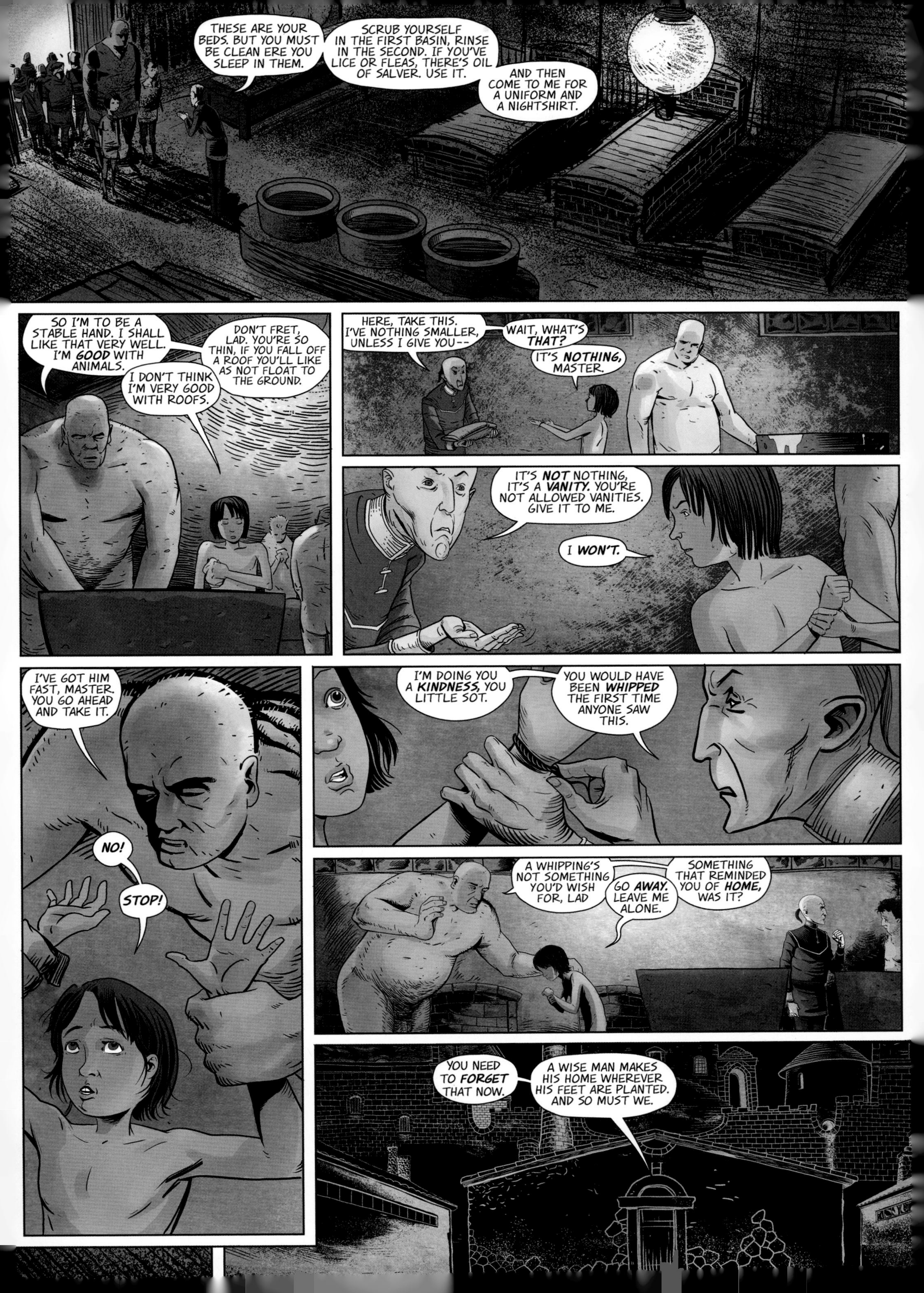
THESE ARE YOUR BEDS. BUT YOU MUST BE CLEAN ERE YOU SLEEP IN THEM.
SCRUB YOURSELF IN THE FIRST BASIN, RINSE IN THE SECOND. IF YOU'VE LICE OR FLEAS, THERE'S OIL OF SALVER. USE IT.
AND THEN COME TO ME FOR A UNIFORM AND A NIGHTSHIRT.
SO I'M TO BE A STABLE HAND. I SHALL LIKE THAT VERY WELL. I'M **GOOD** WITH ANIMALS.
DON'T FRET, LAD. YOU'RE SO THIN, IF YOU FALL OFF A ROOF YOU'LL LIKE AS NOT FLOAT TO THE GROUND.
I DON'T THINK I'M VERY GOOD WITH ROOFS.
HERE, TAKE THIS. I'VE NOTHING SMALLER, UNLESS I GIVE YOU--
WAIT, WHAT'S **THAT?**
IT'S **NOTHING,** MASTER.
IT'S **NOT** NOTHING, IT'S A **VANITY.** YOU'RE NOT ALLOWED VANITIES. GIVE IT TO ME.
I **WON'T.**
I'VE GOT HIM FAST, MASTER. YOU GO AHEAD AND TAKE IT.
NO!
STOP!
I'M DOING YOU A **KINDNESS,** YOU LITTLE SOT.
YOU WOULD HAVE BEEN **WHIPPED** THE FIRST TIME ANYONE SAW THIS.
A WHIPPING'S NOT SOMETHING YOU'D WISH FOR, LAD
GO **AWAY.** LEAVE ME ALONE.
SOMETHING THAT REMINDED YOU OF **HOME,** WAS IT?
YOU NEED TO **FORGET** THAT NOW.
A WISE MAN MAKES HIS HOME WHEREVER HIS FEET ARE PLANTED. AND SO MUST WE.

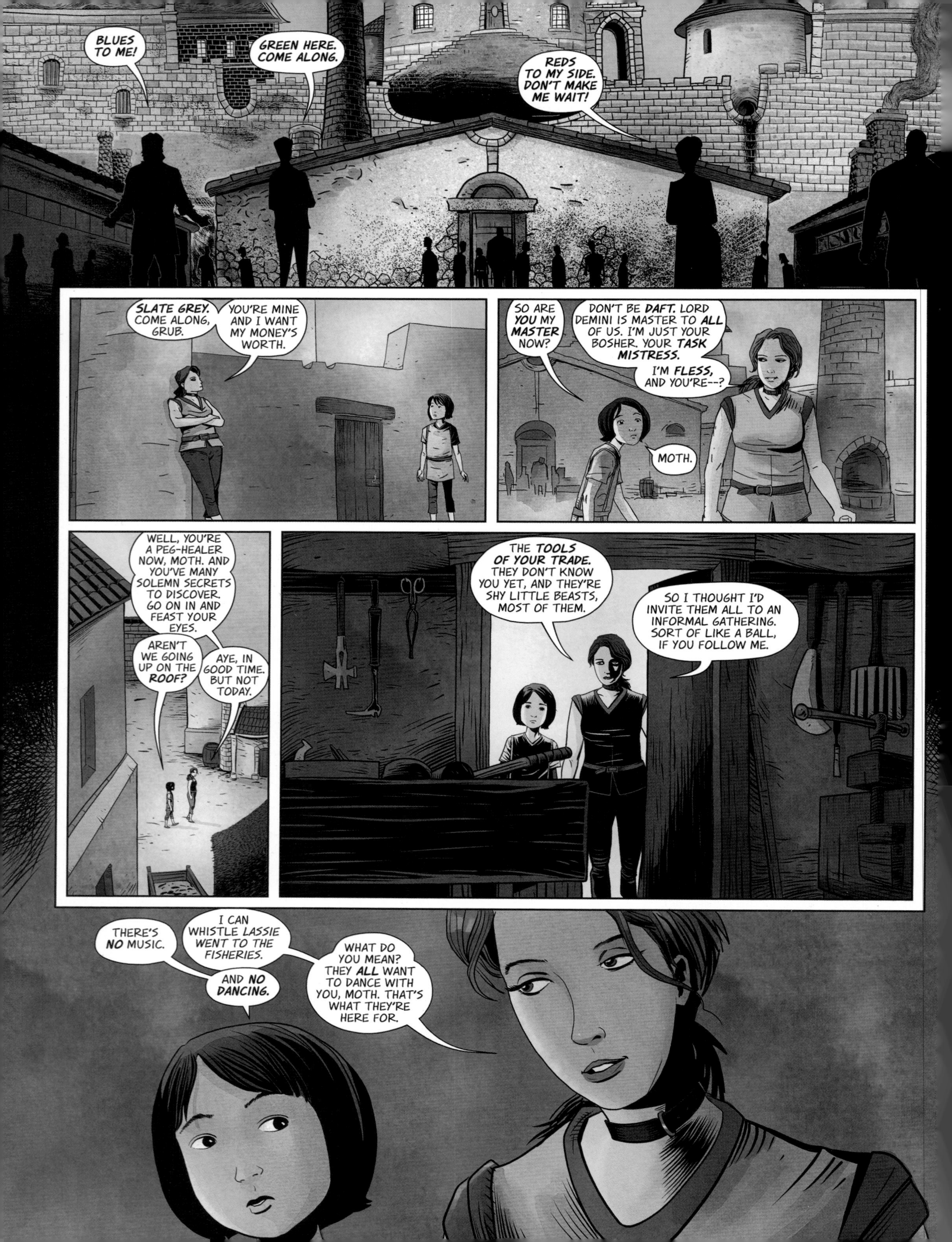
BLUES TO ME!
GREEN HERE. COME ALONG.
REDS TO MY SIDE. DON'T MAKE ME WAIT!
SLATE GREY. COME ALONG, GRUB.
YOU'RE MINE AND I WANT MY MONEY'S WORTH.
SO ARE YOU MY MASTER NOW?
DON'T BE DAFT. LORD DEMINI IS MASTER TO ALL OF US. I'M JUST YOUR BOSHER. YOUR TASK MISTRESS.
I'M FLESS, AND YOU'RE--?
MOTH.
WELL, YOU'RE A PEG-HEALER NOW, MOTH. AND YOU'VE MANY SOLEMN SECRETS TO DISCOVER. GO ON IN AND FEAST YOUR EYES.
AREN'T WE GOING UP ON THE ROOF?
AYE, IN GOOD TIME. BUT NOT TODAY.
THE TOOLS OF YOUR TRADE. THEY DON'T KNOW YOU YET, AND THEY'RE SHY LITTLE BEASTS, MOST OF THEM.
SO I THOUGHT I'D INVITE THEM ALL TO AN INFORMAL GATHERING. SORT OF LIKE A BALL, IF YOU FOLLOW ME.
THERE'S NO MUSIC.
I CAN WHISTLE LASSIE WENT TO THE FISHERIES.
AND NO DANCING.
WHAT DO YOU MEAN? THEY ALL WANT TO DANCE WITH YOU, MOTH. THAT'S WHAT THEY'RE HERE FOR.

  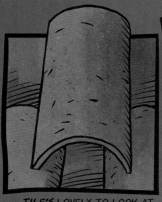 

SHINGLES ARE SHINGLES, WHETHER THEY BE WOOD OR SLATE OR TILE. WE'VE ALL THREE OF THOSE ON HIGHEST HOUSE, AND EACH HAS GOT ITS LITTLE WAYS.

SLATE LASTS LONGEST, BUT IT'S HEAVY.

TILE'S LOVELY TO LOOK AT BUT IT'S FRAGILE.

WOOD IS LIGHT AND CHEAP BUT IT WARPS AND ROTS AND INSECTS BORE THROUGH IT.

THIS IS A SCANTLE STICK. YOU USE IT TO SORT YOUR SHINGLES TO SIZE AND TO LAY THE COURSES RIGHT. EACH SIZE HAS A NAME, FROM THIRTEENS TO FAIRINGS, BUT I'LL TELL YOU THOSE LATER. YOU'LL USUALLY LAY YOUR LONGEST SLATES NEXT TO THE EAVES, THEN DIMINISH AS YOU GO UP THE ROOF.

YOU'LL HEAR SOME HEALERS TALK OF PENDLE. PENDLE IS JUST SLATE OR STONE, ESPECIALLY STUFF THAT SPLITS. BUT IT'S AN OLD WORD AND YOU WON'T HEAR IT MUCH ANY MORE.

  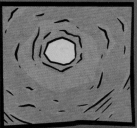 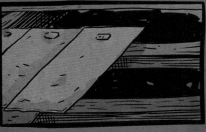

THE SHINGLES HANG FROM WOODEN PEGS, LIKE THESE.

YOU USE A SLATE HAMMER OR A MARTLE TO DRIVE HOLES THROUGH THE SHINGLES,

THEN YOU PUSH THE PEGS THROUGH. JUST AT THE TOP HERE, SO THEY CAN HANG FROM THE LATHS IN THE ROOF.

THEN THERE'S THATCH, WHICH WE STILL USE ON SOME OF THE OUTBUILDINGS.

IT BREATHES BETTER THAN ANYTHING. HOLDS THE HEAT IN WINTER, LETS IT OUT WHEN THE SUN SHINES. THATCHING'S THE HARDEST THING WE DO BECAUSE YOU'VE GOT TO BUNDLE AND BIND IT BY HAND. TAKES A WHILE TO GET YOUR EYE IN.

AND ONCE THEY'RE HUNG YOU CAN PUSH MOSS BETWEEN THEM TO MAKE THEM TIGHT AGAINST THE WIND. FOR THAT YOU'D USE YOUR MOSSING IRONS. OR IF THE GAP WAS TOO BIG YOU'D MIX A MORTAR OUT OF LIME AND OX-HAIR. THAT'S CALLED TORCHING. TORCHING THE GAP.

THESE WILL HELP, THOUGH. THE HOOKS WILL HOLD THE STRAW IN PLACE WHILE YOU BIND IT WITH A SWAY AND COMB IT INTO LINE WITH YOUR LEGGETT.

YOU THINK YOU GOT ALL THAT?

NO!

WELL, YOU WILL. A LITTLE BIT AT A TIME. WE'LL CUT SLATE FIRST.

BUT THIS IS A BALL SO ANYTHING COULD HAPPEN AFTER THAT.

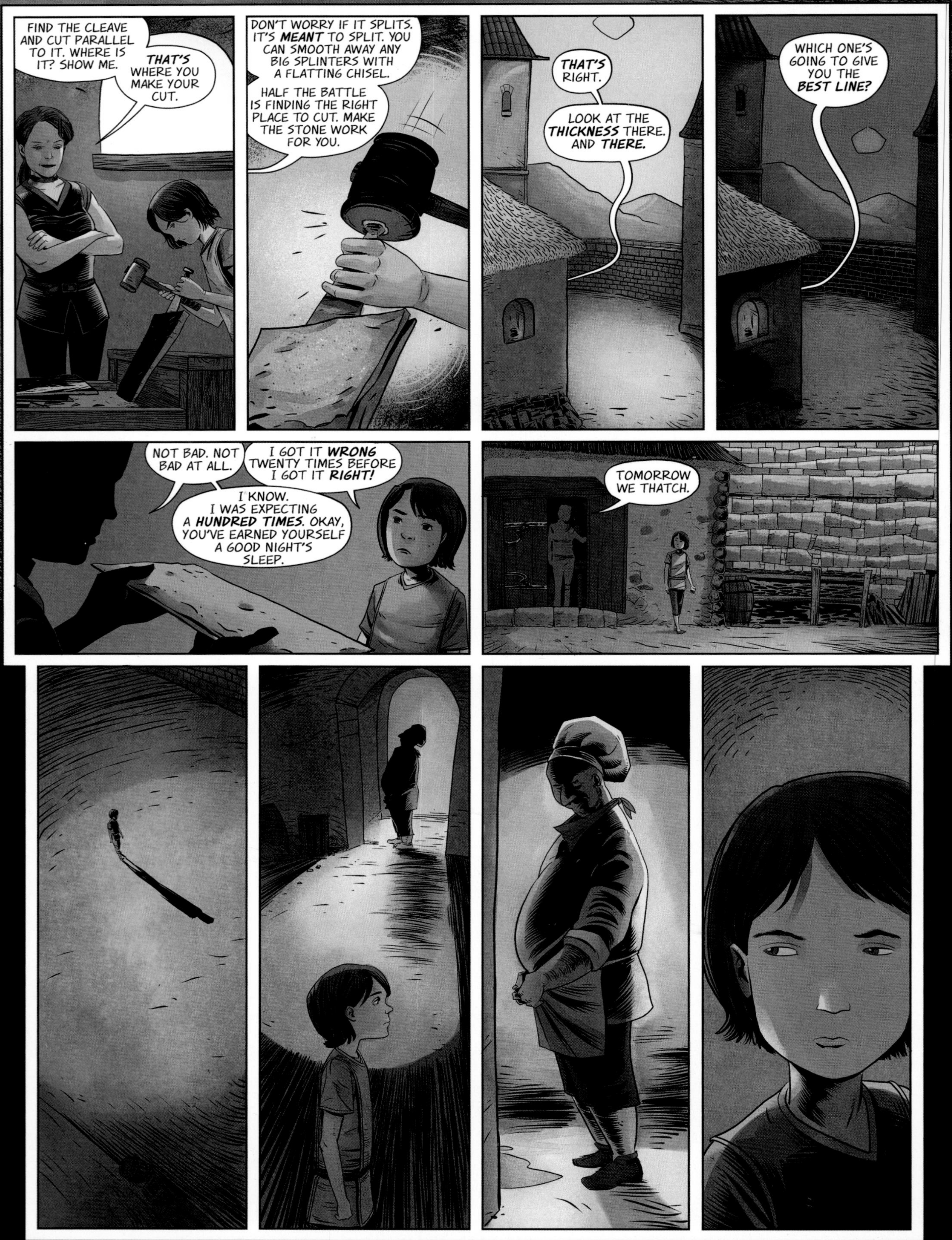
FIND THE CLEAVE AND CUT PARALLEL TO IT. WHERE IS IT? SHOW ME.
THAT'S WHERE YOU MAKE YOUR CUT.
DON'T WORRY IF IT SPLITS. IT'S MEANT TO SPLIT. YOU CAN SMOOTH AWAY ANY BIG SPLINTERS WITH A FLATTING CHISEL.
HALF THE BATTLE IS FINDING THE RIGHT PLACE TO CUT. MAKE THE STONE WORK FOR YOU.
THAT'S RIGHT.
LOOK AT THE THICKNESS THERE. AND THERE.
WHICH ONE'S GOING TO GIVE YOU THE BEST LINE?
NOT BAD. NOT BAD AT ALL.
I GOT IT WRONG TWENTY TIMES BEFORE I GOT IT RIGHT!
I KNOW. I WAS EXPECTING A HUNDRED TIMES. OKAY, YOU'VE EARNED YOURSELF A GOOD NIGHT'S SLEEP.
TOMORROW WE THATCH.

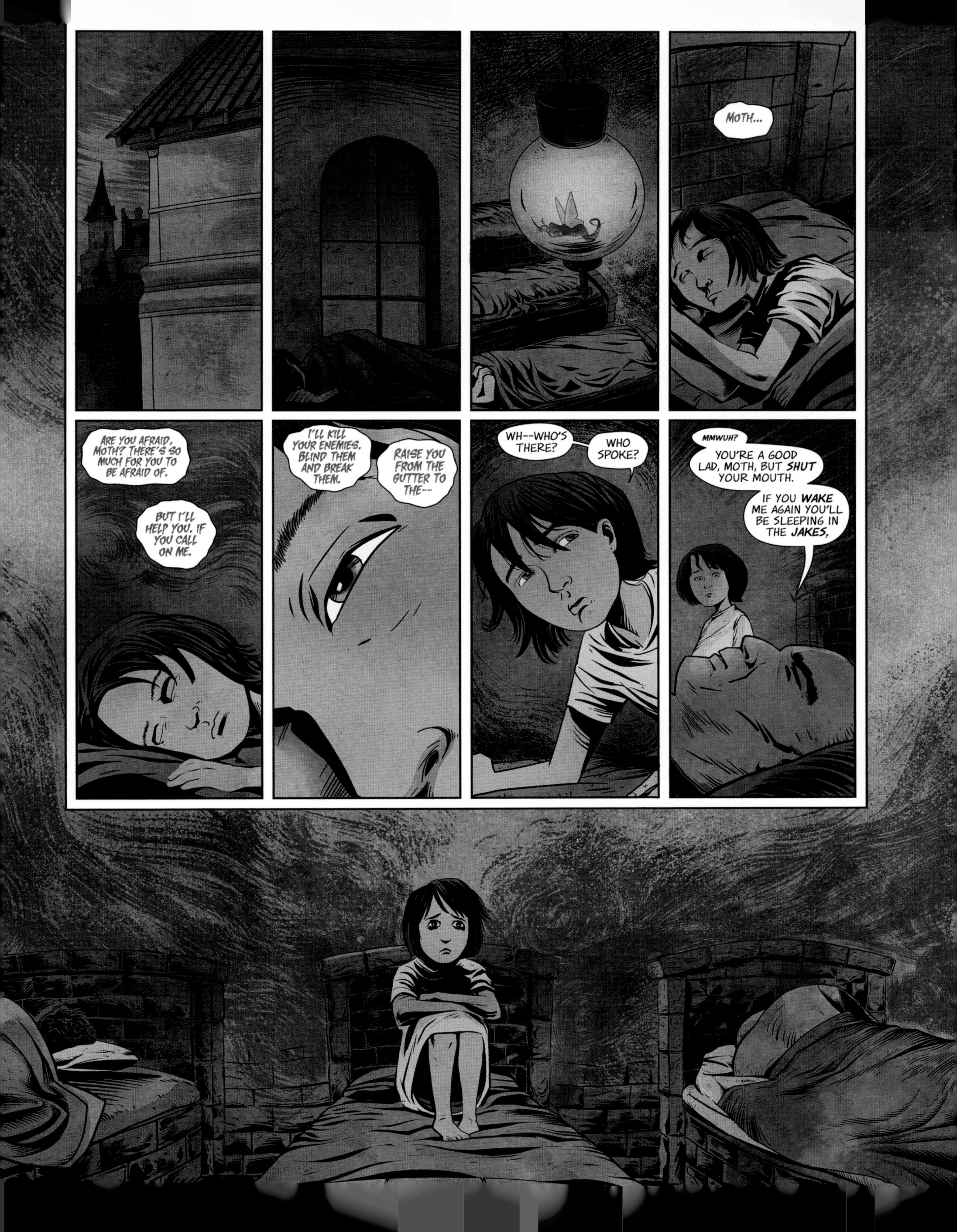
MOTH...
ARE YOU AFRAID, MOTH? THERE'S SO MUCH FOR YOU TO BE AFRAID OF.
BUT I'LL HELP YOU. IF YOU CALL ON ME.
I'LL KILL YOUR ENEMIES. BLIND THEM AND BREAK THEM.
RAISE YOU FROM THE GUTTER TO THE--
WH--WHO'S THERE?
WHO SPOKE?
MMWUH?
YOU'RE A GOOD LAD, MOTH, BUT SHUT YOUR MOUTH.
IF YOU WAKE ME AGAIN YOU'LL BE SLEEPING IN THE JAKES.

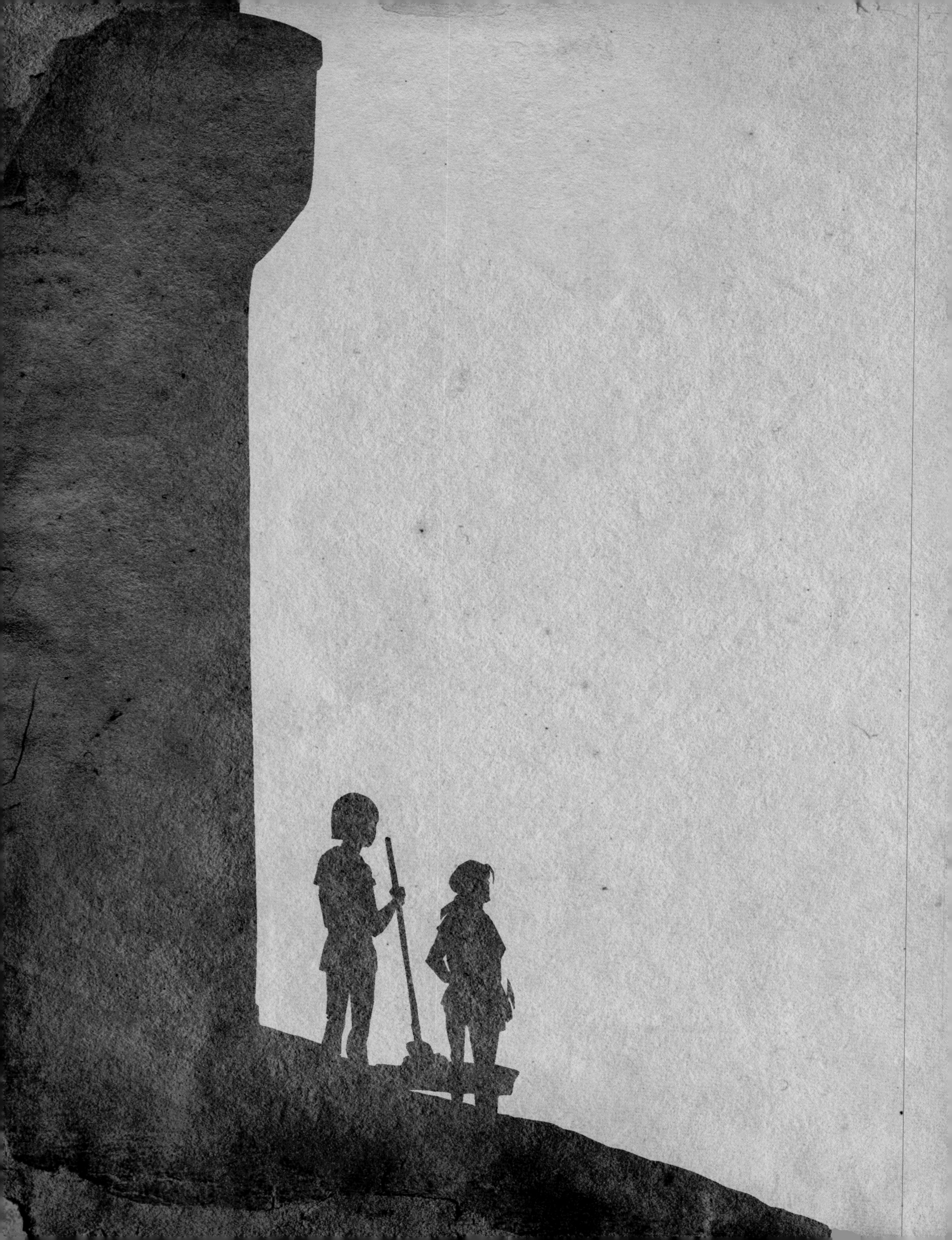

Chapter Two

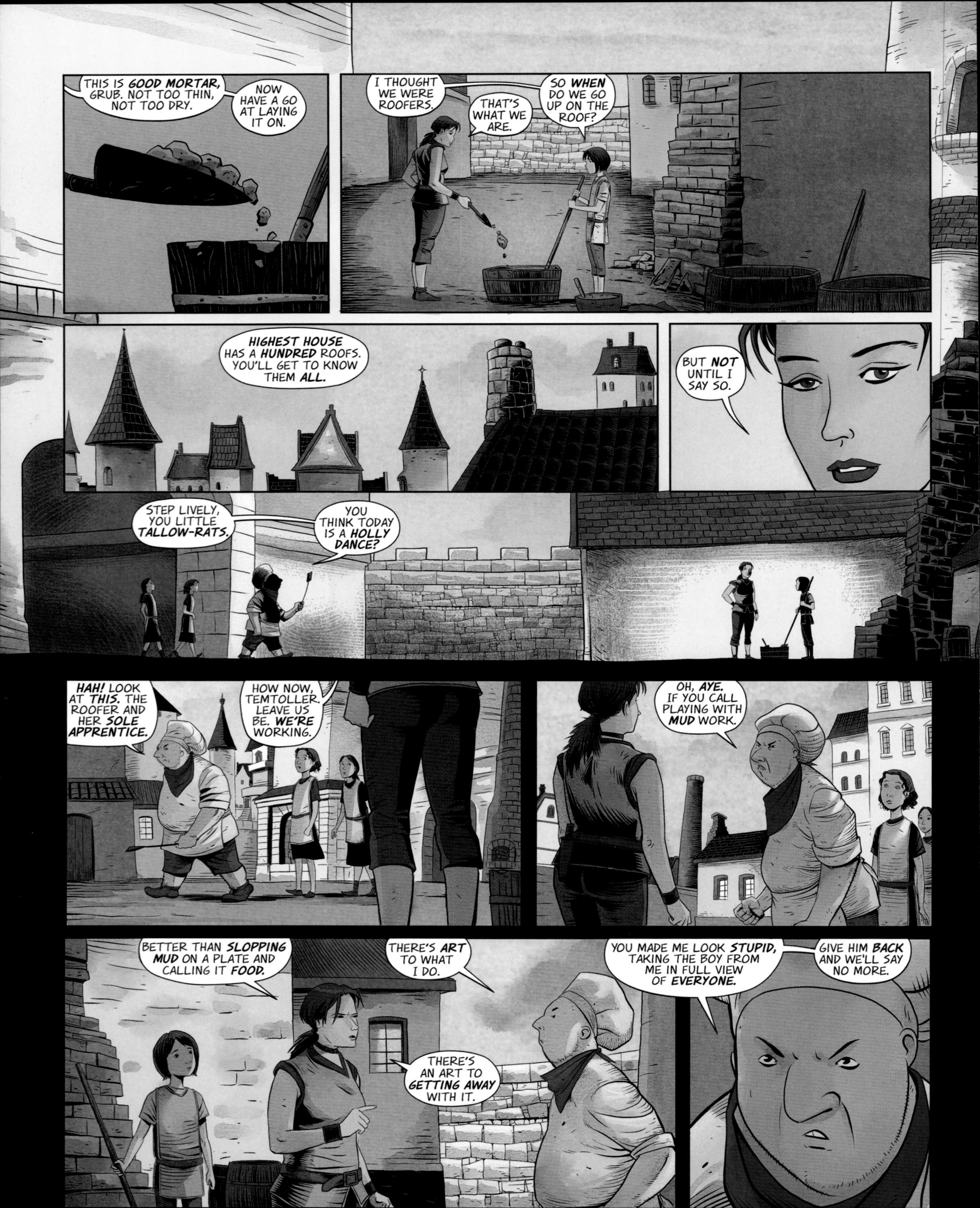

THIS IS GOOD MORTAR, GRUB. NOT TOO THIN, NOT TOO DRY.
NOW HAVE A GO AT LAYING IT ON.
I THOUGHT WE WERE ROOFERS.
THAT'S WHAT WE ARE.
SO WHEN DO WE GO UP ON THE ROOF?
HIGHEST HOUSE HAS A HUNDRED ROOFS. YOU'LL GET TO KNOW THEM ALL.
BUT NOT UNTIL I SAY SO.
STEP LIVELY, YOU LITTLE TALLOW-RATS.
YOU THINK TODAY IS A HOLLY DANCE?
HAH! LOOK AT THIS. THE ROOFER AND HER SOLE APPRENTICE.
HOW NOW, TEMTOLLER. LEAVE US BE. WE'RE WORKING.
OH, AYE. IF YOU CALL PLAYING WITH MUD WORK.
BETTER THAN SLOPPING MUD ON A PLATE AND CALLING IT FOOD.
THERE'S ART TO WHAT I DO.
THERE'S AN ART TO GETTING AWAY WITH IT.
YOU MADE ME LOOK STUPID, TAKING THE BOY FROM ME IN FULL VIEW OF EVERYONE.
GIVE HIM BACK AND WE'LL SAY NO MORE.

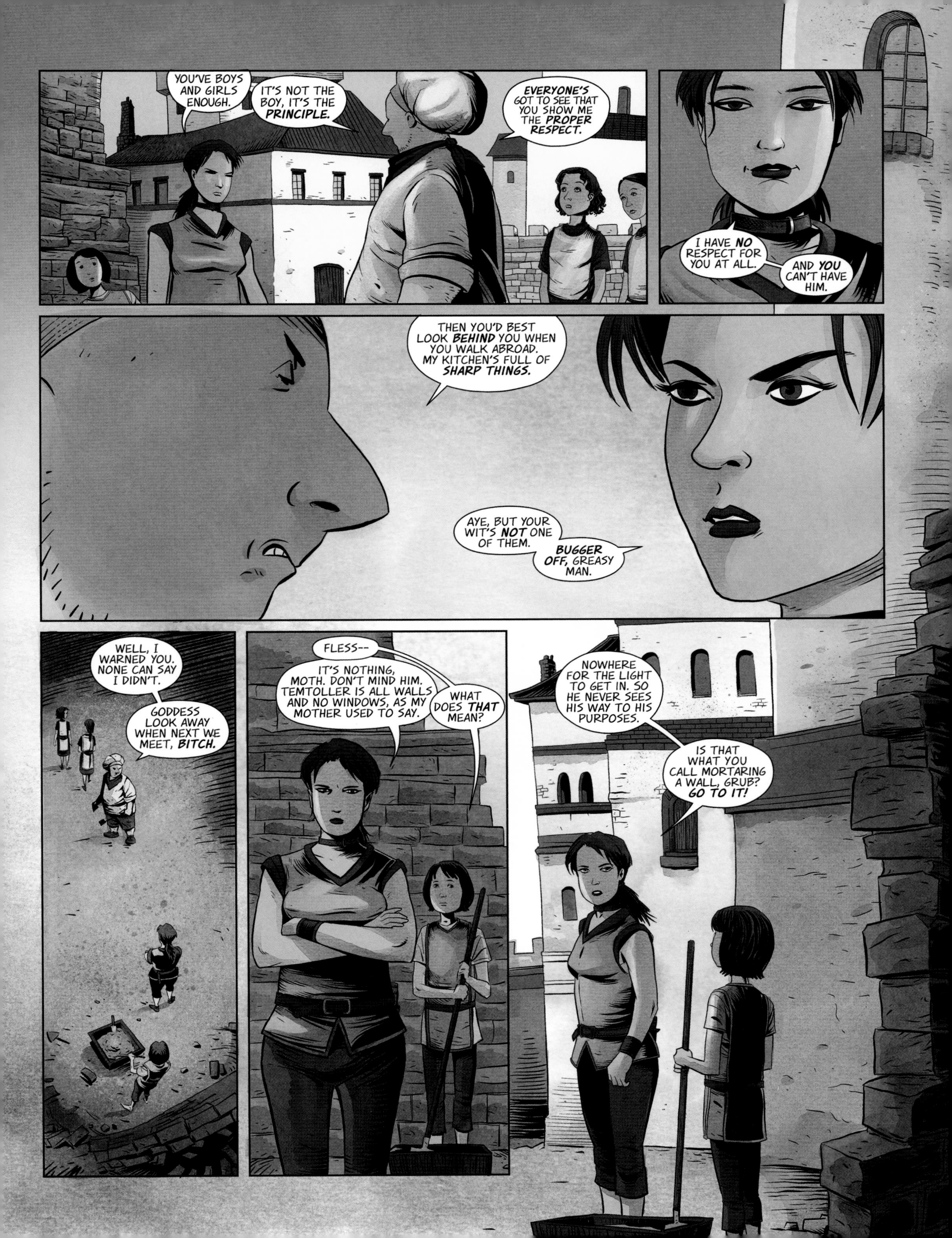

YOU'VE BOYS AND GIRLS ENOUGH.
IT'S NOT THE BOY, IT'S THE **PRINCIPLE.**
EVERYONE'S GOT TO SEE THAT YOU SHOW ME THE **PROPER RESPECT.**
I HAVE **NO** RESPECT FOR YOU AT ALL.
AND **YOU** CAN'T HAVE HIM.
THEN YOU'D BEST LOOK **BEHIND** YOU WHEN YOU WALK ABROAD. MY KITCHEN'S FULL OF **SHARP THINGS.**
AYE, BUT YOUR WIT'S **NOT** ONE OF THEM.
BUGGER OFF, GREASY MAN.
WELL, I WARNED YOU. NONE CAN SAY I DIDN'T.
GODDESS LOOK AWAY WHEN NEXT WE MEET, **BITCH.**
FLESS--
IT'S NOTHING, MOTH. DON'T MIND HIM. TEMTOLLER IS ALL WALLS AND NO WINDOWS, AS MY MOTHER USED TO SAY.
WHAT DOES **THAT** MEAN?
NOWHERE FOR THE LIGHT TO GET IN. SO HE NEVER SEES HIS WAY TO HIS PURPOSES.
IS THAT WHAT YOU CALL MORTARING A WALL, GRUB? **GO TO IT!**

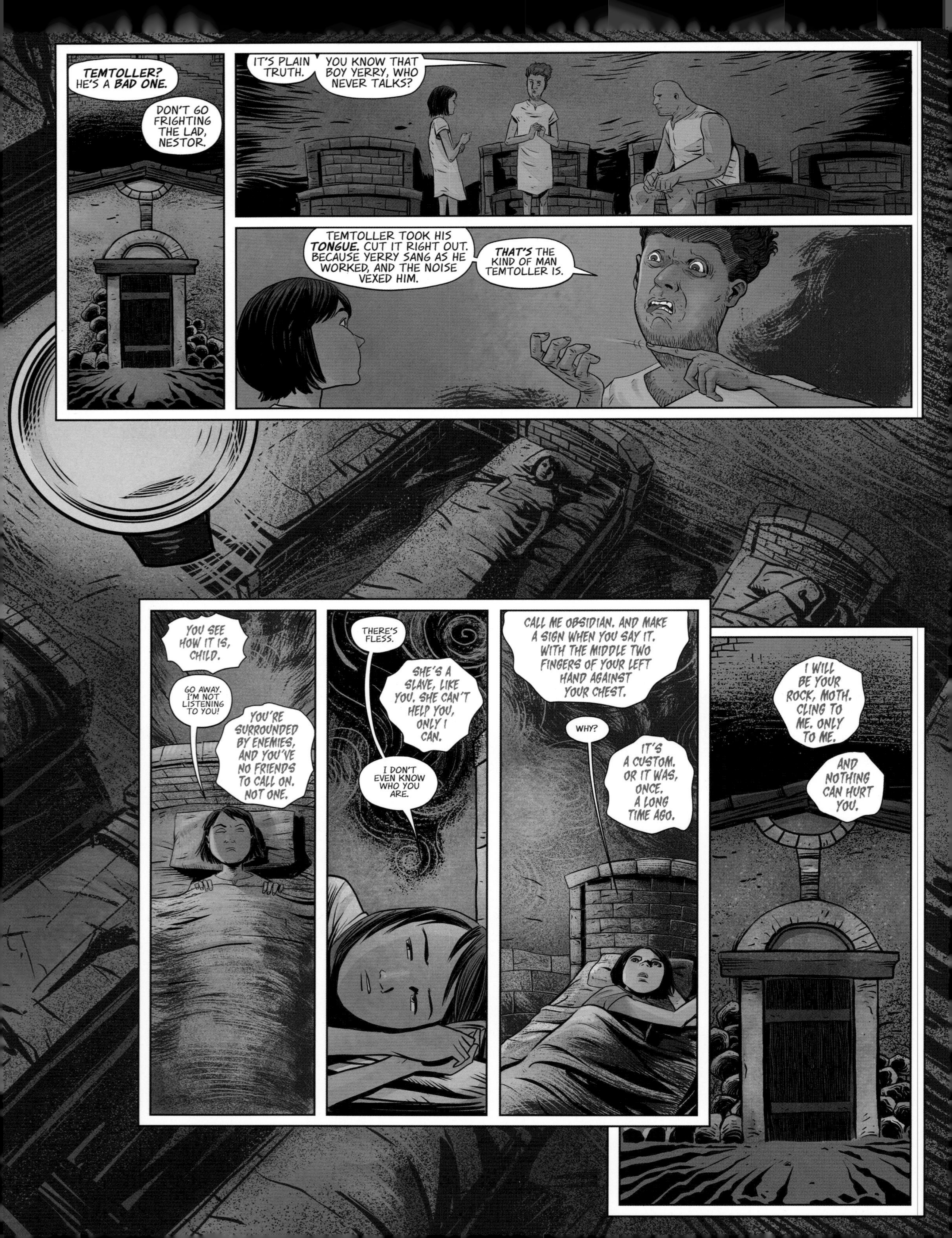
TEMTOLLER? HE'S A BAD ONE.
DON'T GO FRIGHTING THE LAD, NESTOR.
IT'S PLAIN TRUTH.
YOU KNOW THAT BOY YERRY, WHO NEVER TALKS?
TEMTOLLER TOOK HIS TONGUE. CUT IT RIGHT OUT. BECAUSE YERRY SANG AS HE WORKED, AND THE NOISE VEXED HIM.
THAT'S THE KIND OF MAN TEMTOLLER IS.
YOU SEE HOW IT IS, CHILD.
GO AWAY. I'M NOT LISTENING TO YOU!
YOU'RE SURROUNDED BY ENEMIES, AND YOU'VE NO FRIENDS TO CALL ON. NOT ONE.
THERE'S FLESS.
SHE'S A SLAVE, LIKE YOU. SHE CAN'T HELP YOU, ONLY I CAN.
I DON'T EVEN KNOW WHO YOU ARE.
CALL ME OBSIDIAN. AND MAKE A SIGN WHEN YOU SAY IT. WITH THE MIDDLE TWO FINGERS OF YOUR LEFT HAND AGAINST YOUR CHEST.
WHY?
IT'S A CUSTOM. OR IT WAS, ONCE. A LONG TIME AGO.
I WILL BE YOUR ROCK, MOTH. CLING TO ME. ONLY TO ME.
AND NOTHING CAN HURT YOU.

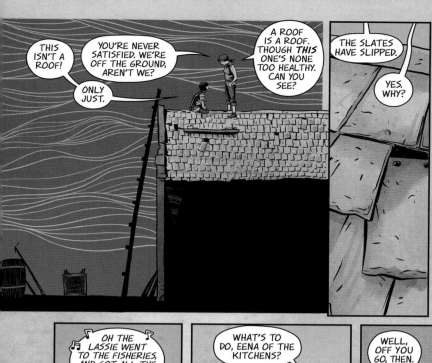

THIS ISN'T A ROOF!

YOU'RE NEVER SATISFIED. WE'RE OFF THE GROUND, AREN'T WE?

ONLY JUST.

A ROOF IS A ROOF. THOUGH *THIS* ONE'S NONE TOO HEALTHY. CAN YOU SEE?

THE SLATES HAVE SLIPPED.

YES. WHY?

BECAUSE THE PEGS HAVE *ROTTED*.

THEN LET'S *FIX* THEM. WHAT SAY YOU?

🎵 OH THE LASSIE WENT TO THE FISHERIES, AND GOT ALL THE FISH SHE COULD HOLD. 🎵

🎵 "TWAS BOLDLY DONE," HER MOTHER SAID, "BUT WHAT DID YOU USE FOR GOLD?" 🎵

WHAT'S TO DO, EENA OF THE KITCHENS?

SIEUR EXTAT SENT ME TO FETCH YOUR BOY TO HIM.

HE'S TO COME *RIGHT* NOW AND NOT TO TARRY ON THE WAY.

WELL, OFF YOU GO, THEN.

WHY WOULD THE STEWARD WANT TO SPEAK TO *ME*?

LIKE AS NOT HE'LL TELL YOU HIMSELF. SPEAK HIM FAIR, BE OBEDIENT AND HE'LL NOT HURT YOU.

WAS HIS FACE ANGRY, OR--?

I DIDN'T LOOK AT HIS FACE, RAGAMUFFIN BOY. SIEUR EXTAT IS A *WIZARD* AND HE CAN PLUCK YOUR SOUL OUT OF YOUR EYES.

I LOOKED AT THE GROUND.

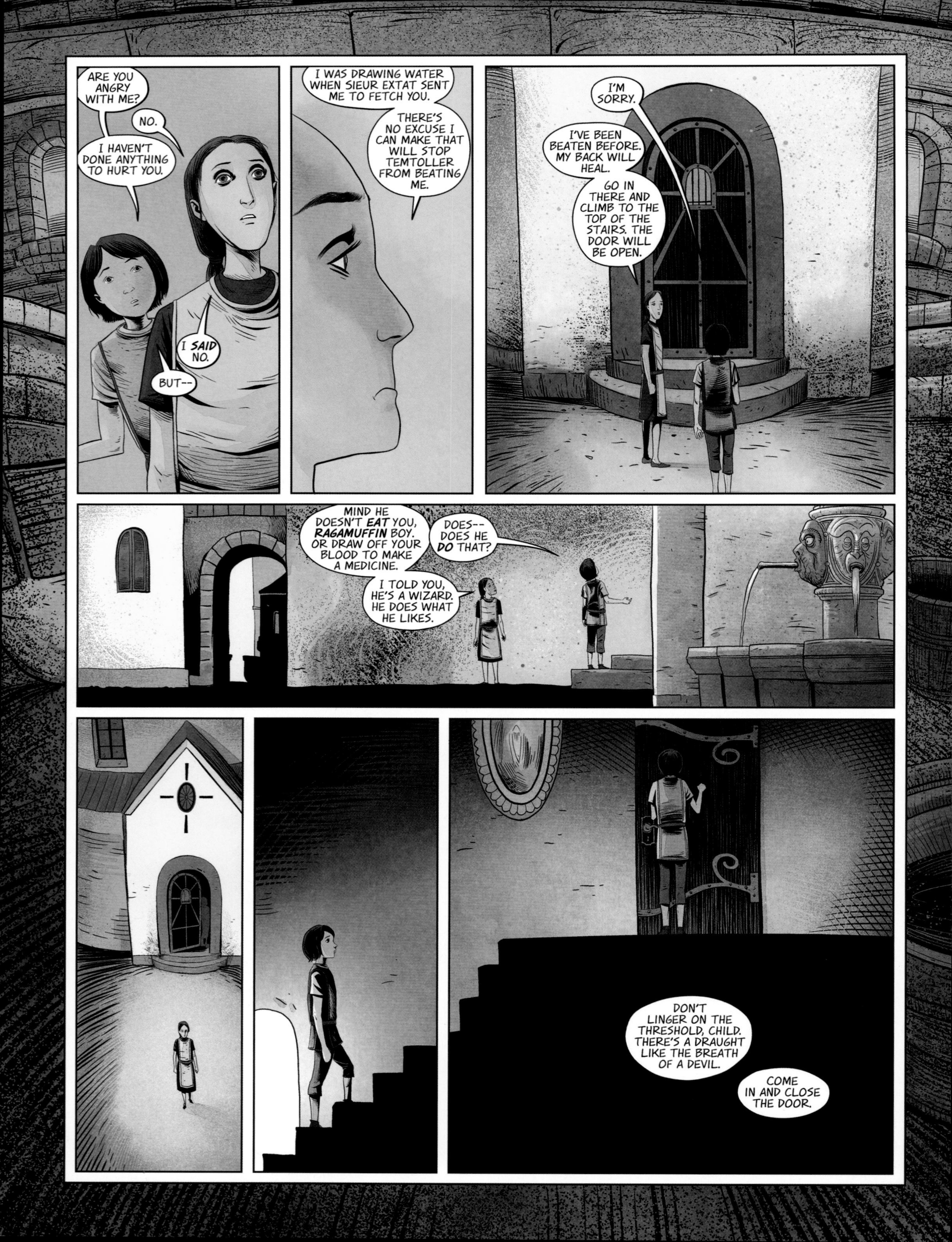

ARE YOU ANGRY WITH ME?
NO.
I HAVEN'T DONE ANYTHING TO HURT YOU.
I SAID NO.
BUT--
I WAS DRAWING WATER WHEN SIEUR EXTAT SENT ME TO FETCH YOU.
THERE'S NO EXCUSE I CAN MAKE THAT WILL STOP TEMTOLLER FROM BEATING ME.
I'M SORRY.
I'VE BEEN BEATEN BEFORE. MY BACK WILL HEAL.
GO IN THERE AND CLIMB TO THE TOP OF THE STAIRS. THE DOOR WILL BE OPEN.
MIND HE DOESN'T EAT YOU, RAGAMUFFIN BOY. OR DRAW OFF YOUR BLOOD TO MAKE A MEDICINE.
DOES-- DOES HE DO THAT?
I TOLD YOU, HE'S A WIZARD. HE DOES WHAT HE LIKES.
DON'T LINGER ON THE THRESHOLD, CHILD. THERE'S A DRAUGHT LIKE THE BREATH OF A DEVIL.
COME IN AND CLOSE THE DOOR.

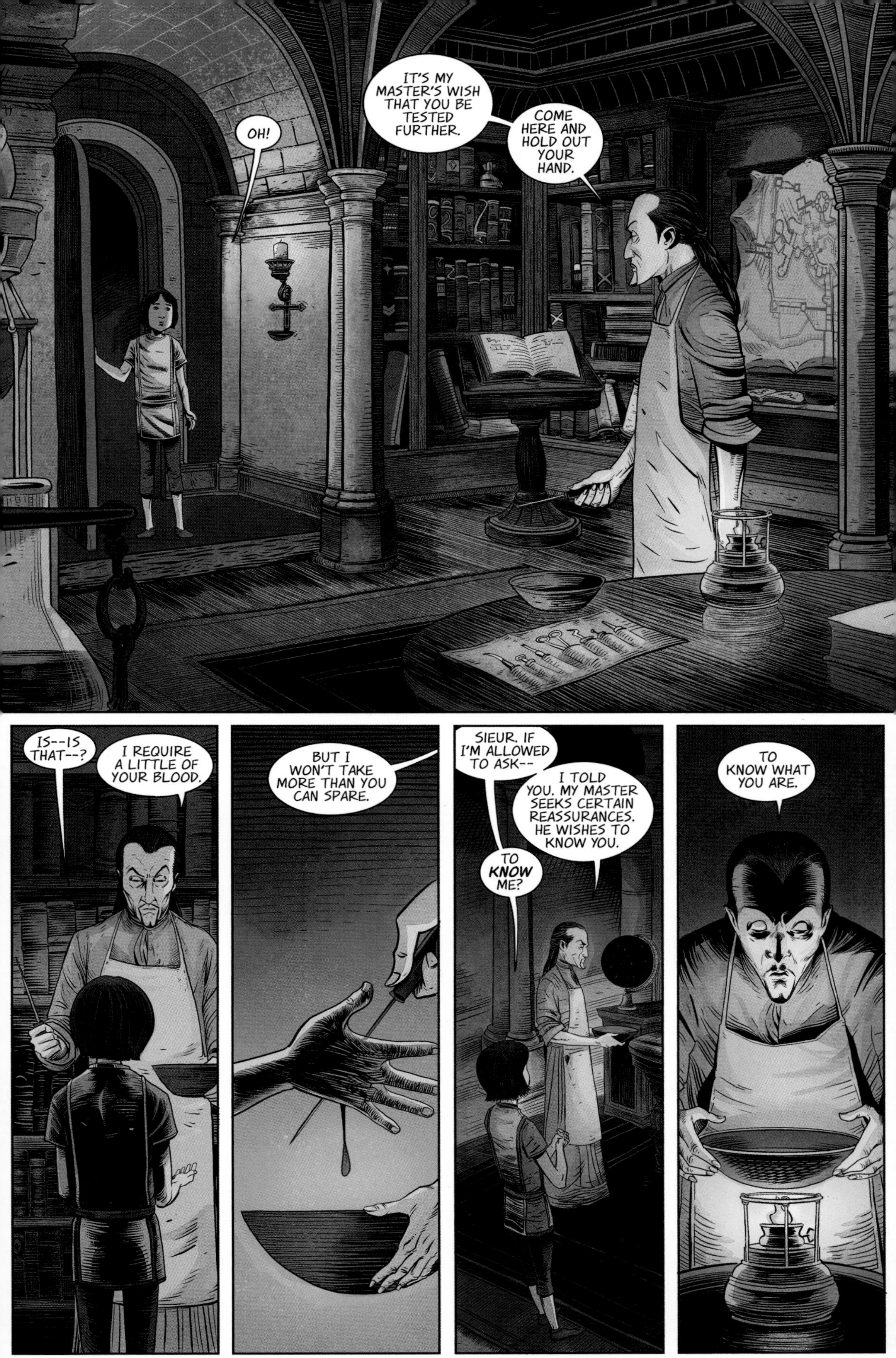
OH!
IT'S MY MASTER'S WISH THAT YOU BE TESTED FURTHER.
COME HERE AND HOLD OUT YOUR HAND.
IS--IS THAT--?
I REQUIRE A LITTLE OF YOUR BLOOD.
BUT I WON'T TAKE MORE THAN YOU CAN SPARE.
SIEUR. IF I'M ALLOWED TO ASK--
I TOLD YOU. MY MASTER SEEKS CERTAIN REASSURANCES. HE WISHES TO KNOW YOU.
TO KNOW ME?
TO KNOW WHAT YOU ARE.

YOU **SEE** THAT? OF COURSE YOU DO. I KNOW. I KNEW AS SOON AS I SAW HIM.

HE HAS THEIR **EYES.**

THIS SALVE WILL MAKE THE CUT HEAL MORE QUICKLY. SAY **NOTHING** OF WHAT WAS DONE HERE. TO **ANYONE.**

BUT YOU MAY ASK **ONE** QUESTION OF ME, IF YOU WISH.

NO, MAGISTER.

ONE QUESTION?

AYE.

THEN--IF IT PLEASE YOU, SIEUR-- WHAT IS THIS A PICTURE OF?

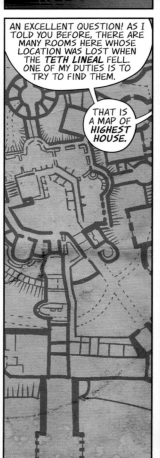

AN EXCELLENT QUESTION! AS I TOLD YOU BEFORE, THERE ARE MANY ROOMS HERE WHOSE LOCATION WAS LOST WHEN THE **TETH LINEAL** FELL. ONE OF MY DUTIES IS TO TRY TO FIND THEM.

THAT IS A MAP OF **HIGHEST HOUSE.**

A MAP?

A SCHEMATIC DIAGRAM. SEEN AS THOUGH ONE LOOKED AT EACH ROOM, EACH COURTYARD FROM ABOVE.

IT IS A WORK IN PROGRESS. **LORD DEMINI** HIMSELF BID ME MAKE IT.

IS IT MAGIC?

OF COURSE IT IS. ALL HUMAN THOUGHT IS MAGIC.

THESE BOOKS THAT SURROUND US, IF YOU COULD BUT UNDERSTAND THEM, WOULD GIVE YOU THE POWER TO UNMAKE THE WORLD AND BUILD IT ANEW.

A SLAVE WITH A **BOOK?** THE SKIES WOULD FALL! THAT IS WHERE THE REAL WALL IS SET BETWEEN THE POWERFUL AND THE POWERLESS, CHILD.

BAZAD MEG! I WISH I COULD READ, THEN!

NOT IN THE **WORLD,** BUT IN THE **MIND.**

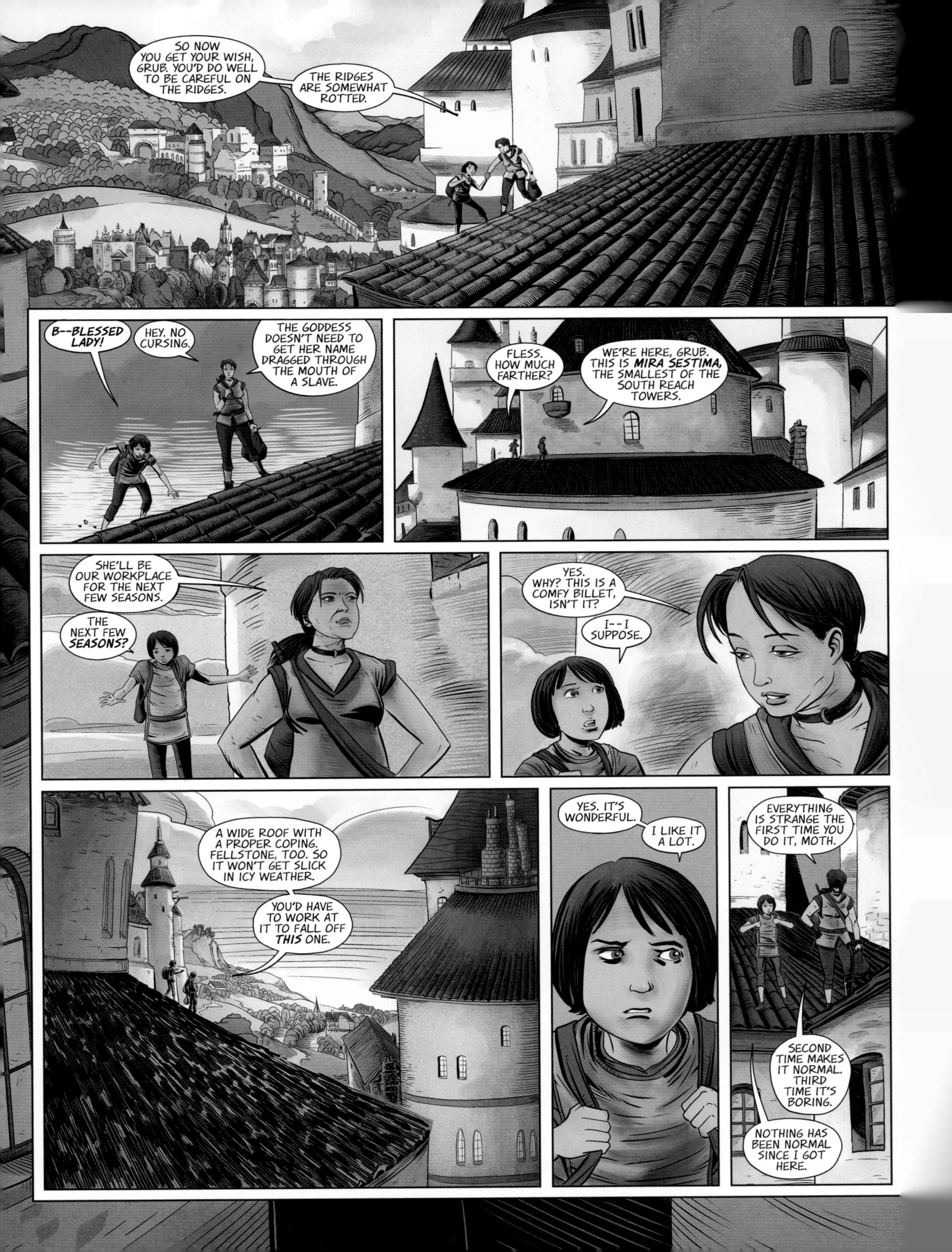
SO NOW YOU GET YOUR WISH, GRUB. YOU'D DO WELL TO BE CAREFUL ON THE RIDGES.
THE RIDGES ARE SOMEWHAT ROTTED.
B--BLESSED LADY!
HEY. NO CURSING.
THE GODDESS DOESN'T NEED TO GET HER NAME DRAGGED THROUGH THE MOUTH OF A SLAVE.
FLESS. HOW MUCH FARTHER?
WE'RE HERE, GRUB. THIS IS MIRA SESTIMA, THE SMALLEST OF THE SOUTH REACH TOWERS.
SHE'LL BE OUR WORKPLACE FOR THE NEXT FEW SEASONS.
THE NEXT FEW SEASONS?
YES. WHY? THIS IS A COMFY BILLET, ISN'T IT?
I--I SUPPOSE.
A WIDE ROOF WITH A PROPER COPING. FELLSTONE, TOO. SO IT WON'T GET SLICK IN ICY WEATHER.
YOU'D HAVE TO WORK AT IT TO FALL OFF THIS ONE.
YES. IT'S WONDERFUL.
I LIKE IT A LOT.
EVERYTHING IS STRANGE THE FIRST TIME YOU DO IT, MOTH.
SECOND TIME MAKES IT NORMAL. THIRD TIME IT'S BORING.
NOTHING HAS BEEN NORMAL SINCE I GOT HERE.

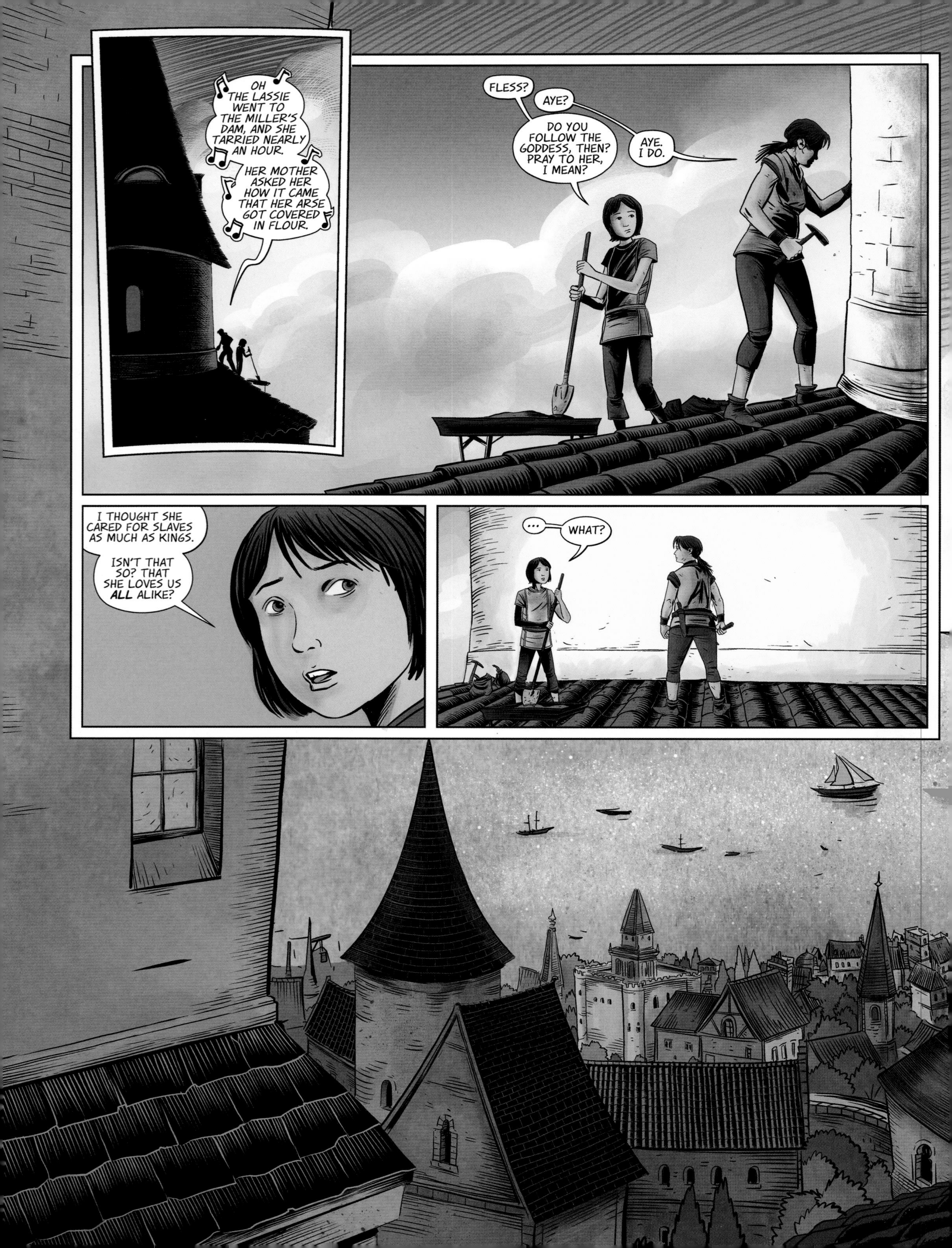
OH THE LASSIE WENT TO THE MILLER'S DAM, AND SHE TARRIED NEARLY AN HOUR.
HER MOTHER ASKED HER HOW IT CAME THAT HER ARSE GOT COVERED IN FLOUR.
FLESS?
AYE?
DO YOU FOLLOW THE GODDESS, THEN? PRAY TO HER, I MEAN?
AYE. I DO.
I THOUGHT SHE CARED FOR SLAVES AS MUCH AS KINGS.
ISN'T THAT SO? THAT SHE LOVES US ALL ALIKE?
...
WHAT?

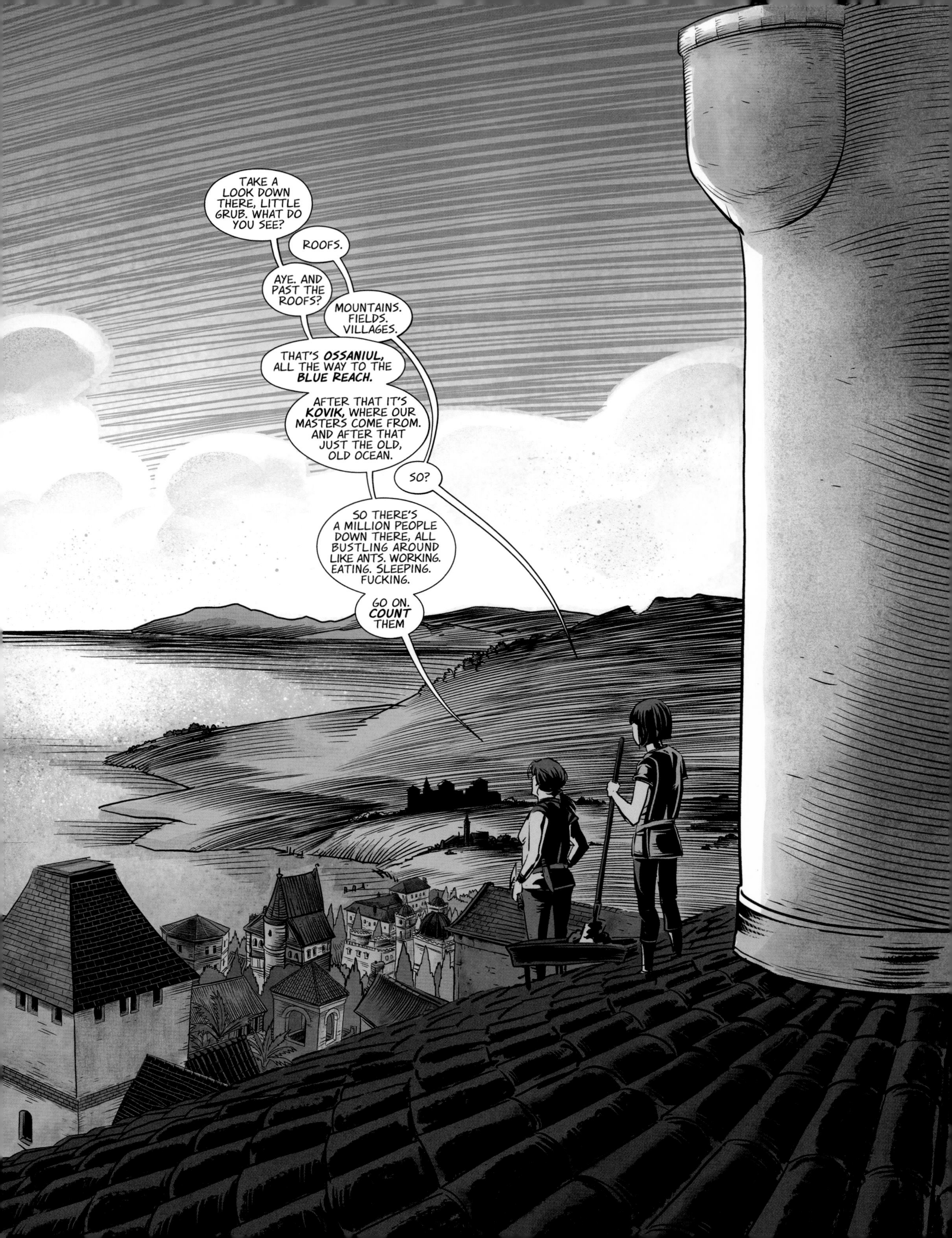
TAKE A LOOK DOWN THERE, LITTLE GRUB. WHAT DO YOU SEE?
ROOFS.
AYE. AND PAST THE ROOFS?
MOUNTAINS. FIELDS. VILLAGES.
THAT'S **OSSANIUL,** ALL THE WAY TO THE **BLUE REACH.**
AFTER THAT IT'S **KOVIK,** WHERE OUR MASTERS COME FROM. AND AFTER THAT JUST THE OLD, OLD OCEAN.
SO?
SO THERE'S A MILLION PEOPLE DOWN THERE, ALL BUSTLING AROUND LIKE ANTS. WORKING. EATING. SLEEPING. FUCKING.
GO ON. **COUNT** THEM

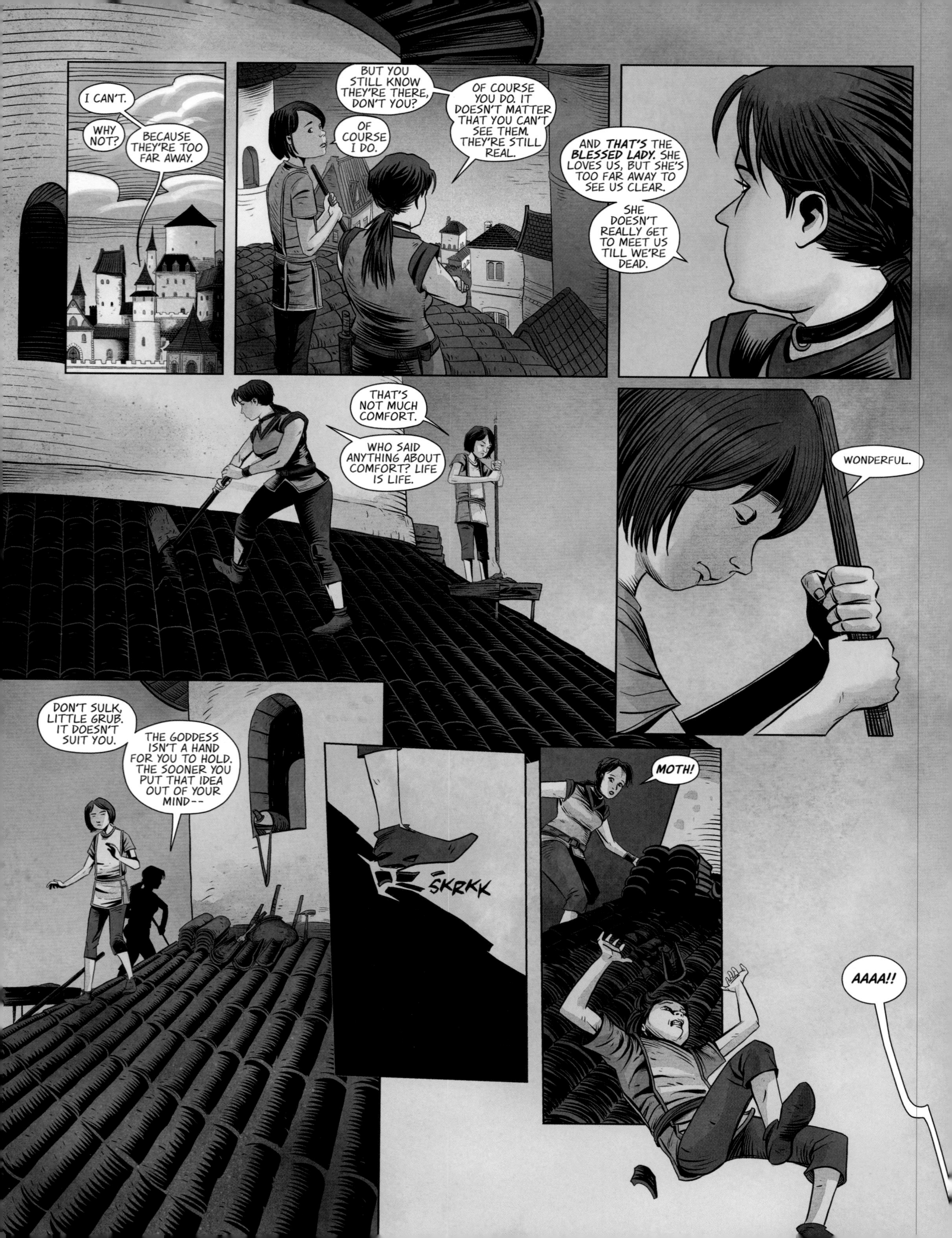
I CAN'T.
WHY NOT?
BECAUSE THEY'RE TOO FAR AWAY.
BUT YOU STILL KNOW THEY'RE THERE, DON'T YOU?
OF COURSE I DO.
OF COURSE YOU DO. IT DOESN'T MATTER THAT YOU CAN'T SEE THEM. THEY'RE STILL REAL.
AND THAT'S THE BLESSED LADY. SHE LOVES US, BUT SHE'S TOO FAR AWAY TO SEE US CLEAR.
SHE DOESN'T REALLY GET TO MEET US TILL WE'RE DEAD.
THAT'S NOT MUCH COMFORT.
WHO SAID ANYTHING ABOUT COMFORT? LIFE IS LIFE.
WONDERFUL.
DON'T SULK, LITTLE GRUB. IT DOESN'T SUIT YOU.
THE GODDESS ISN'T A HAND FOR YOU TO HOLD. THE SOONER YOU PUT THAT IDEA OUT OF YOUR MIND--
SKRKK
MOTH!
AAAA!!

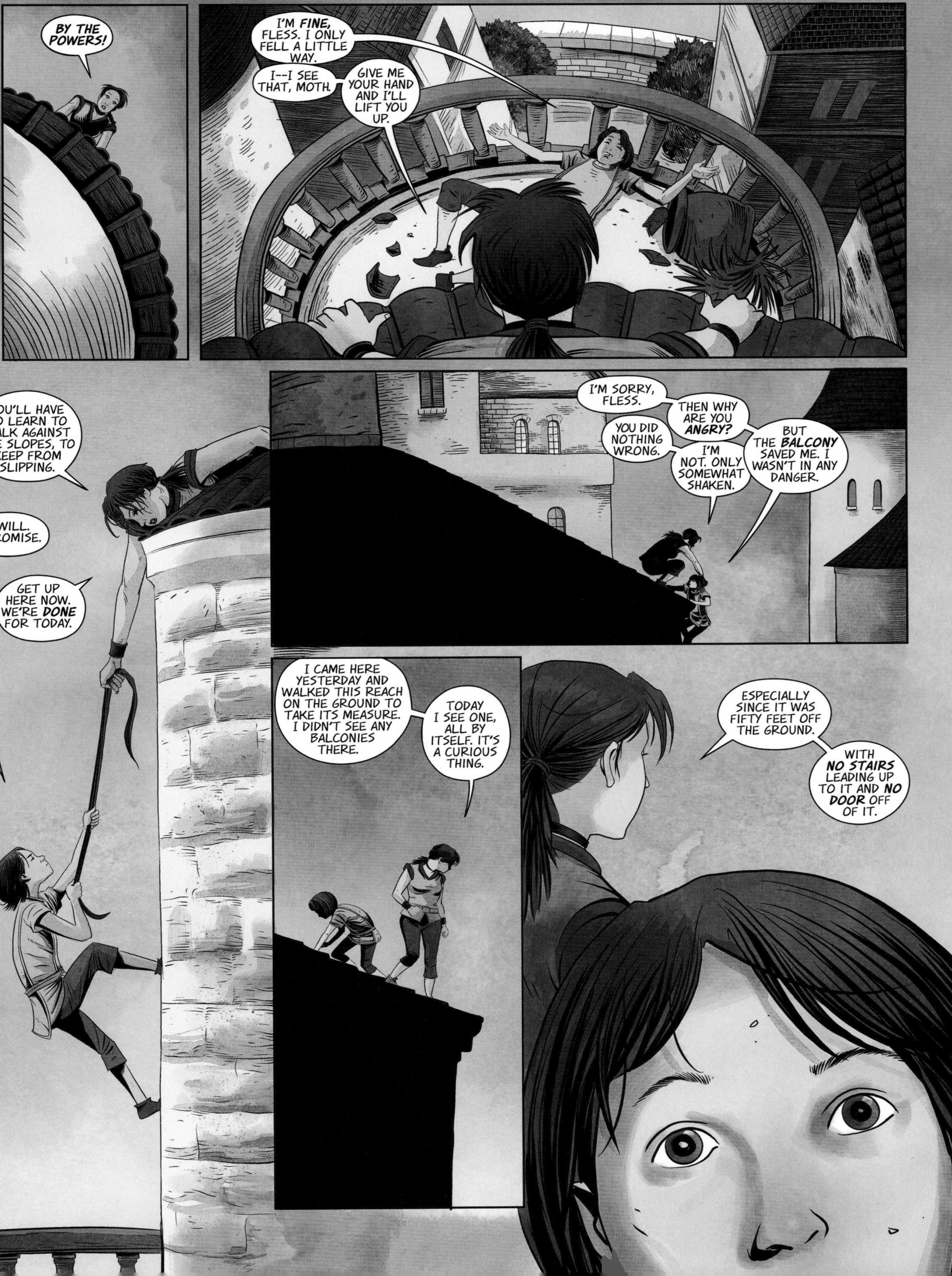

BY THE POWERS!
I'M FINE, FLESS. I ONLY FELL A LITTLE WAY.
I--I SEE THAT, MOTH.
GIVE ME YOUR HAND AND I'LL LIFT YOU UP.
YOU'LL HAVE TO LEARN TO WALK AGAINST THE SLOPES, TO KEEP FROM SLIPPING.
I WILL. I PROMISE.
GET UP HERE NOW. WE'RE DONE FOR TODAY.
I'M SORRY, FLESS.
YOU DID NOTHING WRONG.
THEN WHY ARE YOU ANGRY?
I'M NOT. ONLY SOMEWHAT SHAKEN.
BUT THE BALCONY SAVED ME. I WASN'T IN ANY DANGER.
I CAME HERE YESTERDAY AND WALKED THIS REACH ON THE GROUND TO TAKE ITS MEASURE. I DIDN'T SEE ANY BALCONIES THERE.
TODAY I SEE ONE, ALL BY ITSELF. IT'S A CURIOUS THING.
ESPECIALLY SINCE IT WAS FIFTY FEET OFF THE GROUND.
WITH NO STAIRS LEADING UP TO IT AND NO DOOR OFF OF IT.

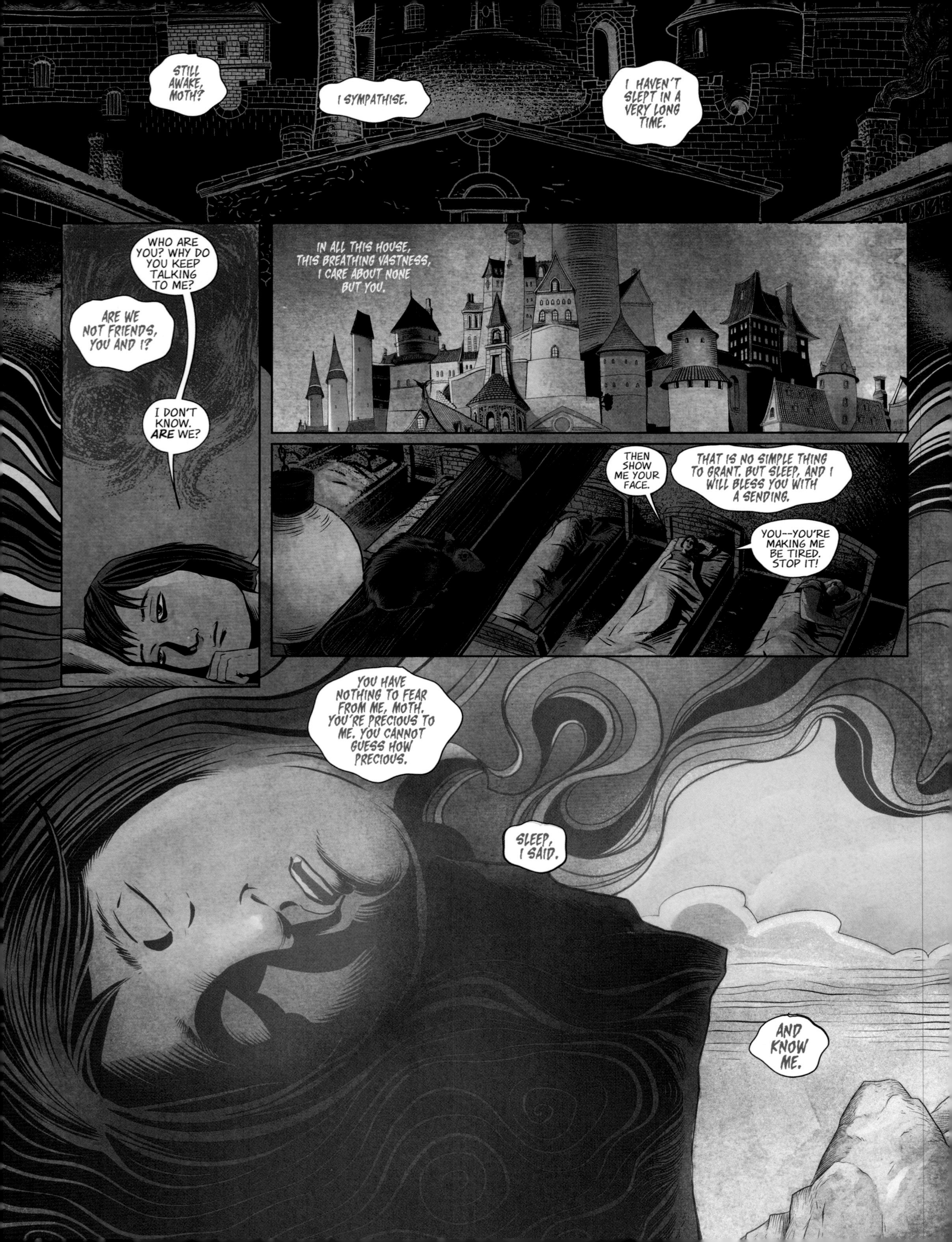
STILL AWAKE, MOTH?
I SYMPATHISE.
I HAVEN'T SLEPT IN A VERY LONG TIME.
WHO ARE YOU? WHY DO YOU KEEP TALKING TO ME?
ARE WE NOT FRIENDS, YOU AND I?
I DON'T KNOW. ARE WE?
IN ALL THIS HOUSE, THIS BREATHING VASTNESS, I CARE ABOUT NONE BUT YOU.
THEN SHOW ME YOUR FACE.
THAT IS NO SIMPLE THING TO GRANT. BUT SLEEP, AND I WILL BLESS YOU WITH A SENDING.
YOU--YOU'RE MAKING ME BE TIRED. STOP IT!
YOU HAVE NOTHING TO FEAR FROM ME, MOTH. YOU'RE PRECIOUS TO ME. YOU CANNOT GUESS HOW PRECIOUS.
SLEEP, I SAID.
AND KNOW ME.

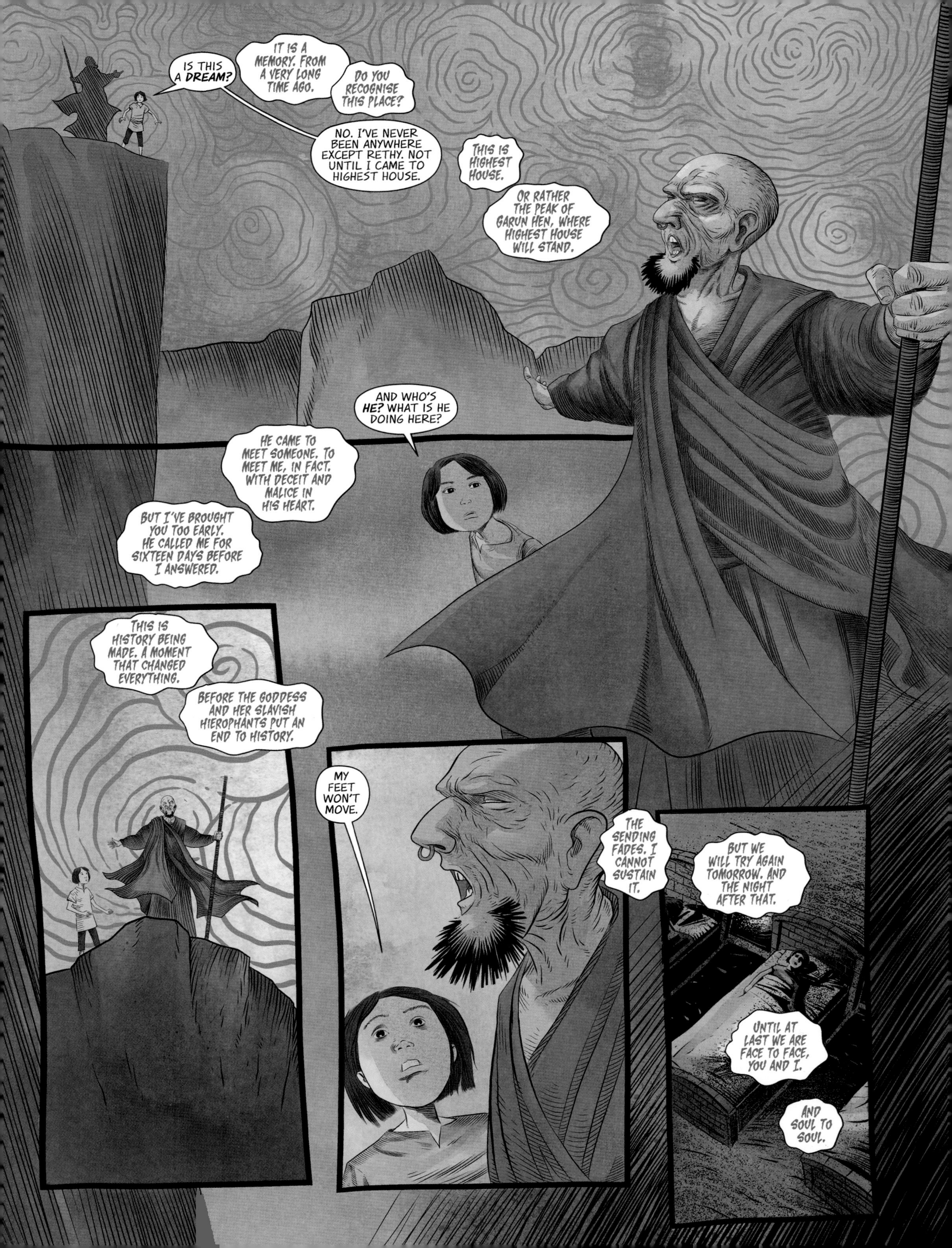
IS THIS A DREAM?
IT IS A MEMORY. FROM A VERY LONG TIME AGO.
DO YOU RECOGNISE THIS PLACE?
NO. I'VE NEVER BEEN ANYWHERE EXCEPT RETHY. NOT UNTIL I CAME TO HIGHEST HOUSE.
THIS IS HIGHEST HOUSE.
OR RATHER THE PEAK OF GARUN HEN, WHERE HIGHEST HOUSE WILL STAND.
AND WHO'S HE? WHAT IS HE DOING HERE?
HE CAME TO MEET SOMEONE. TO MEET ME, IN FACT. WITH DECEIT AND MALICE IN HIS HEART.
BUT I'VE BROUGHT YOU TOO EARLY. HE CALLED ME FOR SIXTEEN DAYS BEFORE I ANSWERED.
THIS IS HISTORY BEING MADE. A MOMENT THAT CHANGED EVERYTHING.
BEFORE THE GODDESS AND HER SLAVISH HIEROPHANTS PUT AN END TO HISTORY.
MY FEET WON'T MOVE.
THE SENDING FADES. I CANNOT SUSTAIN IT.
BUT WE WILL TRY AGAIN TOMORROW. AND THE NIGHT AFTER THAT.
UNTIL AT LAST WE ARE FACE TO FACE, YOU AND I.
AND SOUL TO SOUL.

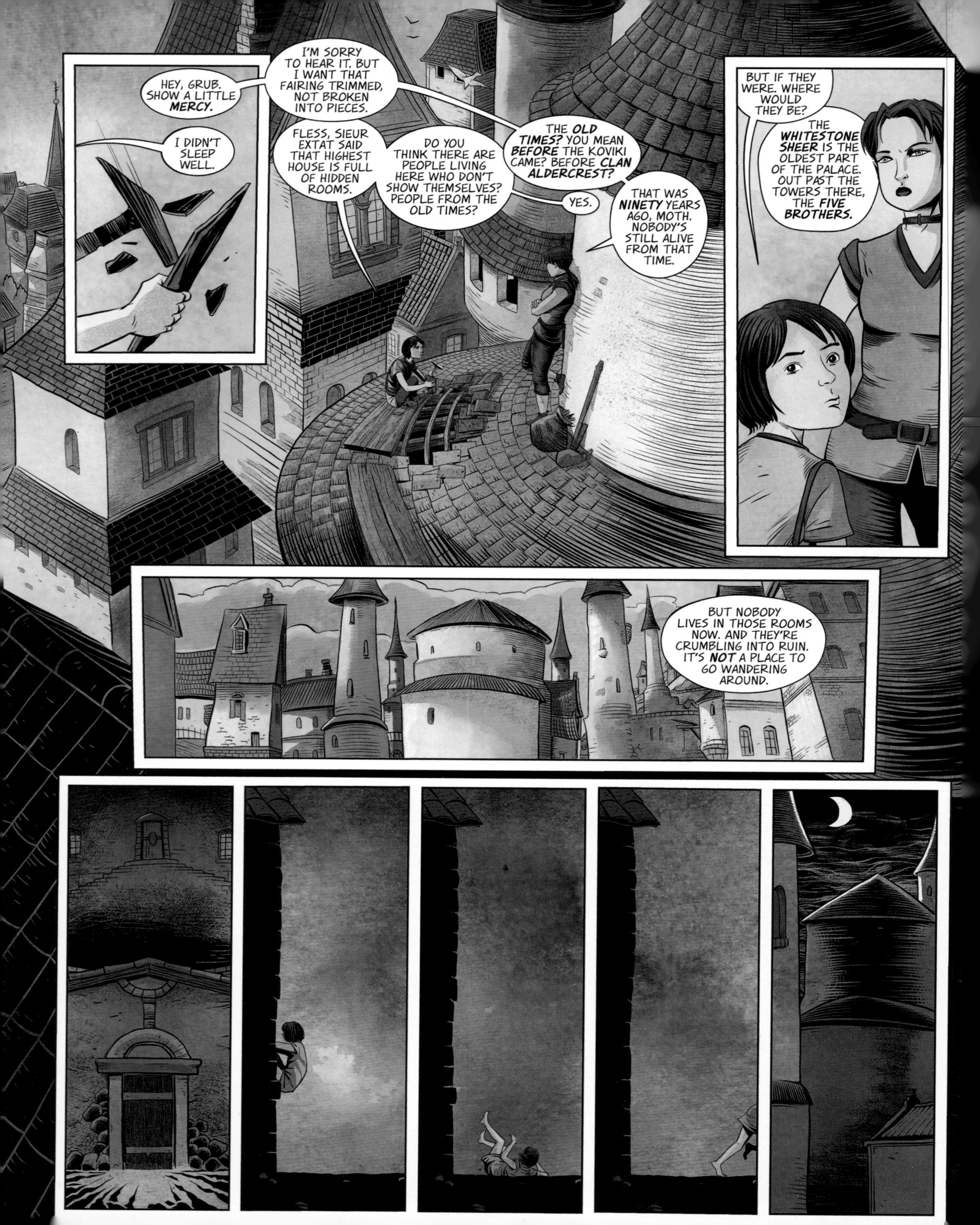
HEY, GRUB. SHOW A LITTLE MERCY.
I'M SORRY TO HEAR IT. BUT I WANT THAT FAIRING TRIMMED, NOT BROKEN INTO PIECES.
I DIDN'T SLEEP WELL.
FLESS, SIEUR EXTAT SAID THAT HIGHEST HOUSE IS FULL OF HIDDEN ROOMS.
DO YOU THINK THERE ARE PEOPLE LIVING HERE WHO DON'T SHOW THEMSELVES? PEOPLE FROM THE OLD TIMES?
THE OLD TIMES? YOU MEAN BEFORE THE KOVIKI CAME? BEFORE CLAN ALDERCREST?
YES.
THAT WAS NINETY YEARS AGO, MOTH. NOBODY'S STILL ALIVE FROM THAT TIME.
BUT IF THEY WERE. WHERE WOULD THEY BE?
THE WHITESTONE SHEER IS THE OLDEST PART OF THE PALACE. OUT PAST THE TOWERS THERE, THE FIVE BROTHERS.
BUT NOBODY LIVES IN THOSE ROOMS NOW. AND THEY'RE CRUMBLING INTO RUIN. IT'S NOT A PLACE TO GO WANDERING AROUND.

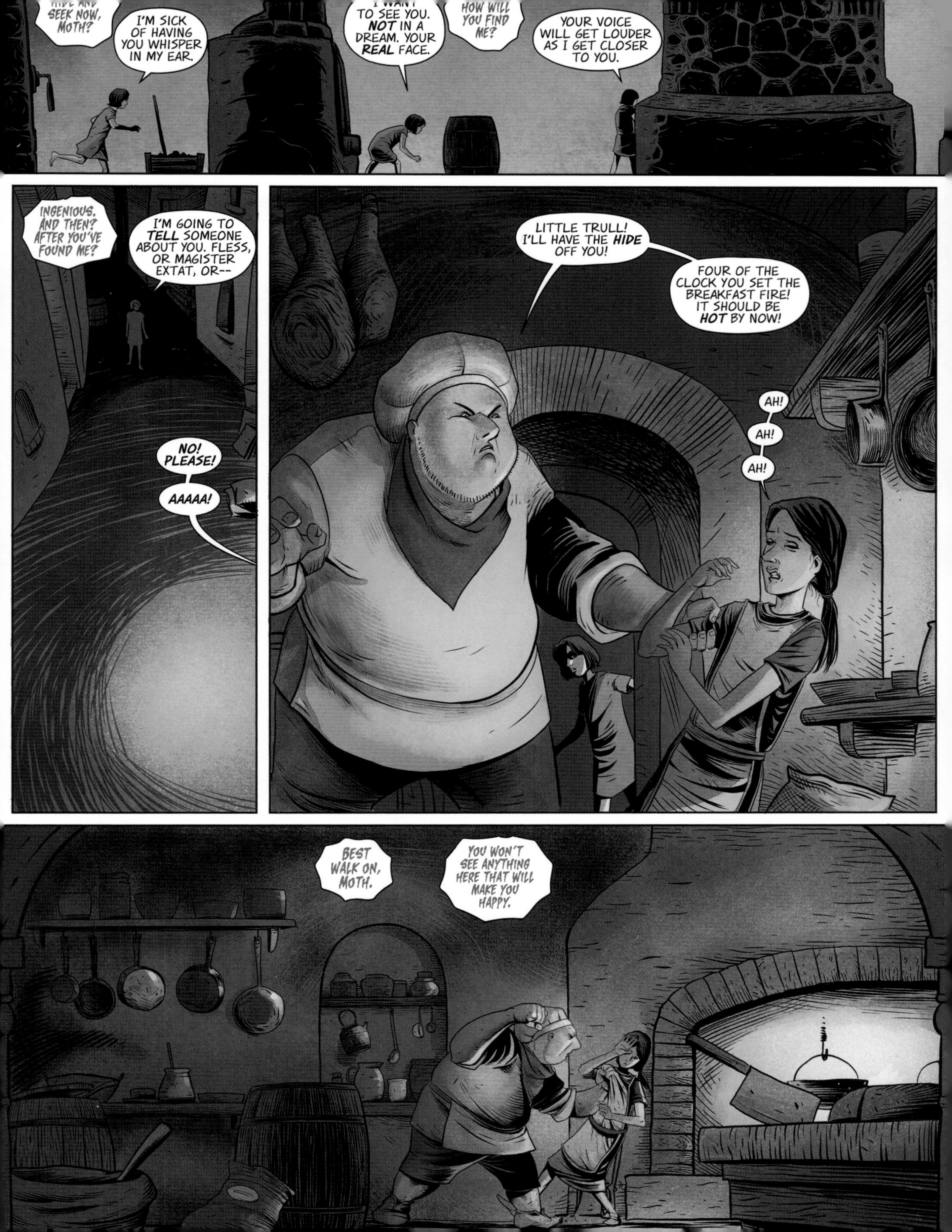
SEEK NOW, MOTH?
I'M SICK OF HAVING YOU WHISPER IN MY EAR.
TO SEE YOU. NOT IN A DREAM. YOUR REAL FACE.
HOW WILL YOU FIND ME?
YOUR VOICE WILL GET LOUDER AS I GET CLOSER TO YOU.
INGENIOUS. AND THEN? AFTER YOU'VE FOUND ME?
I'M GOING TO TELL SOMEONE ABOUT YOU. FLESS, OR MAGISTER EXTAT, OR--
NO! PLEASE!
AAAAA!
LITTLE TRULL! I'LL HAVE THE HIDE OFF YOU!
FOUR OF THE CLOCK YOU SET THE BREAKFAST FIRE! IT SHOULD BE HOT BY NOW!
AH!
AH!
AH!
BEST WALK ON, MOTH.
YOU WON'T SEE ANYTHING HERE THAT WILL MAKE YOU HAPPY.

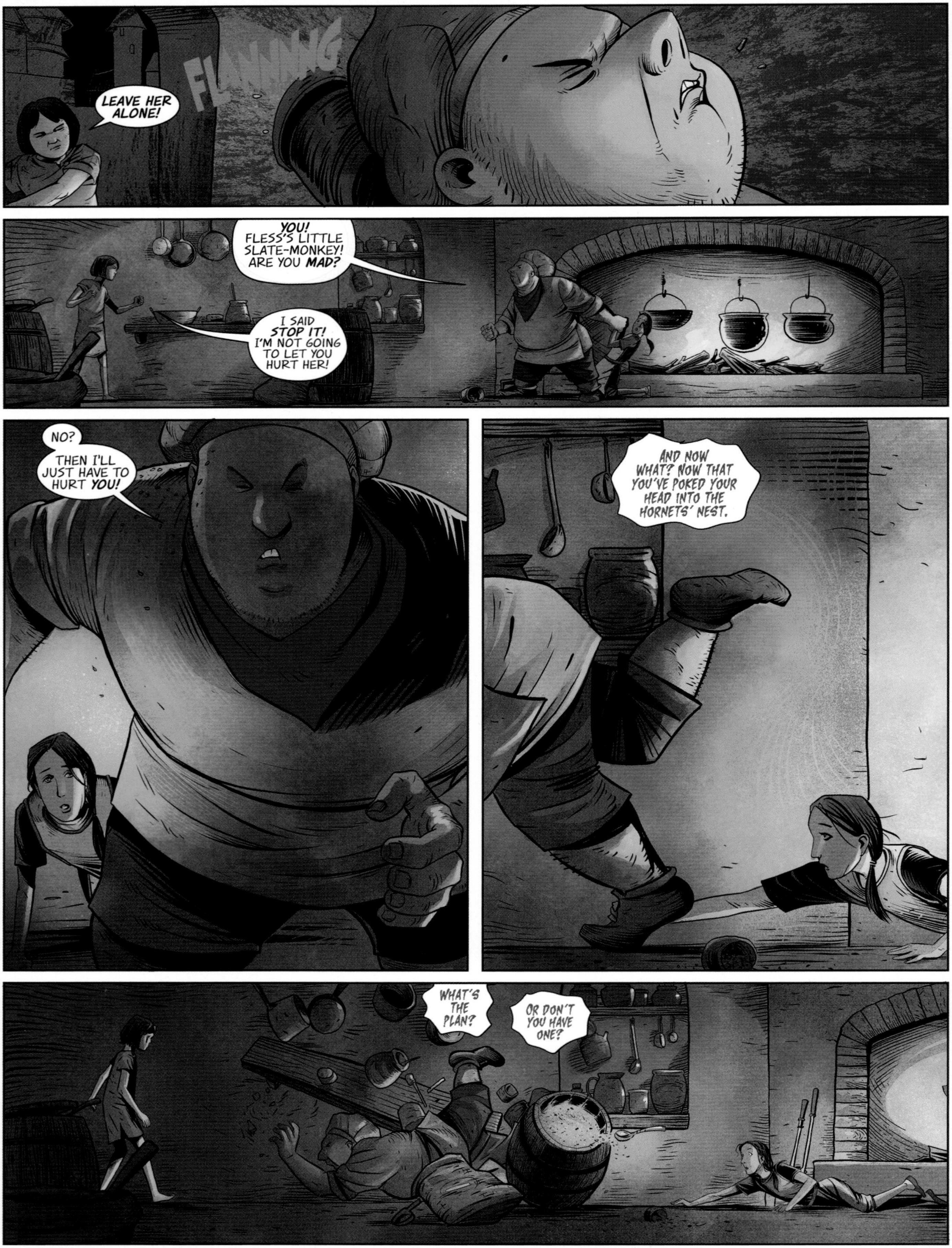
LEAVE HER ALONE!
FLANNNG
YOU! FLESS'S LITTLE SLATE-MONKEY! ARE YOU MAD?
I SAID STOP IT! I'M NOT GOING TO LET YOU HURT HER!
NO?
THEN I'LL JUST HAVE TO HURT YOU!
AND NOW WHAT? NOW THAT YOU'VE POKED YOUR HEAD INTO THE HORNETS' NEST.
WHAT'S THE PLAN?
OR DON'T YOU HAVE ONE?

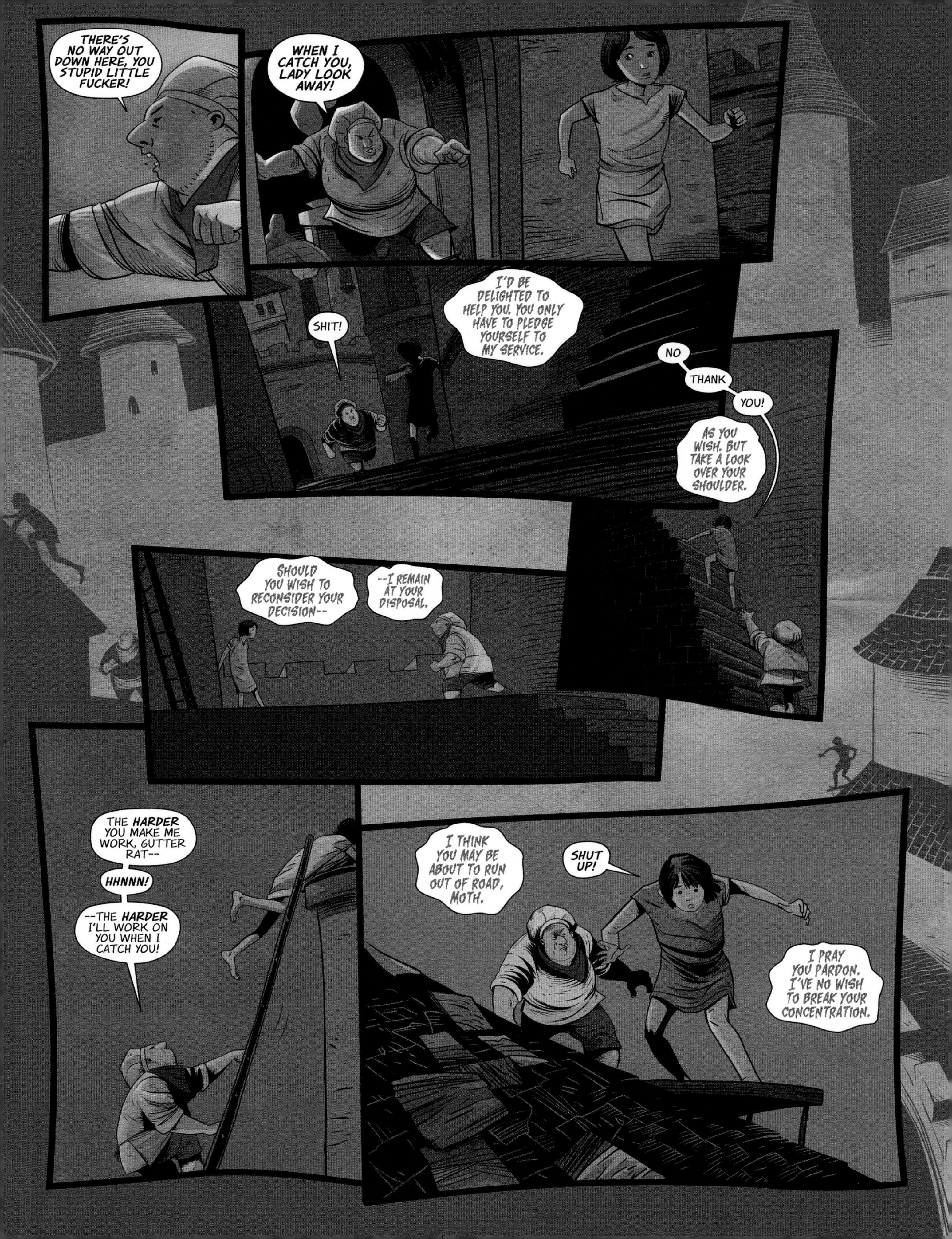
THERE'S NO WAY OUT DOWN HERE, YOU STUPID LITTLE FUCKER!
WHEN I CATCH YOU, LADY LOOK AWAY!
SHIT!
I'D BE DELIGHTED TO HELP YOU. YOU ONLY HAVE TO PLEDGE YOURSELF TO MY SERVICE.
NO
THANK
YOU!
AS YOU WISH. BUT TAKE A LOOK OVER YOUR SHOULDER.
SHOULD YOU WISH TO RECONSIDER YOUR DECISION--
--I REMAIN AT YOUR DISPOSAL.
THE HARDER YOU MAKE ME WORK, GUTTER RAT--
HHNNN!
--THE HARDER I'LL WORK ON YOU WHEN I CATCH YOU!
I THINK YOU MAY BE ABOUT TO RUN OUT OF ROAD, MOTH.
SHUT UP!
I PRAY YOU PARDON. I'VE NO WISH TO BREAK YOUR CONCENTRATION.

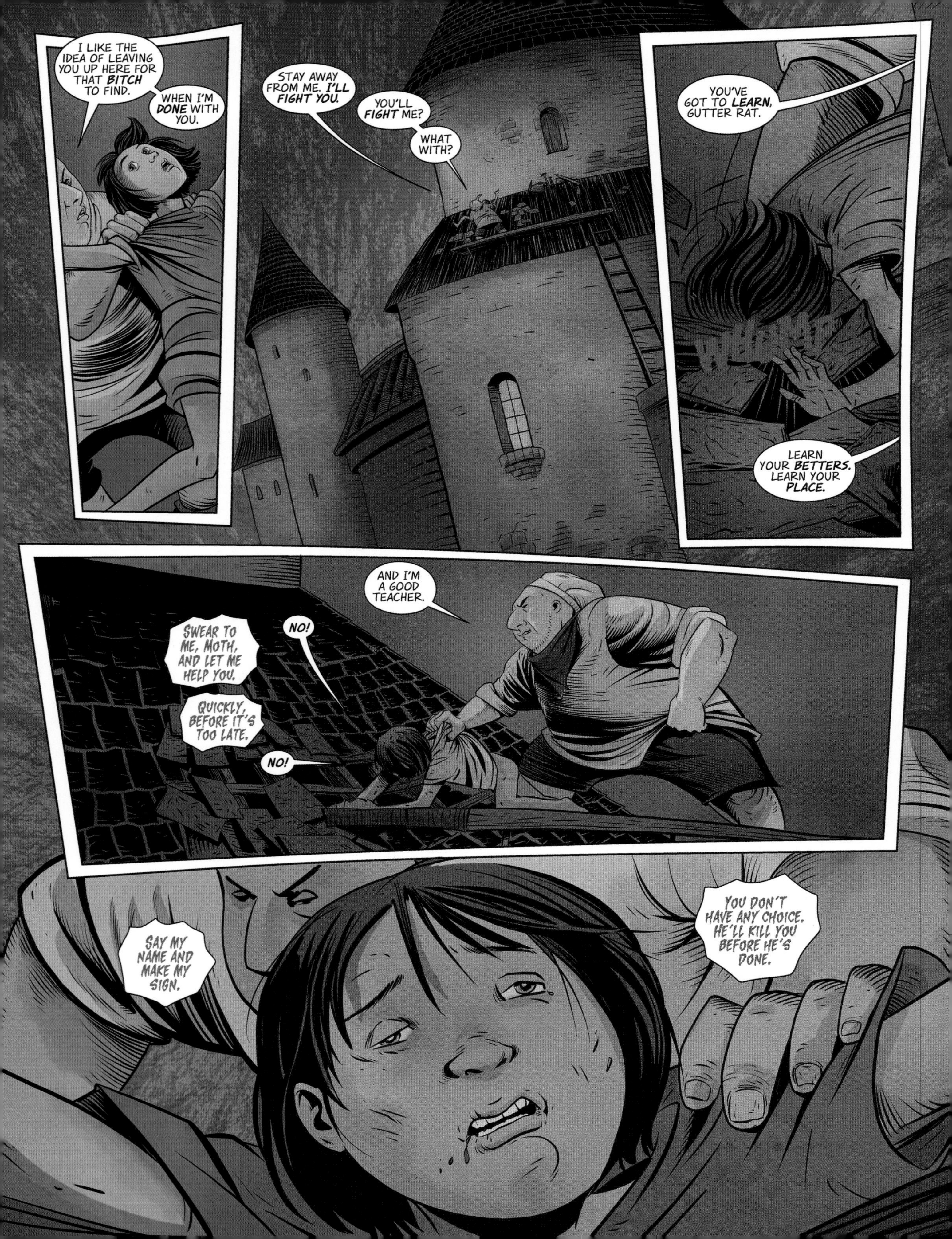
I LIKE THE IDEA OF LEAVING YOU UP HERE FOR THAT BITCH TO FIND.
WHEN I'M DONE WITH YOU.
STAY AWAY FROM ME. I'LL FIGHT YOU.
YOU'LL FIGHT ME?
WHAT WITH?
YOU'VE GOT TO LEARN, GUTTER RAT.
WHUMP
LEARN YOUR BETTERS. LEARN YOUR PLACE.
AND I'M A GOOD TEACHER.
SWEAR TO ME, MOTH, AND LET ME HELP YOU.
NO!
QUICKLY, BEFORE IT'S TOO LATE.
NO!
SAY MY NAME AND MAKE MY SIGN.
YOU DON'T HAVE ANY CHOICE. HE'LL KILL YOU BEFORE HE'S DONE.

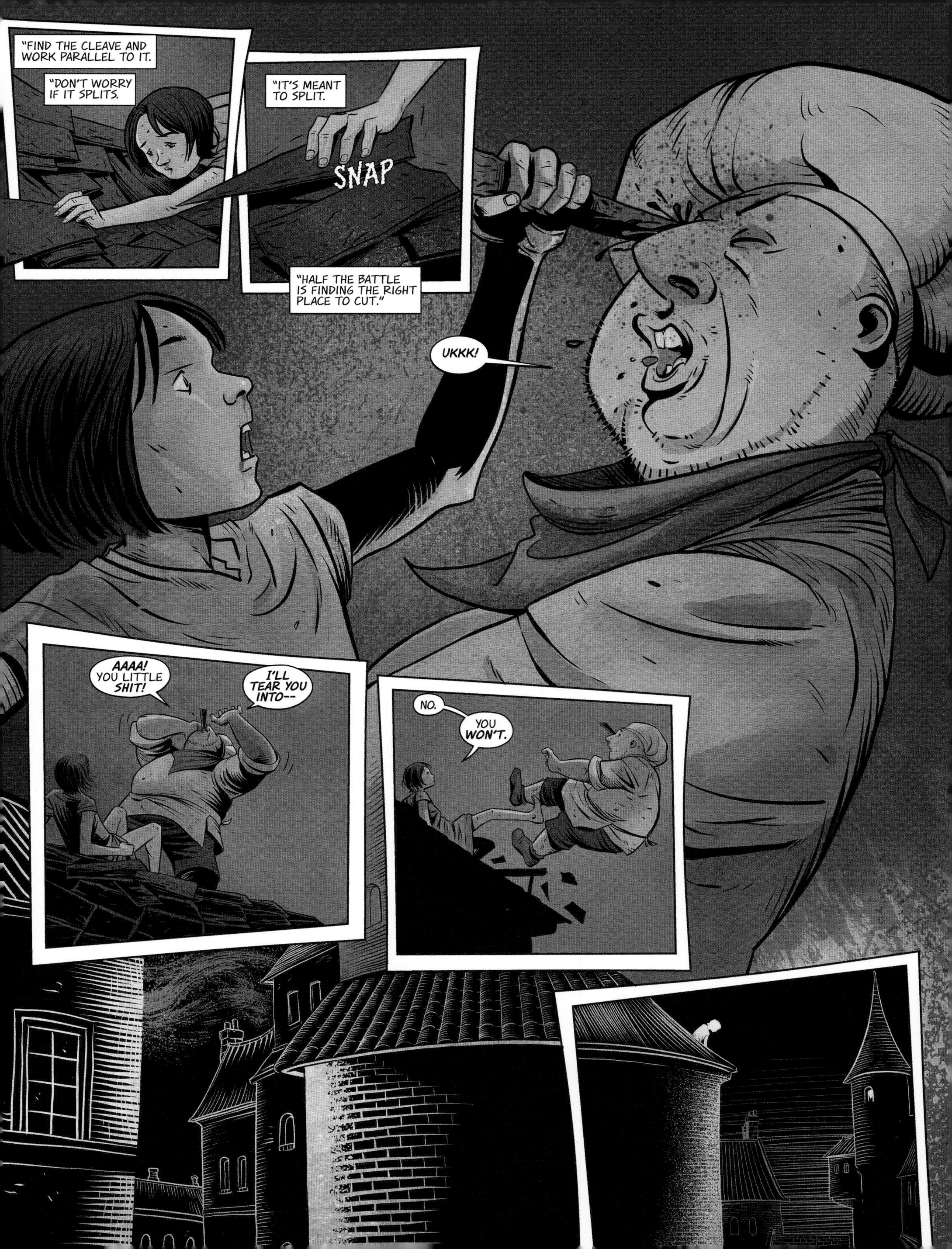

"FIND THE CLEAVE AND WORK PARALLEL TO IT.
"DON'T WORRY IF IT SPLITS.
"IT'S MEANT TO SPLIT.
SNAP
"HALF THE BATTLE IS FINDING THE RIGHT PLACE TO CUT."
UKKK!
AAAA! YOU LITTLE SHIT!
I'LL TEAR YOU INTO--
NO.
YOU WON'T.

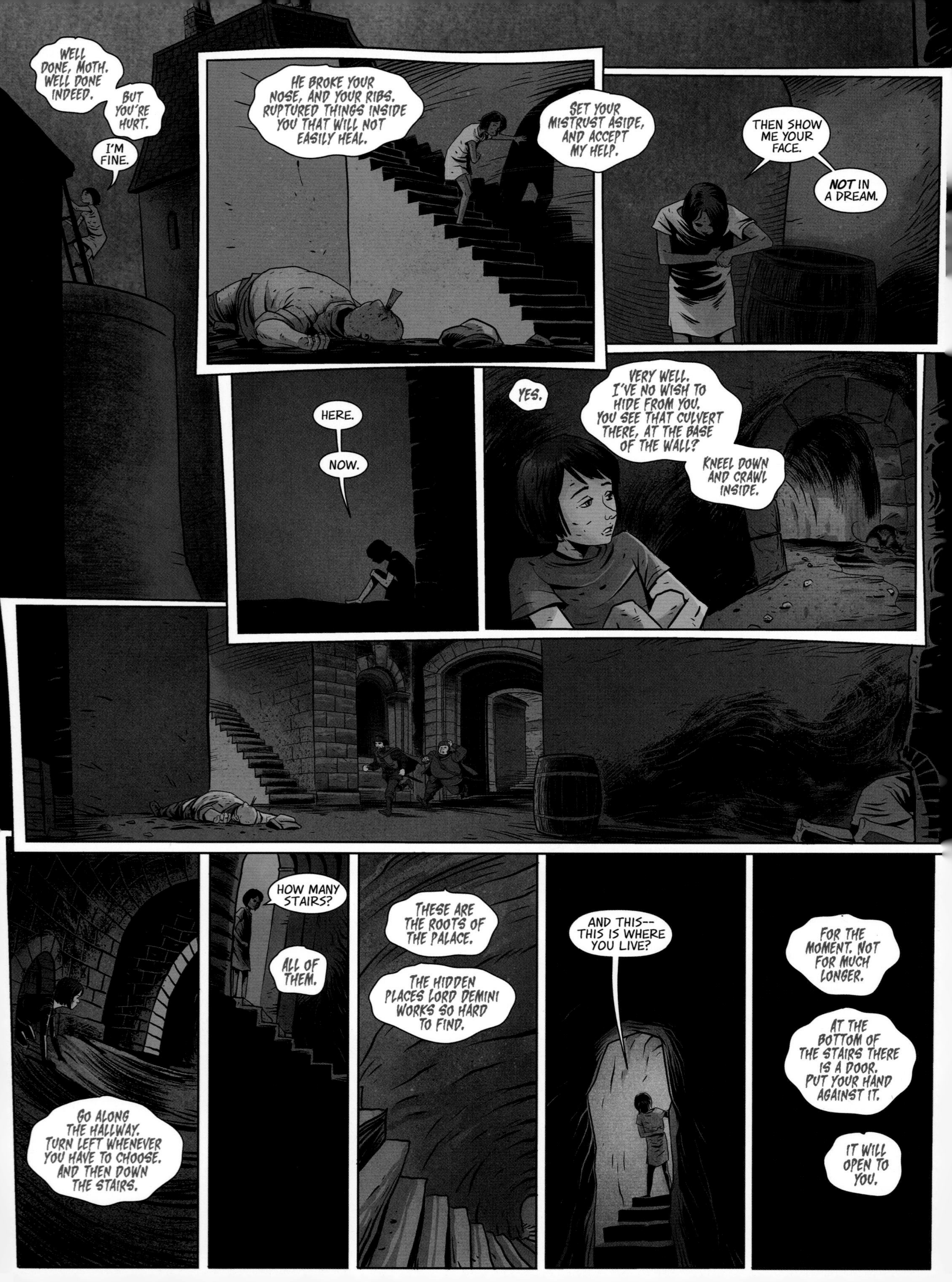
WELL DONE, MOTH. WELL DONE INDEED.
BUT YOU'RE HURT.
I'M FINE.
HE BROKE YOUR NOSE, AND YOUR RIBS. RUPTURED THINGS INSIDE YOU THAT WILL NOT EASILY HEAL.
SET YOUR MISTRUST ASIDE, AND ACCEPT MY HELP.
THEN SHOW ME YOUR FACE.
NOT IN A DREAM.
HERE.
NOW.
YES.
VERY WELL. I'VE NO WISH TO HIDE FROM YOU. YOU SEE THAT CULVERT THERE, AT THE BASE OF THE WALL?
KNEEL DOWN AND CRAWL INSIDE.
GO ALONG THE HALLWAY. TURN LEFT WHENEVER YOU HAVE TO CHOOSE. AND THEN DOWN THE STAIRS.
HOW MANY STAIRS?
ALL OF THEM.
THESE ARE THE ROOTS OF THE PALACE.
THE HIDDEN PLACES LORD DEMINI WORKS SO HARD TO FIND.
AND THIS-- THIS IS WHERE YOU LIVE?
FOR THE MOMENT. NOT FOR MUCH LONGER.
AT THE BOTTOM OF THE STAIRS THERE IS A DOOR. PUT YOUR HAND AGAINST IT.
IT WILL OPEN TO YOU.

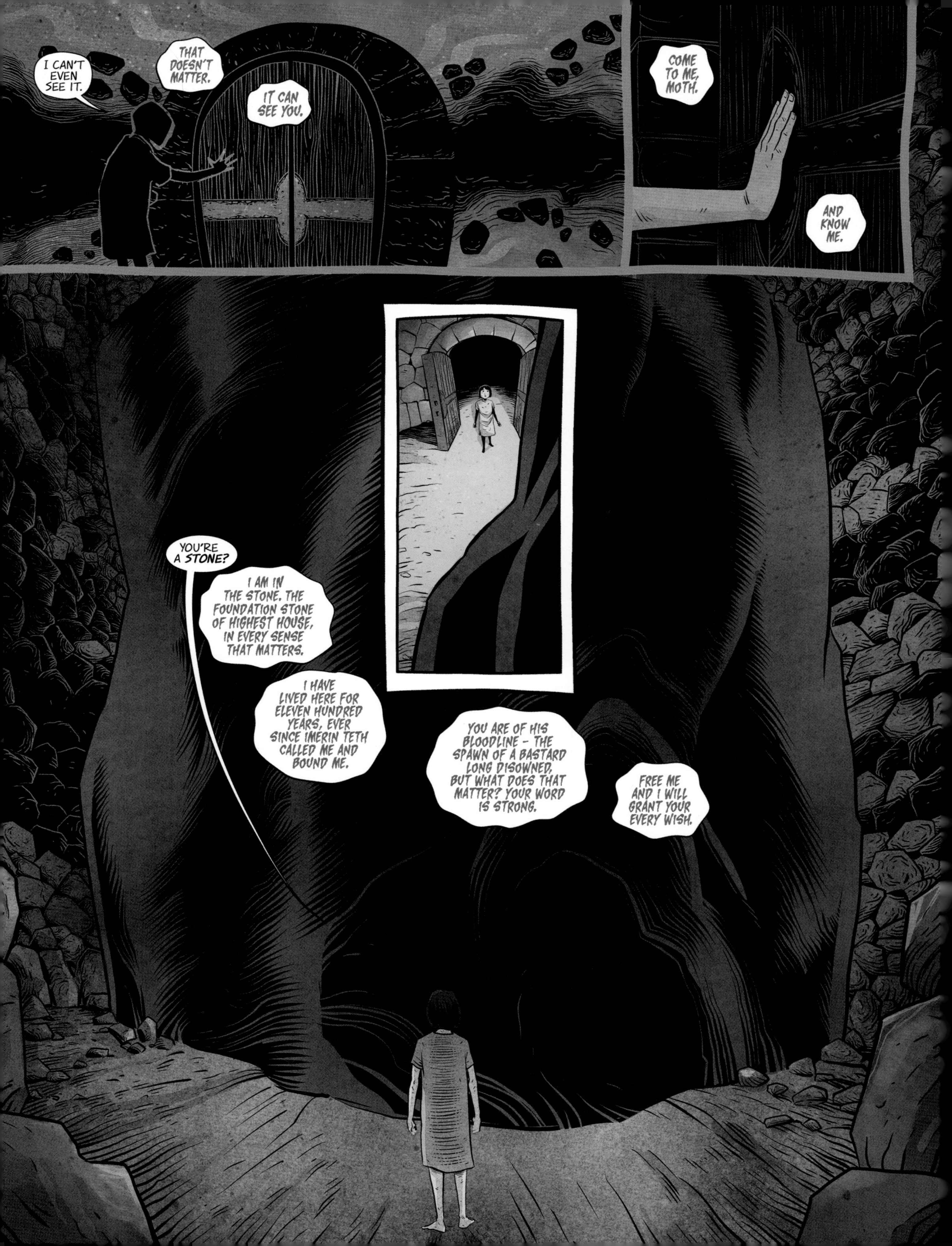
I CAN'T EVEN SEE IT.
THAT DOESN'T MATTER.
IT CAN SEE YOU.
COME TO ME, MOTH.
AND KNOW ME.
YOU'RE A STONE?
I AM IN THE STONE. THE FOUNDATION STONE OF HIGHEST HOUSE, IN EVERY SENSE THAT MATTERS.
I HAVE LIVED HERE FOR ELEVEN HUNDRED YEARS, EVER SINCE IMERIN TETH CALLED ME AND BOUND ME.
YOU ARE OF HIS BLOODLINE – THE SPAWN OF A BASTARD LONG DISOWNED, BUT WHAT DOES THAT MATTER? YOUR WORD IS STRONG.
FREE ME AND I WILL GRANT YOUR EVERY WISH.

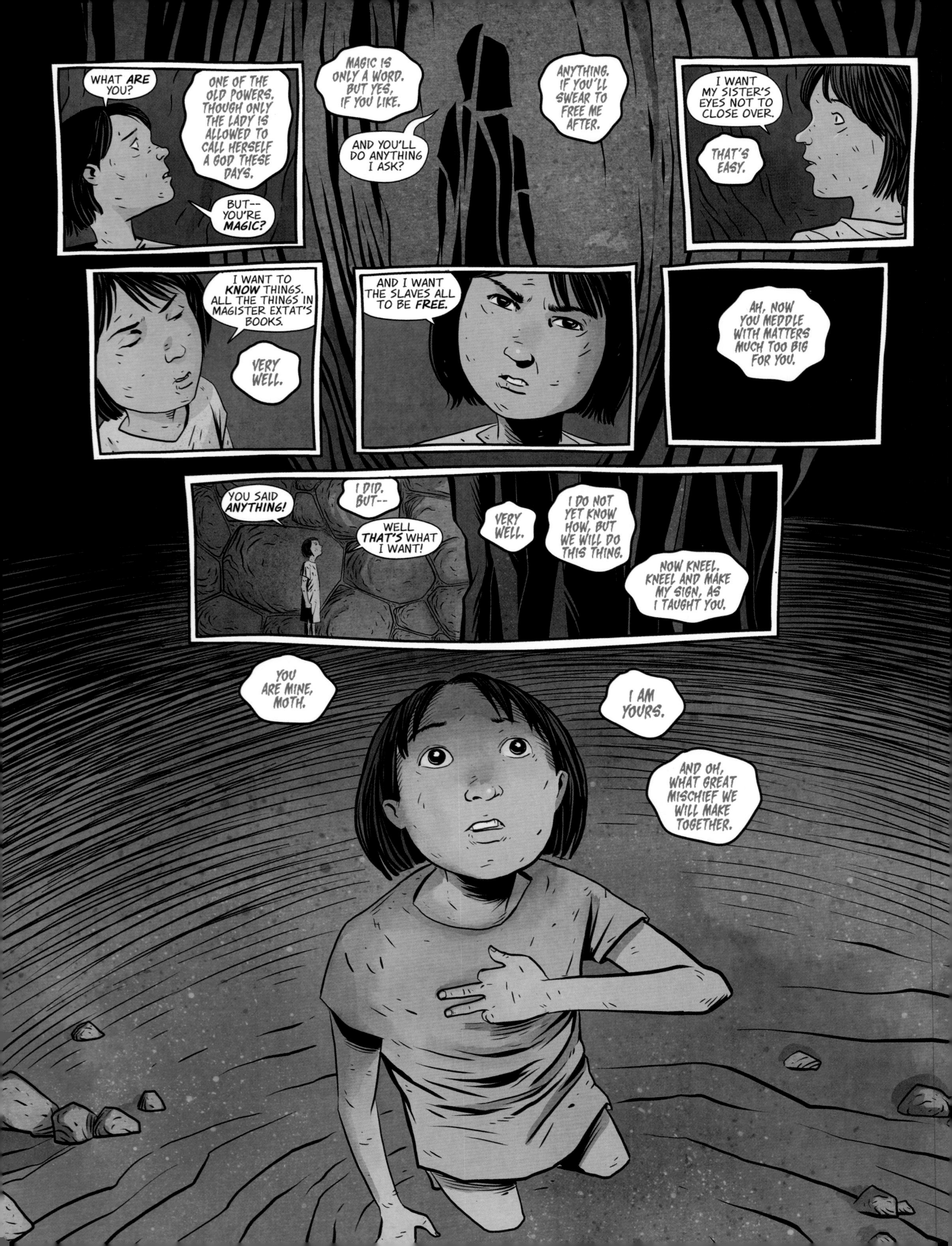
WHAT ARE YOU?
ONE OF THE OLD POWERS. THOUGH ONLY THE LADY IS ALLOWED TO CALL HERSELF A GOD THESE DAYS.
BUT-- YOU'RE MAGIC?
MAGIC IS ONLY A WORD. BUT YES, IF YOU LIKE.
AND YOU'LL DO ANYTHING I ASK?
ANYTHING. IF YOU'LL SWEAR TO FREE ME AFTER.
I WANT MY SISTER'S EYES NOT TO CLOSE OVER.
THAT'S EASY.
I WANT TO KNOW THINGS. ALL THE THINGS IN MAGISTER EXTAT'S BOOKS.
VERY WELL.
AND I WANT THE SLAVES ALL TO BE FREE.
AH, NOW YOU MEDDLE WITH MATTERS MUCH TOO BIG FOR YOU.
YOU SAID ANYTHING!
I DID. BUT--
WELL THAT'S WHAT I WANT!
VERY WELL.
I DO NOT YET KNOW HOW, BUT WE WILL DO THIS THING.
NOW KNEEL. KNEEL AND MAKE MY SIGN, AS I TAUGHT YOU.
YOU ARE MINE, MOTH.
I AM YOURS.
AND OH, WHAT GREAT MISCHIEF WE WILL MAKE TOGETHER.

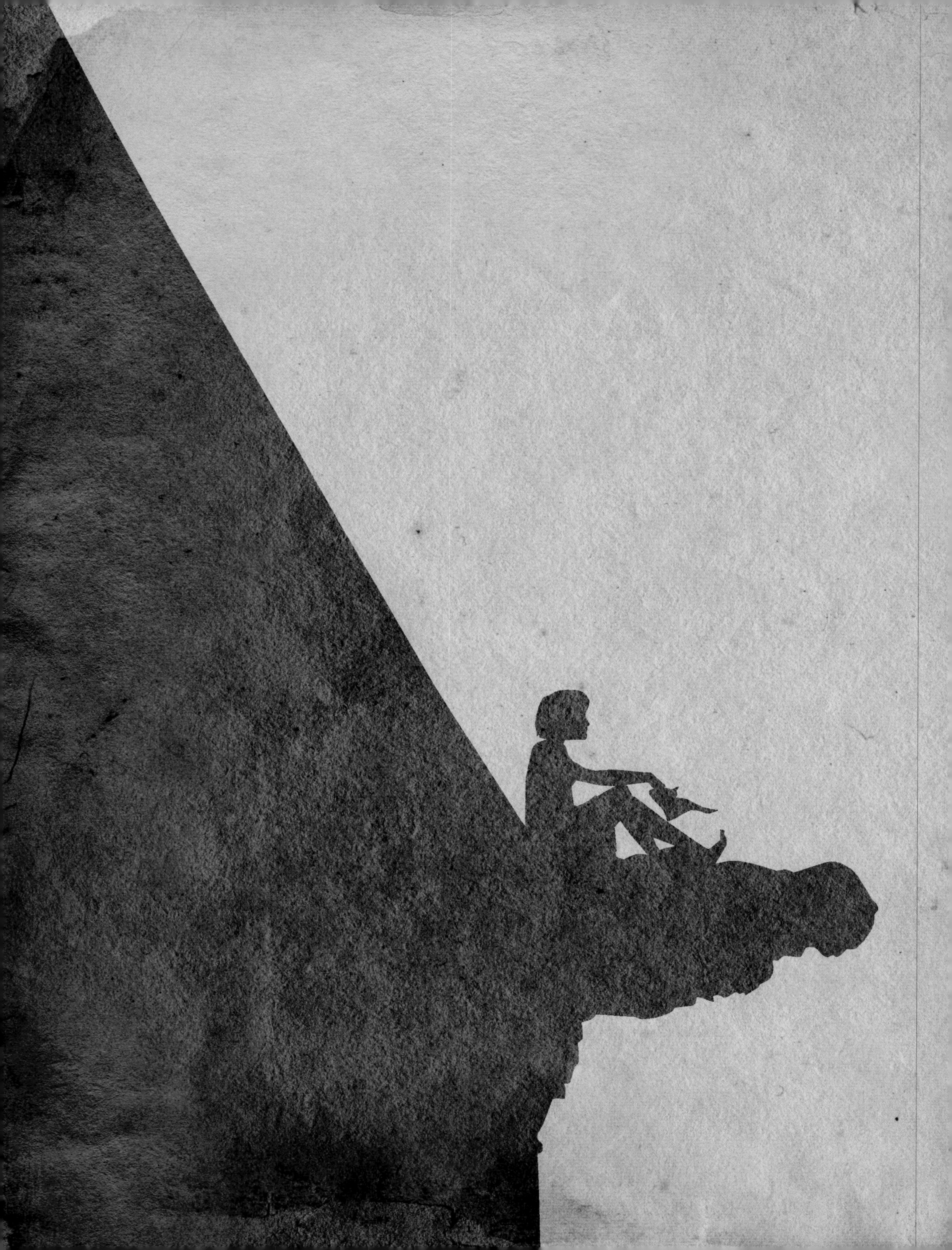

Chapter Three

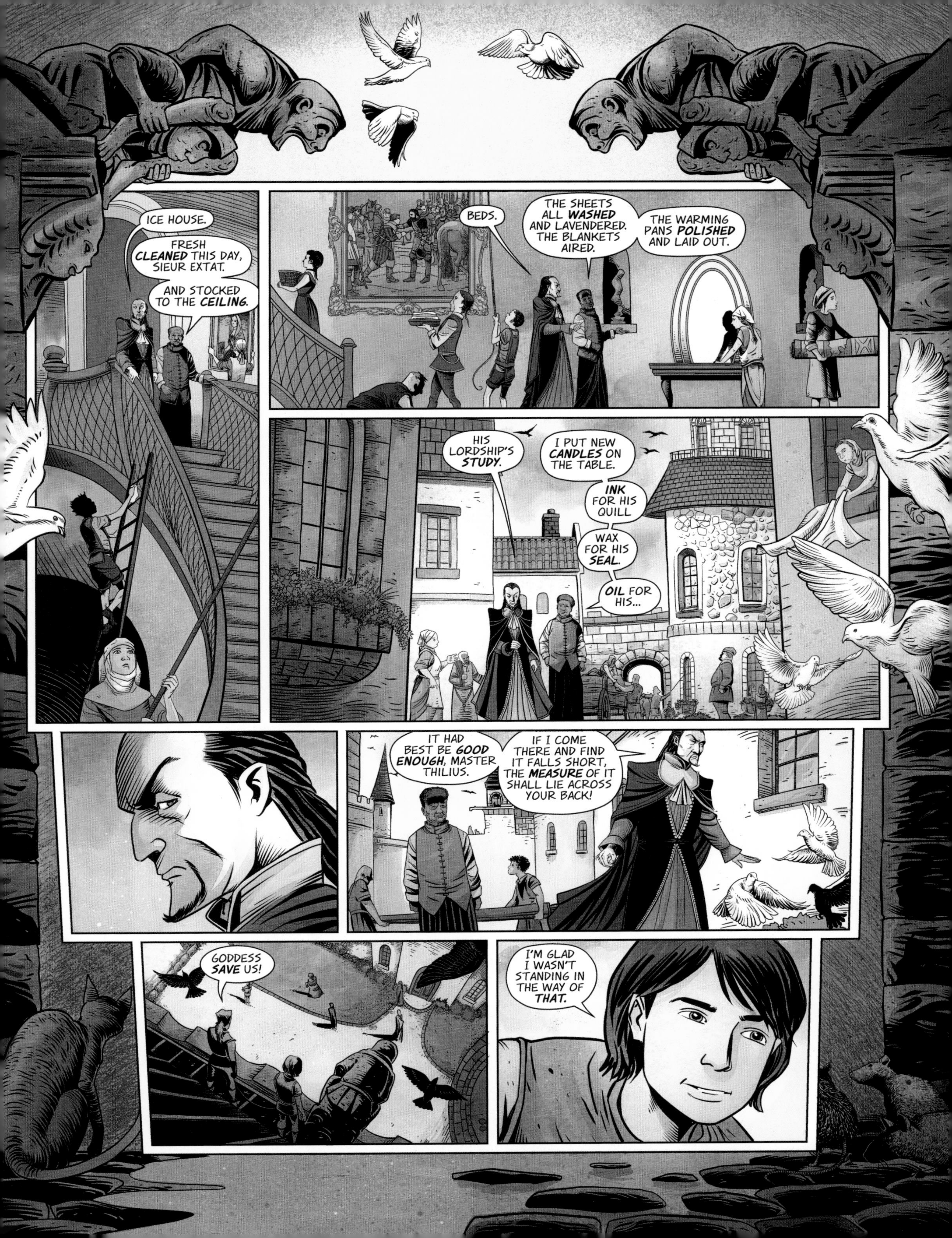
ICE HOUSE.
FRESH CLEANED THIS DAY, SIEUR EXTAT.
AND STOCKED TO THE CEILING.
BEDS.
THE SHEETS ALL WASHED AND LAVENDERED. THE BLANKETS AIRED.
THE WARMING PANS POLISHED AND LAID OUT.
HIS LORDSHIP'S STUDY.
I PUT NEW CANDLES ON THE TABLE.
INK FOR HIS QUILL
WAX FOR HIS SEAL.
OIL FOR HIS...
IT HAD BEST BE GOOD ENOUGH, MASTER THILIUS.
IF I COME THERE AND FIND IT FALLS SHORT, THE MEASURE OF IT SHALL LIE ACROSS YOUR BACK!
GODDESS SAVE US!
I'M GLAD I WASN'T STANDING IN THE WAY OF THAT.

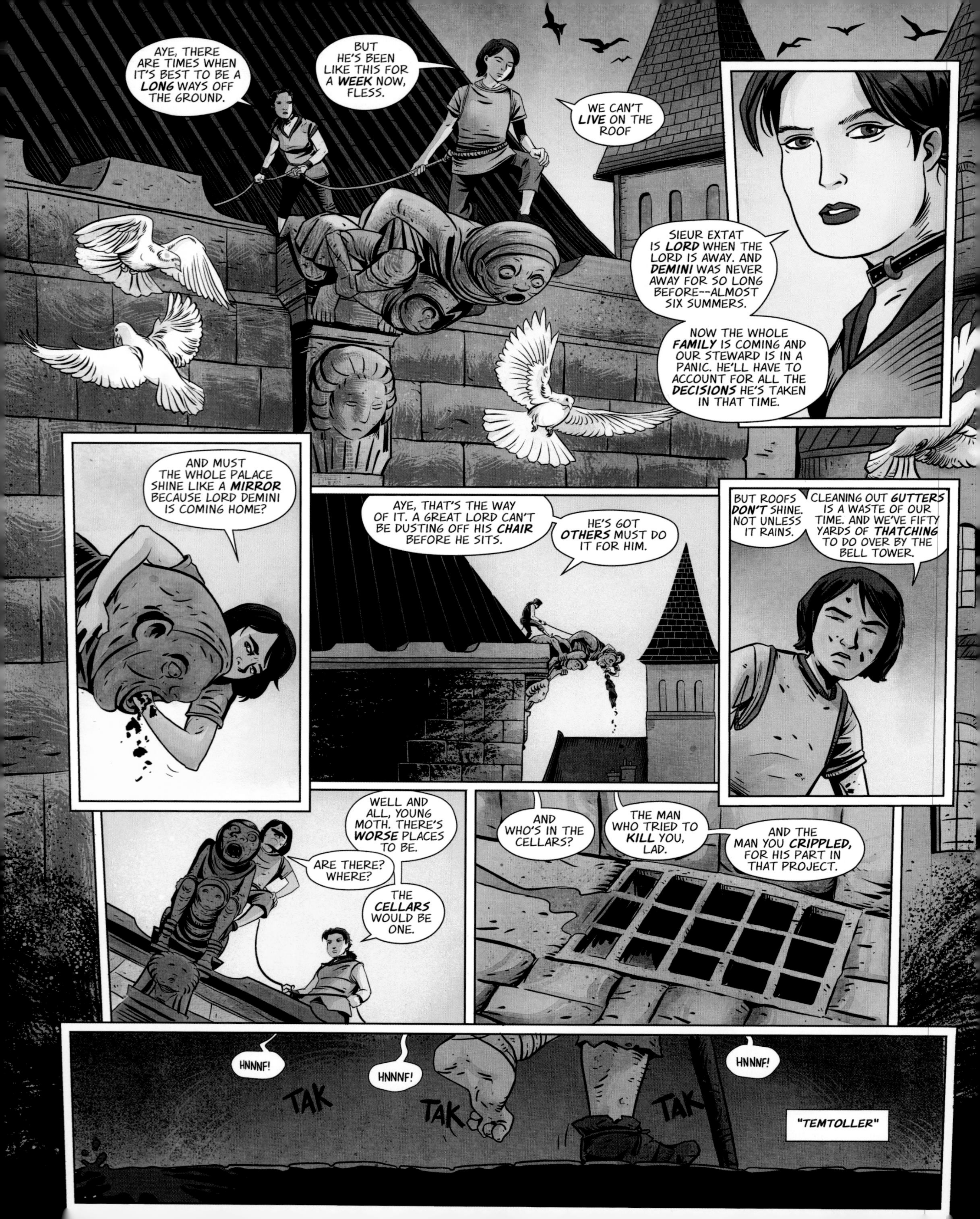
AYE, THERE ARE TIMES WHEN IT'S BEST TO BE A LONG WAYS OFF THE GROUND.
BUT HE'S BEEN LIKE THIS FOR A WEEK NOW, FLESS.
WE CAN'T LIVE ON THE ROOF
SIEUR EXTAT IS LORD WHEN THE LORD IS AWAY. AND DEMINI WAS NEVER AWAY FOR SO LONG BEFORE--ALMOST SIX SUMMERS.
NOW THE WHOLE FAMILY IS COMING AND OUR STEWARD IS IN A PANIC. HE'LL HAVE TO ACCOUNT FOR ALL THE DECISIONS HE'S TAKEN IN THAT TIME.
AND MUST THE WHOLE PALACE SHINE LIKE A MIRROR BECAUSE LORD DEMINI IS COMING HOME?
AYE, THAT'S THE WAY OF IT. A GREAT LORD CAN'T BE DUSTING OFF HIS CHAIR BEFORE HE SITS.
HE'S GOT OTHERS MUST DO IT FOR HIM.
BUT ROOFS DON'T SHINE. NOT UNLESS IT RAINS.
CLEANING OUT GUTTERS IS A WASTE OF OUR TIME. AND WE'VE FIFTY YARDS OF THATCHING TO DO OVER BY THE BELL TOWER.
WELL AND ALL, YOUNG MOTH. THERE'S WORSE PLACES TO BE.
ARE THERE? WHERE?
THE CELLARS WOULD BE ONE.
AND WHO'S IN THE CELLARS?
THE MAN WHO TRIED TO KILL YOU, LAD.
AND THE MAN YOU CRIPPLED, FOR HIS PART IN THAT PROJECT.
HNNNF!
TAK
HNNNF!
TAK
HNNNF!
TAK
"TEMTOLLER"

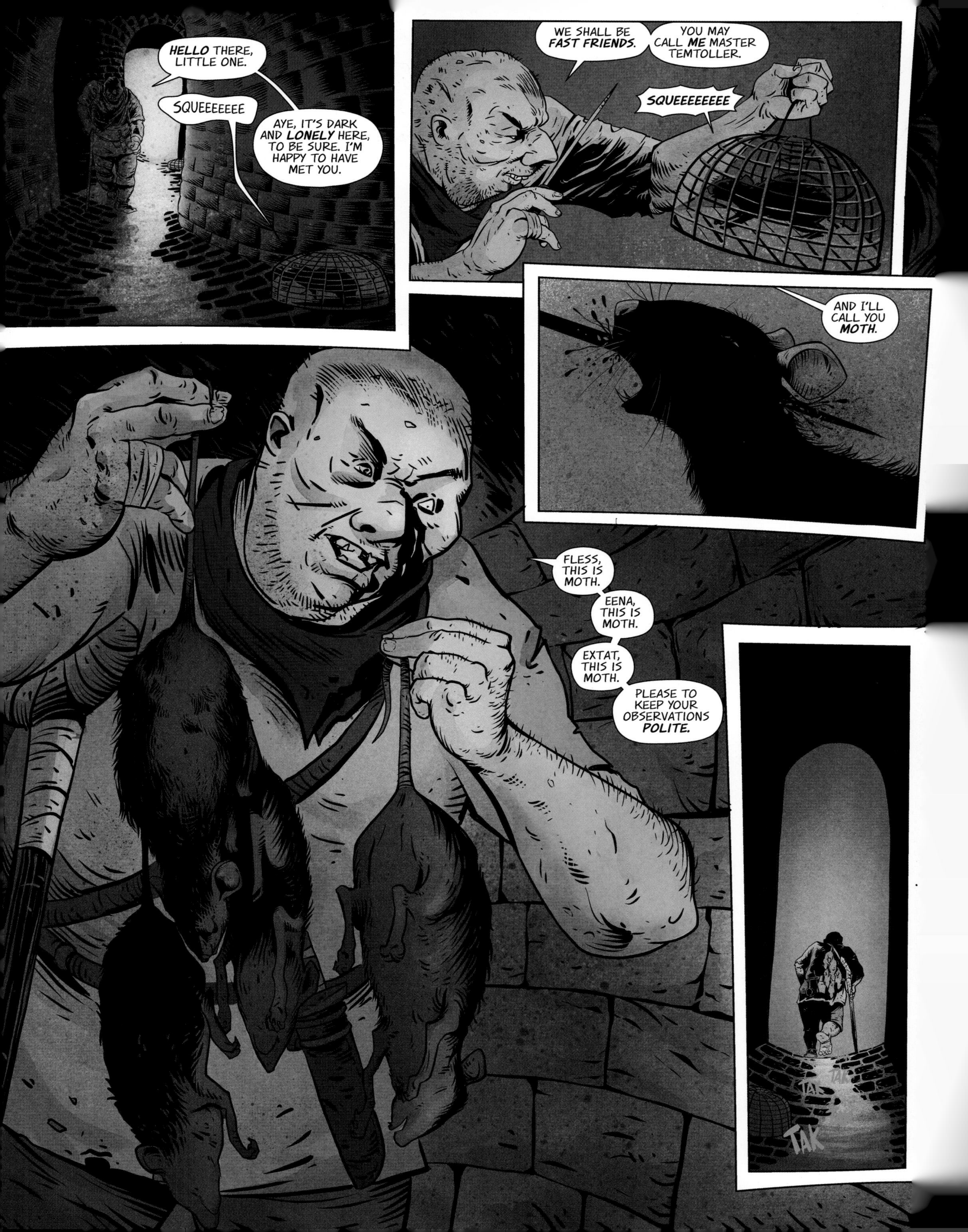
HELLO THERE, LITTLE ONE.
SQUEEEEEEE
AYE, IT'S DARK AND LONELY HERE, TO BE SURE. I'M HAPPY TO HAVE MET YOU.
WE SHALL BE FAST FRIENDS.
YOU MAY CALL ME MASTER TEMTOLLER.
SQUEEEEEEEE
AND I'LL CALL YOU MOTH.
FLESS, THIS IS MOTH.
EENA, THIS IS MOTH.
EXTAT, THIS IS MOTH.
PLEASE TO KEEP YOUR OBSERVATIONS POLITE.
TAK
TAK
TAK

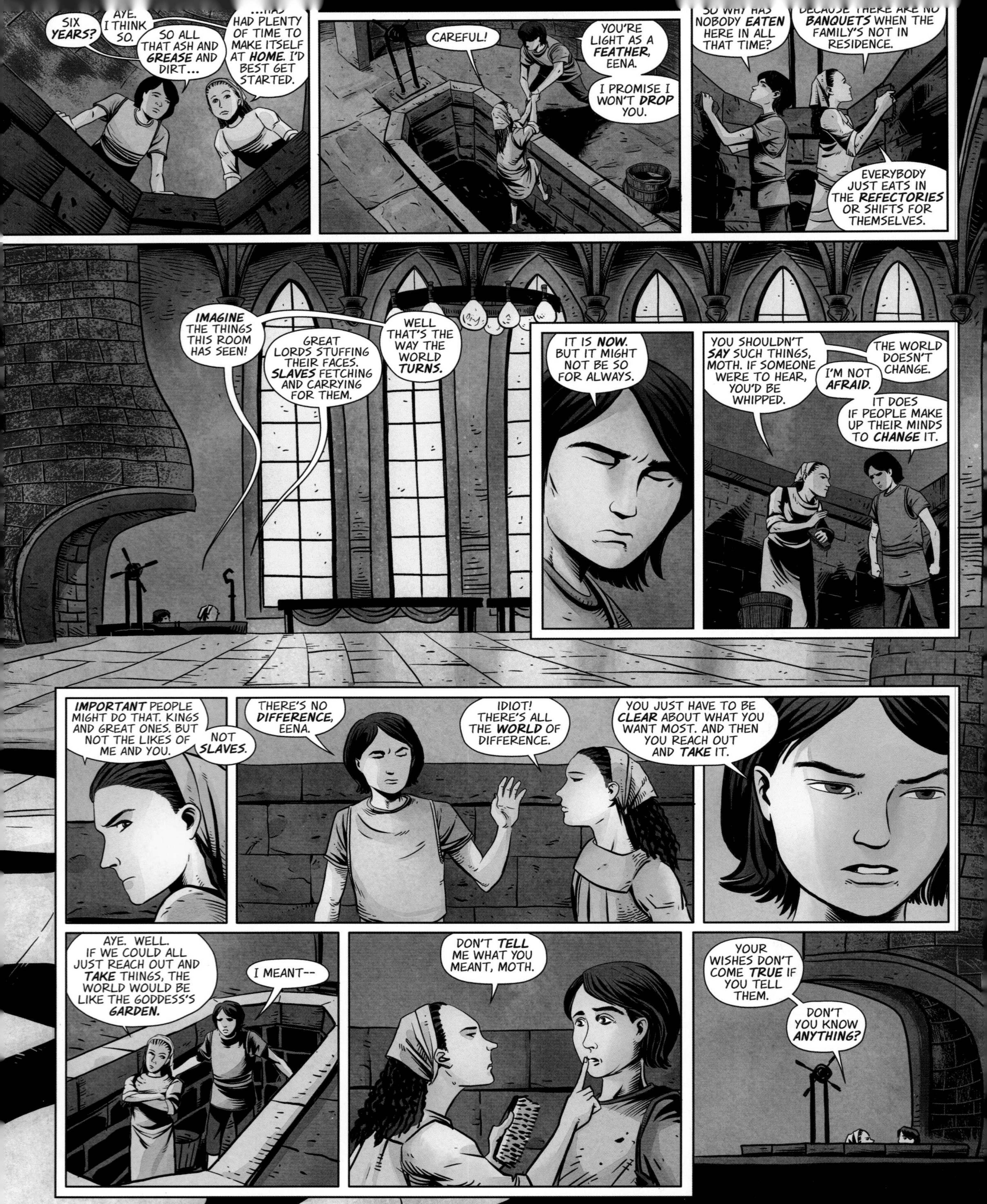
SIX YEARS?
AYE. I THINK SO.
SO ALL THAT ASH AND GREASE AND DIRT...
...HAD PLENTY OF TIME TO MAKE ITSELF AT HOME. I'D BEST GET STARTED.
CAREFUL!
YOU'RE LIGHT AS A FEATHER, EENA.
I PROMISE I WON'T DROP YOU.
SO WHY HAS NOBODY EATEN HERE IN ALL THAT TIME?
BECAUSE THERE ARE NO BANQUETS WHEN THE FAMILY'S NOT IN RESIDENCE.
EVERYBODY JUST EATS IN THE REFECTORIES OR SHIFTS FOR THEMSELVES.
IMAGINE THE THINGS THIS ROOM HAS SEEN!
GREAT LORDS STUFFING THEIR FACES. SLAVES FETCHING AND CARRYING FOR THEM.
WELL THAT'S THE WAY THE WORLD TURNS.
IT IS NOW. BUT IT MIGHT NOT BE SO FOR ALWAYS.
YOU SHOULDN'T SAY SUCH THINGS, MOTH. IF SOMEONE WERE TO HEAR, YOU'D BE WHIPPED.
THE WORLD DOESN'T CHANGE.
I'M NOT AFRAID.
IT DOES IF PEOPLE MAKE UP THEIR MINDS TO CHANGE IT.
IMPORTANT PEOPLE MIGHT DO THAT. KINGS AND GREAT ONES. BUT NOT THE LIKES OF ME AND YOU.
NOT SLAVES.
THERE'S NO DIFFERENCE, EENA.
IDIOT! THERE'S ALL THE WORLD OF DIFFERENCE.
YOU JUST HAVE TO BE CLEAR ABOUT WHAT YOU WANT MOST. AND THEN YOU REACH OUT AND TAKE IT.
AYE. WELL. IF WE COULD ALL JUST REACH OUT AND TAKE THINGS, THE WORLD WOULD BE LIKE THE GODDESS'S GARDEN.
I MEANT--
DON'T TELL ME WHAT YOU MEANT, MOTH.
YOUR WISHES DON'T COME TRUE IF YOU TELL THEM.
DON'T YOU KNOW ANYTHING?

OLD?

AYE! OR **HOUSE-MARKED STEEL**, WHICH IS JUST AS GOOD!

FOR **SLAVES?** FOR **US?**

FOR ANY SLAVE WHOSE BOSHER GIVES GOOD **REPORT** OF HIM.

LORD DEMINI DOES IT WHENEVER HE COMES, THEY SAY. AND THIS TIME HE'LL BE **ESPECIALLY** MINDED TO BE GENEROUS.

HE JUST WON A **WAR**, AFTER ALL.

IT WERE **NO WAR.**

FIVE THOUSAND MEN ON EITHER SIDE! WHAT WOULD **YOU** CALL IT, JADIK?

IT WERE A HOUSE **FEUD.**

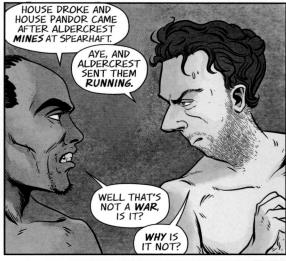

HOUSE DROKE AND HOUSE PANDOR CAME AFTER ALDERCREST **MINES** AT SPEARHAFT.

AYE, AND ALDERCREST SENT THEM **RUNNING.**

WELL THAT'S NOT A **WAR,** IS IT?

WHY IS IT NOT?

WAR IS WHEN COUNTRIES FIGHT **COUNTRIES.** LIKE WHEN KOVIK FOUGHT **OSSANIUL** AND THE KOVIKI BECAME OUR MASTERS.

IT'S NOT WHEN FAMILIES FIGHT **FAMILIES.**

WAS **BLOOD** NOT SPILLED?

AYE, BUT--

AND DID **FLAGS** NOT FLY, BOTH OURS AND THEIRS? IT WAS WAR ENOUGH FOR ME, AND VICTORY ENOUGH.

AYE, BUT STILL--

YOU SHOULD REJOICE THAT ALDERCREST **WON!**

ALL READY?

AYE, MASTER WIMBLE. ALL READY.

GOOD, GOOD. THIS DAY'S LIGHT IS **DONE.**

AND THIS **ROOM'S,** LIKEWISE.

UP WITH YOU, MOTH. YOU CAN SLEEP WHEN YOU'RE DEAD.

ALL OTHER THINGS BEING EQUAL.

COME, COME, MAKE HASTE.

I'VE A GIFT FOR YOU.

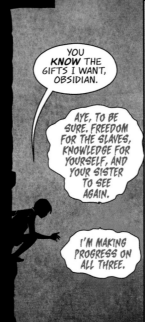

YOU *KNOW* THE GIFTS I WANT, OBSIDIAN.

AYE, TO BE SURE. FREEDOM FOR THE SLAVES, KNOWLEDGE FOR YOURSELF, AND YOUR SISTER TO SEE AGAIN.

I'M MAKING PROGRESS ON ALL THREE.

JET'S *EYES* OUGHT TO BE EASY ENOUGH. I'VE SEEN WHAT YOU CAN DO.

WHAT I CAN DO HERE.

AT FURTHER REMOVES FROM THE HOUSE, MY POWER WORKS DIFFERENTLY. YOU HAVE TO TRUST ME.

TRUST YOU? YOU'RE A BIG BLACK *STONE* THAT DOES MAGIC!

AND DID I NOT HEAL YOUR LUNGS OF THE CONSUMPTION, THAT YOU RUN LIKE A GAZELLE NOW? TO THE LEFT, THE SECOND DOOR THERE. I'VE UNLOCKED IT FOR YOU.

I WILL NOT ASK YOU TO RELEASE ME UNTIL YOU'RE SATISFIED I'VE DONE ALL I PROMISED.

AND I AM NOT THE STONE. I AM BOUND WITHIN THE STONE.

WHO *ARE* THESE PEOPLE?

THE LORDS AND LADIES OF THE TETH LINEAL, WHO LIVED IN THIS HOUSE IN FORMER TIMES.

THEY WERE YOUR FOREBEARS. YOUR FATHER WAS A BASTARD'S BASTARD, BUT HE STOOD IN DIRECT LINE OF DESCENT.

AND THAT'S WHY YOU *BROUGHT* ME HERE.

AYE.

BECAUSE IT'S ONLY *THEIR* BLOOD THAT CAN *FREE* YOU.

AYE. OPEN THE DOOR.

WHAT DO YOU THINK?

AS YOU CA[...] BOY, THE [...] ARE WOR[...] TONIGH[...]

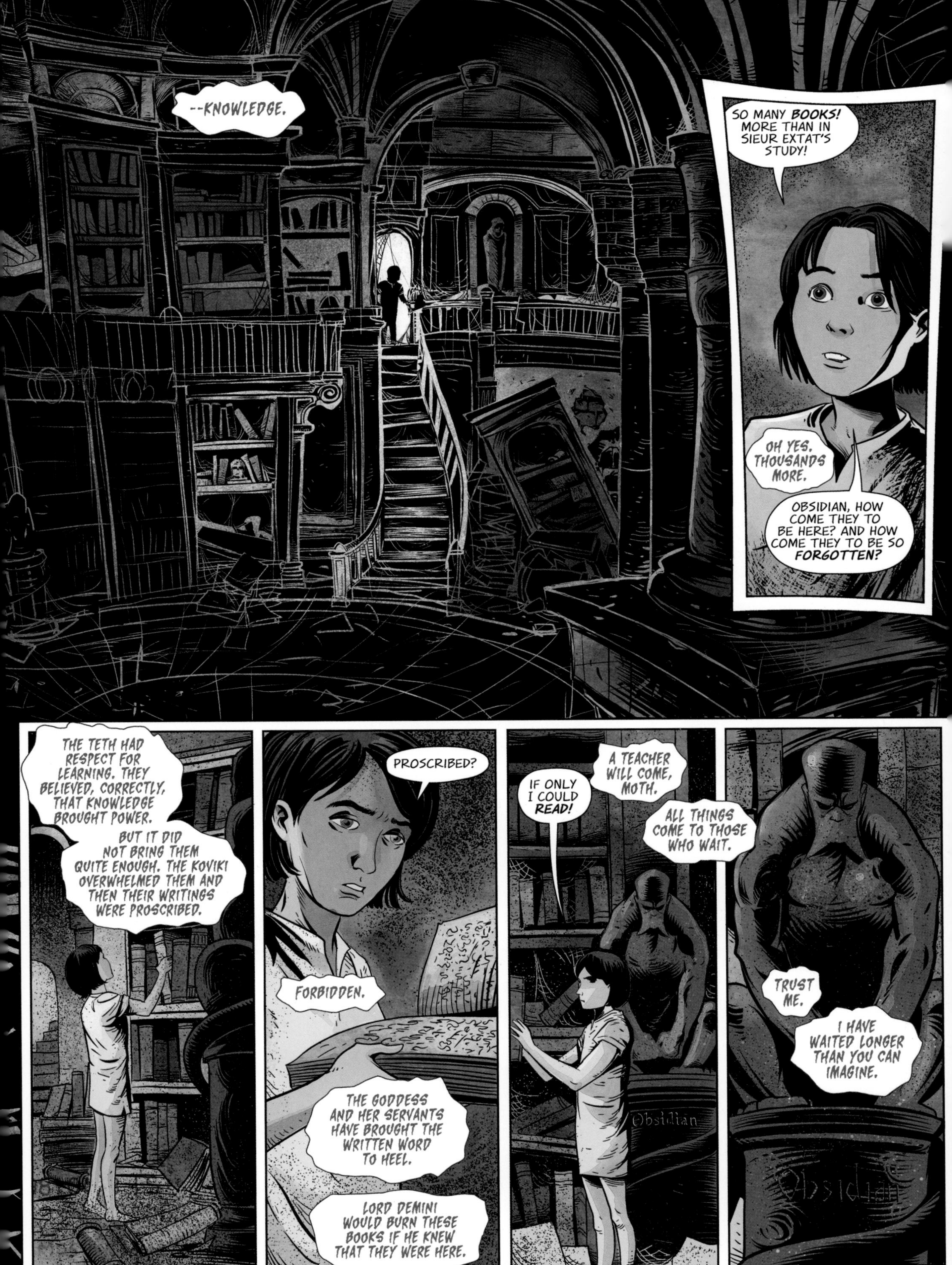
--KNOWLEDGE.
SO MANY BOOKS! MORE THAN IN SIEUR EXTAT'S STUDY!
OH YES. THOUSANDS MORE.
OBSIDIAN, HOW COME THEY TO BE HERE? AND HOW COME THEY TO BE SO FORGOTTEN?
THE TETH HAD RESPECT FOR LEARNING. THEY BELIEVED, CORRECTLY, THAT KNOWLEDGE BROUGHT POWER.
BUT IT DID NOT BRING THEM QUITE ENOUGH. THE KOVIKI OVERWHELMED THEM AND THEN THEIR WRITINGS WERE PROSCRIBED.
PROSCRIBED?
FORBIDDEN.
THE GODDESS AND HER SERVANTS HAVE BROUGHT THE WRITTEN WORD TO HEEL.
LORD DEMINI WOULD BURN THESE BOOKS IF HE KNEW THAT THEY WERE HERE.
IF ONLY I COULD READ!
A TEACHER WILL COME, MOTH.
ALL THINGS COME TO THOSE WHO WAIT.
Obsidian
TRUST ME.
I HAVE WAITED LONGER THAN YOU CAN IMAGINE.
Obsidian

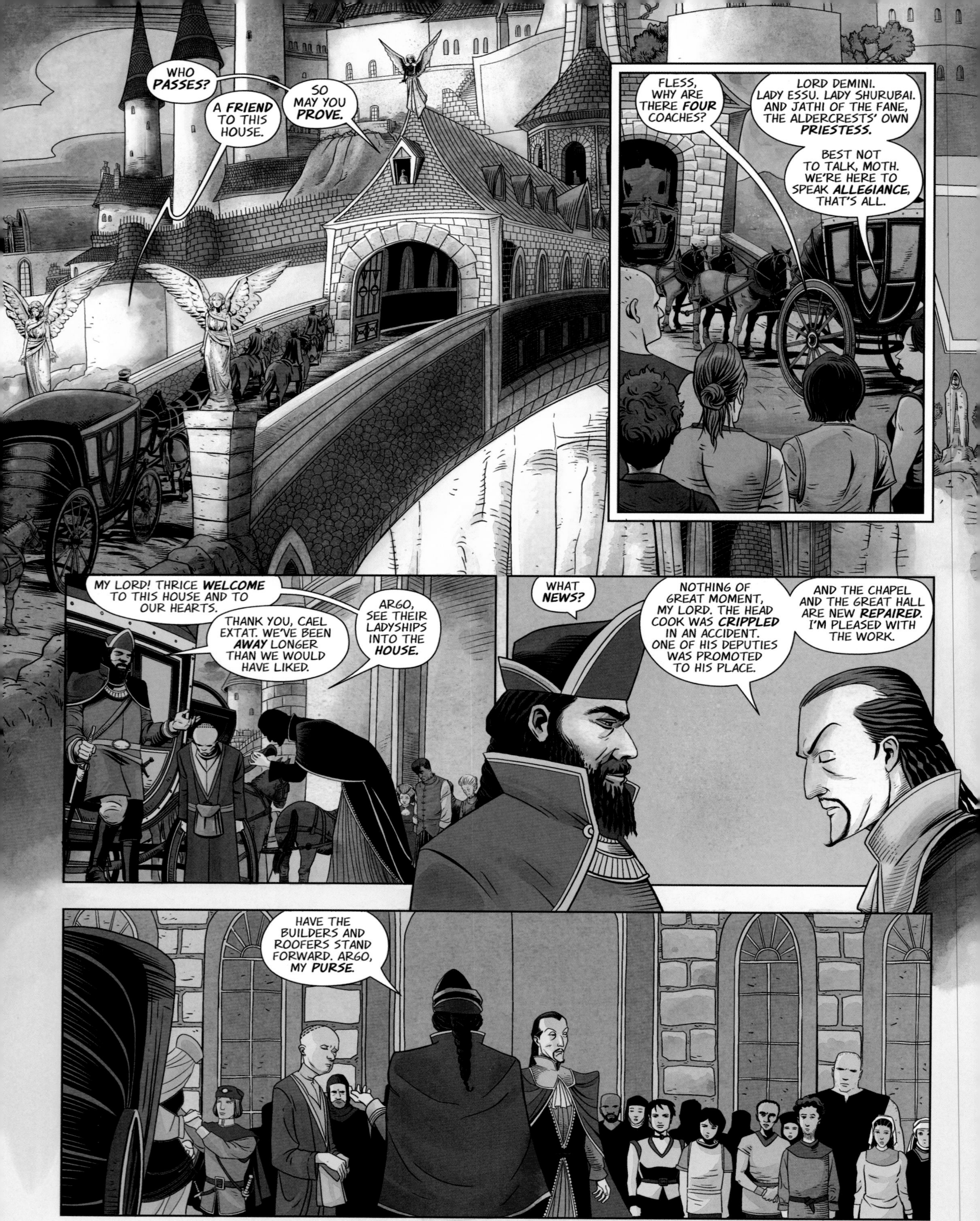
WHO PASSES?
A FRIEND TO THIS HOUSE.
SO MAY YOU PROVE.
FLESS, WHY ARE THERE FOUR COACHES?
LORD DEMINI. LADY ESSU. LADY SHURUBAI. AND JATHI OF THE FANE, THE ALDERCRESTS' OWN PRIESTESS.
BEST NOT TO TALK, MOTH. WE'RE HERE TO SPEAK ALLEGIANCE, THAT'S ALL.
MY LORD! THRICE WELCOME TO THIS HOUSE AND TO OUR HEARTS.
THANK YOU, CAEL EXTAT. WE'VE BEEN AWAY LONGER THAN WE WOULD HAVE LIKED.
ARGO, SEE THEIR LADYSHIPS INTO THE HOUSE.
WHAT NEWS?
NOTHING OF GREAT MOMENT, MY LORD. THE HEAD COOK WAS CRIPPLED IN AN ACCIDENT. ONE OF HIS DEPUTIES WAS PROMOTED TO HIS PLACE.
AND THE CHAPEL AND THE GREAT HALL ARE NEW REPAIRED. I'M PLEASED WITH THE WORK.
HAVE THE BUILDERS AND ROOFERS STAND FORWARD. ARGO, MY PURSE.

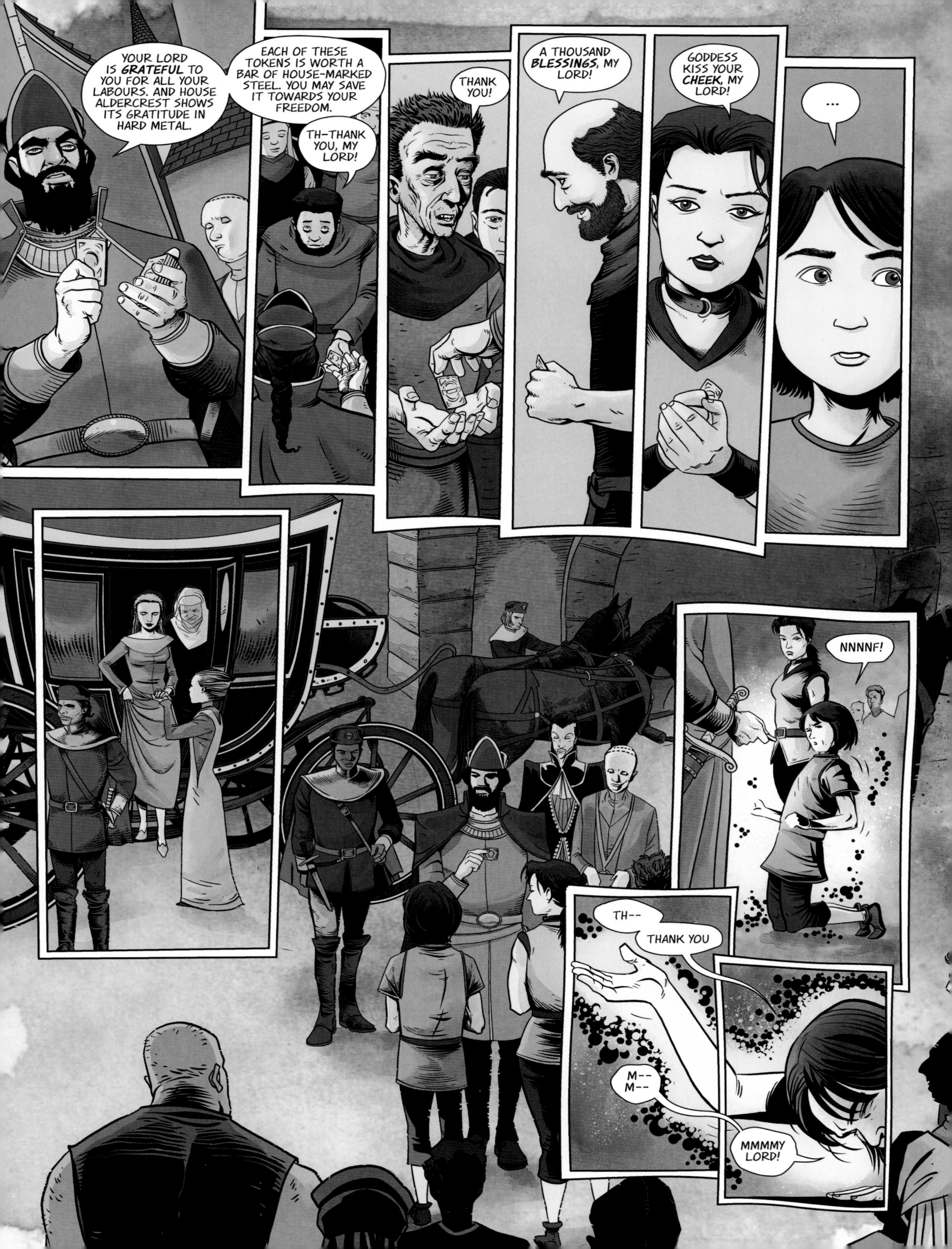
YOUR LORD IS GRATEFUL TO YOU FOR ALL YOUR LABOURS. AND HOUSE ALDERCREST SHOWS ITS GRATITUDE IN HARD METAL.
EACH OF THESE TOKENS IS WORTH A BAR OF HOUSE-MARKED STEEL. YOU MAY SAVE IT TOWARDS YOUR FREEDOM.
TH-THANK YOU, MY LORD!
THANK YOU!
A THOUSAND BLESSINGS, MY LORD!
GODDESS KISS YOUR CHEEK, MY LORD!
...
NNNNF!
TH--
THANK YOU
M--
M--
MMMMY LORD!

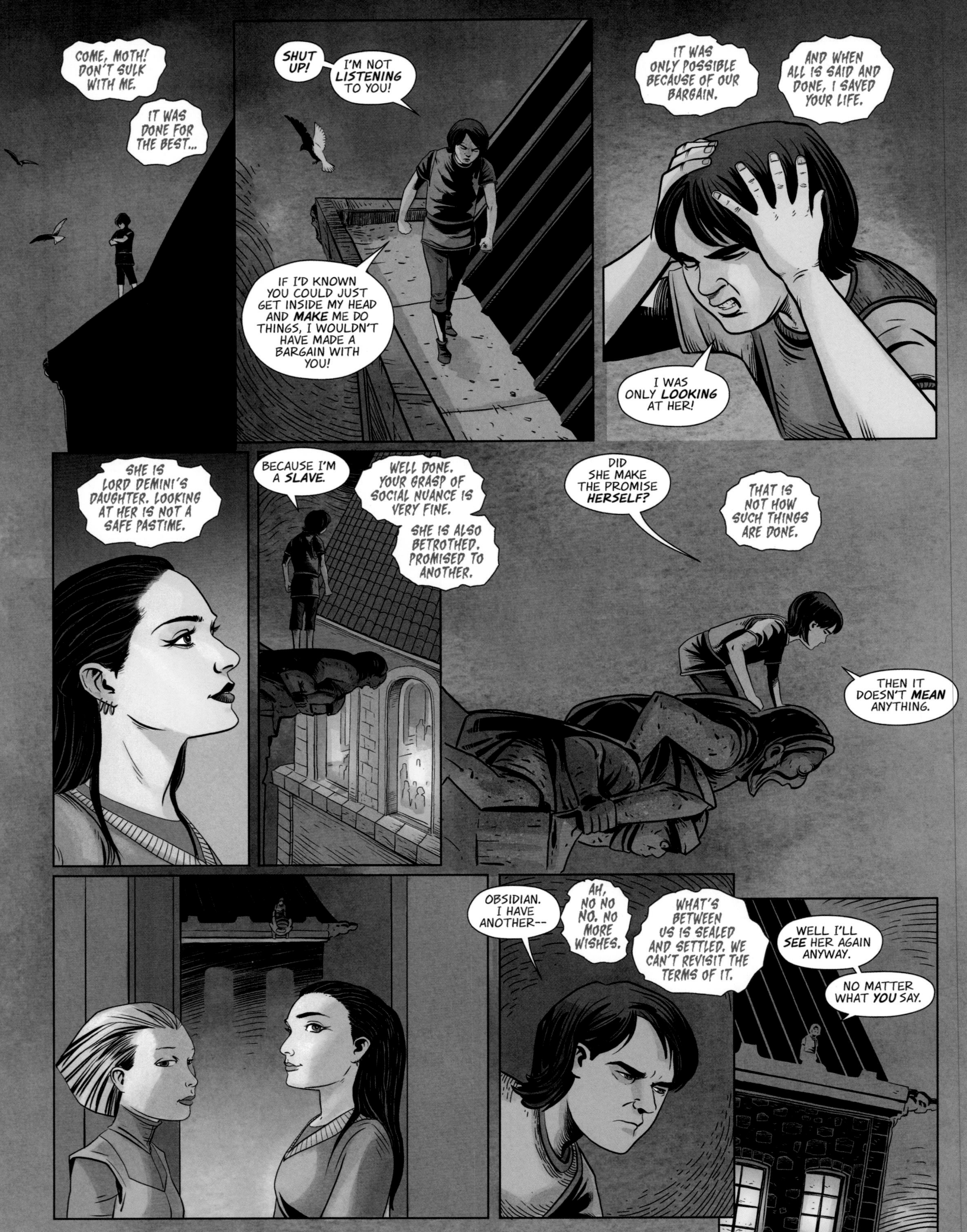
COME, MOTH! DON'T SULK WITH ME.
IT WAS DONE FOR THE BEST...
SHUT UP!
I'M NOT LISTENING TO YOU!
IF I'D KNOWN YOU COULD JUST GET INSIDE MY HEAD AND MAKE ME DO THINGS, I WOULDN'T HAVE MADE A BARGAIN WITH YOU!
IT WAS ONLY POSSIBLE BECAUSE OF OUR BARGAIN.
AND WHEN ALL IS SAID AND DONE, I SAVED YOUR LIFE.
I WAS ONLY LOOKING AT HER!
SHE IS LORD DEMINI'S DAUGHTER. LOOKING AT HER IS NOT A SAFE PASTIME.
BECAUSE I'M A SLAVE.
WELL DONE. YOUR GRASP OF SOCIAL NUANCE IS VERY FINE.
SHE IS ALSO BETROTHED. PROMISED TO ANOTHER.
DID SHE MAKE THE PROMISE HERSELF?
THAT IS NOT HOW SUCH THINGS ARE DONE.
THEN IT DOESN'T MEAN ANYTHING.
OBSIDIAN. I HAVE ANOTHER--
AH, NO NO NO. NO MORE WISHES.
WHAT'S BETWEEN US IS SEALED AND SETTLED. WE CAN'T REVISIT THE TERMS OF IT.
WELL I'LL SEE HER AGAIN ANYWAY.
NO MATTER WHAT YOU SAY.

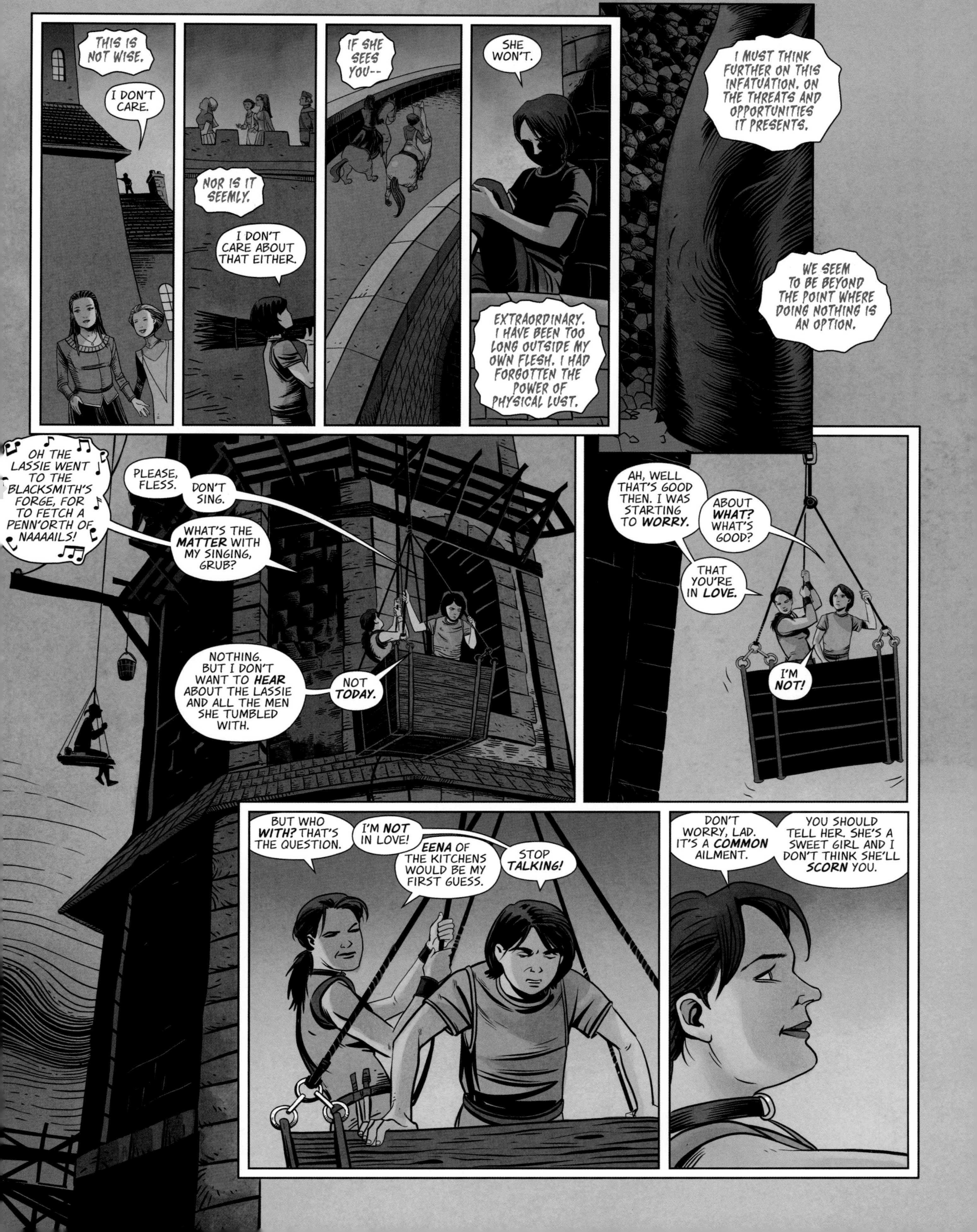
THIS IS NOT WISE.
I DON'T CARE.
NOR IS IT SEEMLY.
I DON'T CARE ABOUT THAT EITHER.
IF SHE SEES YOU--
SHE WON'T.
EXTRAORDINARY. I HAVE BEEN TOO LONG OUTSIDE MY OWN FLESH. I HAD FORGOTTEN THE POWER OF PHYSICAL LUST.
I MUST THINK FURTHER ON THIS INFATUATION. ON THE THREATS AND OPPORTUNITIES IT PRESENTS.
WE SEEM TO BE BEYOND THE POINT WHERE DOING NOTHING IS AN OPTION.
OH THE LASSIE WENT TO THE BLACKSMITH'S FORGE, FOR TO FETCH A PENN'ORTH OF NAAAAILS!
PLEASE, FLESS.
DON'T SING.
WHAT'S THE MATTER WITH MY SINGING, GRUB?
NOTHING. BUT I DON'T WANT TO HEAR ABOUT THE LASSIE AND ALL THE MEN SHE TUMBLED WITH.
NOT TODAY.
AH, WELL THAT'S GOOD THEN. I WAS STARTING TO WORRY.
ABOUT WHAT? WHAT'S GOOD?
THAT YOU'RE IN LOVE.
I'M NOT!
BUT WHO WITH? THAT'S THE QUESTION.
I'M NOT IN LOVE!
EENA OF THE KITCHENS WOULD BE MY FIRST GUESS.
STOP TALKING!
DON'T WORRY, LAD. IT'S A COMMON AILMENT.
YOU SHOULD TELL HER. SHE'S A SWEET GIRL AND I DON'T THINK SHE'LL SCORN YOU.

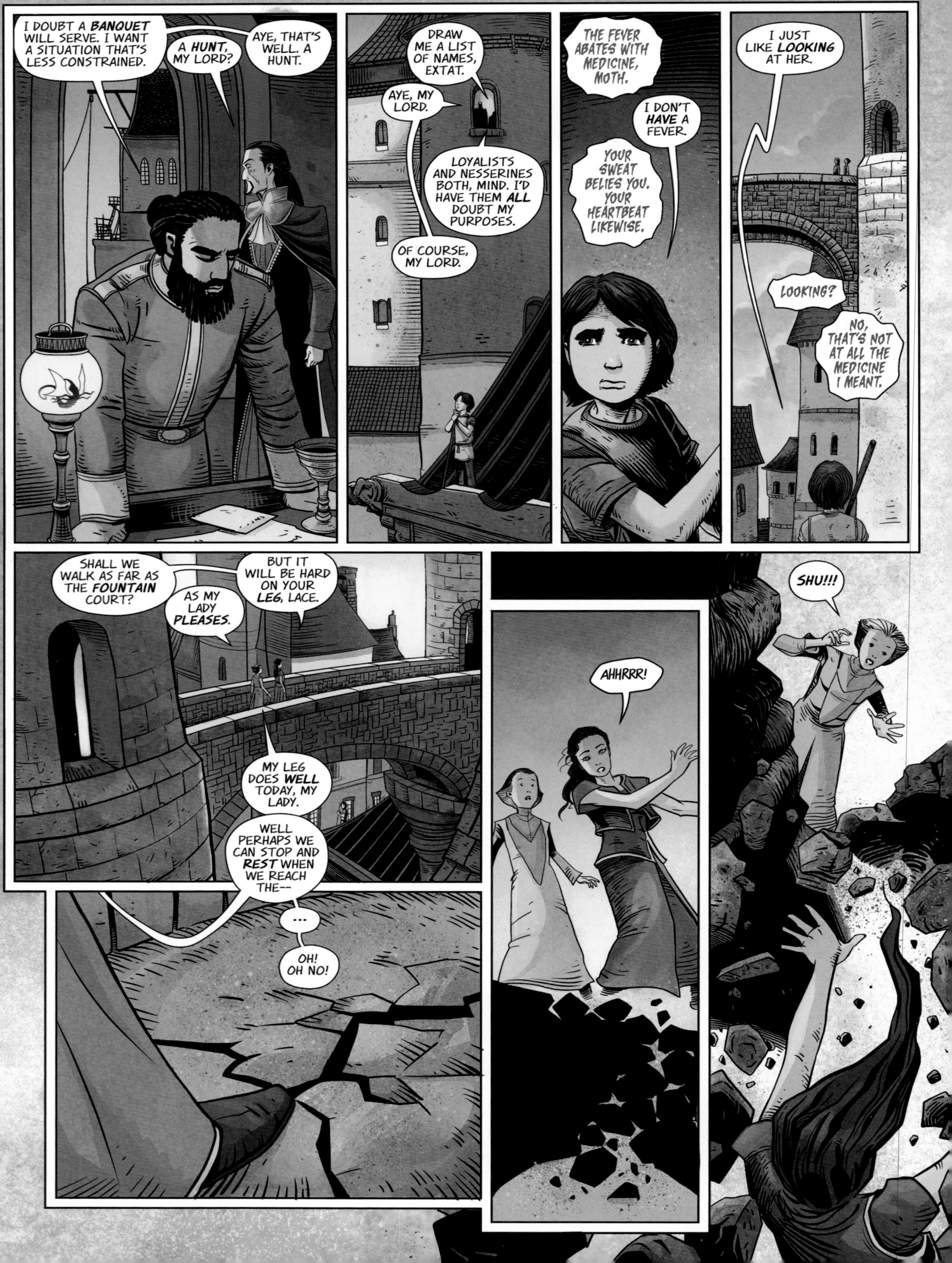
I DOUBT A BANQUET WILL SERVE. I WANT A SITUATION THAT'S LESS CONSTRAINED.
A HUNT, MY LORD?
AYE, THAT'S WELL. A HUNT.
DRAW ME A LIST OF NAMES, EXTAT.
AYE, MY LORD.
LOYALISTS AND NESSERINES BOTH, MIND. I'D HAVE THEM ALL DOUBT MY PURPOSES.
OF COURSE, MY LORD.
THE FEVER ABATES WITH MEDICINE, MOTH.
I DON'T HAVE A FEVER.
YOUR SWEAT BELIES YOU. YOUR HEARTBEAT LIKEWISE.
I JUST LIKE LOOKING AT HER.
LOOKING?
NO, THAT'S NOT AT ALL THE MEDICINE I MEANT.
SHALL WE WALK AS FAR AS THE FOUNTAIN COURT?
AS MY LADY PLEASES.
BUT IT WILL BE HARD ON YOUR LEG, LACE.
MY LEG DOES WELL TODAY, MY LADY.
WELL PERHAPS WE CAN STOP AND REST WHEN WE REACH THE--
...
OH! OH NO!
AHHRRR!
SHU!!!

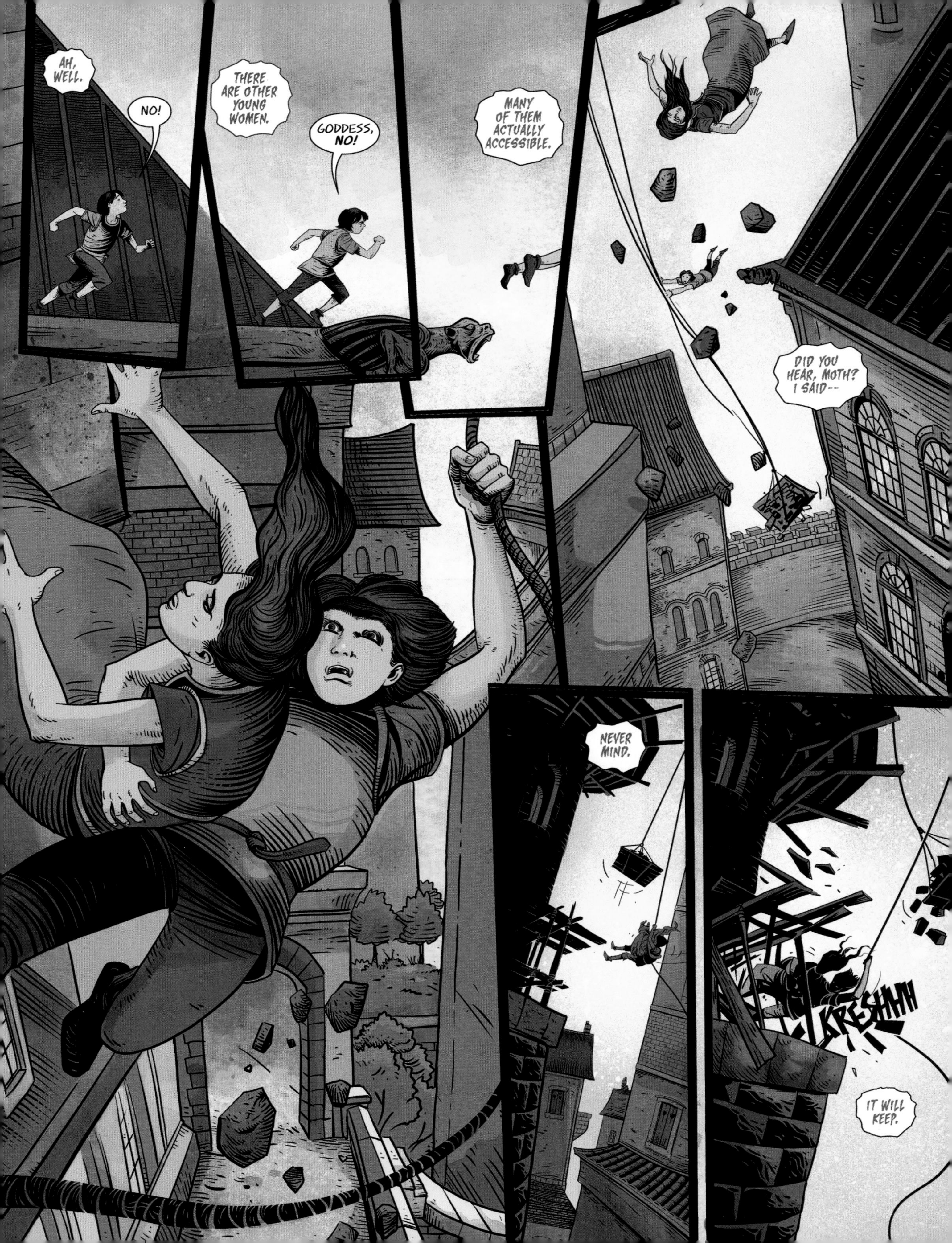
AH, WELL.
NO!
THERE ARE OTHER YOUNG WOMEN.
GODDESS, NO!
MANY OF THEM ACTUALLY ACCESSIBLE.
DID YOU HEAR, MOTH? I SAID--
NEVER MIND.
KRESHHH
IT WILL KEEP.

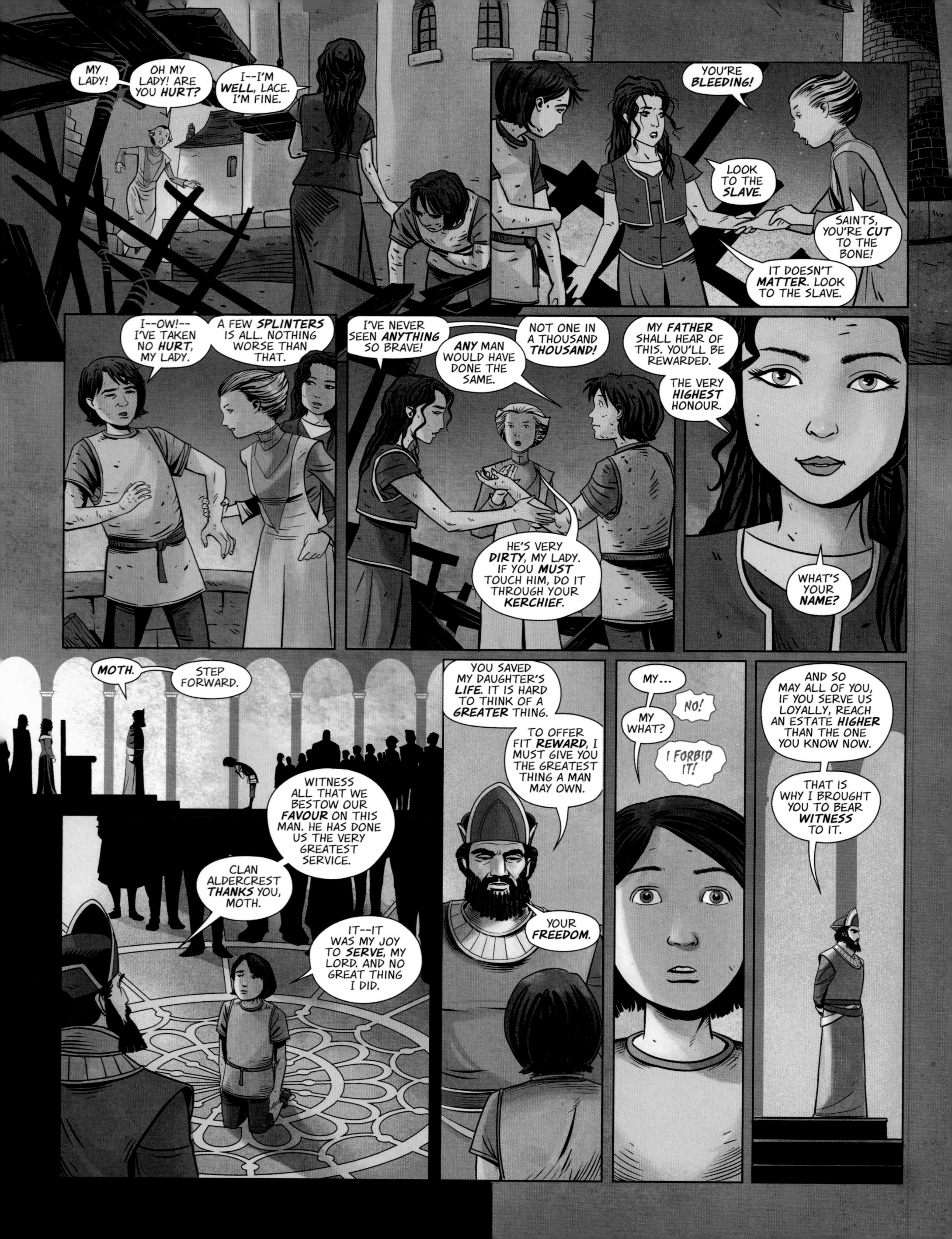

MY LADY!
OH MY LADY! ARE YOU HURT?
I--I'M WELL, LACE. I'M FINE.
YOU'RE BLEEDING!
LOOK TO THE SLAVE.
SAINTS, YOU'RE CUT TO THE BONE!
IT DOESN'T MATTER. LOOK TO THE SLAVE.
I--OW!--I'VE TAKEN NO HURT, MY LADY.
A FEW SPLINTERS IS ALL. NOTHING WORSE THAN THAT.
I'VE NEVER SEEN ANYTHING SO BRAVE!
NOT ONE IN A THOUSAND THOUSAND!
ANY MAN WOULD HAVE DONE THE SAME.
HE'S VERY DIRTY, MY LADY. IF YOU MUST TOUCH HIM, DO IT THROUGH YOUR KERCHIEF.
MY FATHER SHALL HEAR OF THIS. YOU'LL BE REWARDED.
THE VERY HIGHEST HONOUR.
WHAT'S YOUR NAME?
MOTH.
STEP FORWARD.
WITNESS ALL THAT WE BESTOW OUR FAVOUR ON THIS MAN. HE HAS DONE US THE VERY GREATEST SERVICE.
CLAN ALDERCREST THANKS YOU, MOTH.
IT--IT WAS MY JOY TO SERVE, MY LORD. AND NO GREAT THING I DID.
YOU SAVED MY DAUGHTER'S LIFE. IT IS HARD TO THINK OF A GREATER THING.
TO OFFER FIT REWARD, I MUST GIVE YOU THE GREATEST THING A MAN MAY OWN.
YOUR FREEDOM.
MY...
NO!
MY WHAT?
I FORBID IT!
AND SO MAY ALL OF YOU, IF YOU SERVE US LOYALLY, REACH AN ESTATE HIGHER THAN THE ONE YOU KNOW NOW.
THAT IS WHY I BROUGHT YOU TO BEAR WITNESS TO IT.

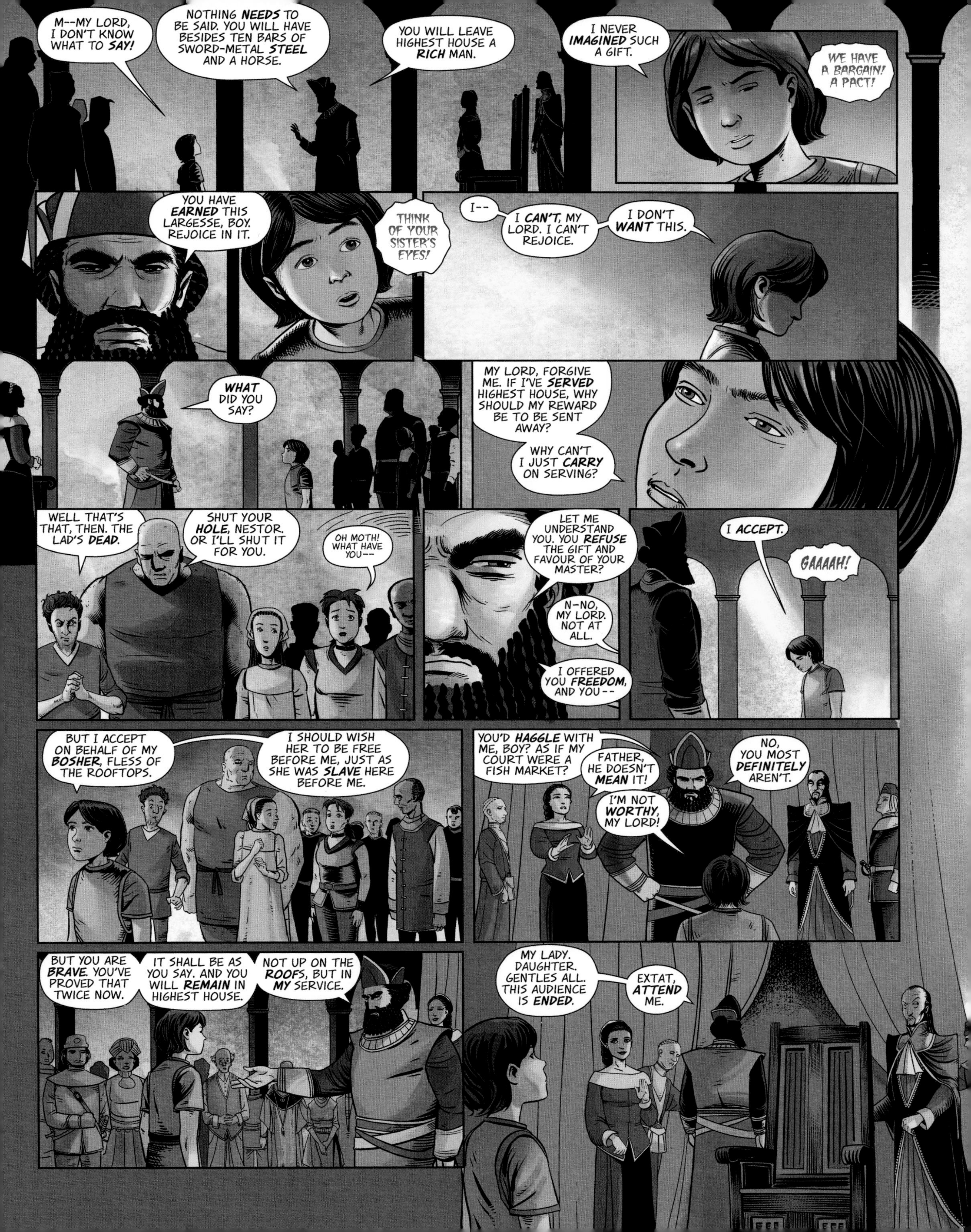
M--MY LORD, I DON'T KNOW WHAT TO SAY!
NOTHING NEEDS TO BE SAID. YOU WILL HAVE BESIDES TEN BARS OF SWORD-METAL STEEL AND A HORSE.
YOU WILL LEAVE HIGHEST HOUSE A RICH MAN.
I NEVER IMAGINED SUCH A GIFT.
WE HAVE A BARGAIN! A PACT!
YOU HAVE EARNED THIS LARGESSE, BOY. REJOICE IN IT.
THINK OF YOUR SISTER'S EYES!
I--
I CAN'T, MY LORD. I CAN'T REJOICE.
I DON'T WANT THIS.
WHAT DID YOU SAY?
MY LORD, FORGIVE ME. IF I'VE SERVED HIGHEST HOUSE, WHY SHOULD MY REWARD BE TO BE SENT AWAY?
WHY CAN'T I JUST CARRY ON SERVING?
WELL THAT'S THAT, THEN. THE LAD'S DEAD.
SHUT YOUR HOLE, NESTOR. OR I'LL SHUT IT FOR YOU.
OH MOTH! WHAT HAVE YOU--
LET ME UNDERSTAND YOU. YOU REFUSE THE GIFT AND FAVOUR OF YOUR MASTER?
N-NO, MY LORD. NOT AT ALL.
I OFFERED YOU FREEDOM, AND YOU--
I ACCEPT.
GAAAAH!
BUT I ACCEPT ON BEHALF OF MY BOSHER, FLESS OF THE ROOFTOPS.
I SHOULD WISH HER TO BE FREE BEFORE ME, JUST AS SHE WAS SLAVE HERE BEFORE ME.
YOU'D HAGGLE WITH ME, BOY? AS IF MY COURT WERE A FISH MARKET?
FATHER, HE DOESN'T MEAN IT!
I'M NOT WORTHY, MY LORD!
NO, YOU MOST DEFINITELY AREN'T.
BUT YOU ARE BRAVE. YOU'VE PROVED THAT TWICE NOW.
IT SHALL BE AS YOU SAY. AND YOU WILL REMAIN IN HIGHEST HOUSE.
NOT UP ON THE ROOFS, BUT IN MY SERVICE.
MY LADY. DAUGHTER. GENTLES ALL. THIS AUDIENCE IS ENDED.
EXTAT, ATTEND ME.

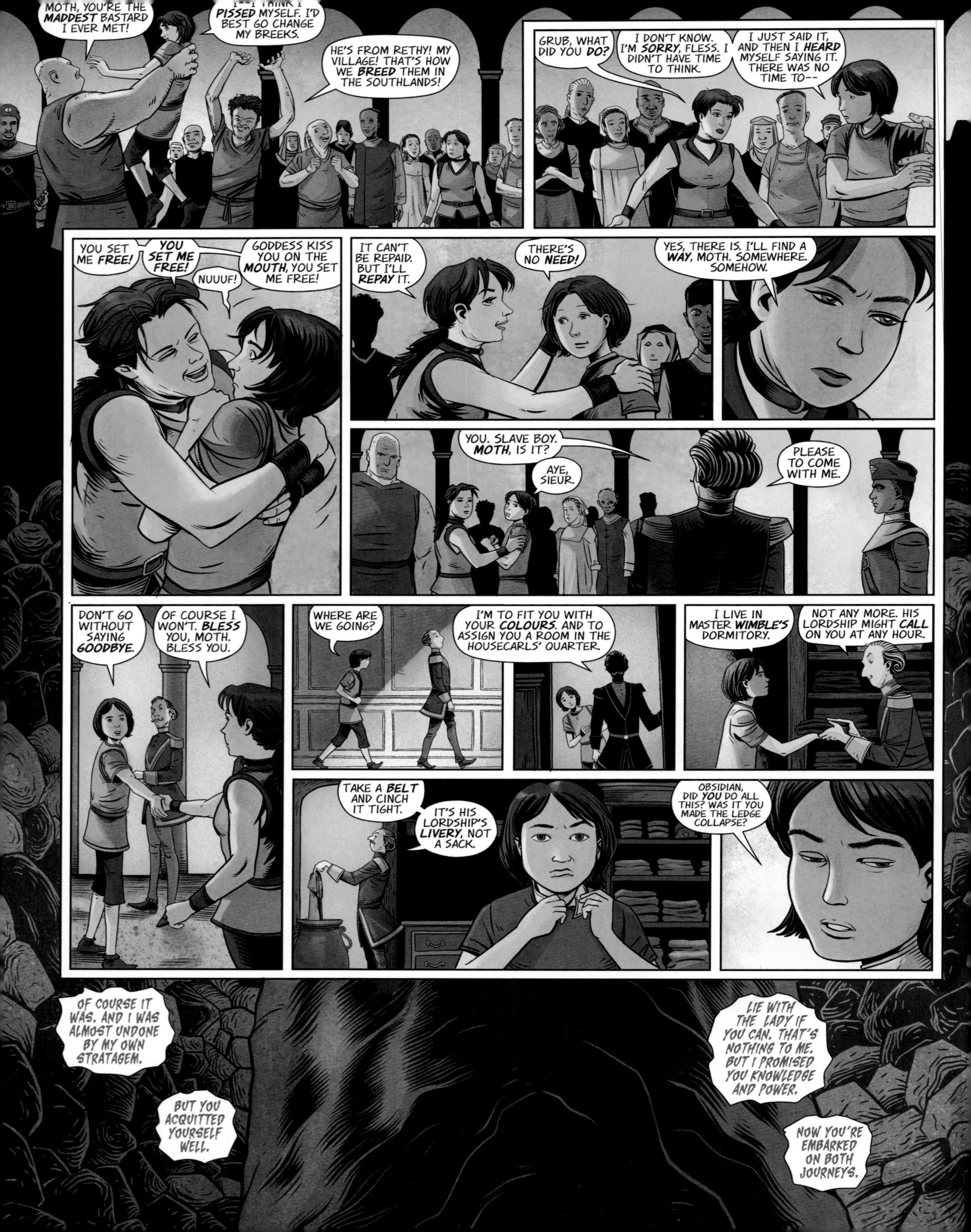
MOTH, YOU'RE THE MADDEST BASTARD I EVER MET!
PISSED MYSELF. I'D BEST GO CHANGE MY BREEKS.
HE'S FROM RETHY! MY VILLAGE! THAT'S HOW WE BREED THEM IN THE SOUTHLANDS!
GRUB, WHAT DID YOU DO?
I DON'T KNOW. I'M SORRY, FLESS. I DIDN'T HAVE TIME TO THINK.
I JUST SAID IT, AND THEN I HEARD MYSELF SAYING IT. THERE WAS NO TIME TO--
YOU SET ME FREE!
YOU SET ME FREE!
GODDESS KISS YOU ON THE MOUTH, YOU SET ME FREE!
NUUUF!
IT CAN'T BE REPAID. BUT I'LL REPAY IT.
THERE'S NO NEED!
YES, THERE IS. I'LL FIND A WAY, MOTH. SOMEWHERE. SOMEHOW.
YOU. SLAVE BOY. MOTH, IS IT?
AYE, SIEUR.
PLEASE TO COME WITH ME.
DON'T GO WITHOUT SAYING GOODBYE.
OF COURSE I WON'T. BLESS YOU, MOTH. BLESS YOU.
WHERE ARE WE GOING?
I'M TO FIT YOU WITH YOUR COLOURS, AND TO ASSIGN YOU A ROOM IN THE HOUSECARLS' QUARTER.
I LIVE IN MASTER WIMBLE'S DORMITORY.
NOT ANY MORE. HIS LORDSHIP MIGHT CALL ON YOU AT ANY HOUR.
TAKE A BELT AND CINCH IT TIGHT.
IT'S HIS LORDSHIP'S LIVERY, NOT A SACK.
OBSIDIAN, DID YOU DO ALL THIS? WAS IT YOU MADE THE LEDGE COLLAPSE?
OF COURSE IT WAS. AND I WAS ALMOST UNDONE BY MY OWN STRATAGEM.
BUT YOU ACQUITTED YOURSELF WELL.
LIE WITH THE LADY IF YOU CAN. THAT'S NOTHING TO ME. BUT I PROMISED YOU KNOWLEDGE AND POWER.
NOW YOU'RE EMBARKED ON BOTH JOURNEYS.

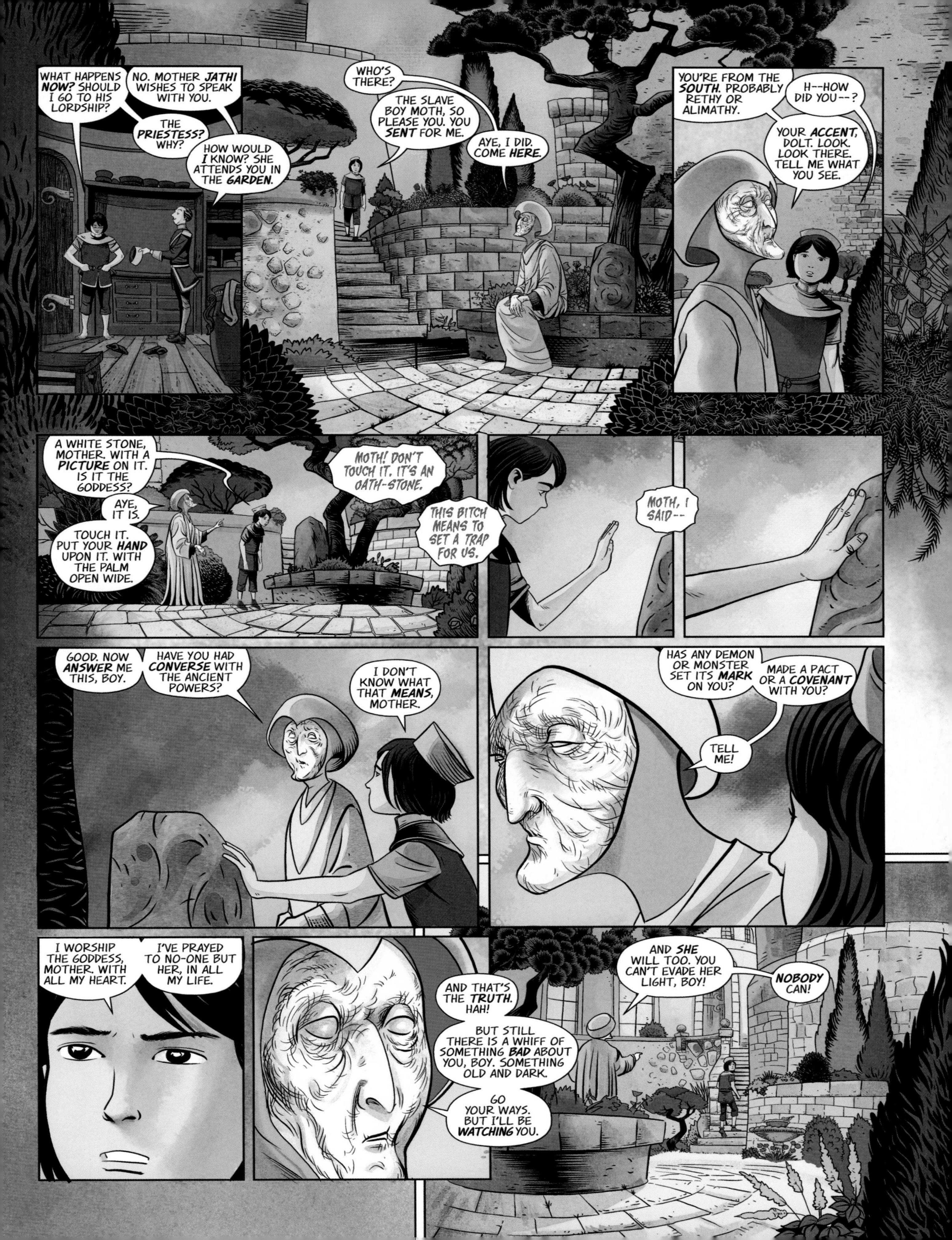
WHAT HAPPENS NOW? SHOULD I GO TO HIS LORDSHIP?
NO. MOTHER JATHI WISHES TO SPEAK WITH YOU.
THE PRIESTESS? WHY?
HOW WOULD I KNOW? SHE ATTENDS YOU IN THE GARDEN.
WHO'S THERE?
THE SLAVE BOY MOTH, SO PLEASE YOU. YOU SENT FOR ME.
AYE, I DID. COME HERE.
YOU'RE FROM THE SOUTH. PROBABLY RETHY OR ALIMATHY.
H--HOW DID YOU--?
YOUR ACCENT, DOLT. LOOK. LOOK THERE. TELL ME WHAT YOU SEE.
A WHITE STONE, MOTHER. WITH A PICTURE ON IT. IS IT THE GODDESS?
AYE, IT IS.
TOUCH IT. PUT YOUR HAND UPON IT. WITH THE PALM OPEN WIDE.
MOTH! DON'T TOUCH IT. IT'S AN OATH-STONE.
THIS BITCH MEANS TO SET A TRAP FOR US.
MOTH, I SAID--
GOOD. NOW ANSWER ME THIS, BOY.
HAVE YOU HAD CONVERSE WITH THE ANCIENT POWERS?
I DON'T KNOW WHAT THAT MEANS, MOTHER.
HAS ANY DEMON OR MONSTER SET ITS MARK ON YOU?
MADE A PACT OR A COVENANT WITH YOU?
TELL ME!
I WORSHIP THE GODDESS, MOTHER. WITH ALL MY HEART.
I'VE PRAYED TO NO-ONE BUT HER, IN ALL MY LIFE.
AND THAT'S THE TRUTH. HAH!
BUT STILL THERE IS A WHIFF OF SOMETHING BAD ABOUT YOU, BOY. SOMETHING OLD AND DARK.
GO YOUR WAYS. BUT I'LL BE WATCHING YOU.
AND SHE WILL TOO. YOU CAN'T EVADE HER LIGHT, BOY!
NOBODY CAN!

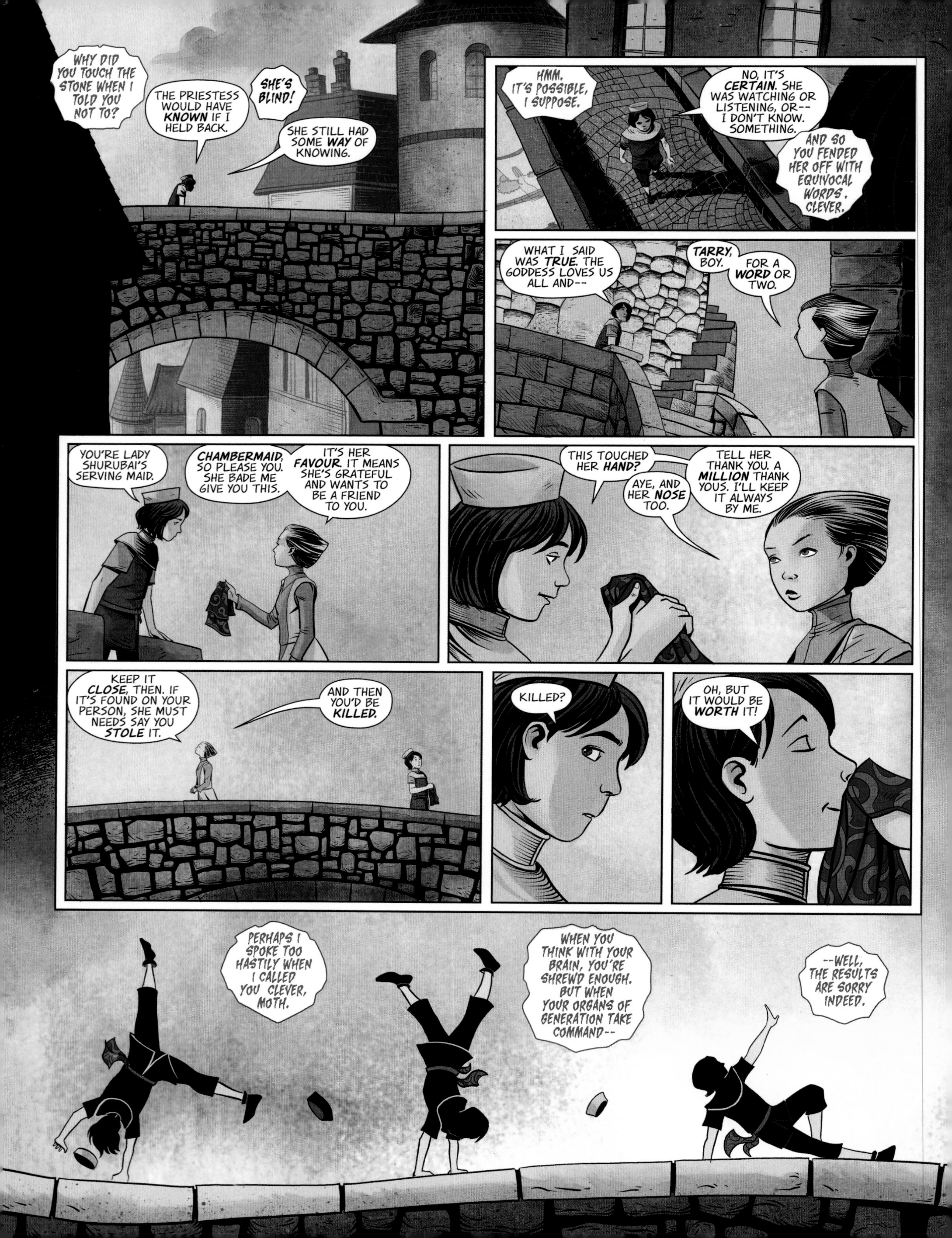
WHY DID YOU TOUCH THE STONE WHEN I TOLD YOU NOT TO?
THE PRIESTESS WOULD HAVE KNOWN IF I HELD BACK.
SHE'S BLIND!
SHE STILL HAD SOME WAY OF KNOWING.
HMM. IT'S POSSIBLE, I SUPPOSE.
NO, IT'S CERTAIN. SHE WAS WATCHING OR LISTENING, OR-- I DON'T KNOW. SOMETHING.
AND SO YOU FENDED HER OFF WITH EQUIVOCAL WORDS. CLEVER.
WHAT I SAID WAS TRUE. THE GODDESS LOVES US ALL AND--
TARRY, BOY.
FOR A WORD OR TWO.
YOU'RE LADY SHURUBAI'S SERVING MAID.
CHAMBERMAID, SO PLEASE YOU. SHE BADE ME GIVE YOU THIS.
IT'S HER FAVOUR. IT MEANS SHE'S GRATEFUL AND WANTS TO BE A FRIEND TO YOU.
THIS TOUCHED HER HAND?
AYE, AND HER NOSE TOO.
TELL HER THANK YOU. A MILLION THANK YOUS. I'LL KEEP IT ALWAYS BY ME.
KEEP IT CLOSE, THEN. IF IT'S FOUND ON YOUR PERSON, SHE MUST NEEDS SAY YOU STOLE IT.
AND THEN YOU'D BE KILLED.
KILLED?
OH, BUT IT WOULD BE WORTH IT!
PERHAPS I SPOKE TOO HASTILY WHEN I CALLED YOU CLEVER, MOTH.
WHEN YOU THINK WITH YOUR BRAIN, YOU'RE SHREWD ENOUGH. BUT WHEN YOUR ORGANS OF GENERATION TAKE COMMAND--
--WELL, THE RESULTS ARE SORRY INDEED.

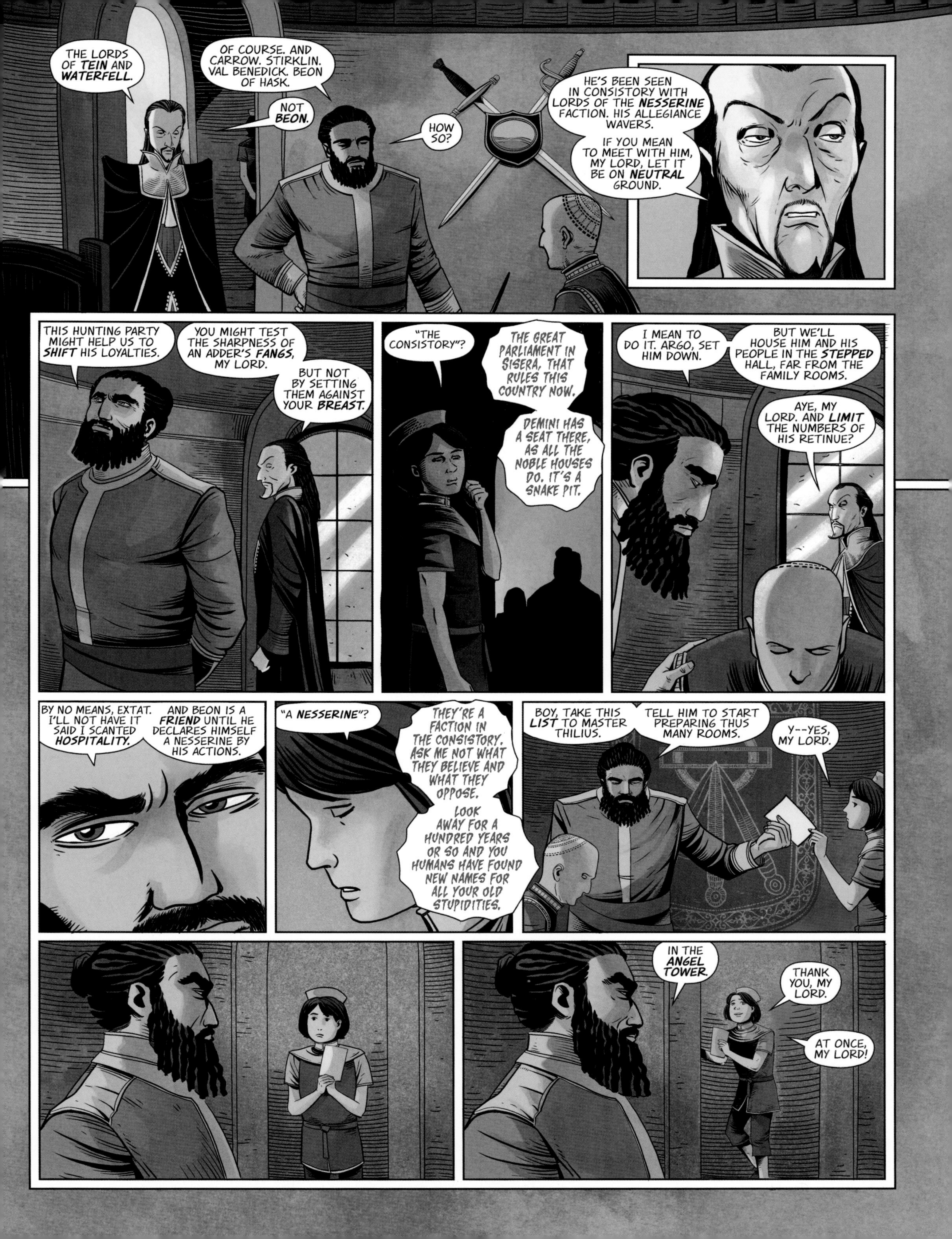
THE LORDS OF TEIN AND WATERFELL.
OF COURSE. AND CARROW. STIRKLIN. VAL BENEDICK. BEON OF HASK.
NOT BEON.
HOW SO?
HE'S BEEN SEEN IN CONSISTORY WITH LORDS OF THE NESSERINE FACTION. HIS ALLEGIANCE WAVERS.
IF YOU MEAN TO MEET WITH HIM, MY LORD, LET IT BE ON NEUTRAL GROUND.
THIS HUNTING PARTY MIGHT HELP US TO SHIFT HIS LOYALTIES.
YOU MIGHT TEST THE SHARPNESS OF AN ADDER'S FANGS, MY LORD.
BUT NOT BY SETTING THEM AGAINST YOUR BREAST.
"THE CONSISTORY"?
THE GREAT PARLIAMENT IN SISERA, THAT RULES THIS COUNTRY NOW.
DEMINI HAS A SEAT THERE, AS ALL THE NOBLE HOUSES DO. IT'S A SNAKE PIT.
I MEAN TO DO IT. ARGO, SET HIM DOWN.
BUT WE'LL HOUSE HIM AND HIS PEOPLE IN THE STEPPED HALL, FAR FROM THE FAMILY ROOMS.
AYE, MY LORD. AND LIMIT THE NUMBERS OF HIS RETINUE?
BY NO MEANS, EXTAT. I'LL NOT HAVE IT SAID I SCANTED HOSPITALITY.
AND BEON IS A FRIEND UNTIL HE DECLARES HIMSELF A NESSERINE BY HIS ACTIONS.
"A NESSERINE"?
THEY'RE A FACTION IN THE CONSISTORY. ASK ME NOT WHAT THEY BELIEVE AND WHAT THEY OPPOSE.
LOOK AWAY FOR A HUNDRED YEARS OR SO AND YOU HUMANS HAVE FOUND NEW NAMES FOR ALL YOUR OLD STUPIDITIES.
BOY, TAKE THIS LIST TO MASTER THILIUS.
TELL HIM TO START PREPARING THUS MANY ROOMS.
Y--YES, MY LORD.
IN THE ANGEL TOWER.
THANK YOU, MY LORD.
AT ONCE, MY LORD!

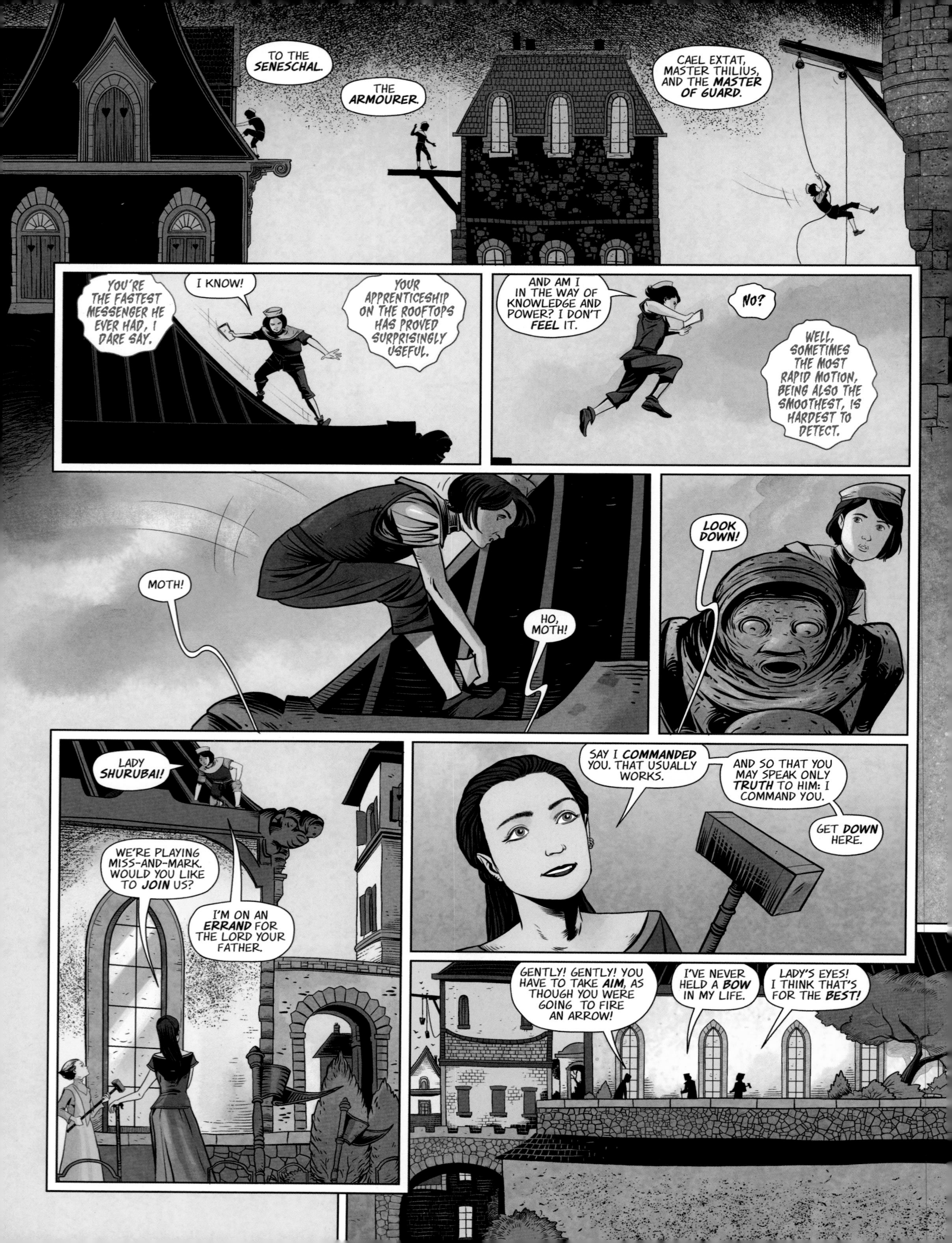
TO THE SENESCHAL.
THE ARMOURER.
CAEL EXTAT, MASTER THILIUS, AND THE MASTER OF GUARD.
YOU'RE THE FASTEST MESSENGER HE EVER HAD, I DARE SAY.
I KNOW!
YOUR APPRENTICESHIP ON THE ROOFTOPS HAS PROVED SURPRISINGLY USEFUL.
AND AM I IN THE WAY OF KNOWLEDGE AND POWER? I DON'T FEEL IT.
NO?
WELL, SOMETIMES THE MOST RAPID MOTION, BEING ALSO THE SMOOTHEST, IS HARDEST TO DETECT.
MOTH!
HO, MOTH!
LOOK DOWN!
LADY SHURUBAI!
WE'RE PLAYING MISS-AND-MARK. WOULD YOU LIKE TO JOIN US?
I'M ON AN ERRAND FOR THE LORD YOUR FATHER.
SAY I COMMANDED YOU. THAT USUALLY WORKS.
AND SO THAT YOU MAY SPEAK ONLY TRUTH TO HIM: I COMMAND YOU.
GET DOWN HERE.
GENTLY! GENTLY! YOU HAVE TO TAKE AIM, AS THOUGH YOU WERE GOING TO FIRE AN ARROW!
I'VE NEVER HELD A BOW IN MY LIFE.
LADY'S EYES! I THINK THAT'S FOR THE BEST!

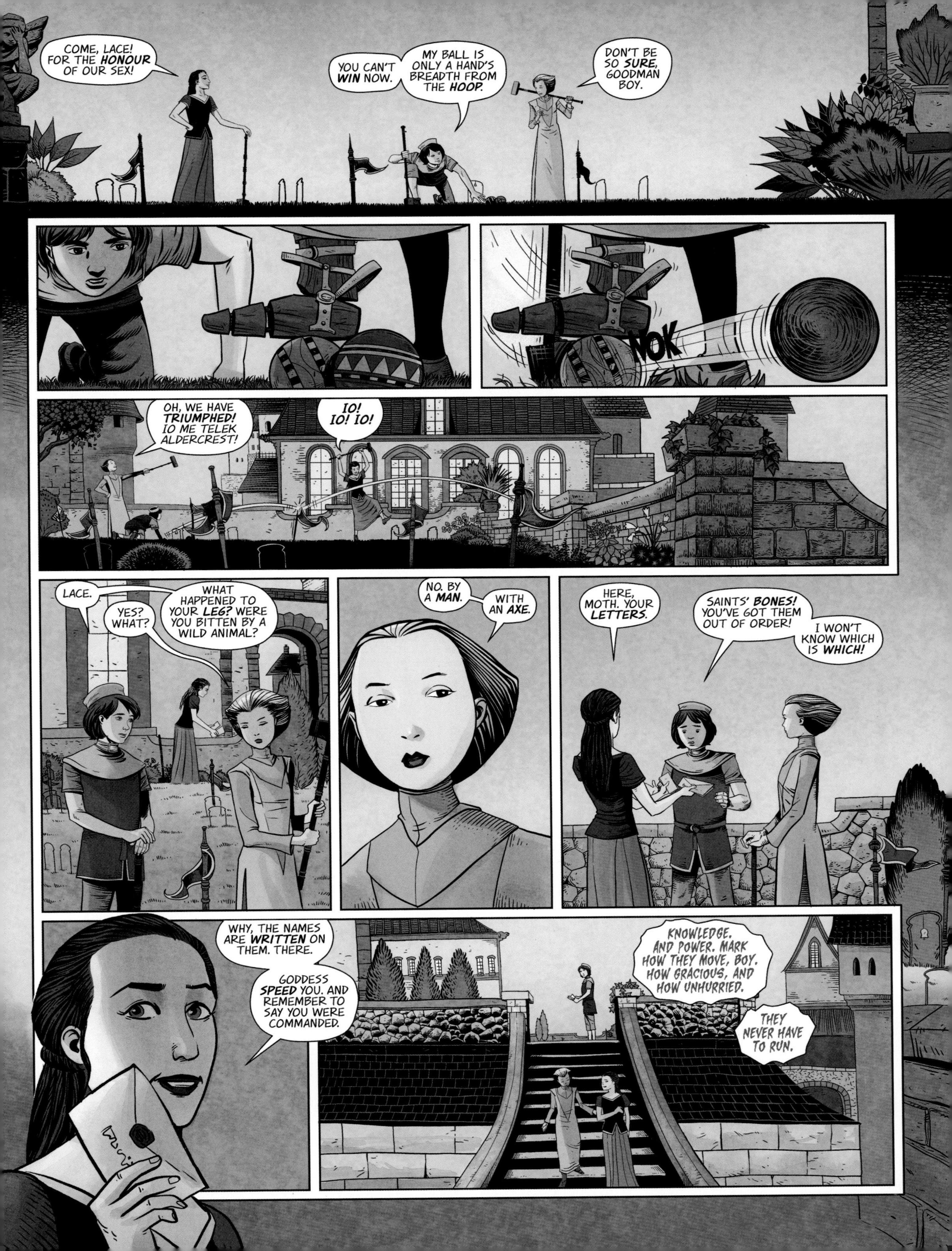
COME, LACE! FOR THE HONOUR OF OUR SEX!
YOU CAN'T WIN NOW.
MY BALL IS ONLY A HAND'S BREADTH FROM THE HOOP.
DON'T BE SO SURE, GOODMAN BOY.
NOK
OH, WE HAVE TRIUMPHED! IO ME TELEK ALDERCREST!
IO! IO! IO!
LACE.
YES? WHAT?
WHAT HAPPENED TO YOUR LEG? WERE YOU BITTEN BY A WILD ANIMAL?
NO. BY A MAN.
WITH AN AXE.
HERE, MOTH. YOUR LETTERS.
SAINTS' BONES! YOU'VE GOT THEM OUT OF ORDER!
I WON'T KNOW WHICH IS WHICH!
WHY, THE NAMES ARE WRITTEN ON THEM. THERE.
GODDESS SPEED YOU. AND REMEMBER TO SAY YOU WERE COMMANDED.
KNOWLEDGE. AND POWER. MARK HOW THEY MOVE, BOY. HOW GRACIOUS, AND HOW UNHURRIED.
THEY NEVER HAVE TO RUN.

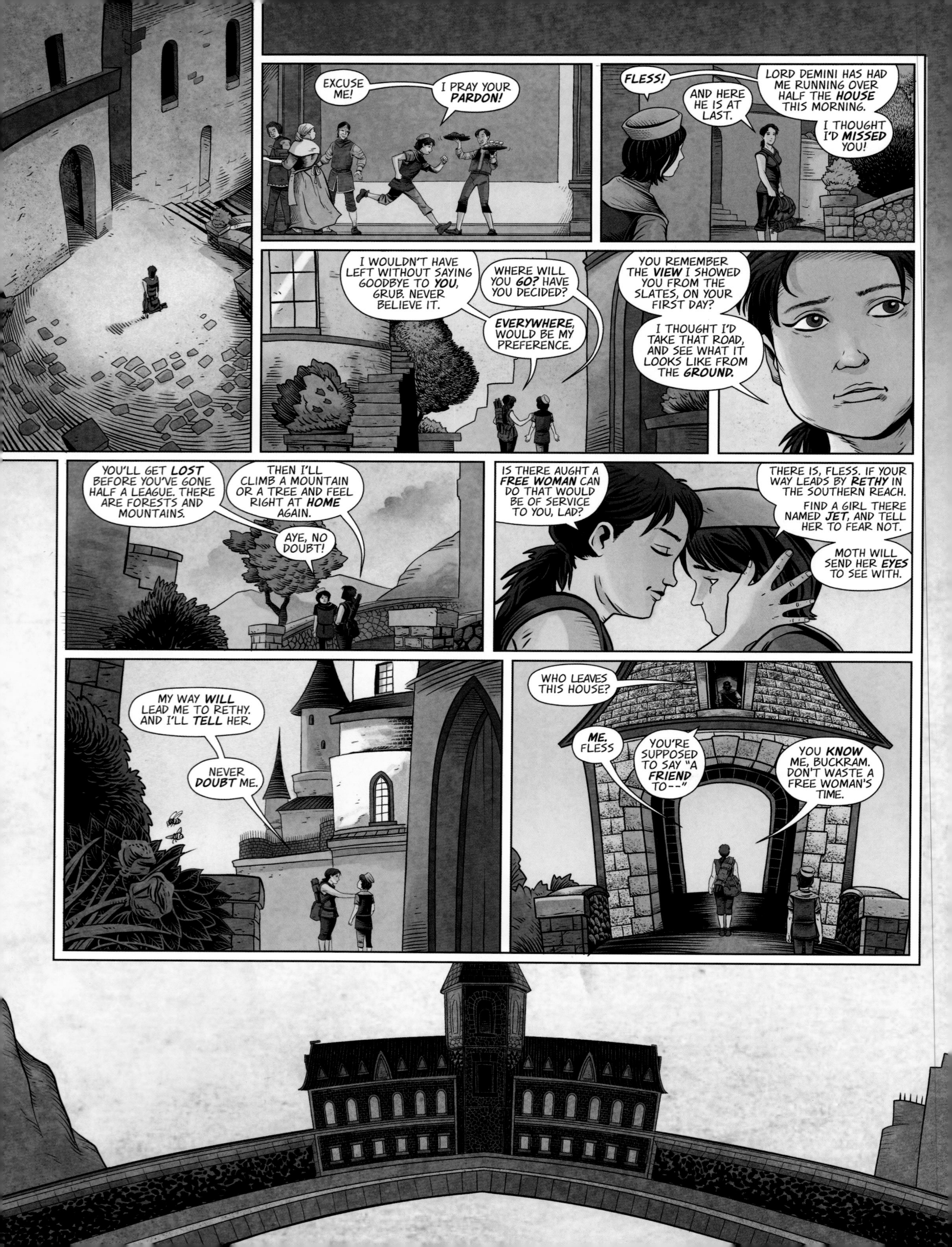
EXCUSE ME!
I PRAY YOUR PARDON!
FLESS!
LORD DEMINI HAS HAD ME RUNNING OVER HALF THE HOUSE THIS MORNING.
AND HERE HE IS AT LAST.
I THOUGHT I'D MISSED YOU!
I WOULDN'T HAVE LEFT WITHOUT SAYING GOODBYE TO YOU, GRUB. NEVER BELIEVE IT.
WHERE WILL YOU GO? HAVE YOU DECIDED?
EVERYWHERE, WOULD BE MY PREFERENCE.
YOU REMEMBER THE VIEW I SHOWED YOU FROM THE SLATES, ON YOUR FIRST DAY?
I THOUGHT I'D TAKE THAT ROAD, AND SEE WHAT IT LOOKS LIKE FROM THE GROUND.
YOU'LL GET LOST BEFORE YOU'VE GONE HALF A LEAGUE. THERE ARE FORESTS AND MOUNTAINS.
THEN I'LL CLIMB A MOUNTAIN OR A TREE AND FEEL RIGHT AT HOME AGAIN.
AYE, NO DOUBT!
IS THERE AUGHT A FREE WOMAN CAN DO THAT WOULD BE OF SERVICE TO YOU, LAD?
THERE IS, FLESS. IF YOUR WAY LEADS BY RETHY IN THE SOUTHERN REACH.
FIND A GIRL THERE NAMED JET, AND TELL HER TO FEAR NOT.
MOTH WILL SEND HER EYES TO SEE WITH.
MY WAY WILL LEAD ME TO RETHY. AND I'LL TELL HER.
NEVER DOUBT ME.
WHO LEAVES THIS HOUSE?
ME. FLESS
YOU'RE SUPPOSED TO SAY "A FRIEND TO--"
YOU KNOW ME, BUCKRAM. DON'T WASTE A FREE WOMAN'S TIME.

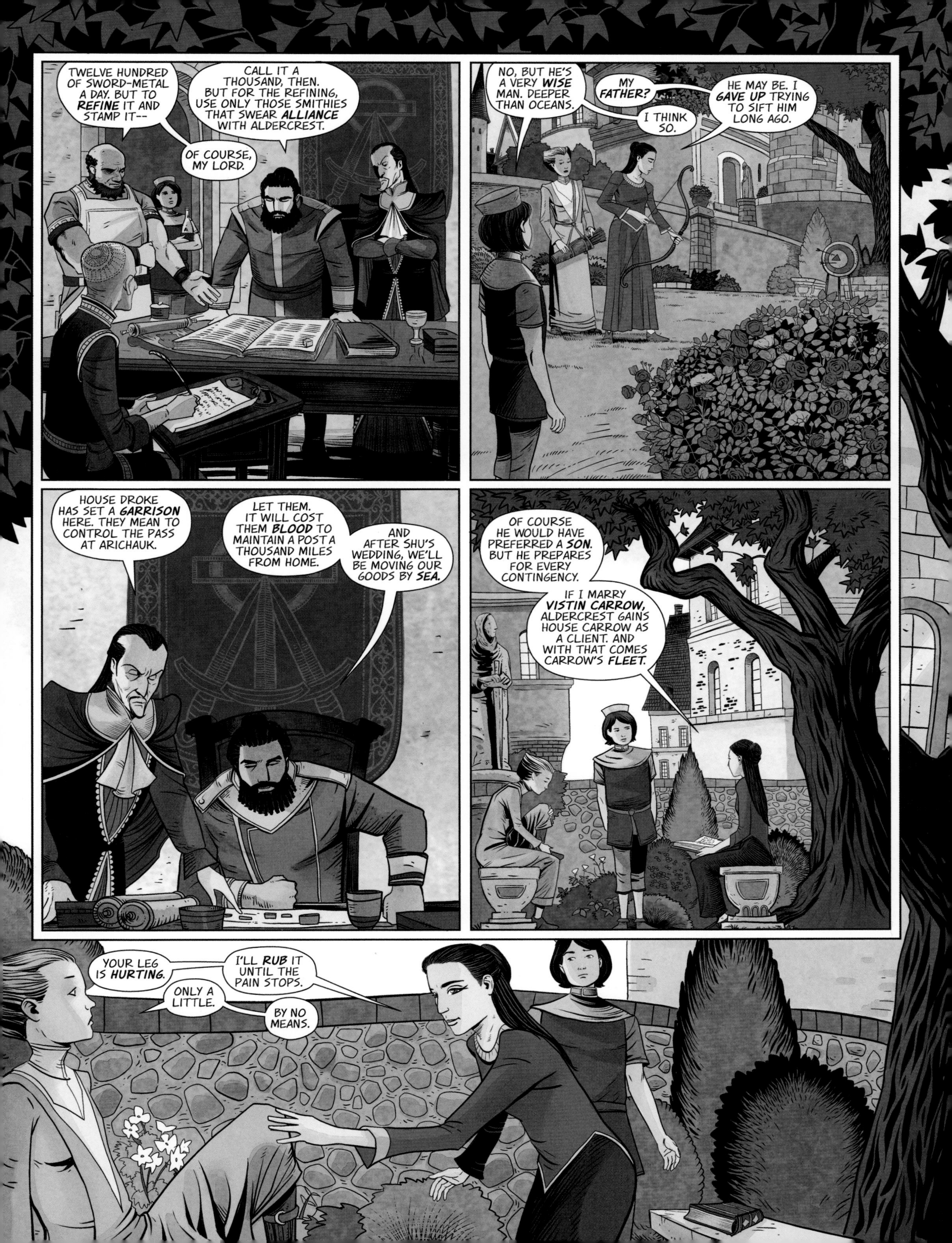
TWELVE HUNDRED OF SWORD-METAL A DAY. BUT TO **REFINE** IT AND STAMP IT--
CALL IT A THOUSAND, THEN. BUT FOR THE REFINING, USE ONLY THOSE SMITHIES THAT SWEAR **ALLIANCE** WITH ALDERCREST.
OF COURSE, MY LORD.
NO, BUT HE'S A VERY **WISE** MAN. DEEPER THAN OCEANS.
MY ***FATHER?***
I THINK SO.
HE MAY BE. I **GAVE UP** TRYING TO SIFT HIM LONG AGO.
HOUSE DROKE HAS SET A **GARRISON** HERE. THEY MEAN TO CONTROL THE PASS AT ARICHAUK.
LET THEM. IT WILL COST THEM **BLOOD** TO MAINTAIN A POST A THOUSAND MILES FROM HOME.
AND AFTER SHU'S WEDDING, WE'LL BE MOVING OUR GOODS BY ***SEA.***
OF COURSE HE WOULD HAVE PREFERRED A **SON**. BUT HE PREPARES FOR EVERY CONTINGENCY.
IF I MARRY **VISTIN CARROW,** ALDERCREST GAINS HOUSE CARROW AS A CLIENT. AND WITH THAT COMES CARROW'S **FLEET**.
YOUR LEG IS **HURTING**.
ONLY A LITTLE.
I'LL **RUB** IT UNTIL THE PAIN STOPS.
BY NO MEANS.

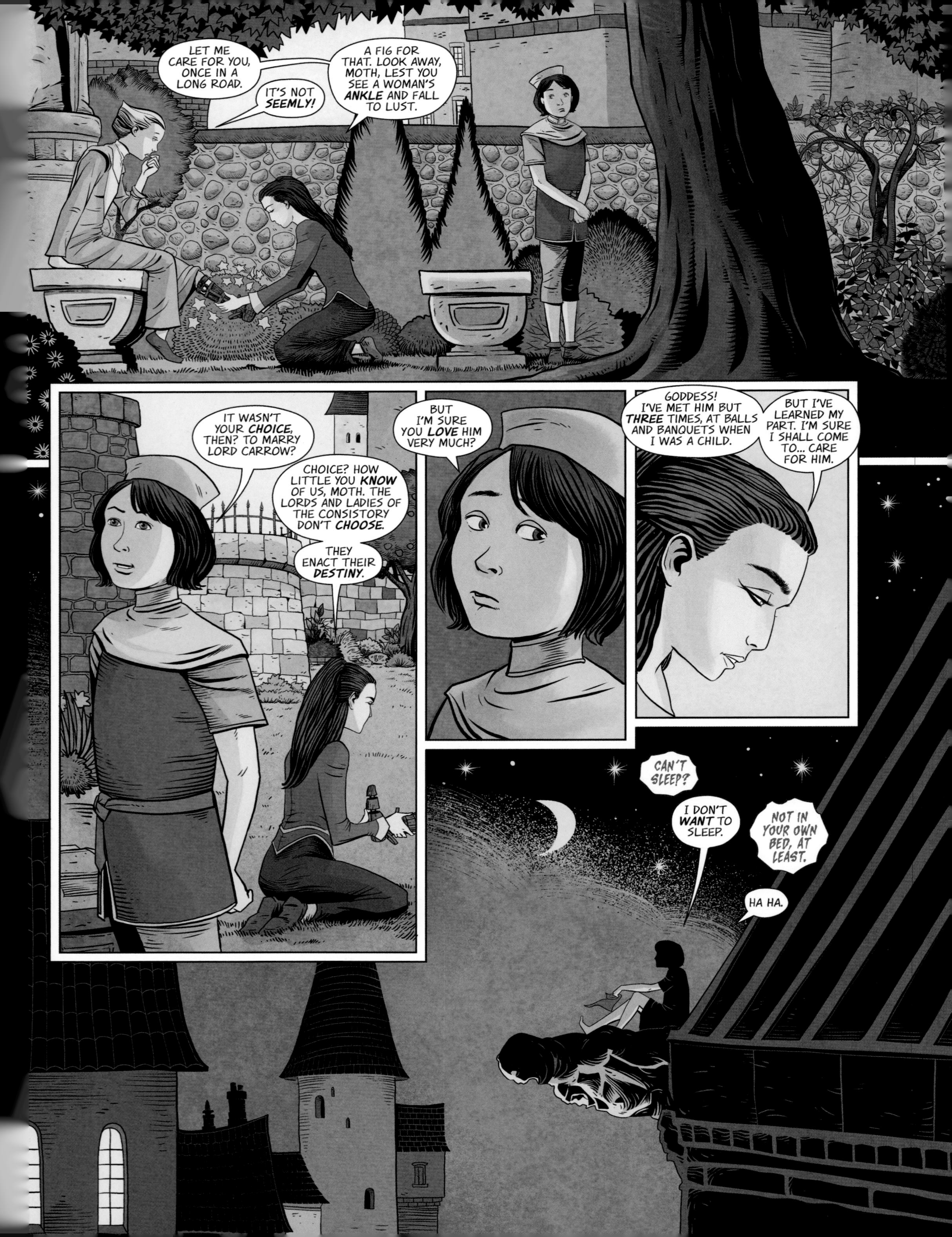
LET ME CARE FOR YOU, ONCE IN A LONG ROAD.
IT'S NOT SEEMLY!
A FIG FOR THAT. LOOK AWAY, MOTH, LEST YOU SEE A WOMAN'S ANKLE AND FALL TO LUST.
IT WASN'T YOUR CHOICE, THEN? TO MARRY LORD CARROW?
CHOICE? HOW LITTLE YOU KNOW OF US, MOTH. THE LORDS AND LADIES OF THE CONSISTORY DON'T CHOOSE.
THEY ENACT THEIR DESTINY.
BUT I'M SURE YOU LOVE HIM VERY MUCH?
GODDESS! I'VE MET HIM BUT THREE TIMES, AT BALLS AND BANQUETS WHEN I WAS A CHILD.
BUT I'VE LEARNED MY PART. I'M SURE I SHALL COME TO... CARE FOR HIM.
CAN'T SLEEP?
I DON'T WANT TO SLEEP.
NOT IN YOUR OWN BED, AT LEAST.
HA HA.

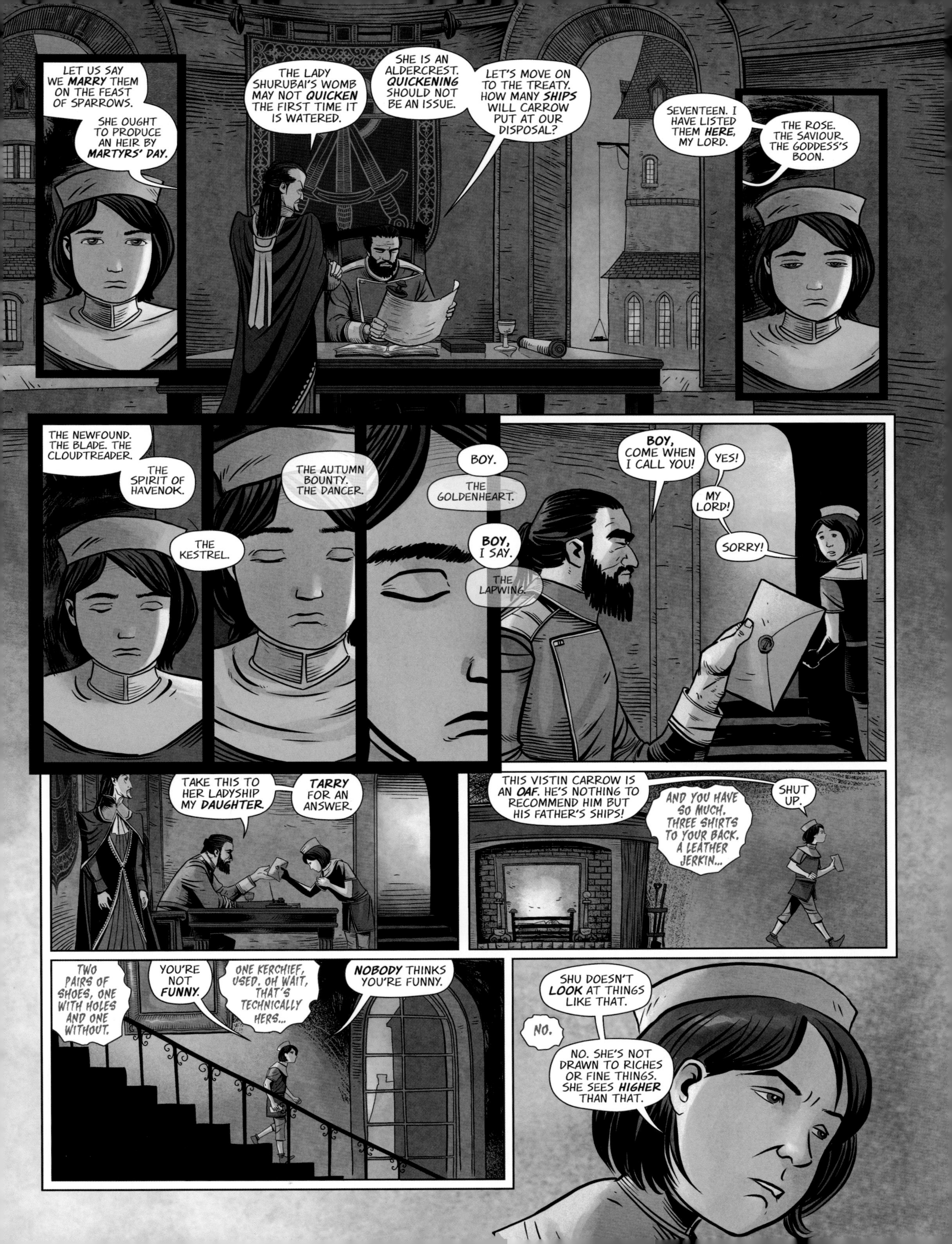
LET US SAY WE MARRY THEM ON THE FEAST OF SPARROWS.
SHE OUGHT TO PRODUCE AN HEIR BY MARTYRS' DAY.
THE LADY SHURUBAI'S WOMB MAY NOT QUICKEN THE FIRST TIME IT IS WATERED.
SHE IS AN ALDERCREST. QUICKENING SHOULD NOT BE AN ISSUE.
LET'S MOVE ON TO THE TREATY. HOW MANY SHIPS WILL CARROW PUT AT OUR DISPOSAL?
SEVENTEEN. I HAVE LISTED THEM HERE, MY LORD.
THE ROSE. THE SAVIOUR. THE GODDESS'S BOON.
THE NEWFOUND. THE BLADE. THE CLOUDTREADER.
THE SPIRIT OF HAVENOK.
THE KESTREL.
THE AUTUMN BOUNTY. THE DANCER.
BOY.
THE GOLDENHEART.
BOY, I SAY.
THE LAPWING.
BOY, COME WHEN I CALL YOU!
YES!
MY LORD!
SORRY!
TAKE THIS TO HER LADYSHIP MY DAUGHTER.
TARRY FOR AN ANSWER.
THIS VISTIN CARROW IS AN OAF. HE'S NOTHING TO RECOMMEND HIM BUT HIS FATHER'S SHIPS!
AND YOU HAVE SO MUCH. THREE SHIRTS TO YOUR BACK. A LEATHER JERKIN...
SHUT UP.
TWO PAIRS OF SHOES, ONE WITH HOLES AND ONE WITHOUT.
YOU'RE NOT FUNNY.
ONE KERCHIEF, USED. OH WAIT, THAT'S TECHNICALLY HERS...
NOBODY THINKS YOU'RE FUNNY.
SHU DOESN'T LOOK AT THINGS LIKE THAT.
NO.
NO. SHE'S NOT DRAWN TO RICHES OR FINE THINGS. SHE SEES HIGHER THAN THAT.

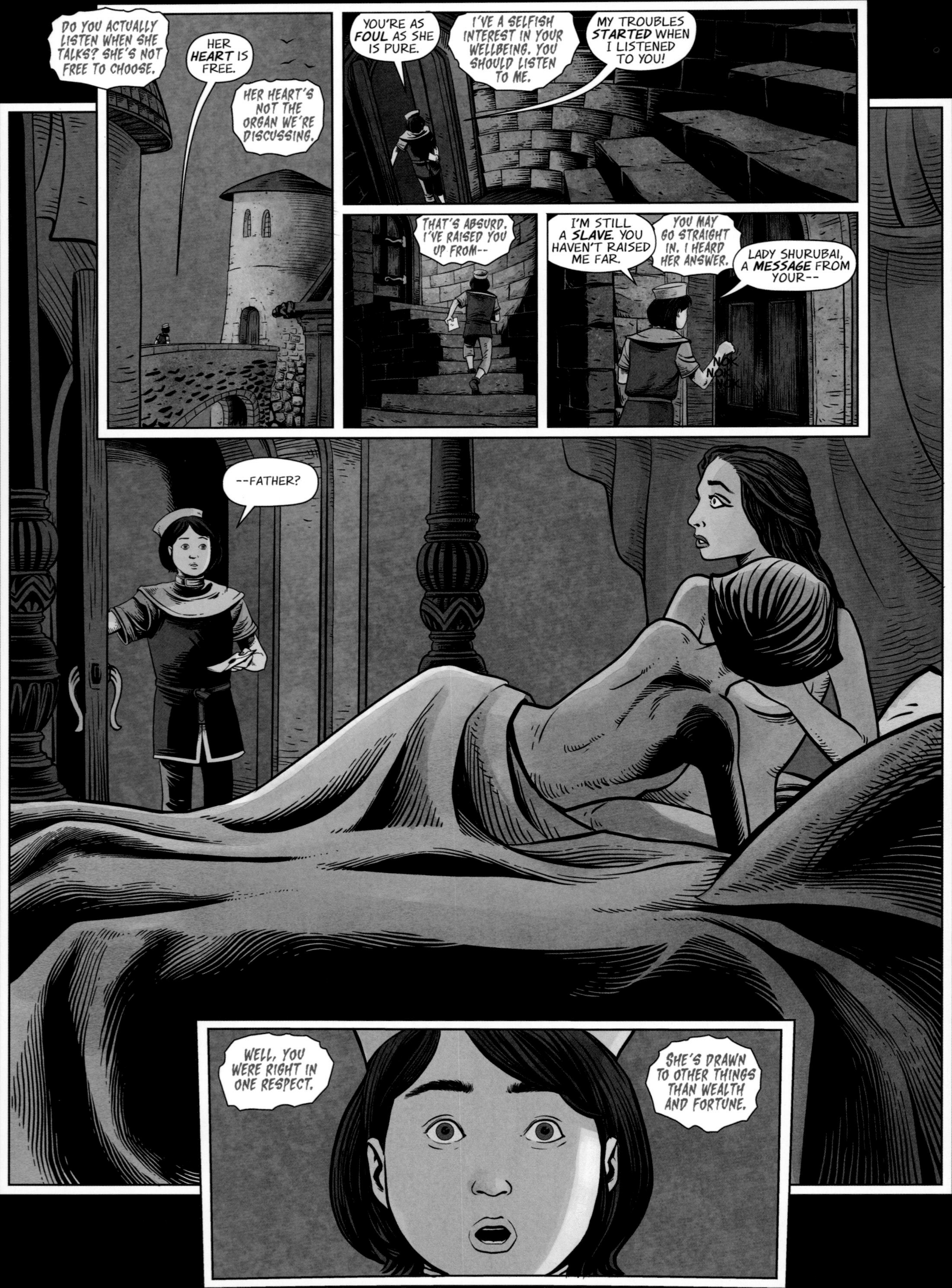
DO YOU ACTUALLY LISTEN WHEN SHE TALKS? SHE'S NOT FREE TO CHOOSE.
HER **HEART** IS FREE.
HER HEART'S NOT THE ORGAN WE'RE DISCUSSING.
YOU'RE AS **FOUL** AS SHE IS PURE.
I'VE A SELFISH INTEREST IN YOUR WELLBEING. YOU SHOULD LISTEN TO ME.
MY TROUBLES **STARTED** WHEN I LISTENED TO YOU!
THAT'S ABSURD. I'VE RAISED YOU UP FROM--
I'M STILL A **SLAVE**. YOU HAVEN'T RAISED ME FAR.
YOU MAY GO STRAIGHT IN. I HEARD HER ANSWER.
LADY SHURUBAI, A **MESSAGE** FROM YOUR--
NOK NOK NOK
--FATHER?
WELL, YOU WERE RIGHT IN ONE RESPECT.
SHE'S DRAWN TO OTHER THINGS THAN WEALTH AND FORTUNE.

Chapter Four

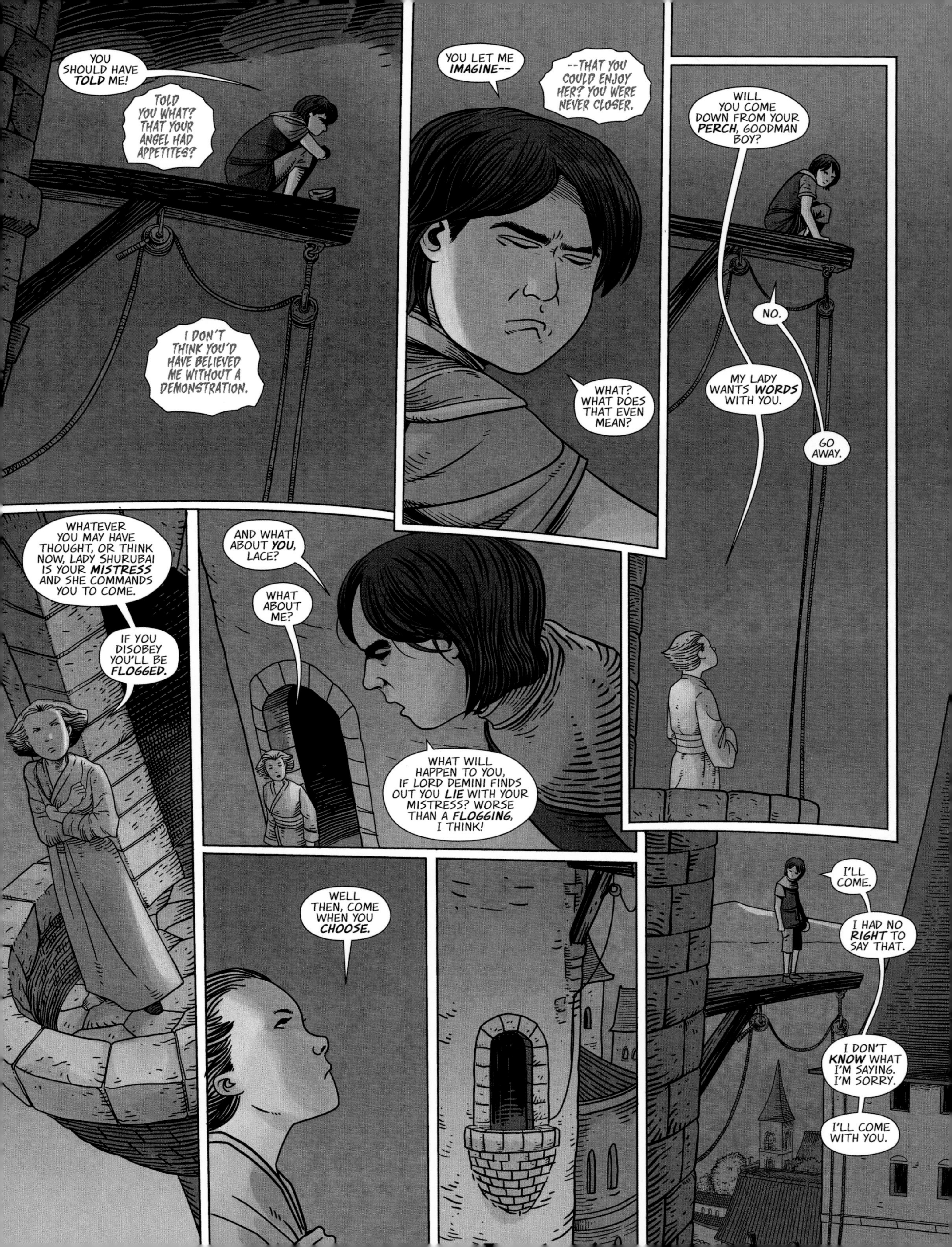
YOU SHOULD HAVE TOLD ME!
TOLD YOU WHAT? THAT YOUR ANGEL HAD APPETITES?
I DON'T THINK YOU'D HAVE BELIEVED ME WITHOUT A DEMONSTRATION.
YOU LET ME IMAGINE--
--THAT YOU COULD ENJOY HER? YOU WERE NEVER CLOSER.
WHAT? WHAT DOES THAT EVEN MEAN?
WILL YOU COME DOWN FROM YOUR PERCH, GOODMAN BOY?
NO.
MY LADY WANTS WORDS WITH YOU.
GO AWAY.
WHATEVER YOU MAY HAVE THOUGHT, OR THINK NOW, LADY SHURUBAI IS YOUR MISTRESS AND SHE COMMANDS YOU TO COME.
IF YOU DISOBEY YOU'LL BE FLOGGED.
AND WHAT ABOUT YOU, LACE?
WHAT ABOUT ME?
WHAT WILL HAPPEN TO YOU, IF LORD DEMINI FINDS OUT YOU LIE WITH YOUR MISTRESS? WORSE THAN A FLOGGING, I THINK!
WELL THEN, COME WHEN YOU CHOOSE.
I'LL COME.
I HAD NO RIGHT TO SAY THAT.
I DON'T KNOW WHAT I'M SAYING. I'M SORRY.
I'LL COME WITH YOU.

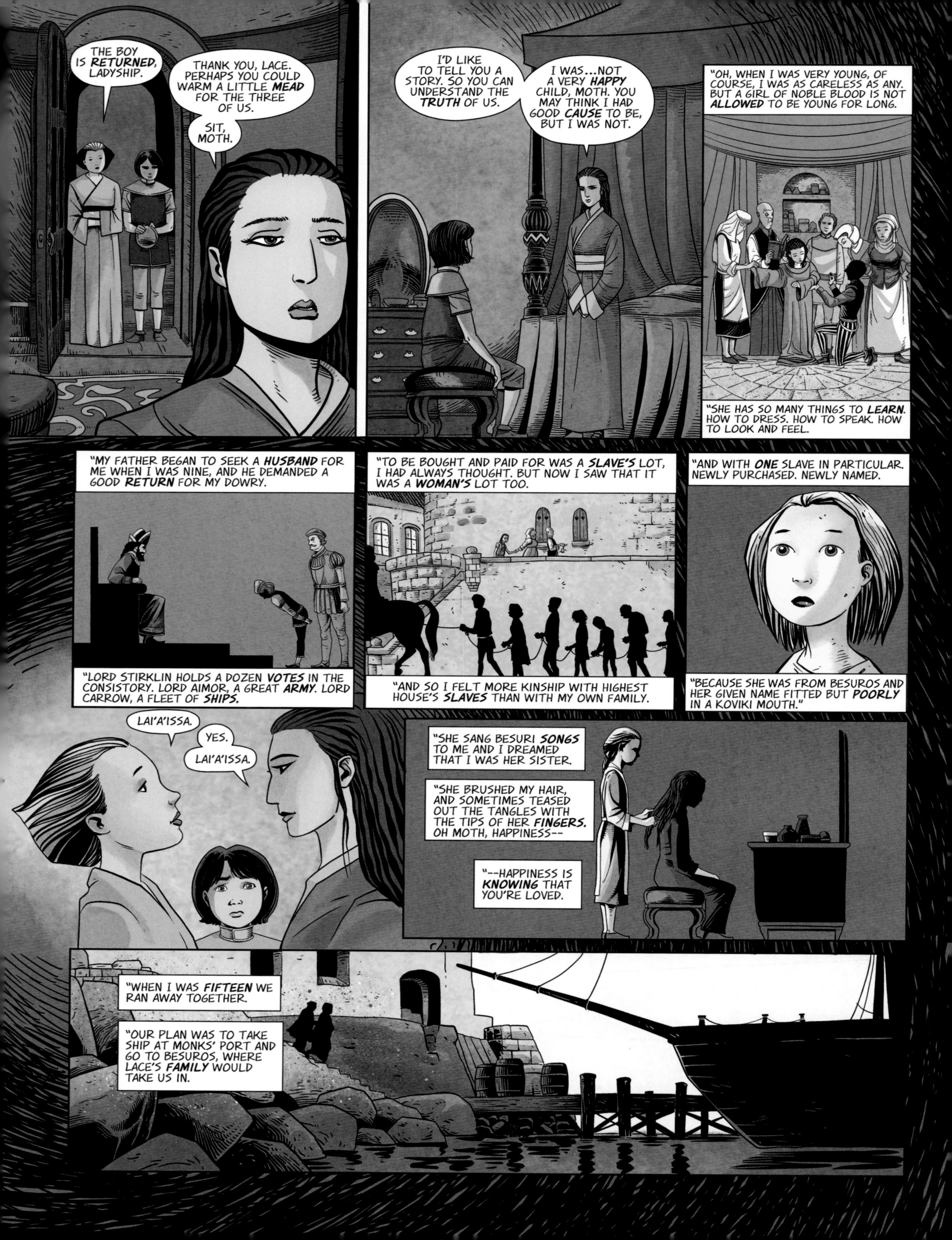
THE BOY IS RETURNED, LADYSHIP.
THANK YOU, LACE. PERHAPS YOU COULD WARM A LITTLE MEAD FOR THE THREE OF US.
SIT, MOTH.
I'D LIKE TO TELL YOU A STORY. SO YOU CAN UNDERSTAND THE TRUTH OF US.
I WAS...NOT A VERY HAPPY CHILD, MOTH. YOU MAY THINK I HAD GOOD CAUSE TO BE, BUT I WAS NOT.
"OH, WHEN I WAS VERY YOUNG, OF COURSE, I WAS AS CARELESS AS ANY. BUT A GIRL OF NOBLE BLOOD IS NOT ALLOWED TO BE YOUNG FOR LONG.
"SHE HAS SO MANY THINGS TO LEARN. HOW TO DRESS. HOW TO SPEAK. HOW TO LOOK AND FEEL.
"MY FATHER BEGAN TO SEEK A HUSBAND FOR ME WHEN I WAS NINE, AND HE DEMANDED A GOOD RETURN FOR MY DOWRY.
"LORD STIRKLIN HOLDS A DOZEN VOTES IN THE CONSISTORY. LORD AIMOR, A GREAT ARMY. LORD CARROW, A FLEET OF SHIPS.
"TO BE BOUGHT AND PAID FOR WAS A SLAVE'S LOT, I HAD ALWAYS THOUGHT. BUT NOW I SAW THAT IT WAS A WOMAN'S LOT TOO.
"AND SO I FELT MORE KINSHIP WITH HIGHEST HOUSE'S SLAVES THAN WITH MY OWN FAMILY.
"AND WITH ONE SLAVE IN PARTICULAR. NEWLY PURCHASED. NEWLY NAMED.
"BECAUSE SHE WAS FROM BESUROS AND HER GIVEN NAME FITTED BUT POORLY IN A KOVIKI MOUTH."
LAI'A'ISSA.
YES. LAI'A'ISSA.
"SHE SANG BESURI SONGS TO ME AND I DREAMED THAT I WAS HER SISTER.
"SHE BRUSHED MY HAIR, AND SOMETIMES TEASED OUT THE TANGLES WITH THE TIPS OF HER FINGERS. OH MOTH, HAPPINESS--
"--HAPPINESS IS KNOWING THAT YOU'RE LOVED.
"WHEN I WAS FIFTEEN WE RAN AWAY TOGETHER.
"OUR PLAN WAS TO TAKE SHIP AT MONKS' PORT AND GO TO BESUROS, WHERE LACE'S FAMILY WOULD TAKE US IN.

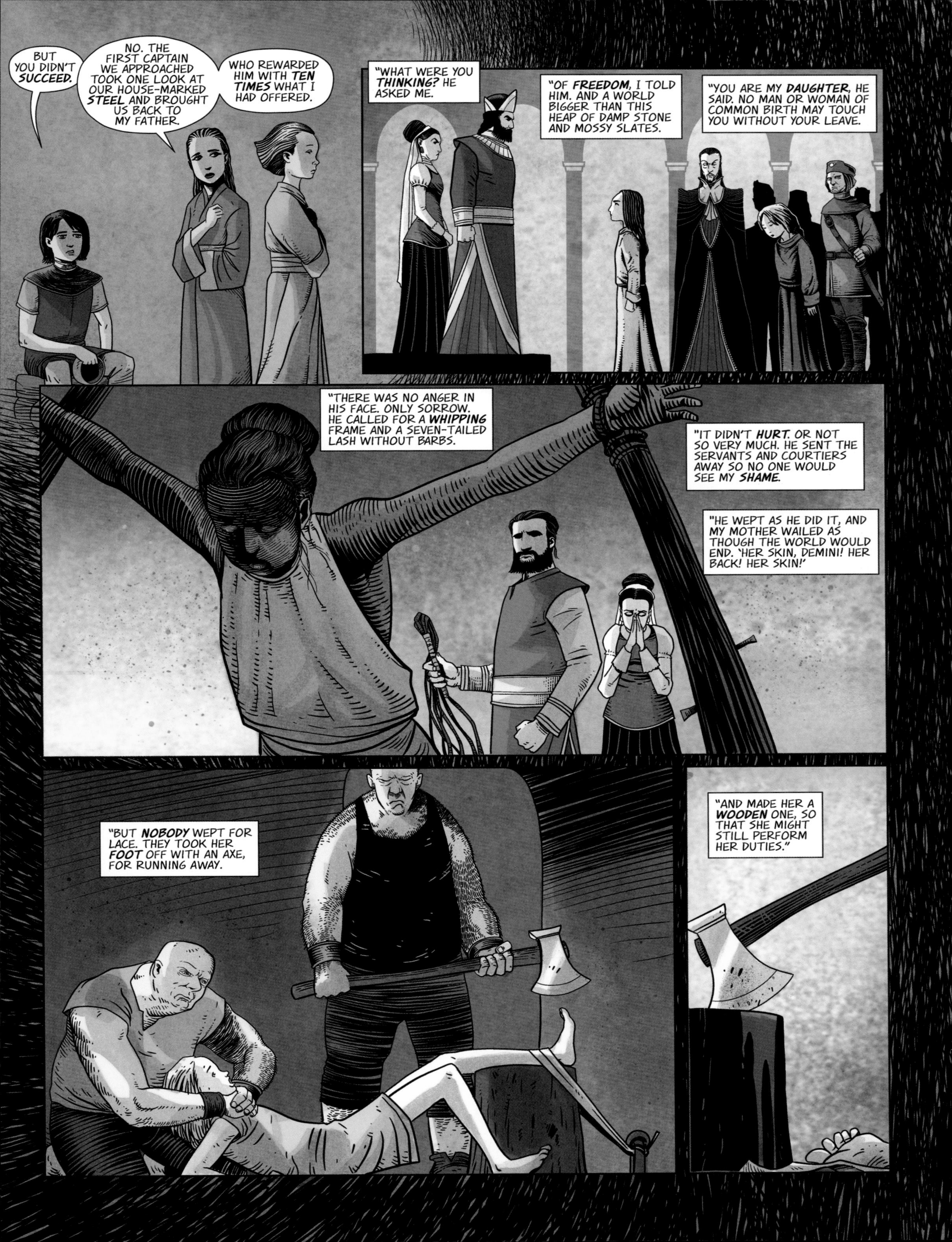

BUT YOU DIDN'T SUCCEED.
NO. THE FIRST CAPTAIN WE APPROACHED TOOK ONE LOOK AT OUR HOUSE-MARKED STEEL AND BROUGHT US BACK TO MY FATHER.
WHO REWARDED HIM WITH TEN TIMES WHAT I HAD OFFERED.
"WHAT WERE YOU THINKING? HE ASKED ME.
"OF FREEDOM, I TOLD HIM. AND A WORLD BIGGER THAN THIS HEAP OF DAMP STONE AND MOSSY SLATES.
"YOU ARE MY DAUGHTER, HE SAID. NO MAN OR WOMAN OF COMMON BIRTH MAY TOUCH YOU WITHOUT YOUR LEAVE.
"THERE WAS NO ANGER IN HIS FACE. ONLY SORROW. HE CALLED FOR A WHIPPING FRAME AND A SEVEN-TAILED LASH WITHOUT BARBS.
"IT DIDN'T HURT. OR NOT SO VERY MUCH. HE SENT THE SERVANTS AND COURTIERS AWAY SO NO ONE WOULD SEE MY SHAME.
"HE WEPT AS HE DID IT, AND MY MOTHER WAILED AS THOUGH THE WORLD WOULD END. 'HER SKIN, DEMINI! HER BACK! HER SKIN!'
"BUT NOBODY WEPT FOR LACE. THEY TOOK HER FOOT OFF WITH AN AXE, FOR RUNNING AWAY.
"AND MADE HER A WOODEN ONE, SO THAT SHE MIGHT STILL PERFORM HER DUTIES."

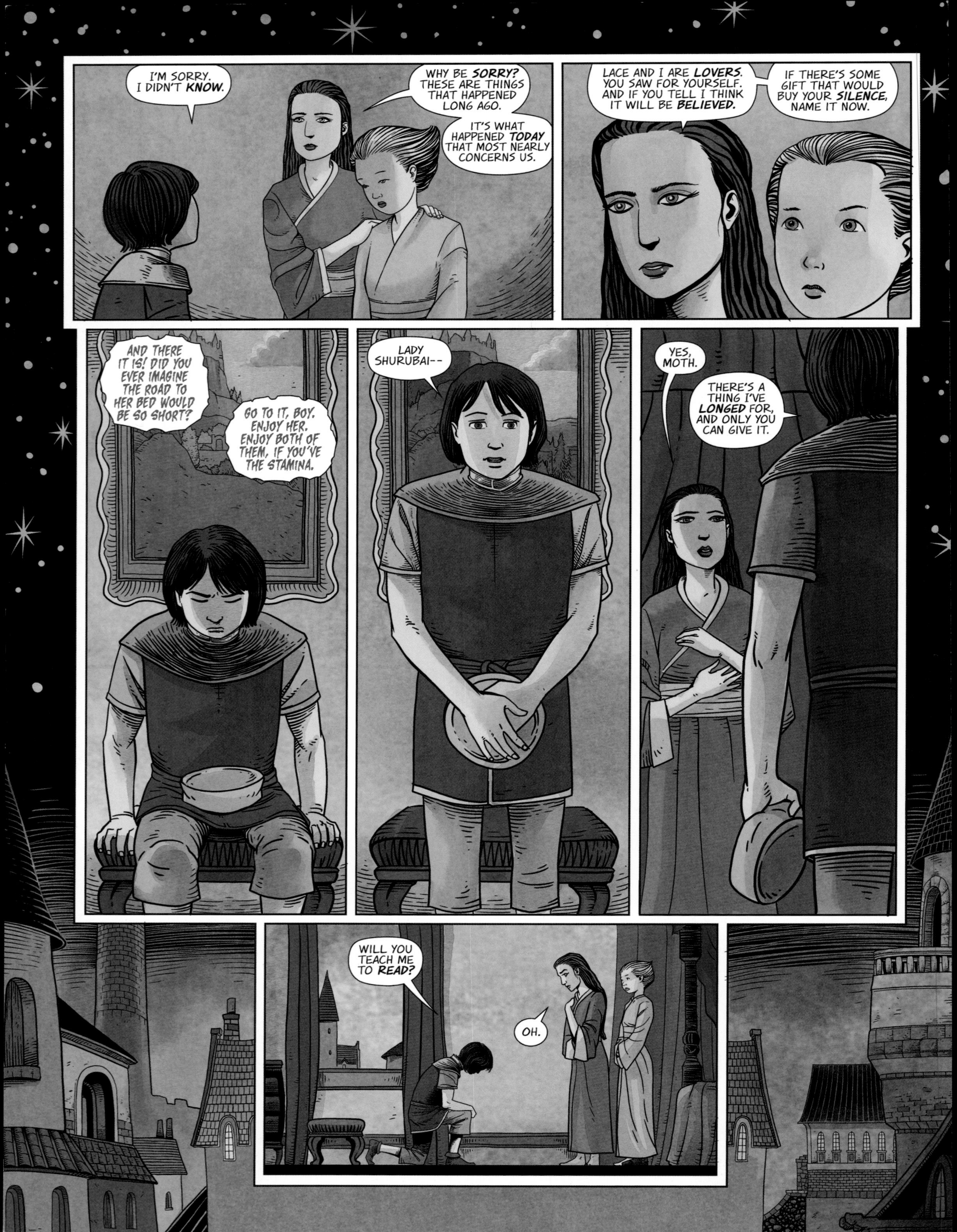
I'M SORRY. I DIDN'T KNOW.
WHY BE SORRY? THESE ARE THINGS THAT HAPPENED LONG AGO.
IT'S WHAT HAPPENED TODAY THAT MOST NEARLY CONCERNS US.
LACE AND I ARE LOVERS. YOU SAW FOR YOURSELF. AND IF YOU TELL I THINK IT WILL BE BELIEVED.
IF THERE'S SOME GIFT THAT WOULD BUY YOUR SILENCE, NAME IT NOW.
AND THERE IT IS! DID YOU EVER IMAGINE THE ROAD TO HER BED WOULD BE SO SHORT?
GO TO IT, BOY. ENJOY HER. ENJOY BOTH OF THEM, IF YOU'VE THE STAMINA.
LADY SHURUBAI--
YES, MOTH.
THERE'S A THING I'VE LONGED FOR, AND ONLY YOU CAN GIVE IT.
WILL YOU TEACH ME TO READ?
OH.

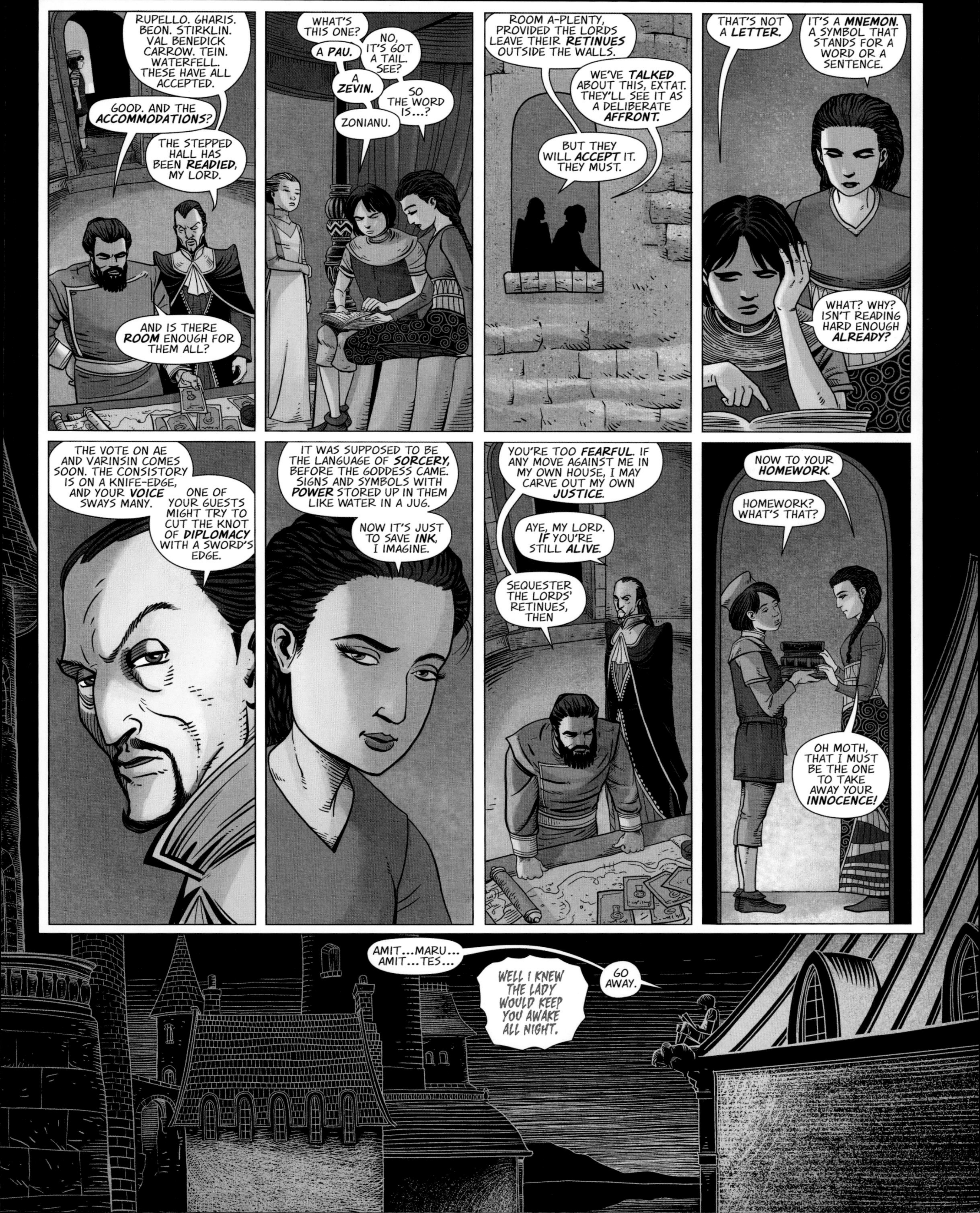
RUPELLO. GHARIS. BEON. STIRKLIN. VAL BENEDICK CARROW. TEIN. WATERFELL. THESE HAVE ALL ACCEPTED.
GOOD. AND THE ACCOMMODATIONS?
THE STEPPED HALL HAS BEEN READIED, MY LORD.
AND IS THERE ROOM ENOUGH FOR THEM ALL?
WHAT'S THIS ONE?
A PAU.
NO, IT'S GOT A TAIL. SEE?
A ZEVIN.
SO THE WORD IS...?
ZONIANU.
ROOM A-PLENTY, PROVIDED THE LORDS LEAVE THEIR RETINUES OUTSIDE THE WALLS.
WE'VE TALKED ABOUT THIS, EXTAT. THEY'LL SEE IT AS A DELIBERATE AFFRONT.
BUT THEY WILL ACCEPT IT. THEY MUST.
THAT'S NOT A LETTER.
IT'S A MNEMON. A SYMBOL THAT STANDS FOR A WORD OR A SENTENCE.
WHAT? WHY? ISN'T READING HARD ENOUGH ALREADY?
THE VOTE ON AE AND VARINSIN COMES SOON. THE CONSISTORY IS ON A KNIFE-EDGE, AND YOUR VOICE SWAYS MANY.
ONE OF YOUR GUESTS MIGHT TRY TO CUT THE KNOT OF DIPLOMACY WITH A SWORD'S EDGE.
IT WAS SUPPOSED TO BE THE LANGUAGE OF SORCERY, BEFORE THE GODDESS CAME. SIGNS AND SYMBOLS WITH POWER STORED UP IN THEM LIKE WATER IN A JUG.
NOW IT'S JUST TO SAVE INK, I IMAGINE.
YOU'RE TOO FEARFUL. IF ANY MOVE AGAINST ME IN MY OWN HOUSE, I MAY CARVE OUT MY OWN JUSTICE.
AYE, MY LORD. IF YOU'RE STILL ALIVE.
SEQUESTER THE LORDS' RETINUES, THEN
NOW TO YOUR HOMEWORK.
HOMEWORK? WHAT'S THAT?
OH MOTH, THAT I MUST BE THE ONE TO TAKE AWAY YOUR INNOCENCE!
AMIT...MARU... AMIT...TES...
WELL I KNEW THE LADY WOULD KEEP YOU AWAKE ALL NIGHT.
GO AWAY.

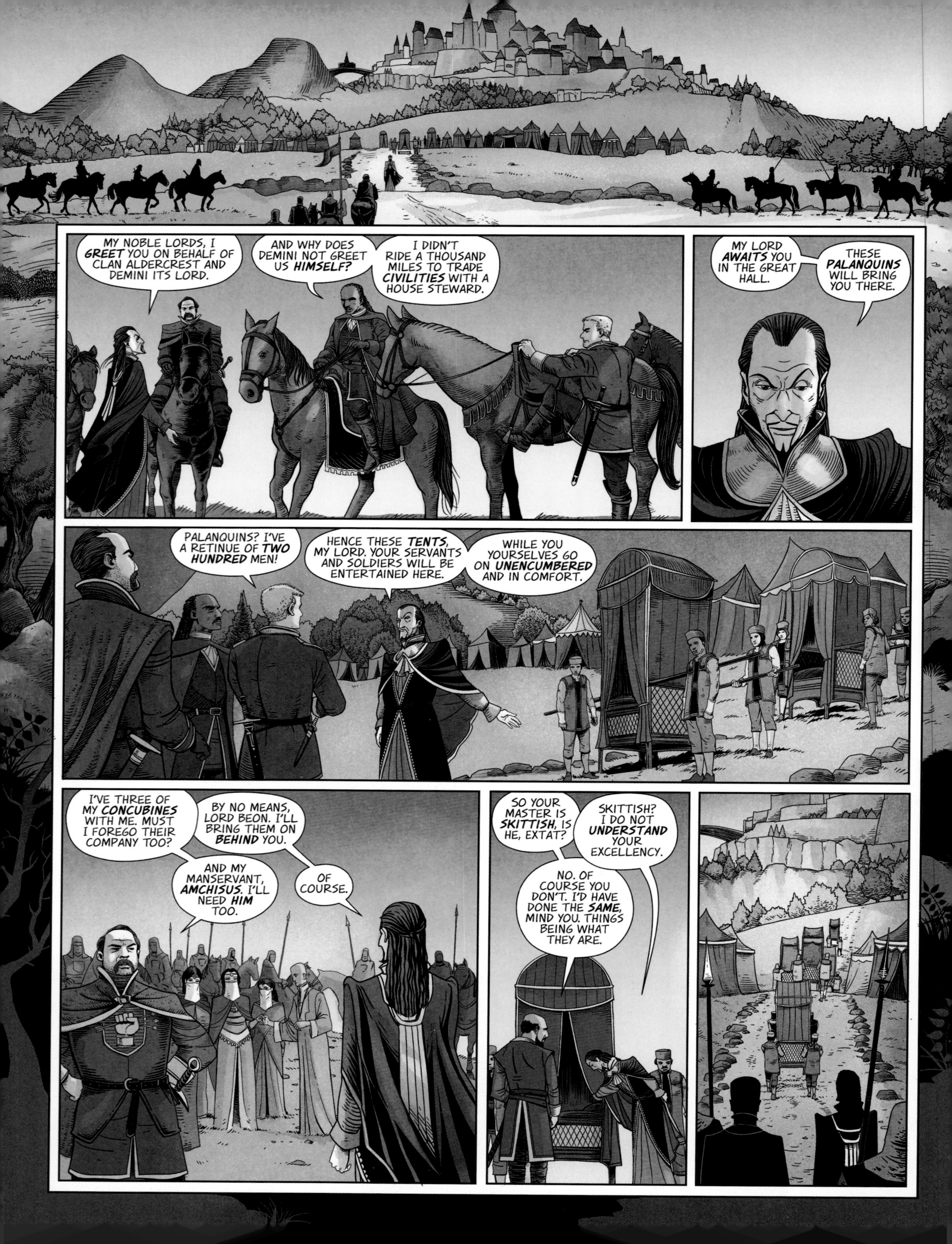

MY NOBLE LORDS, I GREET YOU ON BEHALF OF CLAN ALDERCREST AND DEMINI ITS LORD.
AND WHY DOES DEMINI NOT GREET US HIMSELF?
I DIDN'T RIDE A THOUSAND MILES TO TRADE CIVILITIES WITH A HOUSE STEWARD.
MY LORD AWAITS YOU IN THE GREAT HALL.
THESE PALANQUINS WILL BRING YOU THERE.
PALANQUINS? I'VE A RETINUE OF TWO HUNDRED MEN!
HENCE THESE TENTS, MY LORD. YOUR SERVANTS AND SOLDIERS WILL BE ENTERTAINED HERE.
WHILE YOU YOURSELVES GO ON UNENCUMBERED AND IN COMFORT.
I'VE THREE OF MY CONCUBINES WITH ME. MUST I FOREGO THEIR COMPANY TOO?
BY NO MEANS, LORD BEON. I'LL BRING THEM ON BEHIND YOU.
AND MY MANSERVANT, AMCHISUS. I'LL NEED HIM TOO.
OF COURSE.
SO YOUR MASTER IS SKITTISH, IS HE, EXTAT?
SKITTISH? I DO NOT UNDERSTAND YOUR EXCELLENCY.
NO. OF COURSE YOU DON'T. I'D HAVE DONE THE SAME, MIND YOU. THINGS BEING WHAT THEY ARE.

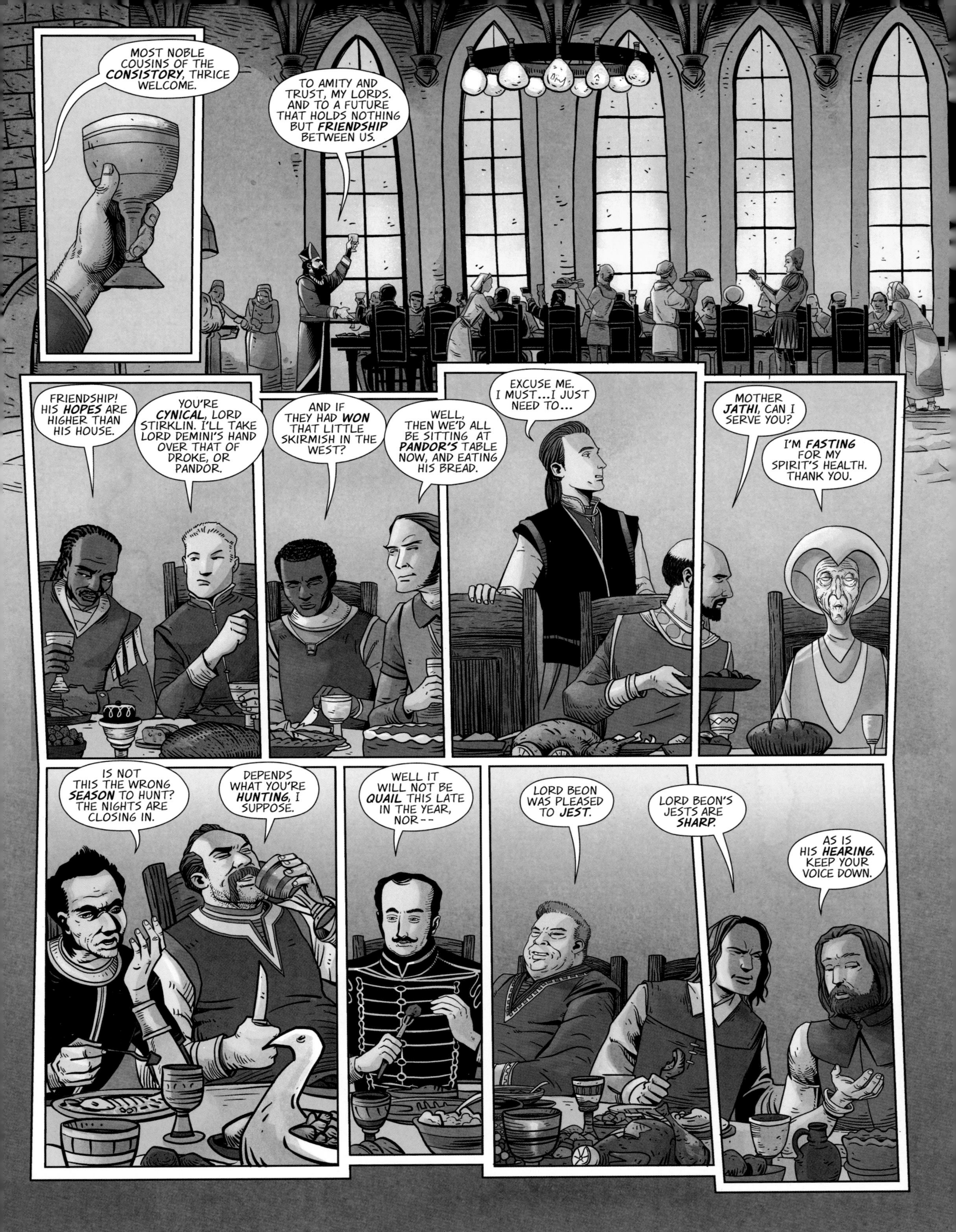
MOST NOBLE COUSINS OF THE CONSISTORY, THRICE WELCOME.
TO AMITY AND TRUST, MY LORDS. AND TO A FUTURE THAT HOLDS NOTHING BUT FRIENDSHIP BETWEEN US.
FRIENDSHIP! HIS HOPES ARE HIGHER THAN HIS HOUSE.
YOU'RE CYNICAL, LORD STIRKLIN. I'LL TAKE LORD DEMINI'S HAND OVER THAT OF DROKE, OR PANDOR.
AND IF THEY HAD WON THAT LITTLE SKIRMISH IN THE WEST?
WELL, THEN WE'D ALL BE SITTING AT PANDOR'S TABLE NOW, AND EATING HIS BREAD.
EXCUSE ME. I MUST...I JUST NEED TO...
MOTHER JATHI, CAN I SERVE YOU?
I'M FASTING FOR MY SPIRIT'S HEALTH. THANK YOU.
IS NOT THIS THE WRONG SEASON TO HUNT? THE NIGHTS ARE CLOSING IN.
DEPENDS WHAT YOU'RE HUNTING, I SUPPOSE.
WELL IT WILL NOT BE QUAIL THIS LATE IN THE YEAR, NOR--
LORD BEON WAS PLEASED TO JEST.
LORD BEON'S JESTS ARE SHARP.
AS IS HIS HEARING. KEEP YOUR VOICE DOWN.

SHURUBAI!

LORD **CARROW.** I THOUGHT YOU WERE AT DINNER.

I WAS. BUT YOU **WEREN'T.** SO I CAME TO SEEK YOU OUT.

YOUR HOUSE HAS A VERY PLEASANT PROSPECT. I **ENVY** YOU THIS VIEW.

OH, YOU WOULDN'T ENVY US OUR **WINTERS.**

NO. PERHAPS NOT.

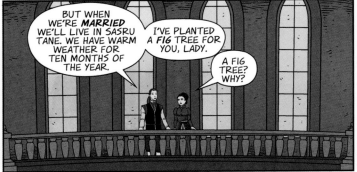

BUT WHEN WE'RE **MARRIED** WE'LL LIVE IN SASRU TANE. WE HAVE WARM WEATHER FOR TEN MONTHS OF THE YEAR.

I'VE PLANTED A **FIG** TREE FOR YOU, LADY.

A FIG TREE? WHY?

BECAUSE FIGS ARE THE MOST **DELICIOUS** FRUIT THERE IS. AS SOFT AS BUTTER IN YOUR MOUTH.

IT'S ALSO SAID TO MAKE YOU **AMOROUS,** BUT YOUR EYES ARE ALL I NEED IN THAT REGARD.

I'M SORRY. THAT WAS **COARSE.** BUT I MEANT NO OFFENCE, SHURUBAI.

I'M NOT **OFFENDED.** ONLY COLD.

LET'S GO BACK **INSIDE.**

YOUNG CARROW SEEMS **SMITTEN.** THE LADY SOMEWHAT LESS SO.

THE LADY WILL PART HER **LEGS** WHEN SHE'S TOLD TO, I SUPPOSE.

BUT TO YOUR **REPORT.** WHAT HAVE YOU FOUND?

AS OUR **INFORMANT** SAID, THERE ARE SCARCELY THREE DOZEN SOLDIERY WITHIN THE WALLS. THE REST ARE BARRACKED ELSEWHERE.

BUT **VEHI** SAYS THERE'S SOMETHING ELSE HERE. SOMETHING THAT SMELLS OF MAGIC.

THAT'S NONSENSE. DEMINI'S DEVOUT AND LILY-WHITE. HE EVEN KEEPS HIS OWN **PRIESTESS.**

THE OSSANI MADE PACTS WITH **DEMONS,** IN TIMES PAST. PERHAPS ONE OF THEM LEFT ITS **SPOOR** HERE, BUT IT LEFT NOTHING ELSE.

WE'LL PROCEED AS PLANNED. MAKE HIS DEATH A PLAUSIBLE **ACCIDENT,** IF WE CAN. AND IF NOT--

--MAKE IT **BLOODY** ENOUGH THAT EVERYONE WILL MARK IT.

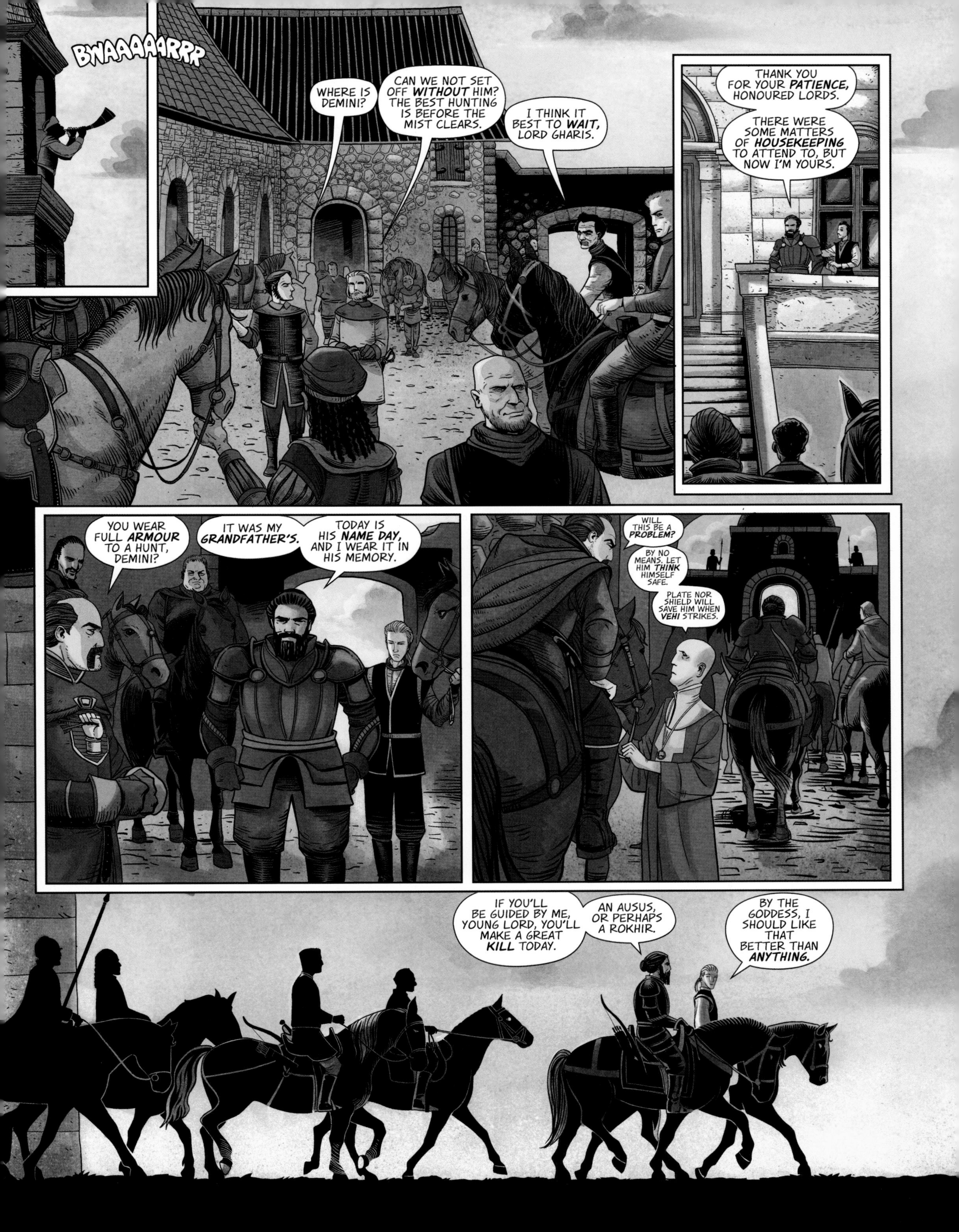

BWAAAAARRR
WHERE IS DEMINI?
CAN WE NOT SET OFF WITHOUT HIM? THE BEST HUNTING IS BEFORE THE MIST CLEARS.
I THINK IT BEST TO WAIT, LORD GHARIS.
THANK YOU FOR YOUR PATIENCE, HONOURED LORDS.
THERE WERE SOME MATTERS OF HOUSEKEEPING TO ATTEND TO, BUT NOW I'M YOURS.
YOU WEAR FULL ARMOUR TO A HUNT, DEMINI?
IT WAS MY GRANDFATHER'S.
TODAY IS HIS NAME DAY, AND I WEAR IT IN HIS MEMORY.
WILL THIS BE A PROBLEM?
BY NO MEANS. LET HIM THINK HIMSELF SAFE.
PLATE NOR SHIELD WILL SAVE HIM WHEN VEHI STRIKES.
IF YOU'LL BE GUIDED BY ME, YOUNG LORD, YOU'LL MAKE A GREAT KILL TODAY.
AN AUSUS, OR PERHAPS A ROKHIR.
BY THE GODDESS, I SHOULD LIKE THAT BETTER THAN ANYTHING.

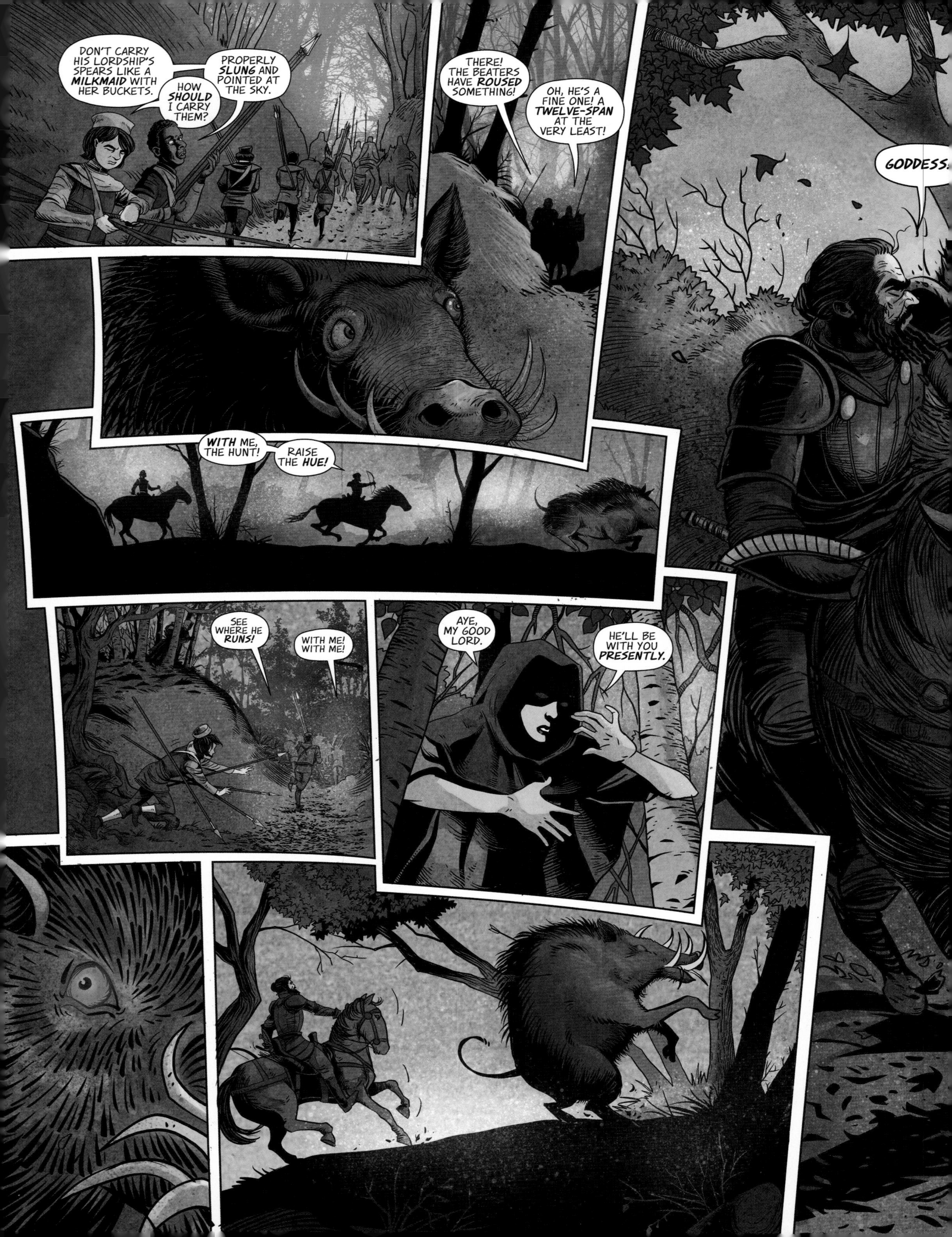
DON'T CARRY HIS LORDSHIP'S SPEARS LIKE A MILKMAID WITH HER BUCKETS.
HOW SHOULD I CARRY THEM?
PROPERLY SLUNG AND POINTED AT THE SKY.
THERE! THE BEATERS HAVE ROUSED SOMETHING!
OH, HE'S A FINE ONE! A TWELVE-SPAN AT THE VERY LEAST!
GODDESS.
WITH ME, THE HUNT!
RAISE THE HUE!
SEE WHERE HE RUNS!
WITH ME! WITH ME!
AYE, MY GOOD LORD.
HE'LL BE WITH YOU PRESENTLY.

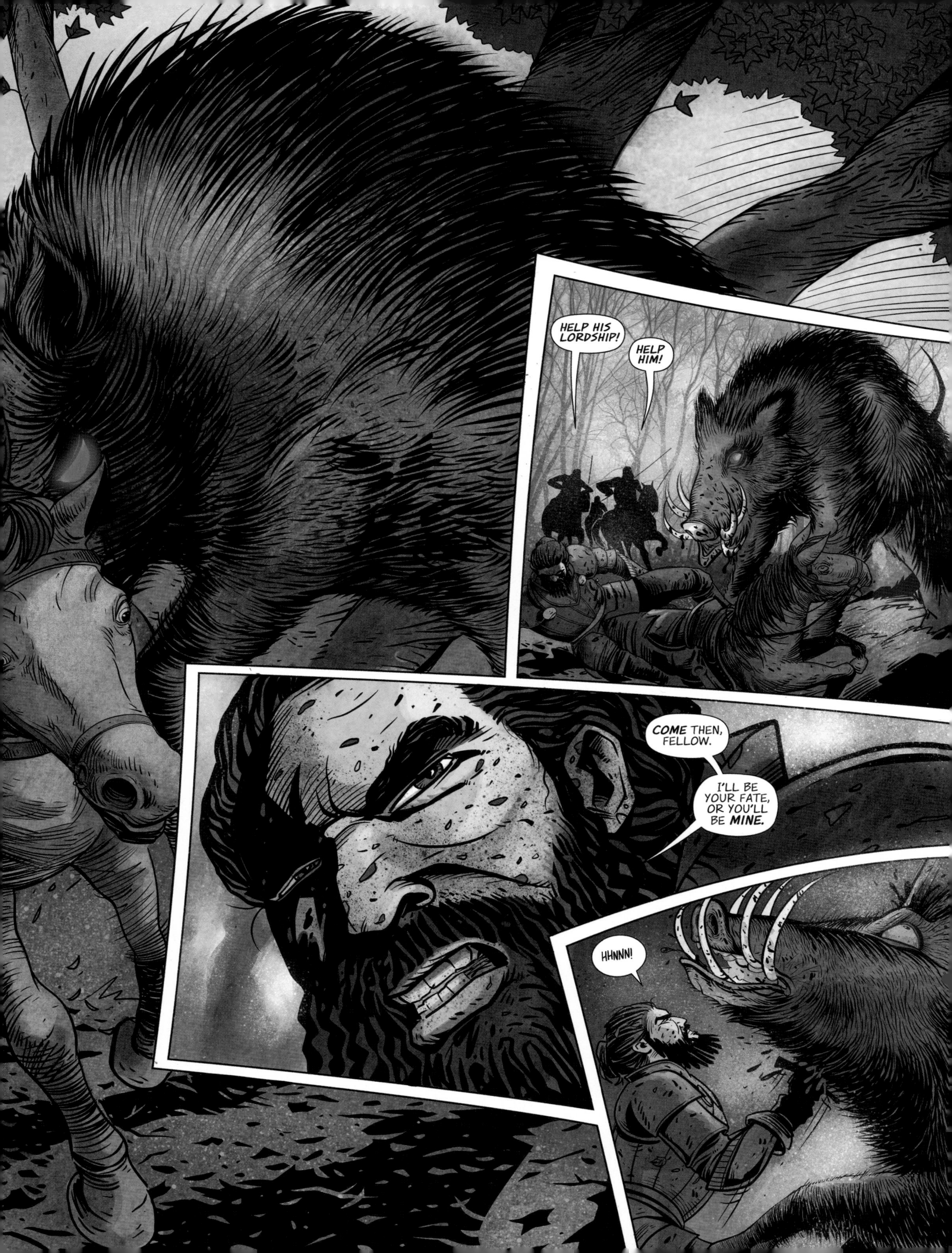
HELP HIS LORDSHIP!
HELP HIM!
COME THEN, FELLOW.
I'LL BE YOUR FATE, OR YOU'LL BE MINE.
HHNNN!

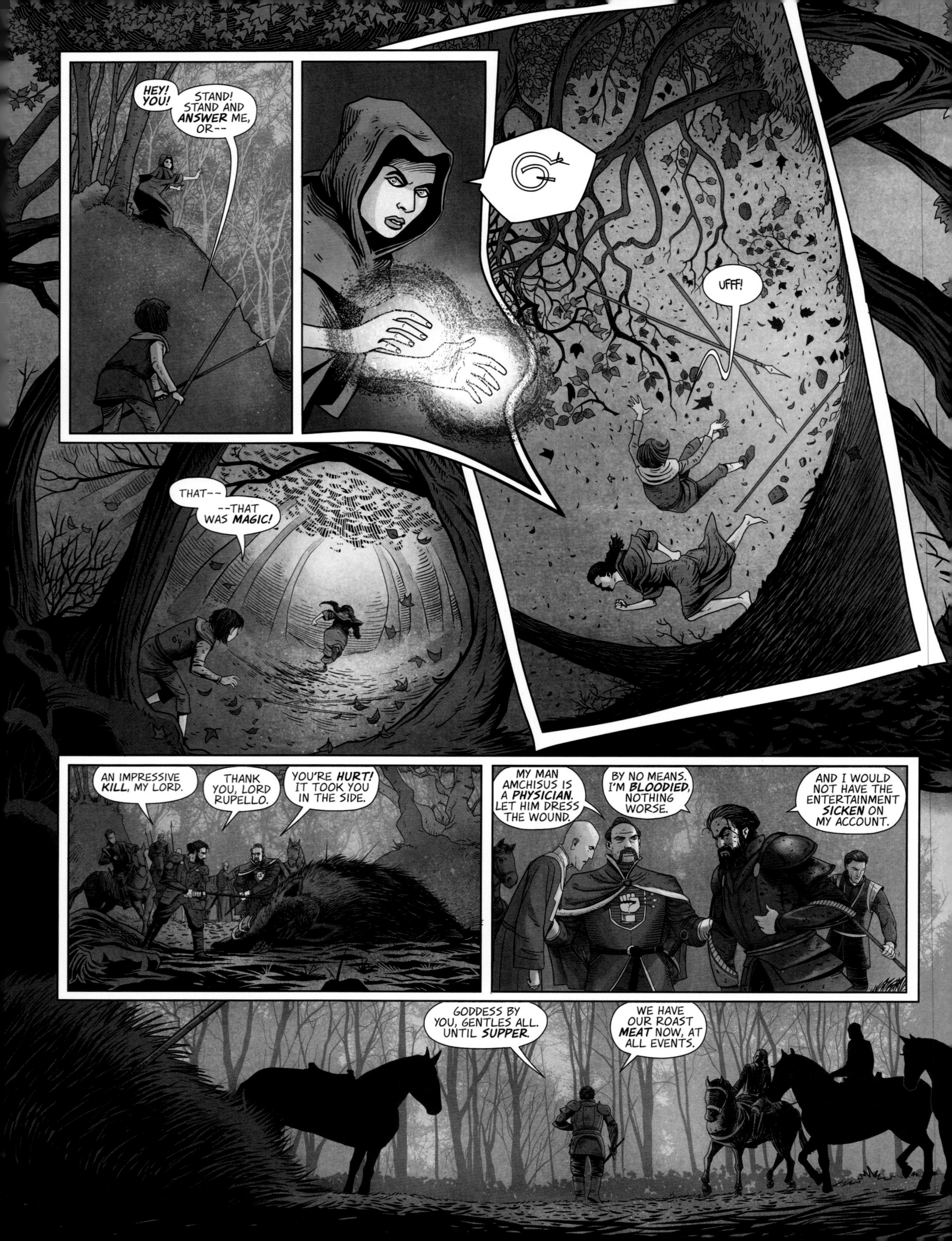

HEY! YOU!
STAND! STAND AND ANSWER ME, OR--
UFFF!
THAT--
--THAT WAS MAGIC!
AN IMPRESSIVE KILL, MY LORD.
THANK YOU, LORD RUPELLO.
YOU'RE HURT! IT TOOK YOU IN THE SIDE.
MY MAN AMCHISUS IS A PHYSICIAN. LET HIM DRESS THE WOUND.
BY NO MEANS. I'M BLOODIED, NOTHING WORSE.
AND I WOULD NOT HAVE THE ENTERTAINMENT SICKEN ON MY ACCOUNT.
GODDESS BY YOU, GENTLES ALL. UNTIL SUPPER.
WE HAVE OUR ROAST MEAT NOW, AT ALL EVENTS.

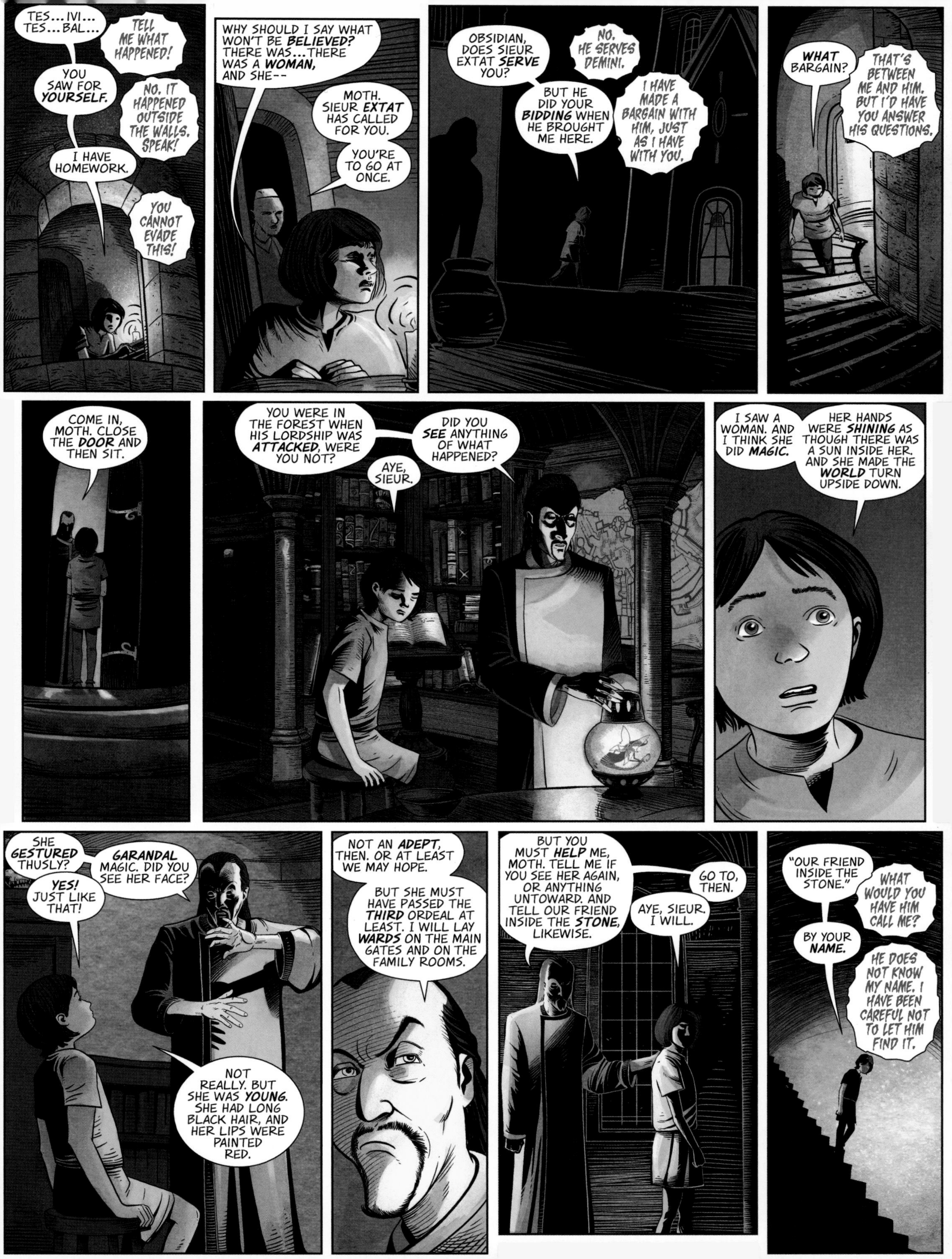
TES...IVI... TES...BAL...
TELL ME WHAT HAPPENED!
YOU SAW FOR YOURSELF.
NO. IT HAPPENED OUTSIDE THE WALLS. SPEAK!
I HAVE HOMEWORK.
YOU CANNOT EVADE THIS!
WHY SHOULD I SAY WHAT WON'T BE BELIEVED? THERE WAS...THERE WAS A WOMAN, AND SHE--
MOTH. SIEUR EXTAT HAS CALLED FOR YOU.
YOU'RE TO GO AT ONCE.
OBSIDIAN, DOES SIEUR EXTAT SERVE YOU?
NO. HE SERVES DEMINI.
BUT HE DID YOUR BIDDING WHEN HE BROUGHT ME HERE.
I HAVE MADE A BARGAIN WITH HIM, JUST AS I HAVE WITH YOU.
WHAT BARGAIN?
THAT'S BETWEEN ME AND HIM. BUT I'D HAVE YOU ANSWER HIS QUESTIONS.
COME IN, MOTH. CLOSE THE DOOR AND THEN SIT.
YOU WERE IN THE FOREST WHEN HIS LORDSHIP WAS ATTACKED, WERE YOU NOT?
AYE, SIEUR.
DID YOU SEE ANYTHING OF WHAT HAPPENED?
I SAW A WOMAN. AND I THINK SHE DID MAGIC.
HER HANDS WERE SHINING AS THOUGH THERE WAS A SUN INSIDE HER. AND SHE MADE THE WORLD TURN UPSIDE DOWN.
SHE GESTURED THUSLY?
YES! JUST LIKE THAT!
GARANDAL MAGIC. DID YOU SEE HER FACE?
NOT REALLY. BUT SHE WAS YOUNG. SHE HAD LONG BLACK HAIR, AND HER LIPS WERE PAINTED RED.
NOT AN ADEPT, THEN. OR AT LEAST WE MAY HOPE.
BUT SHE MUST HAVE PASSED THE THIRD ORDEAL AT LEAST. I WILL LAY WARDS ON THE MAIN GATES AND ON THE FAMILY ROOMS.
BUT YOU MUST HELP ME, MOTH. TELL ME IF YOU SEE HER AGAIN, OR ANYTHING UNTOWARD. AND TELL OUR FRIEND INSIDE THE STONE, LIKEWISE.
GO TO, THEN.
AYE, SIEUR. I WILL.
"OUR FRIEND INSIDE THE STONE."
WHAT WOULD YOU HAVE HIM CALL ME?
BY YOUR NAME.
HE DOES NOT KNOW MY NAME. I HAVE BEEN CAREFUL NOT TO LET HIM FIND IT.

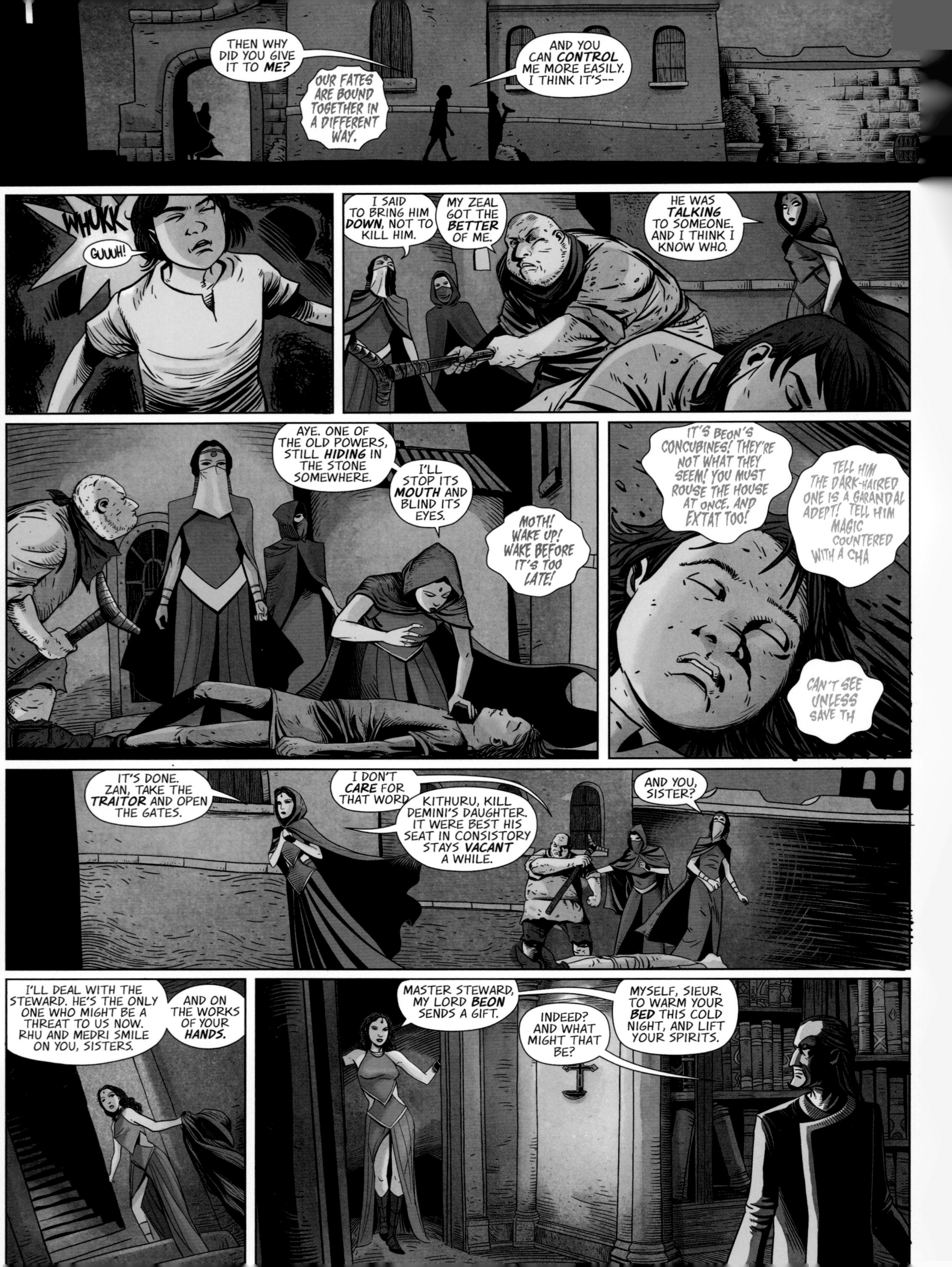
THEN WHY DID YOU GIVE IT TO ME?
OUR FATES ARE BOUND TOGETHER IN A DIFFERENT WAY.
AND YOU CAN CONTROL ME MORE EASILY. I THINK IT'S--
WHUKK
GUUUH!
I SAID TO BRING HIM DOWN, NOT TO KILL HIM.
MY ZEAL GOT THE BETTER OF ME.
HE WAS TALKING TO SOMEONE. AND I THINK I KNOW WHO.
AYE. ONE OF THE OLD POWERS, STILL HIDING IN THE STONE SOMEWHERE.
I'LL STOP ITS MOUTH AND BLIND ITS EYES.
MOTH! WAKE UP! WAKE BEFORE IT'S TOO LATE!
IT'S BEON'S CONCUBINES! THEY'RE NOT WHAT THEY SEEM! YOU MUST ROUSE THE HOUSE AT ONCE. AND EXTAT TOO!
TELL HIM THE DARK-HAIRED ONE IS A GARANDAL ADEPT! TELL HIM MAGIC COUNTERED WITH A CHA
CAN'T SEE UNLESS SAVE TH
IT'S DONE. ZAN, TAKE THE TRAITOR AND OPEN THE GATES.
I DON'T CARE FOR THAT WORD.
KITHURU, KILL DEMINI'S DAUGHTER. IT WERE BEST HIS SEAT IN CONSISTORY STAYS VACANT A WHILE.
AND YOU, SISTER?
I'LL DEAL WITH THE STEWARD. HE'S THE ONLY ONE WHO MIGHT BE A THREAT TO US NOW. RHU AND MEDRI SMILE ON YOU, SISTERS.
AND ON THE WORKS OF YOUR HANDS.
MASTER STEWARD, MY LORD BEON SENDS A GIFT.
INDEED? AND WHAT MIGHT THAT BE?
MYSELF, SIEUR. TO WARM YOUR BED THIS COLD NIGHT, AND LIFT YOUR SPIRITS.

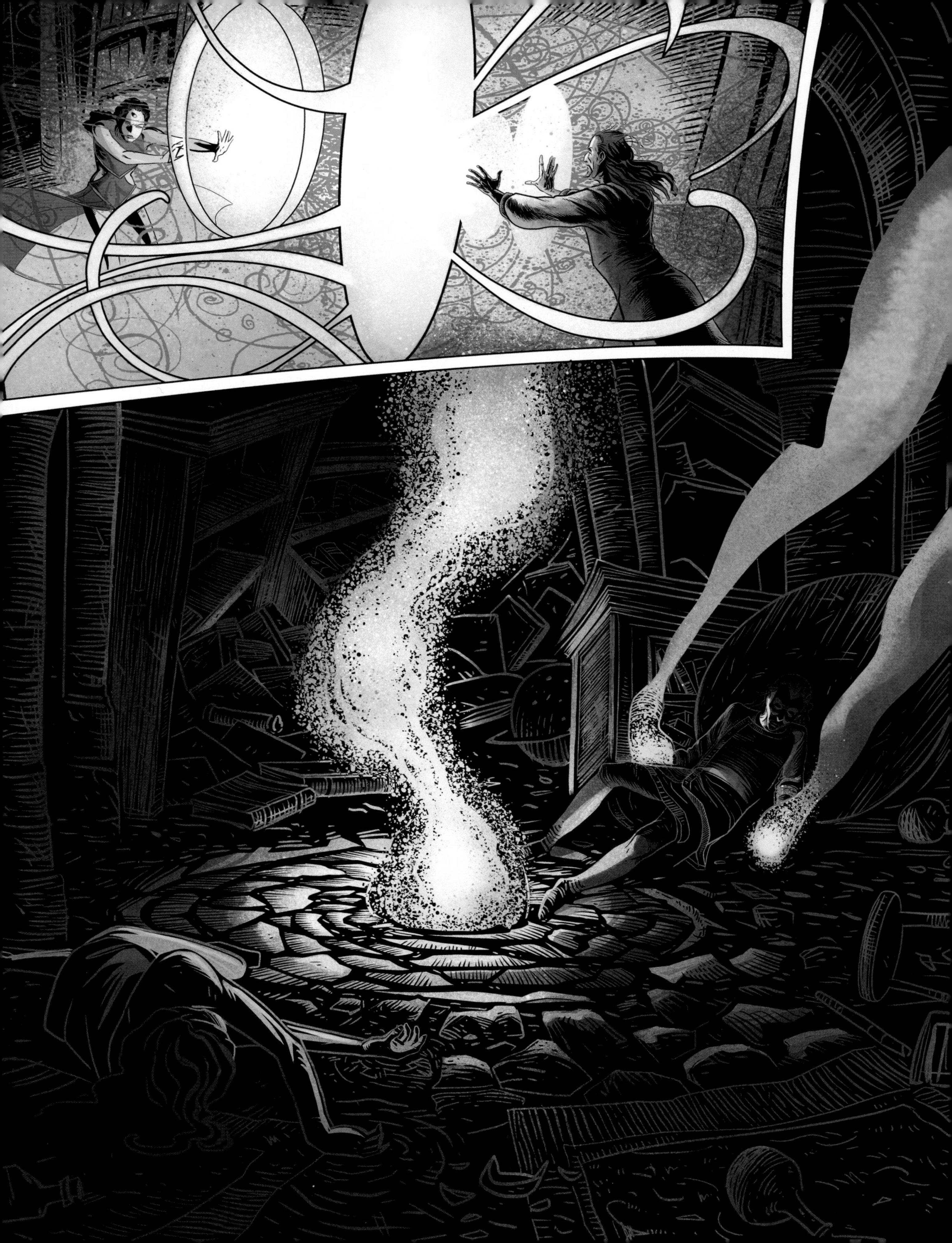

TEMTOLLER?

YOU'RE NOT MEANT TO COME UP HERE.

YOU LOOKED COLD. I'VE BROUGHT A STOUP OF BRANDY.

BRANDY? PERHAPS JUST A SIP, THEN, TO KEEP OFF THE--

NUUUH!

ENEMIES!

ENEMIES WITHIN THE GATES!

OH GODDESS!

ENEMIES WITHIN THE--

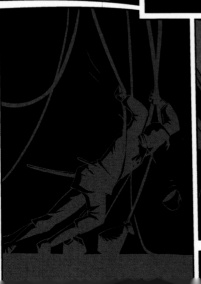

BONNNNNNG

THE--THE HOUSE GUARDS WILL WAKE! WE HAVE TO HIDE!

THROW THE LEVER, YOU POX-EATEN LUMP.

NOW! QUICKLY!

CHUNK

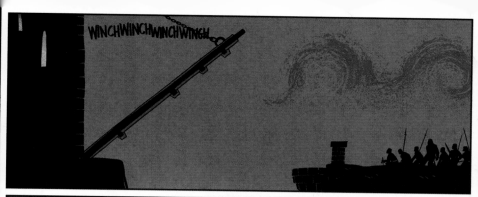

WINCHWINCHWINCHWINGH

FOR BEON, HASK AND THE HEARTH STONE!

TAKE NO PRISONERS!

THE TOCSIN BELL! DEMINI, WE'RE *ATTACKED!*

I *HEAR* IT, ESSU. HAND ME MY SWORD.

BOLT THE *DOOR* AFTER I LEAVE AND OPEN IT TO NO VOICE BUT MINE.

DEMINI! WHAT'S THE *ALARM?*

I GO NOW TO FIND *OUT.* STAY WITHIN DOORS.

I'LL *FIGHT,* MY LORD, SO PLEASE YOU.

I OWE YOUR FATHER *BETTER.*

AND I YOUR *DAUGHTER.*

I WON'T HIDE IN MY *CHAMBER* WHILE YOUR HOUSE AND FAMILY ARE ATTACKED.

COME, THEN, AND GODDESS RIDE YOUR SWORD.

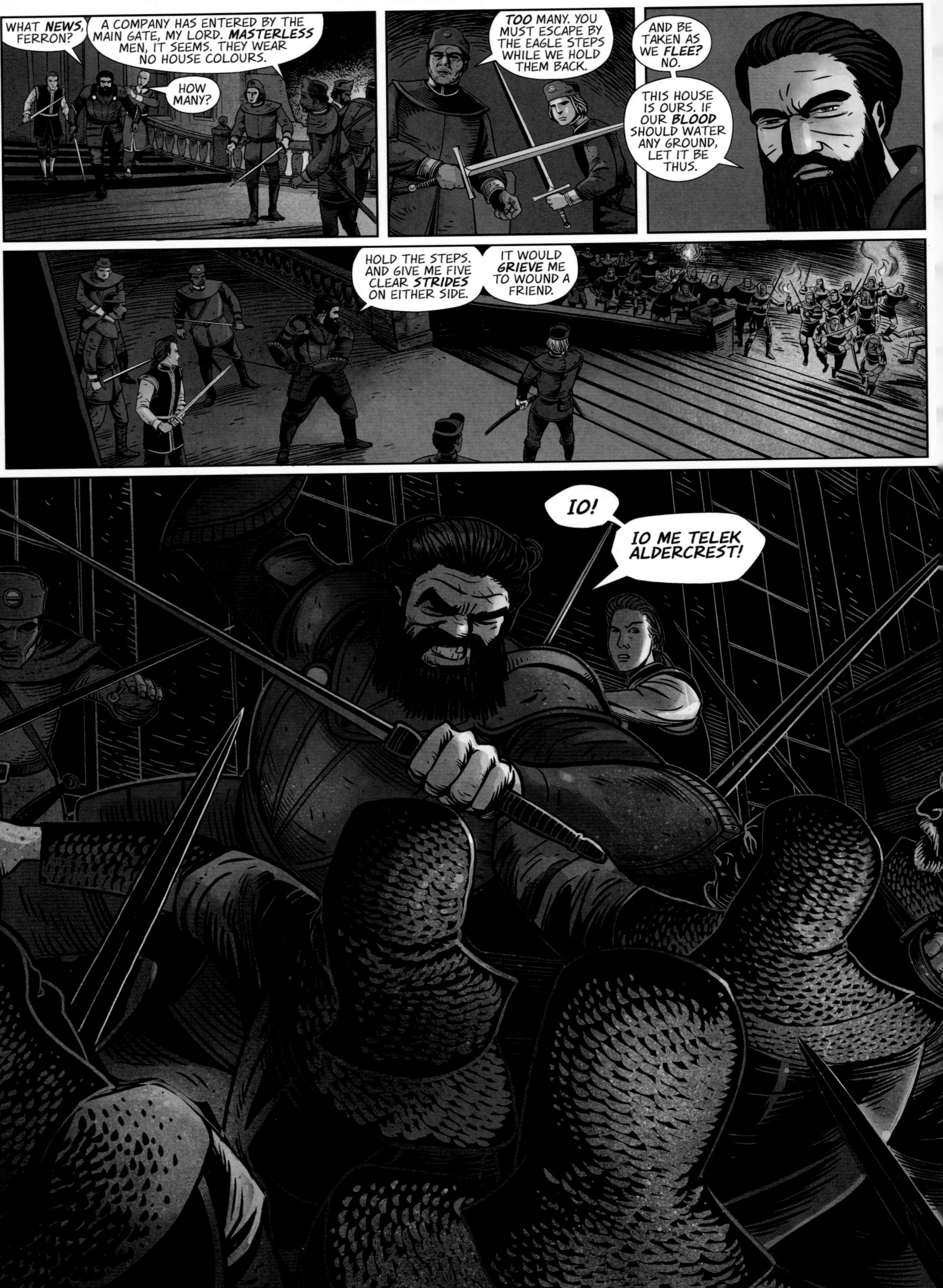
WHAT NEWS, FERRON?
A COMPANY HAS ENTERED BY THE MAIN GATE, MY LORD. MASTERLESS MEN, IT SEEMS. THEY WEAR NO HOUSE COLOURS.
HOW MANY?
TOO MANY. YOU MUST ESCAPE BY THE EAGLE STEPS WHILE WE HOLD THEM BACK.
AND BE TAKEN AS WE FLEE? NO.
THIS HOUSE IS OURS. IF OUR BLOOD SHOULD WATER ANY GROUND, LET IT BE THUS.
HOLD THE STEPS. AND GIVE ME FIVE CLEAR STRIDES ON EITHER SIDE.
IT WOULD GRIEVE ME TO WOUND A FRIEND.
IO!
IO ME TELEK ALDERCREST!

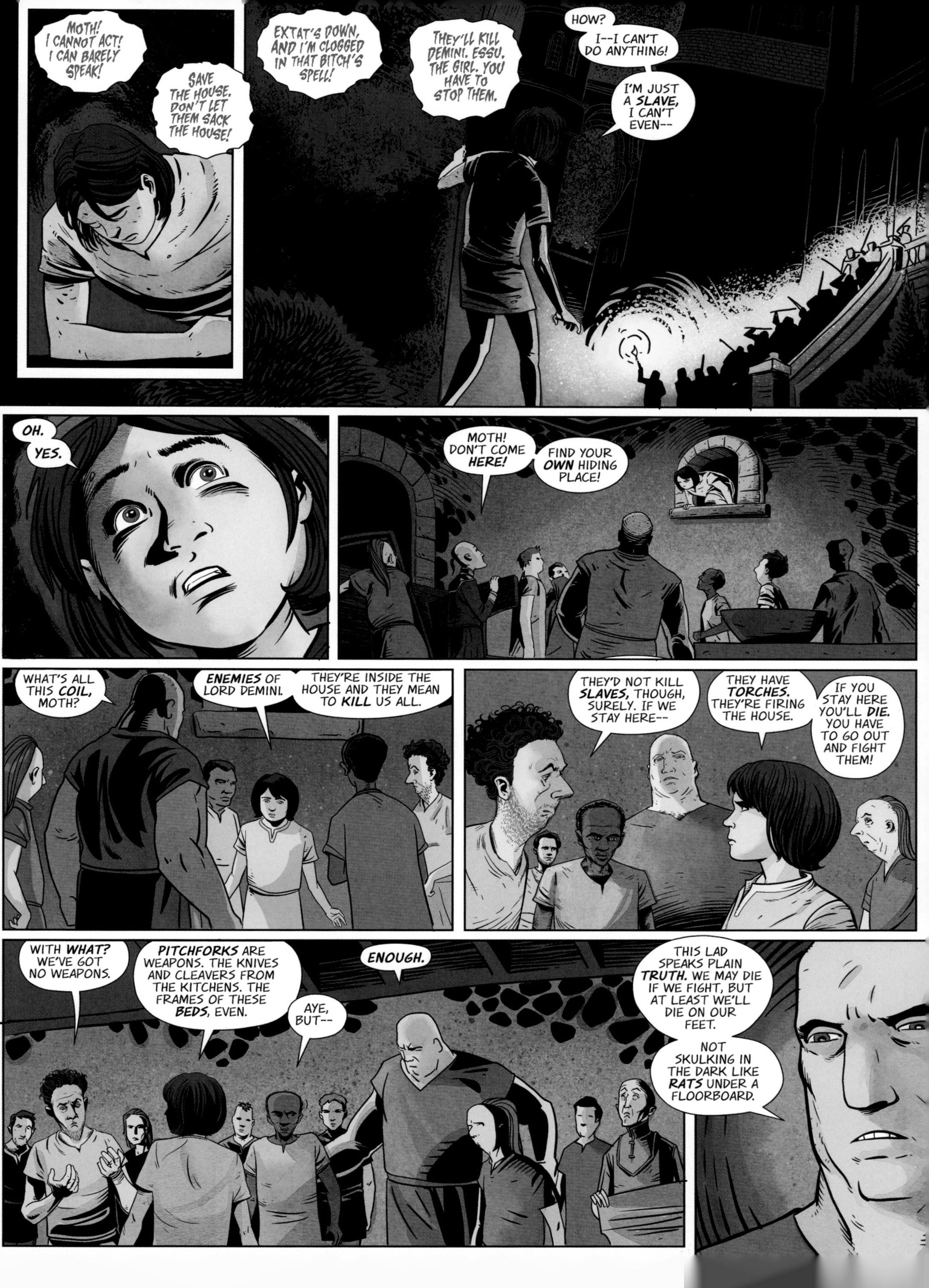
MOTH! I CANNOT ACT! I CAN BARELY SPEAK!
SAVE THE HOUSE. DON'T LET THEM SACK THE HOUSE!
EXTAT'S DOWN, AND I'M CLOGGED IN THAT BITCH'S SPELL!
THEY'LL KILL DEMINI. ESSU. THE GIRL. YOU HAVE TO STOP THEM.
HOW?
I--I CAN'T DO ANYTHING!
I'M JUST A SLAVE, I CAN'T EVEN--
OH.
YES.
MOTH! DON'T COME HERE!
FIND YOUR OWN HIDING PLACE!
WHAT'S ALL THIS COIL, MOTH?
ENEMIES OF LORD DEMINI.
THEY'RE INSIDE THE HOUSE AND THEY MEAN TO KILL US ALL.
THEY'D NOT KILL SLAVES, THOUGH, SURELY. IF WE STAY HERE--
THEY HAVE TORCHES. THEY'RE FIRING THE HOUSE.
IF YOU STAY HERE YOU'LL DIE. YOU HAVE TO GO OUT AND FIGHT THEM!
WITH WHAT? WE'VE GOT NO WEAPONS.
PITCHFORKS ARE WEAPONS. THE KNIVES AND CLEAVERS FROM THE KITCHENS. THE FRAMES OF THESE BEDS, EVEN.
AYE, BUT--
ENOUGH.
THIS LAD SPEAKS PLAIN TRUTH. WE MAY DIE IF WE FIGHT, BUT AT LEAST WE'LL DIE ON OUR FEET.
NOT SKULKING IN THE DARK LIKE RATS UNDER A FLOORBOARD.

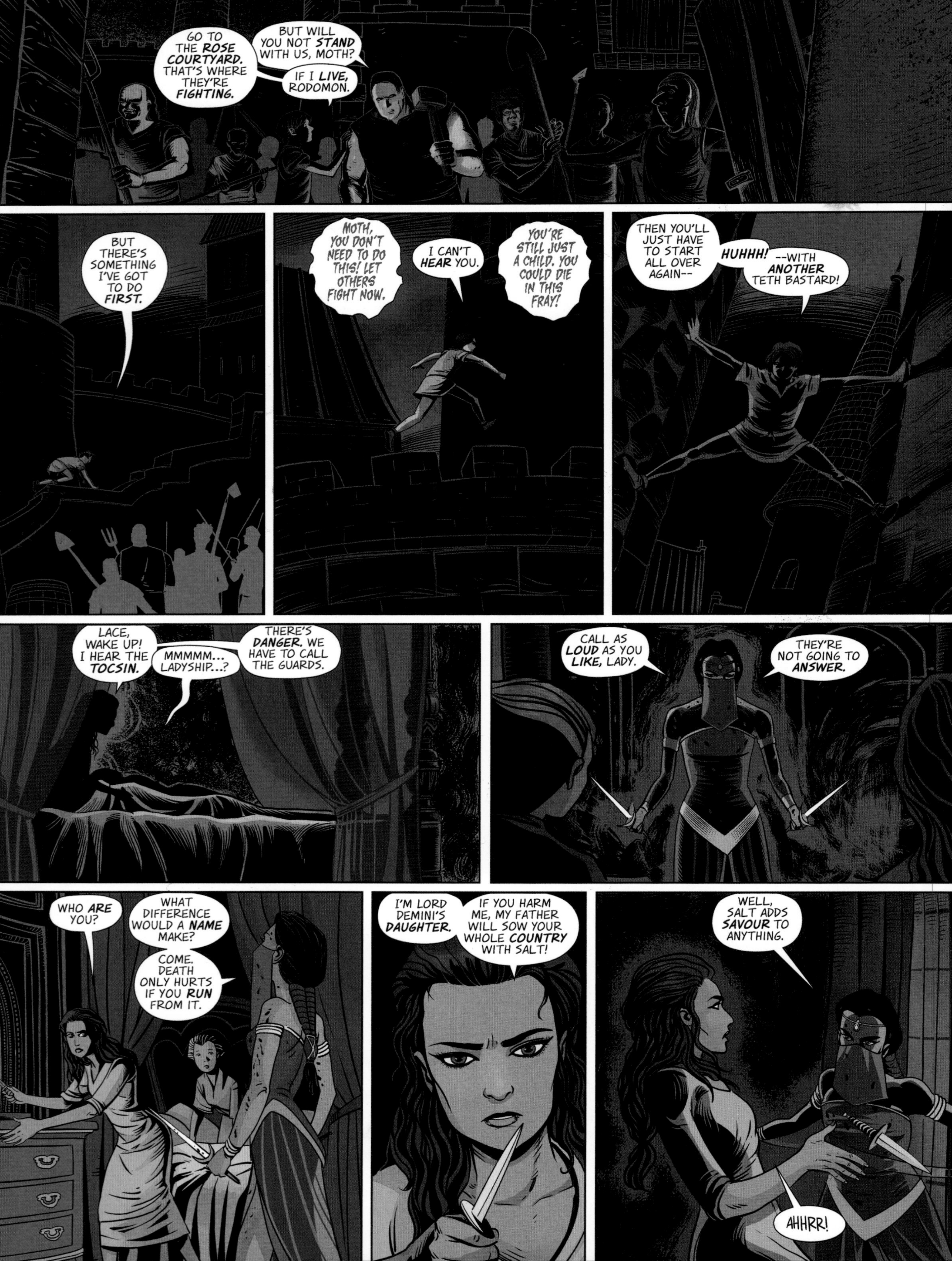
GO TO THE ROSE COURTYARD. THAT'S WHERE THEY'RE FIGHTING.
BUT WILL YOU NOT STAND WITH US, MOTH?
IF I LIVE, RODOMON.
BUT THERE'S SOMETHING I'VE GOT TO DO FIRST.
MOTH, YOU DON'T NEED TO DO THIS! LET OTHERS FIGHT NOW.
I CAN'T HEAR YOU.
YOU'RE STILL JUST A CHILD. YOU COULD DIE IN THIS FRAY!
THEN YOU'LL JUST HAVE TO START ALL OVER AGAIN--
HUHHH!
--WITH ANOTHER TETH BASTARD!
LACE, WAKE UP! I HEAR THE TOCSIN.
MMMMM... LADYSHIP...?
THERE'S DANGER. WE HAVE TO CALL THE GUARDS.
CALL AS LOUD AS YOU LIKE, LADY.
THEY'RE NOT GOING TO ANSWER.
WHO ARE YOU?
WHAT DIFFERENCE WOULD A NAME MAKE?
COME. DEATH ONLY HURTS IF YOU RUN FROM IT.
I'M LORD DEMINI'S DAUGHTER.
IF YOU HARM ME, MY FATHER WILL SOW YOUR WHOLE COUNTRY WITH SALT!
WELL, SALT ADDS SAVOUR TO ANYTHING.
AHHRR!

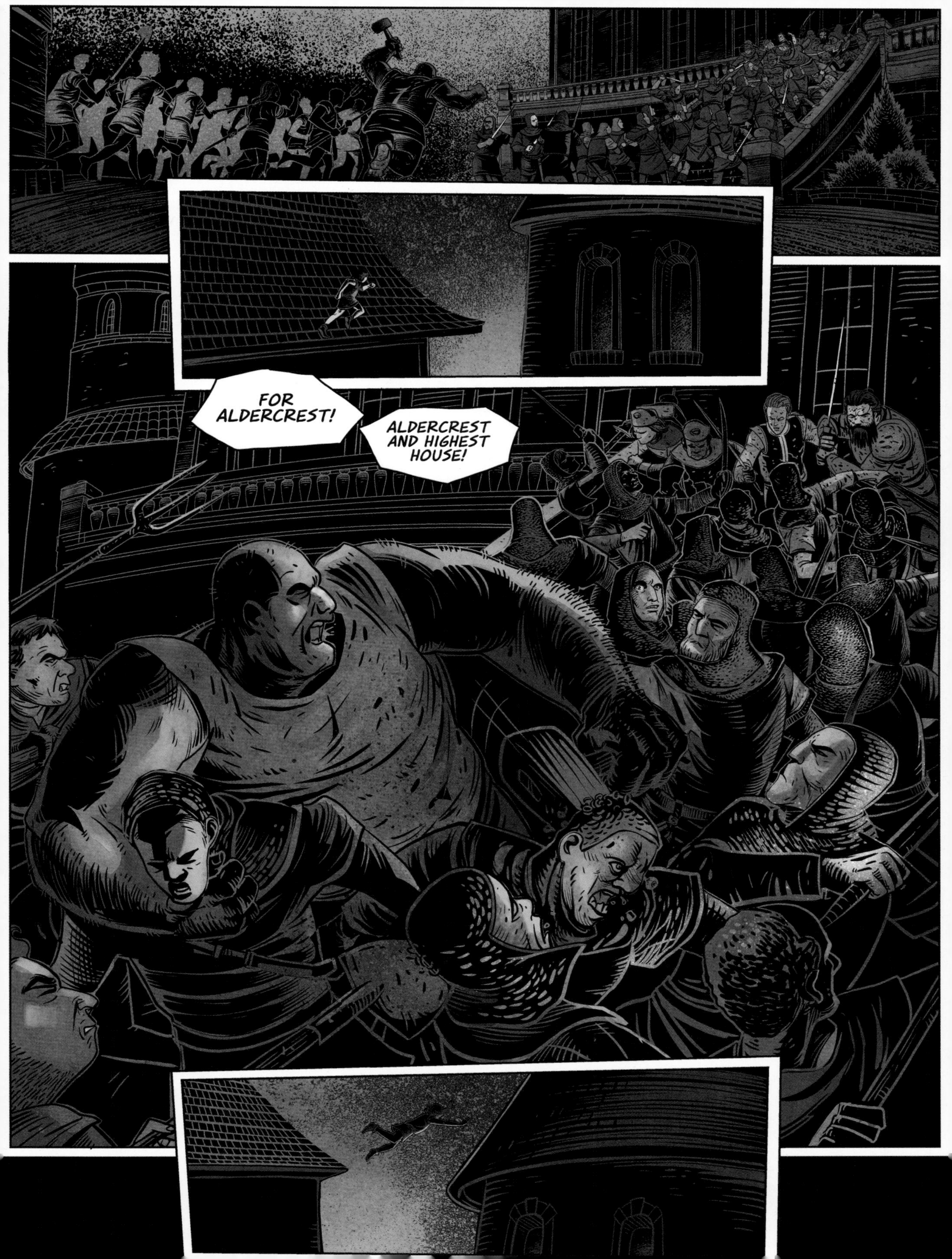
FOR ALDERCREST!
ALDERCREST AND HIGHEST HOUSE!

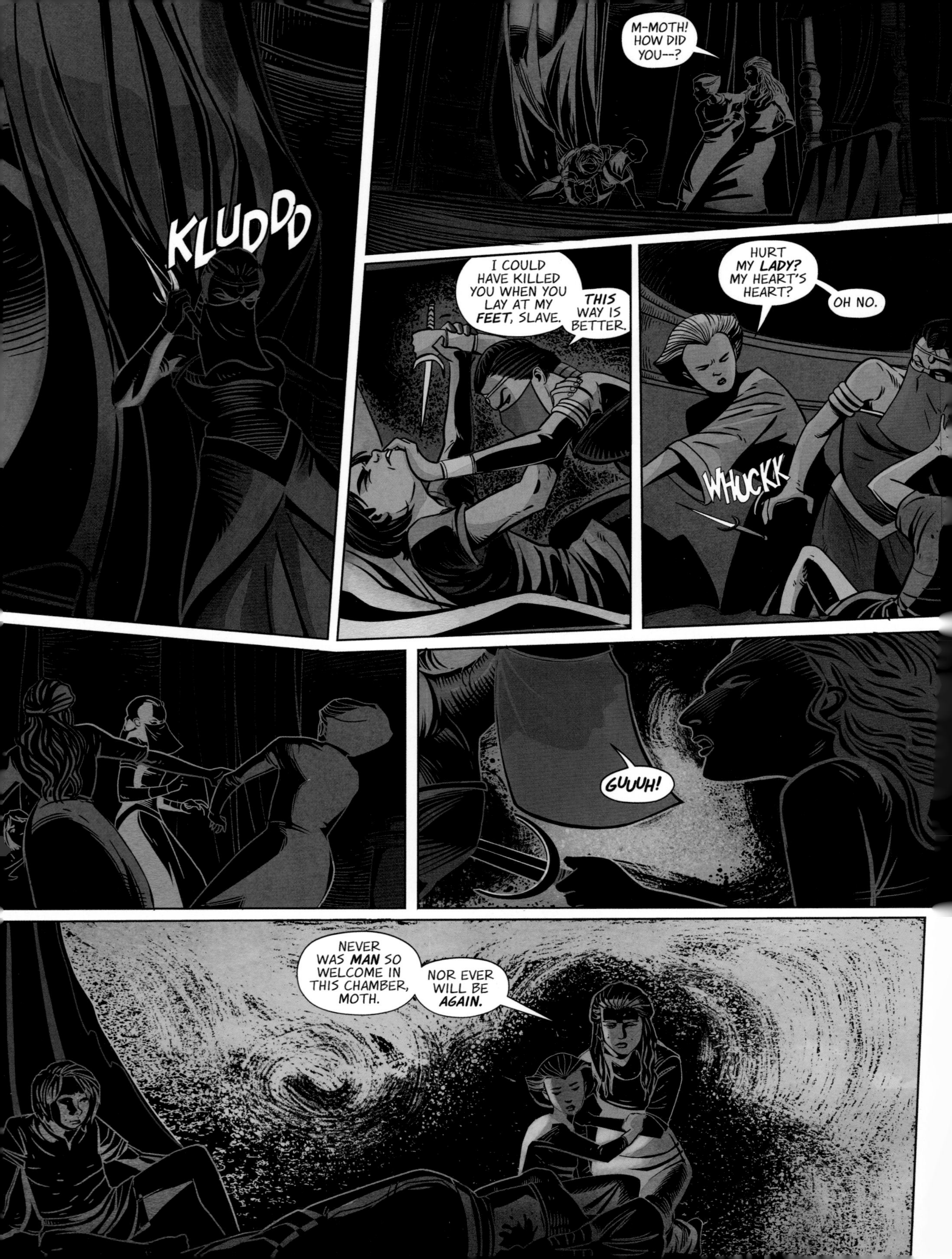
KLUDDD
M-MOTH! HOW DID YOU--?
I COULD HAVE KILLED YOU WHEN YOU LAY AT MY FEET, SLAVE.
THIS WAY IS BETTER.
HURT MY LADY? MY HEART'S HEART?
OH NO.
WHUCKK
GUUUH!
NEVER WAS MAN SO WELCOME IN THIS CHAMBER, MOTH.
NOR EVER WILL BE AGAIN.

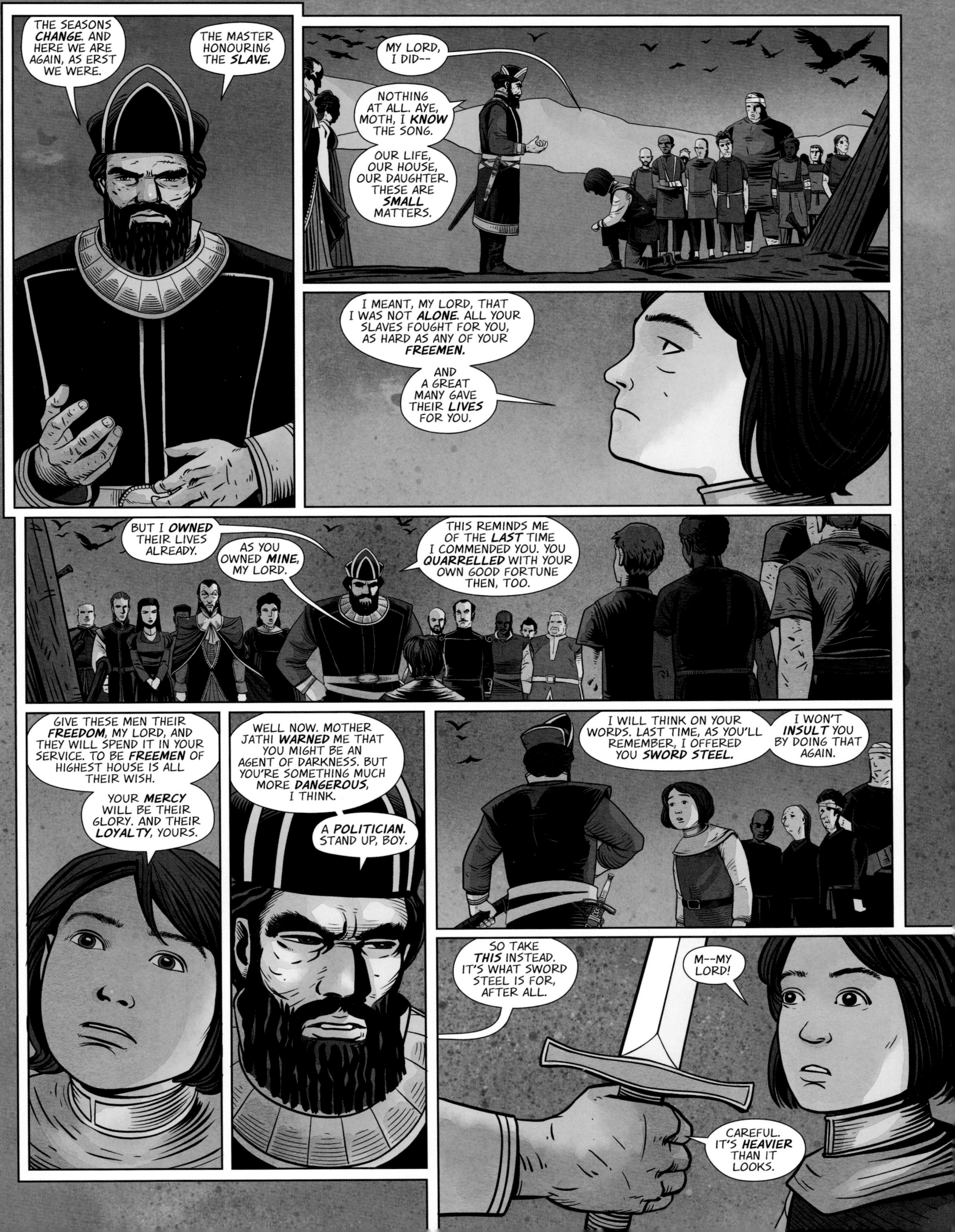

THE SEASONS CHANGE. AND HERE WE ARE AGAIN, AS ERST WE WERE.
THE MASTER HONOURING THE SLAVE.
MY LORD, I DID--
NOTHING AT ALL. AYE, MOTH, I KNOW THE SONG.
OUR LIFE, OUR HOUSE, OUR DAUGHTER. THESE ARE SMALL MATTERS.
I MEANT, MY LORD, THAT I WAS NOT ALONE. ALL YOUR SLAVES FOUGHT FOR YOU, AS HARD AS ANY OF YOUR FREEMEN.
AND A GREAT MANY GAVE THEIR LIVES FOR YOU.
BUT I OWNED THEIR LIVES ALREADY.
AS YOU OWNED MINE, MY LORD.
THIS REMINDS ME OF THE LAST TIME I COMMENDED YOU. YOU QUARRELLED WITH YOUR OWN GOOD FORTUNE THEN, TOO.
GIVE THESE MEN THEIR FREEDOM, MY LORD, AND THEY WILL SPEND IT IN YOUR SERVICE. TO BE FREEMEN OF HIGHEST HOUSE IS ALL THEIR WISH.
YOUR MERCY WILL BE THEIR GLORY. AND THEIR LOYALTY, YOURS.
WELL NOW. MOTHER JATHI WARNED ME THAT YOU MIGHT BE AN AGENT OF DARKNESS. BUT YOU'RE SOMETHING MUCH MORE DANGEROUS, I THINK.
A POLITICIAN. STAND UP, BOY.
I WILL THINK ON YOUR WORDS. LAST TIME, AS YOU'LL REMEMBER, I OFFERED YOU SWORD STEEL.
I WON'T INSULT YOU BY DOING THAT AGAIN.
SO TAKE THIS INSTEAD. IT'S WHAT SWORD STEEL IS FOR, AFTER ALL.
M--MY LORD!
CAREFUL. IT'S HEAVIER THAN IT LOOKS.

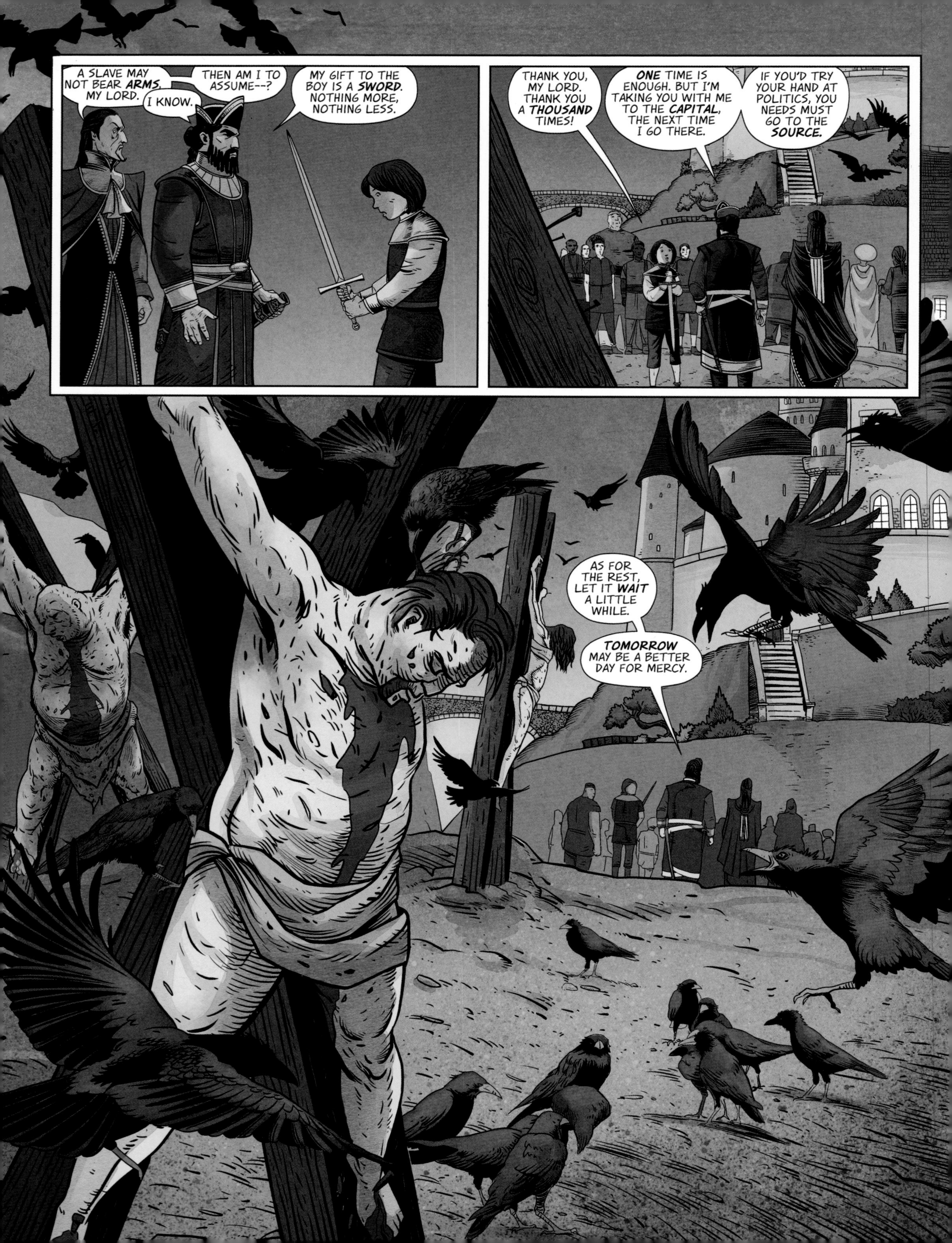
A SLAVE MAY NOT BEAR **ARMS**, MY LORD.
THEN AM I TO ASSUME--?
I KNOW.
MY GIFT TO THE BOY IS A **SWORD**. NOTHING MORE, NOTHING LESS.
THANK YOU, MY LORD. THANK YOU A **THOUSAND** TIMES!
ONE TIME IS ENOUGH. BUT I'M TAKING YOU WITH ME TO THE **CAPITAL**, THE NEXT TIME I GO THERE.
IF YOU'D TRY YOUR HAND AT POLITICS, YOU NEEDS MUST GO TO THE **SOURCE**.
AS FOR THE REST, LET IT **WAIT** A LITTLE WHILE.
TOMORROW MAY BE A BETTER DAY FOR MERCY.

Chapter Five

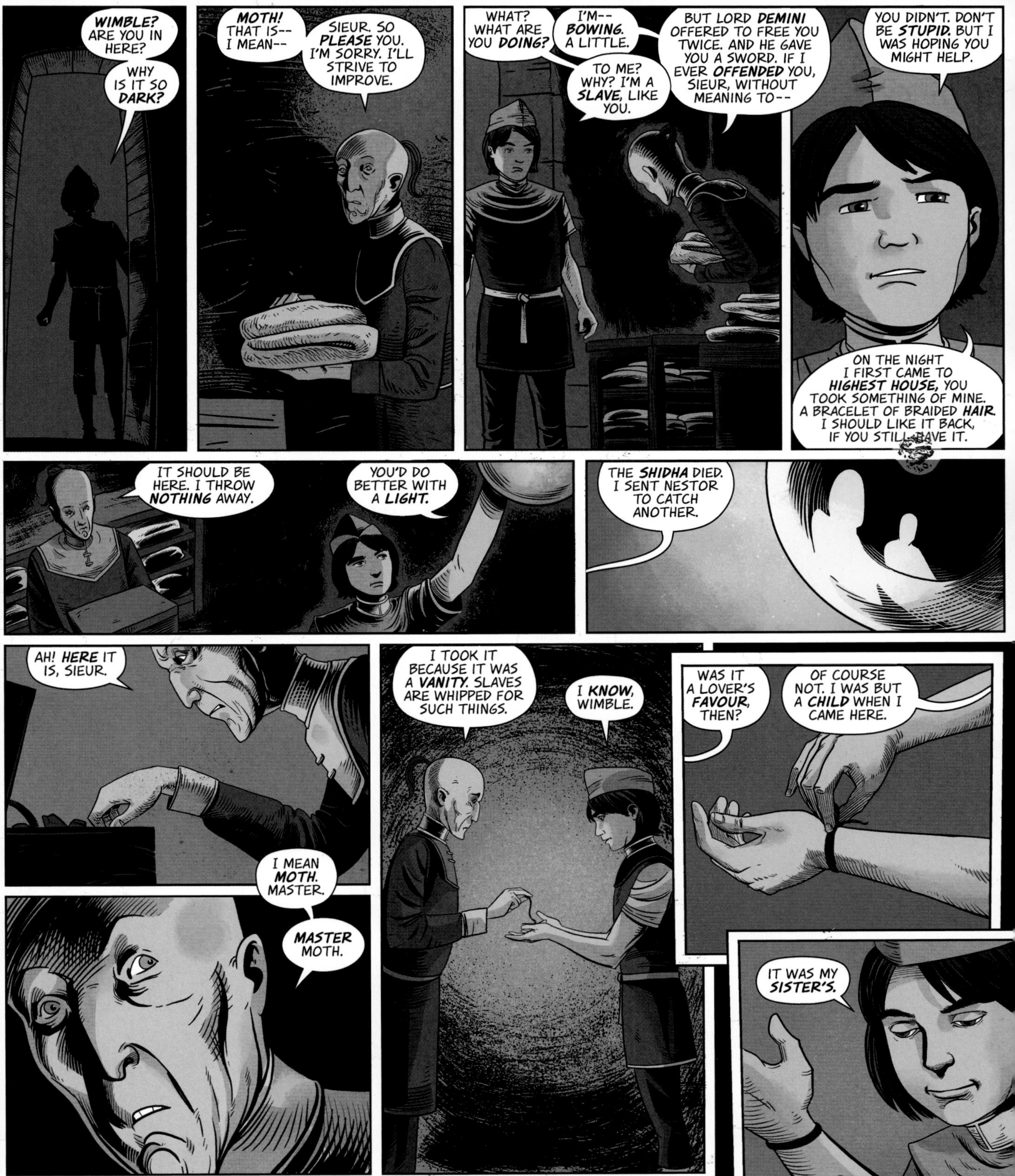

WIMBLE? ARE YOU IN HERE?
WHY IS IT SO DARK?
MOTH! THAT IS-- I MEAN--
SIEUR. SO PLEASE YOU. I'M SORRY. I'LL STRIVE TO IMPROVE.
WHAT? WHAT ARE YOU DOING?
I'M-- BOWING. A LITTLE.
TO ME? WHY? I'M A SLAVE, LIKE YOU.
BUT LORD DEMINI OFFERED TO FREE YOU TWICE. AND HE GAVE YOU A SWORD. IF I EVER OFFENDED YOU, SIEUR, WITHOUT MEANING TO--
YOU DIDN'T. DON'T BE STUPID. BUT I WAS HOPING YOU MIGHT HELP.
ON THE NIGHT I FIRST CAME TO HIGHEST HOUSE, YOU TOOK SOMETHING OF MINE. A BRACELET OF BRAIDED HAIR. I SHOULD LIKE IT BACK, IF YOU STILL HAVE IT.
IT SHOULD BE HERE. I THROW NOTHING AWAY.
YOU'D DO BETTER WITH A LIGHT.
THE SHIDHA DIED. I SENT NESTOR TO CATCH ANOTHER.
AH! HERE IT IS, SIEUR.
I MEAN MOTH. MASTER.
MASTER MOTH.
I TOOK IT BECAUSE IT WAS A VANITY. SLAVES ARE WHIPPED FOR SUCH THINGS.
I KNOW, WIMBLE.
WAS IT A LOVER'S FAVOUR, THEN?
OF COURSE NOT. I WAS BUT A CHILD WHEN I CAME HERE.
IT WAS MY SISTER'S.

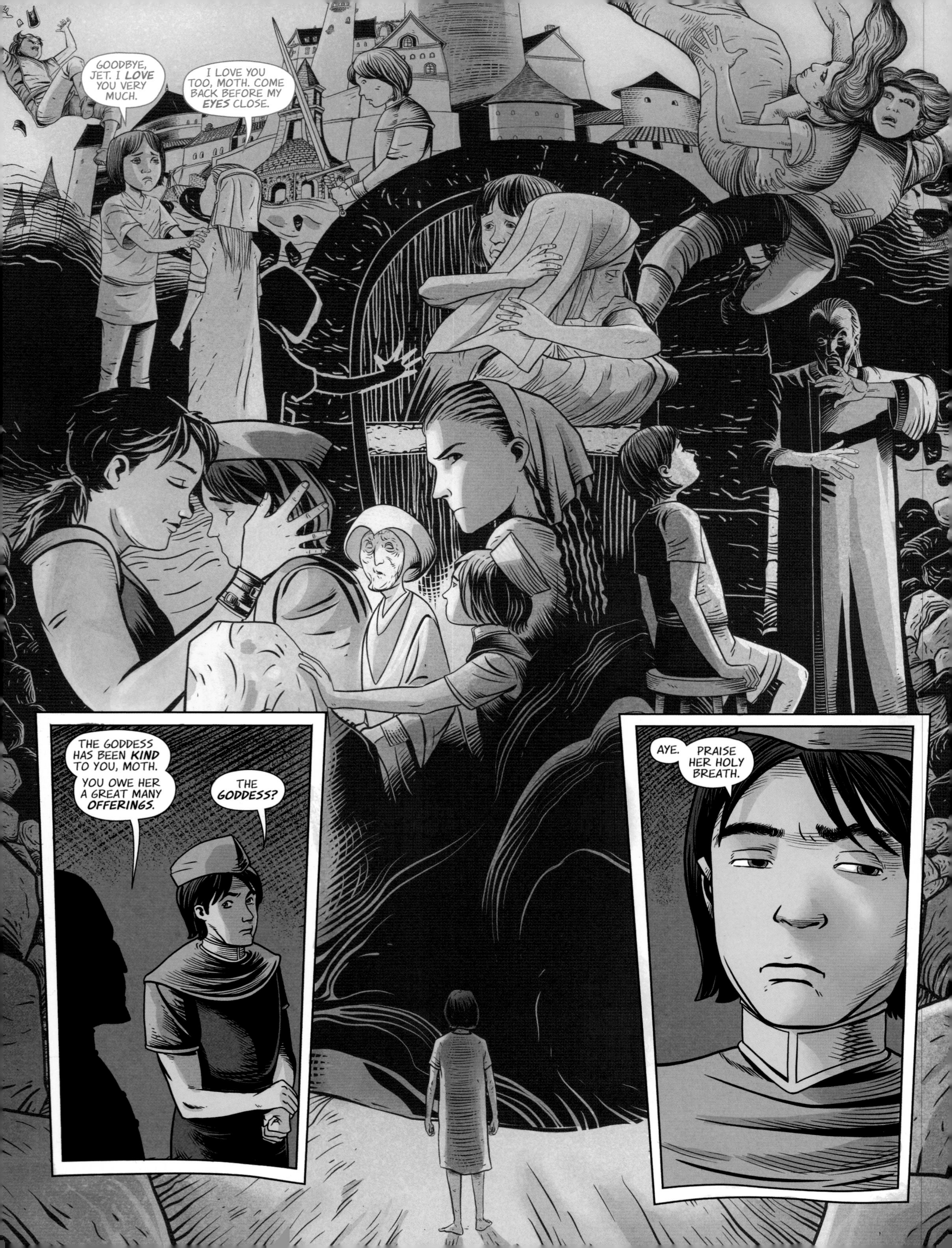
GOODBYE, JET. I LOVE YOU VERY MUCH.
I LOVE YOU TOO, MOTH. COME BACK BEFORE MY EYES CLOSE.
THE GODDESS HAS BEEN KIND TO YOU, MOTH.
YOU OWE HER A GREAT MANY OFFERINGS.
THE GODDESS?
AYE.
PRAISE HER HOLY BREATH.

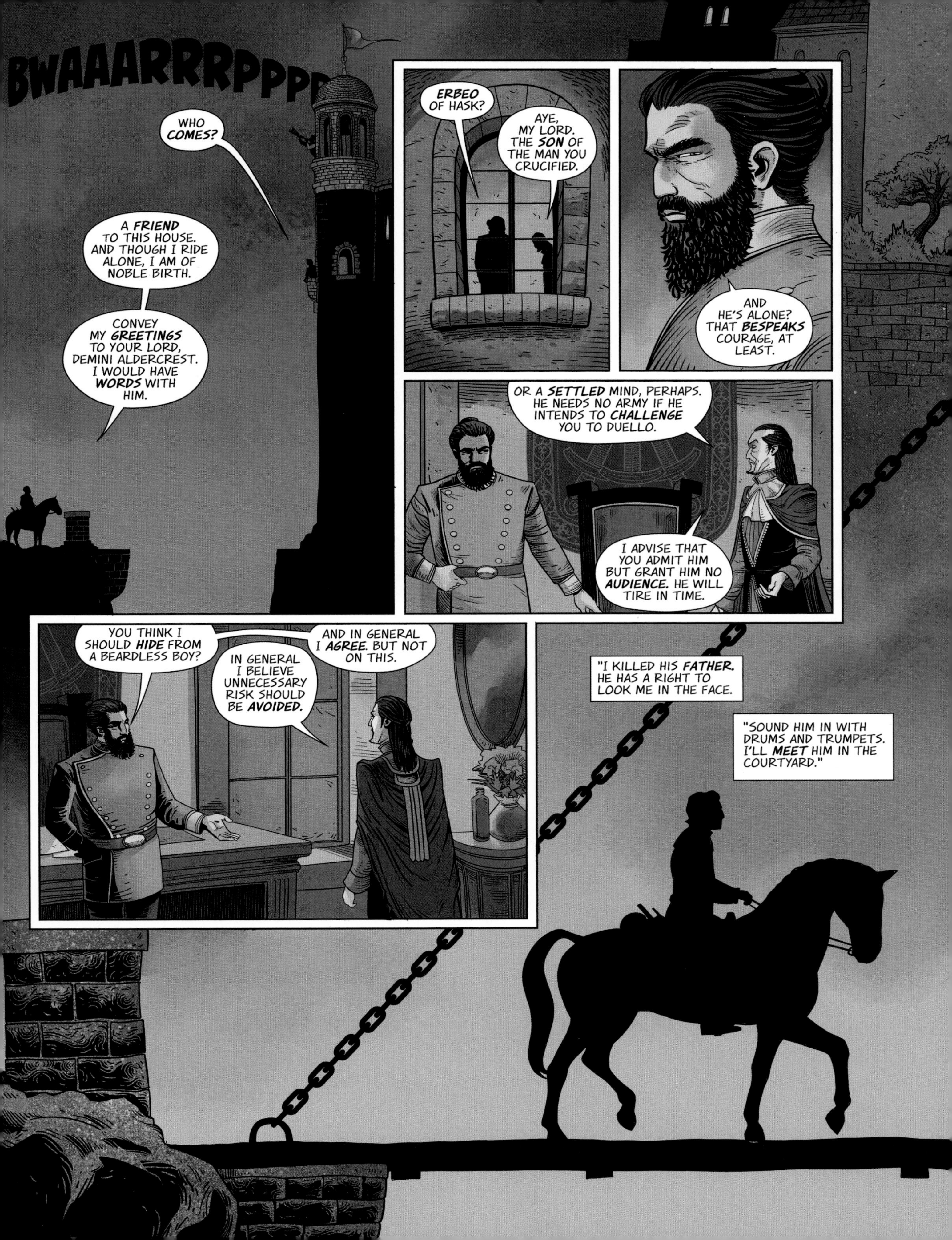

BWAAARRRPPPP
WHO COMES?
A FRIEND TO THIS HOUSE. AND THOUGH I RIDE ALONE, I AM OF NOBLE BIRTH.
CONVEY MY GREETINGS TO YOUR LORD, DEMINI ALDERCREST. I WOULD HAVE WORDS WITH HIM.
ERBEO OF HASK?
AYE, MY LORD. THE SON OF THE MAN YOU CRUCIFIED.
AND HE'S ALONE? THAT BESPEAKS COURAGE, AT LEAST.
OR A SETTLED MIND, PERHAPS. HE NEEDS NO ARMY IF HE INTENDS TO CHALLENGE YOU TO DUELLO.
I ADVISE THAT YOU ADMIT HIM BUT GRANT HIM NO AUDIENCE. HE WILL TIRE IN TIME.
YOU THINK I SHOULD HIDE FROM A BEARDLESS BOY?
IN GENERAL I BELIEVE UNNECESSARY RISK SHOULD BE AVOIDED.
AND IN GENERAL I AGREE. BUT NOT ON THIS.
"I KILLED HIS FATHER. HE HAS A RIGHT TO LOOK ME IN THE FACE.
"SOUND HIM IN WITH DRUMS AND TRUMPETS. I'LL MEET HIM IN THE COURTYARD."

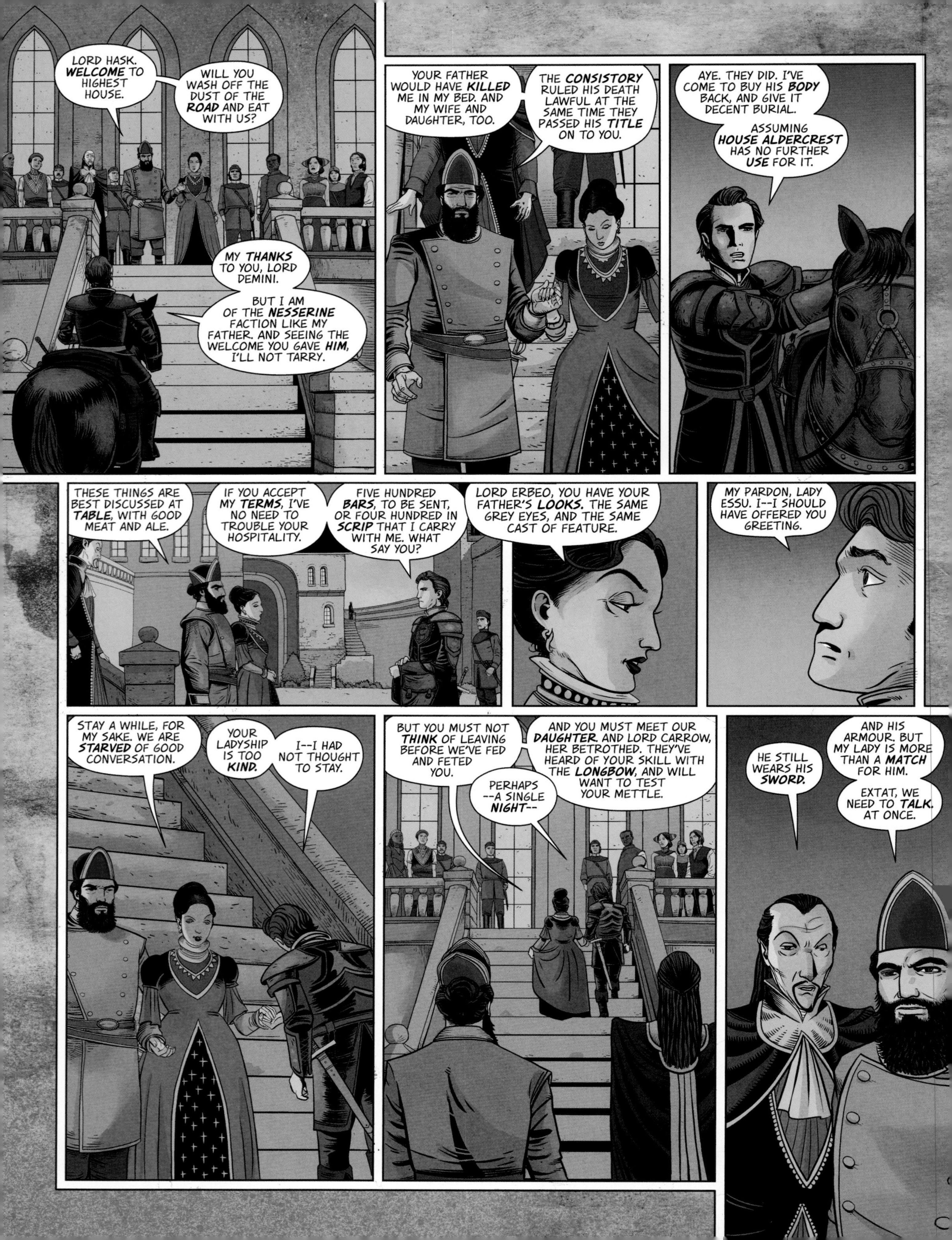
LORD HASK. WELCOME TO HIGHEST HOUSE.
WILL YOU WASH OFF THE DUST OF THE ROAD AND EAT WITH US?
MY THANKS TO YOU, LORD DEMINI.
BUT I AM OF THE NESSERINE FACTION LIKE MY FATHER. AND SEEING THE WELCOME YOU GAVE HIM, I'LL NOT TARRY.
YOUR FATHER WOULD HAVE KILLED ME IN MY BED. AND MY WIFE AND DAUGHTER, TOO.
THE CONSISTORY RULED HIS DEATH LAWFUL AT THE SAME TIME THEY PASSED HIS TITLE ON TO YOU.
AYE. THEY DID. I'VE COME TO BUY HIS BODY BACK, AND GIVE IT DECENT BURIAL.
ASSUMING HOUSE ALDERCREST HAS NO FURTHER USE FOR IT.
THESE THINGS ARE BEST DISCUSSED AT TABLE, WITH GOOD MEAT AND ALE.
IF YOU ACCEPT MY TERMS, I'VE NO NEED TO TROUBLE YOUR HOSPITALITY.
FIVE HUNDRED BARS, TO BE SENT, OR FOUR HUNDRED IN SCRIP THAT I CARRY WITH ME. WHAT SAY YOU?
LORD ERBEO, YOU HAVE YOUR FATHER'S LOOKS. THE SAME GREY EYES, AND THE SAME CAST OF FEATURE.
MY PARDON, LADY ESSU. I--I SHOULD HAVE OFFERED YOU GREETING.
STAY A WHILE, FOR MY SAKE. WE ARE STARVED OF GOOD CONVERSATION.
YOUR LADYSHIP IS TOO KIND.
I--I HAD NOT THOUGHT TO STAY.
BUT YOU MUST NOT THINK OF LEAVING BEFORE WE'VE FED AND FETED YOU.
AND YOU MUST MEET OUR DAUGHTER. AND LORD CARROW, HER BETROTHED. THEY'VE HEARD OF YOUR SKILL WITH THE LONGBOW, AND WILL WANT TO TEST YOUR METTLE.
PERHAPS --A SINGLE NIGHT--
HE STILL WEARS HIS SWORD.
AND HIS ARMOUR. BUT MY LADY IS MORE THAN A MATCH FOR HIM.
EXTAT, WE NEED TO TALK. AT ONCE.

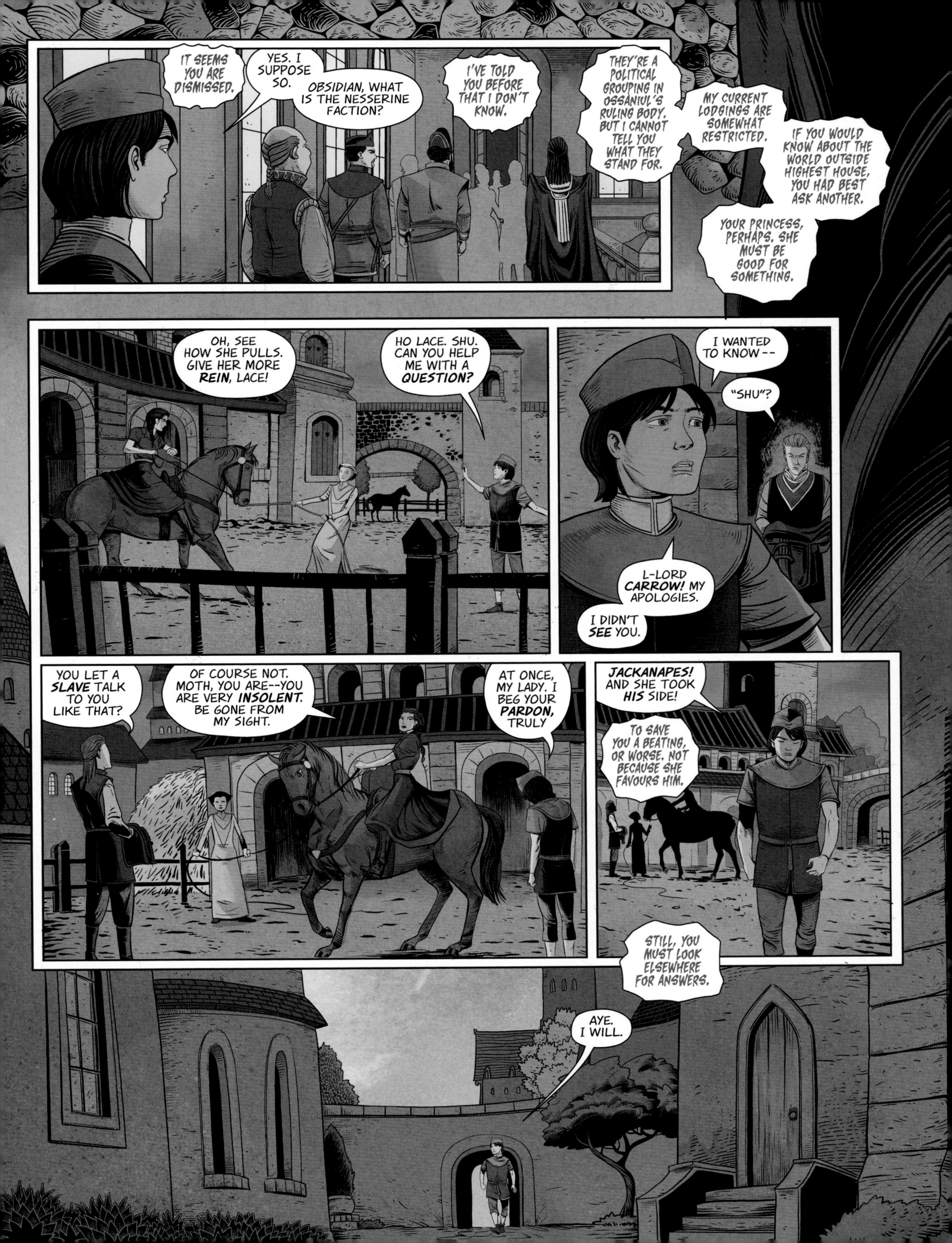
IT SEEMS YOU ARE DISMISSED.
YES. I SUPPOSE SO.
OBSIDIAN, WHAT IS THE NESSERINE FACTION?
I'VE TOLD YOU BEFORE THAT I DON'T KNOW.
THEY'RE A POLITICAL GROUPING IN OSSANIUL'S RULING BODY. BUT I CANNOT TELL YOU WHAT THEY STAND FOR.
MY CURRENT LODGINGS ARE SOMEWHAT RESTRICTED.
IF YOU WOULD KNOW ABOUT THE WORLD OUTSIDE HIGHEST HOUSE, YOU HAD BEST ASK ANOTHER.
YOUR PRINCESS, PERHAPS. SHE MUST BE GOOD FOR SOMETHING.
OH, SEE HOW SHE PULLS. GIVE HER MORE REIN, LACE!
HO LACE. SHU. CAN YOU HELP ME WITH A QUESTION?
I WANTED TO KNOW --
"SHU"?
L-LORD CARROW! MY APOLOGIES.
I DIDN'T SEE YOU.
YOU LET A SLAVE TALK TO YOU LIKE THAT?
OF COURSE NOT. MOTH, YOU ARE--YOU ARE VERY INSOLENT. BE GONE FROM MY SIGHT.
AT ONCE, MY LADY. I BEG YOUR PARDON, TRULY
JACKANAPES! AND SHE TOOK HIS SIDE!
TO SAVE YOU A BEATING, OR WORSE. NOT BECAUSE SHE FAVOURS HIM.
STILL, YOU MUST LOOK ELSEWHERE FOR ANSWERS.
AYE. I WILL.

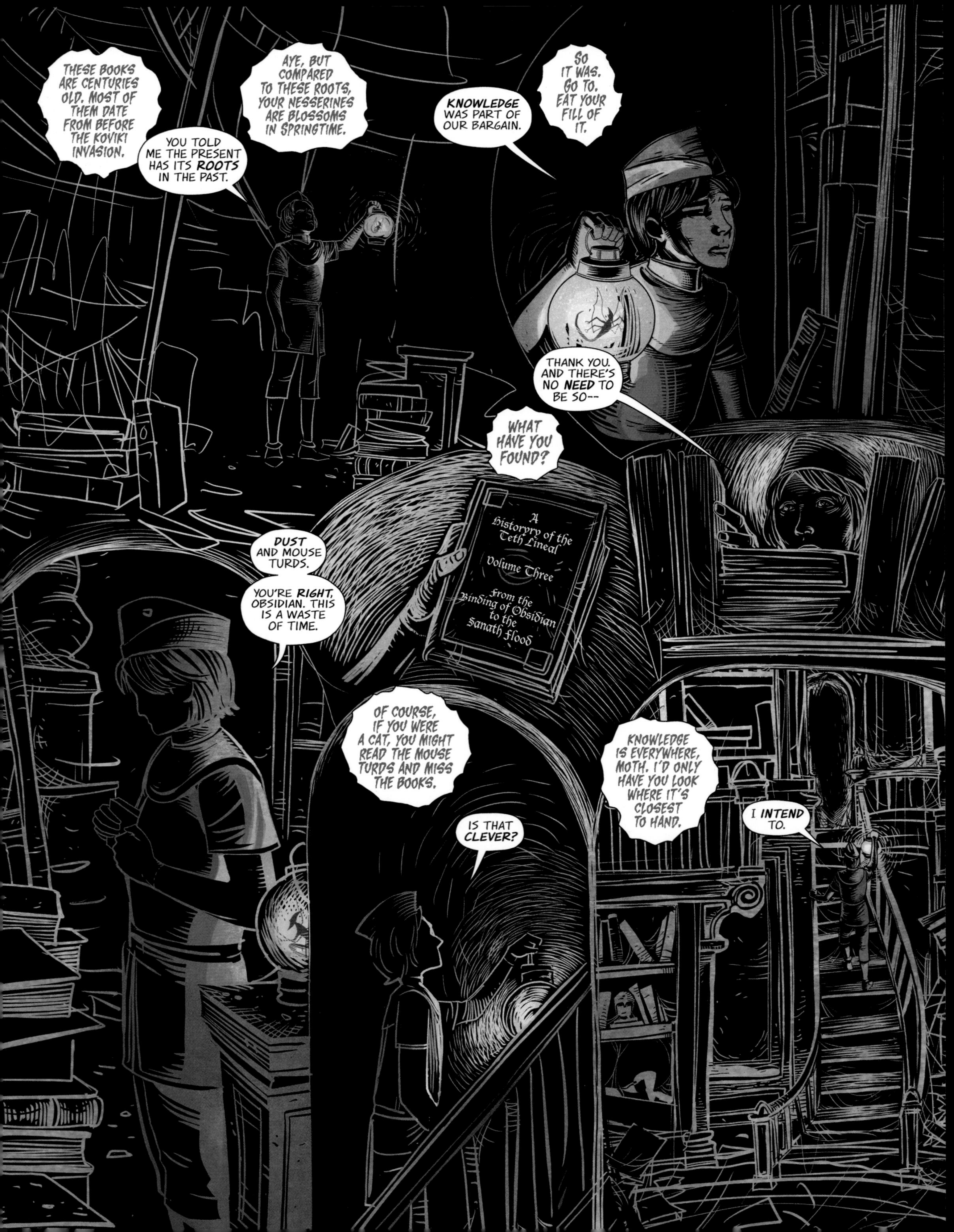
THESE BOOKS ARE CENTURIES OLD. MOST OF THEM DATE FROM BEFORE THE KOVIKI INVASION.
YOU TOLD ME THE PRESENT HAS ITS ROOTS IN THE PAST.
AYE, BUT COMPARED TO THESE ROOTS, YOUR NESSERINES ARE BLOSSOMS IN SPRINGTIME.
KNOWLEDGE WAS PART OF OUR BARGAIN.
SO IT WAS. GO TO. EAT YOUR FILL OF IT.
THANK YOU. AND THERE'S NO NEED TO BE SO--
WHAT HAVE YOU FOUND?
A Historyry of the Teth Lineal
Volume Three
From the Binding of Obsidian to the Sanath Flood
DUST AND MOUSE TURDS.
YOU'RE RIGHT, OBSIDIAN. THIS IS A WASTE OF TIME.
OF COURSE, IF YOU WERE A CAT, YOU MIGHT READ THE MOUSE TURDS AND MISS THE BOOKS.
IS THAT CLEVER?
KNOWLEDGE IS EVERYWHERE, MOTH. I'D ONLY HAVE YOU LOOK WHERE IT'S CLOSEST TO HAND.
I INTEND TO.

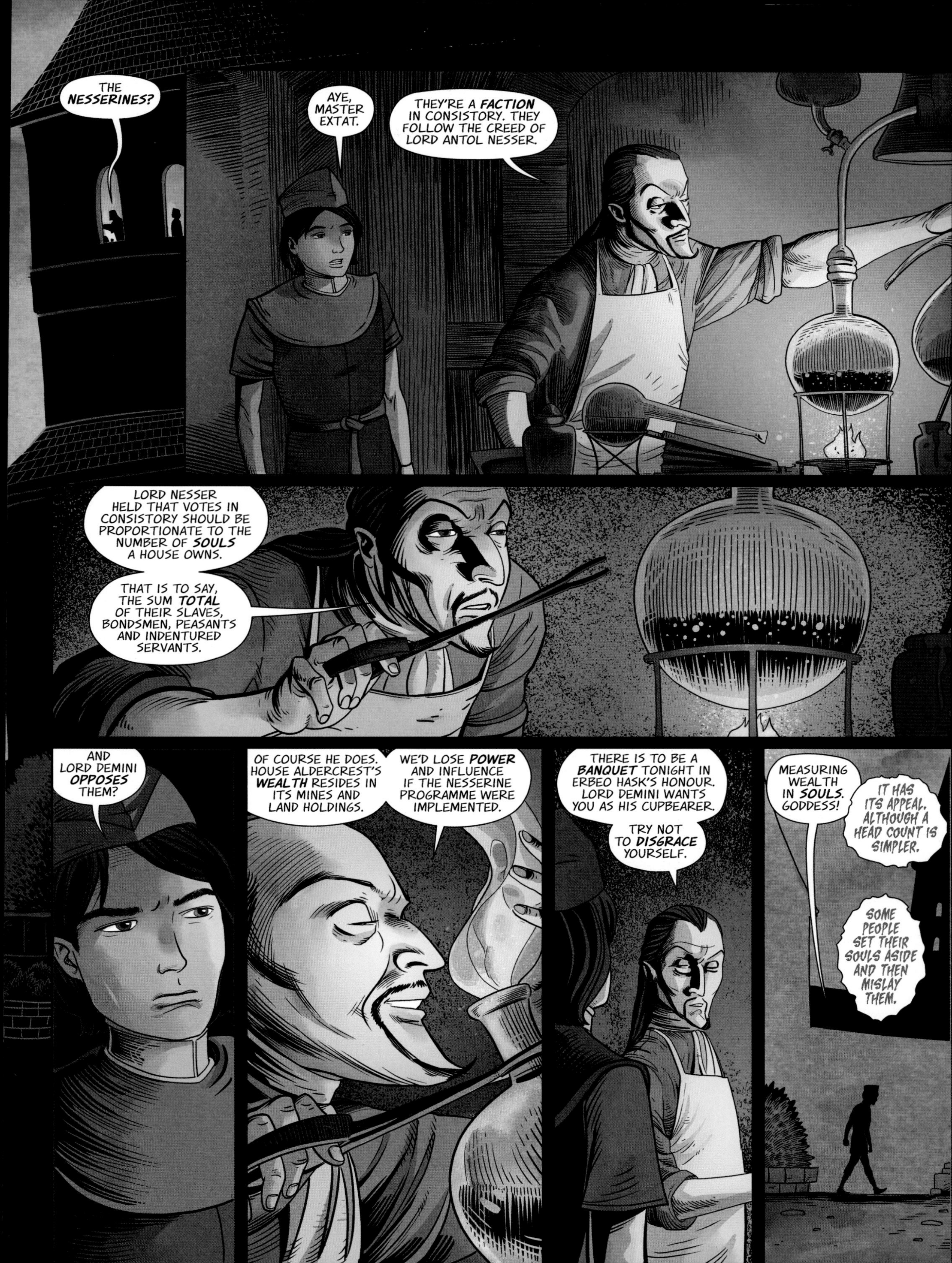
THE NESSERINES?
AYE, MASTER EXTAT.
THEY'RE A FACTION IN CONSISTORY. THEY FOLLOW THE CREED OF LORD ANTOL NESSER.
LORD NESSER HELD THAT VOTES IN CONSISTORY SHOULD BE PROPORTIONATE TO THE NUMBER OF SOULS A HOUSE OWNS.
THAT IS TO SAY, THE SUM TOTAL OF THEIR SLAVES, BONDSMEN, PEASANTS AND INDENTURED SERVANTS.
AND LORD DEMINI OPPOSES THEM?
OF COURSE HE DOES. HOUSE ALDERCREST'S WEALTH RESIDES IN ITS MINES AND LAND HOLDINGS.
WE'D LOSE POWER AND INFLUENCE IF THE NESSERINE PROGRAMME WERE IMPLEMENTED.
THERE IS TO BE A BANQUET TONIGHT IN ERBEO HASK'S HONOUR. LORD DEMINI WANTS YOU AS HIS CUPBEARER.
TRY NOT TO DISGRACE YOURSELF.
MEASURING WEALTH IN SOULS. GODDESS!
IT HAS ITS APPEAL, ALTHOUGH A HEAD COUNT IS SIMPLER.
SOME PEOPLE SET THEIR SOULS ASIDE AND THEN MISLAY THEM.

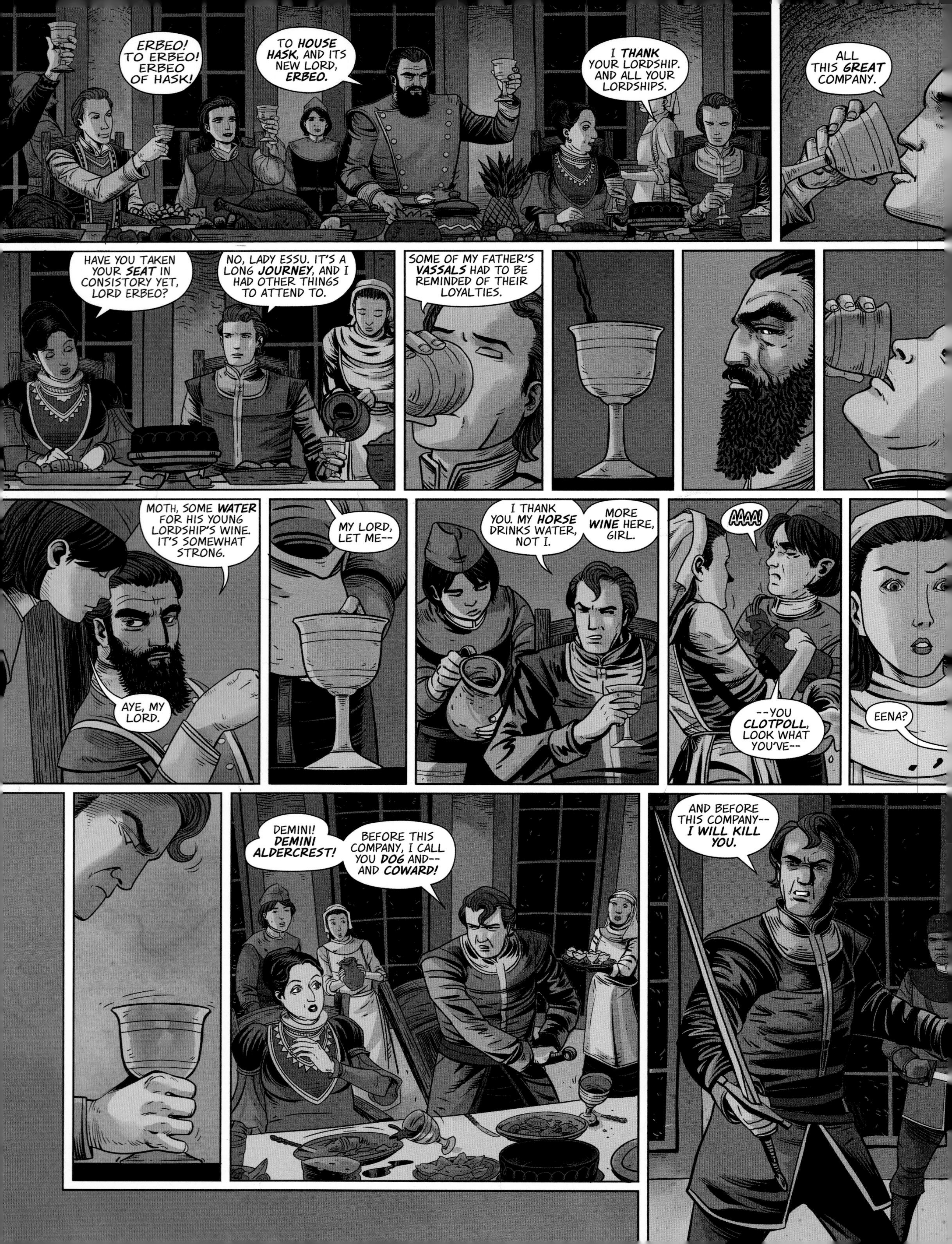
ERBEO! TO ERBEO! ERBEO OF HASK!
TO HOUSE HASK, AND ITS NEW LORD, ERBEO.
I THANK YOUR LORDSHIP. AND ALL YOUR LORDSHIPS.
ALL THIS GREAT COMPANY.
HAVE YOU TAKEN YOUR SEAT IN CONSISTORY YET, LORD ERBEO?
NO, LADY ESSU. IT'S A LONG JOURNEY, AND I HAD OTHER THINGS TO ATTEND TO.
SOME OF MY FATHER'S VASSALS HAD TO BE REMINDED OF THEIR LOYALTIES.
MOTH, SOME WATER FOR HIS YOUNG LORDSHIP'S WINE. IT'S SOMEWHAT STRONG.
AYE, MY LORD.
MY LORD, LET ME--
I THANK YOU. MY HORSE DRINKS WATER, NOT I.
MORE WINE HERE, GIRL.
AAAA!
--YOU CLOTPOLL, LOOK WHAT YOU'VE--
EENA?
DEMINI! DEMINI ALDERCREST!
BEFORE THIS COMPANY, I CALL YOU DOG AND-- AND COWARD!
AND BEFORE THIS COMPANY-- I WILL KILL YOU.

STAND DOWN. HE'S NOT TO BE **HARMED.**

DRAW YOUR **BLADE.**

IF IT **COMES** TO IT, MY LORD, I WILL.

BUT I THINK WE SHOULD **TALK** FIRST.

I SAID-- DRAW YOUR SWORD.

YOU CANNOT **SURVIVE** THIS. AND YOU HAVE NO BROTHERS OR SISTERS.

IF YOU **DIE** HERE, YOUR **HOUSE** DIES WITH YOU.

I OFFERED TO BUY MY FATHER'S BODY BACK. YOU DIDN'T EVEN DEIGN TO **ANSWER ME.**

MY ANSWER IS NO, ERBEO. I WILL NOT **SELL** HIM.

THEN-- THEN I'LL--

THE BODY IS **YOURS.** I OFFER IT FREELY. WITH TWENTY OF MY GUARD TO BEAR IT TO **IDMIOK** IN STATE, AS IT SHOULD BE BORNE.

WE WILL ALSO SPEAK OF WHAT **REPARATIONS** MIGHT BE DUE FOR HIS DEATH AND THAT OF HIS SERVANTS.

OR ELSE WE WILL **FIGHT,** AND I WILL KILL YOU. AND THE NAME OF HASK WILL GO INTO THE DUST.

IT IS **YOUR** CHOICE, AND I CAN'T MAKE IT FOR YOU.

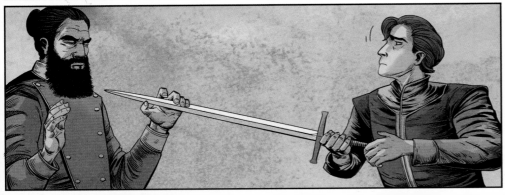

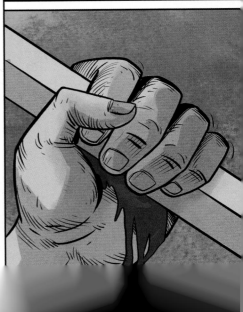

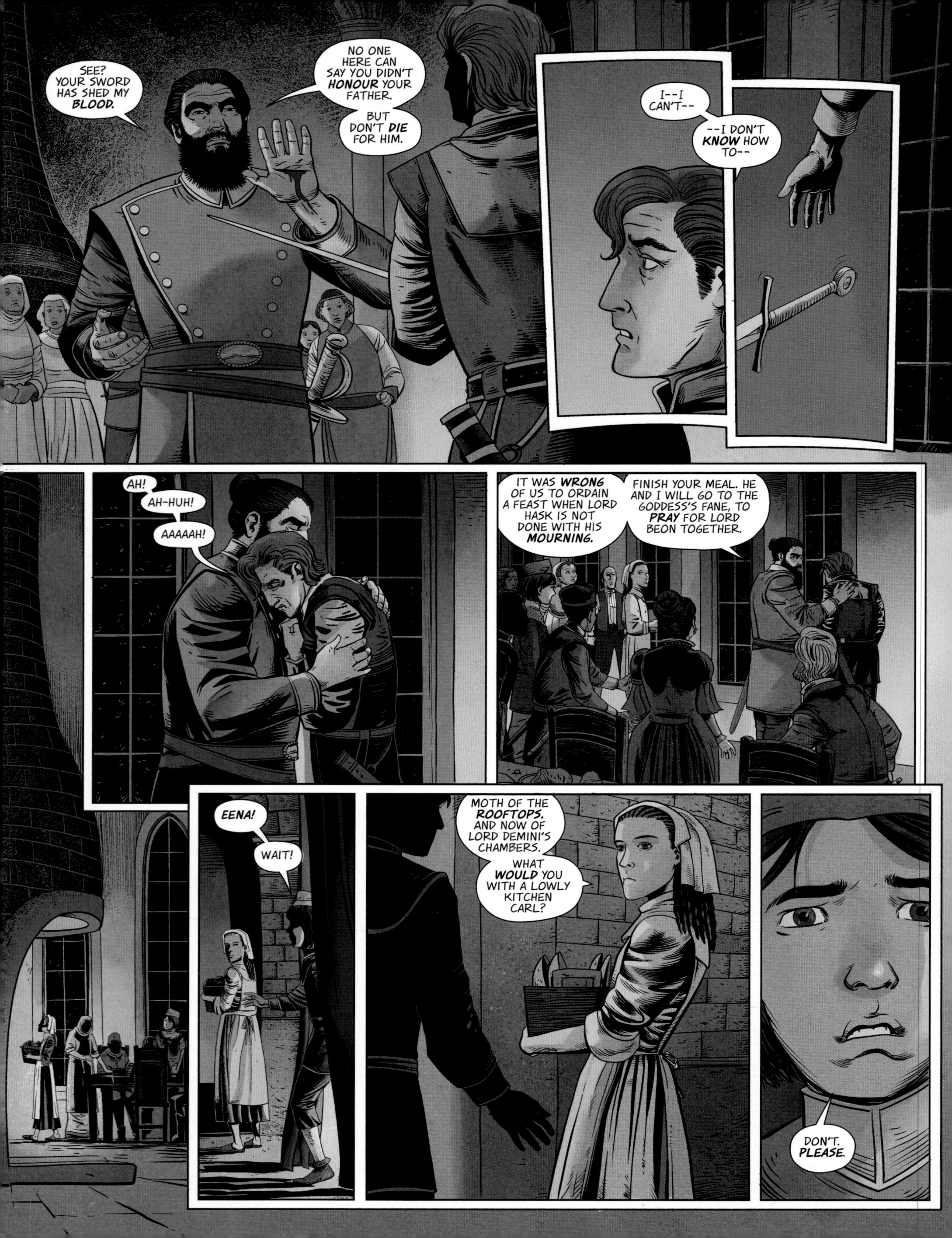
SEE? YOUR SWORD HAS SHED MY **BLOOD.**
NO ONE HERE CAN SAY YOU DIDN'T **HONOUR** YOUR FATHER.
BUT DON'T **DIE** FOR HIM.
I--I CAN'T--
--I DON'T **KNOW** HOW TO--
AH!
AH-HUH!
AAAAAH!
IT WAS **WRONG** OF US TO ORDAIN A FEAST WHEN LORD HASK IS NOT DONE WITH HIS **MOURNING.**
FINISH YOUR MEAL. HE AND I WILL GO TO THE GODDESS'S FANE, TO **PRAY** FOR LORD BEON TOGETHER.
EENA!
WAIT!
MOTH OF THE **ROOFTOPS.** AND NOW OF LORD DEMINI'S CHAMBERS.
WHAT **WOULD** YOU WITH A LOWLY KITCHEN CARL?
DON'T. **PLEASE.**

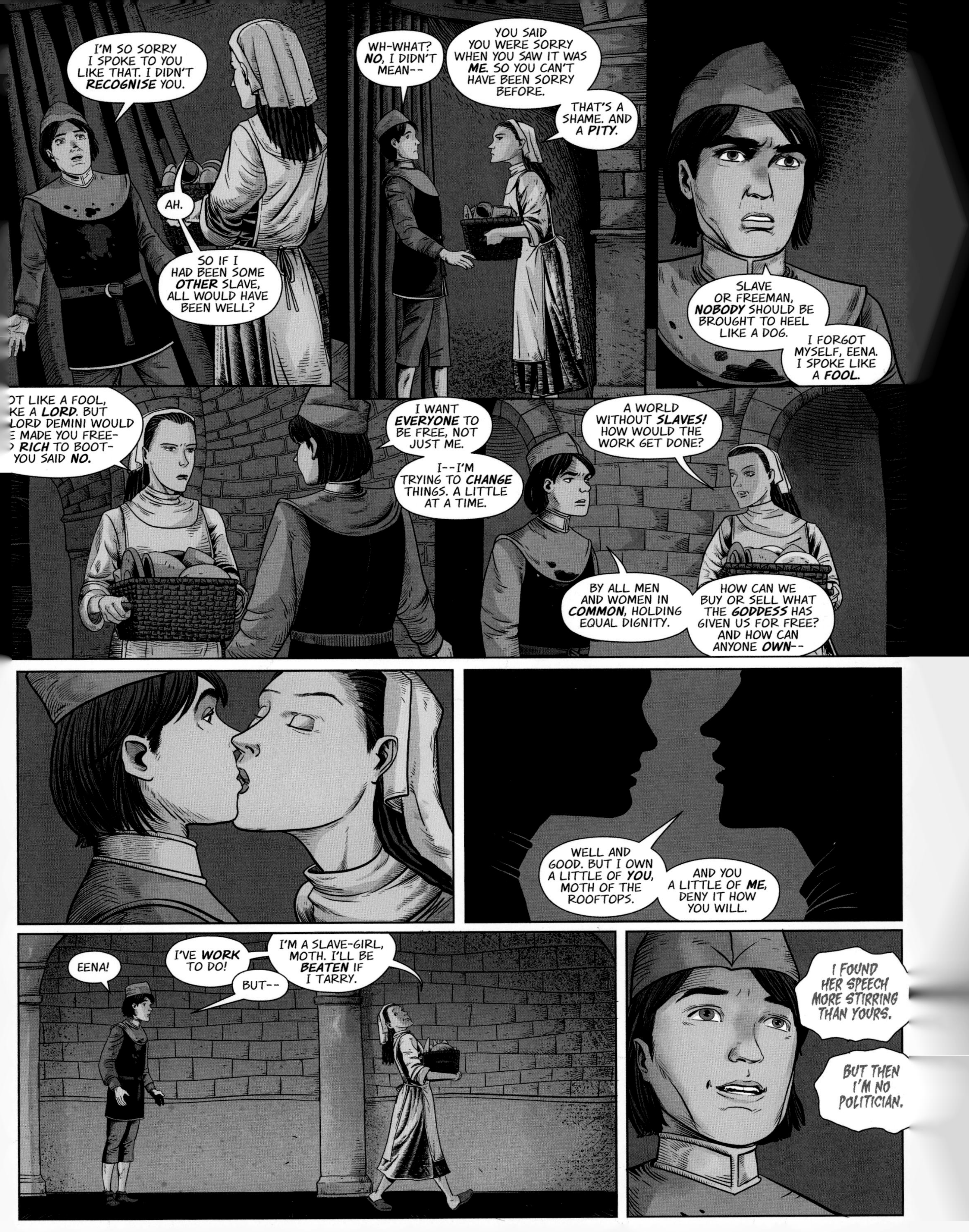
I'M SO SORRY I SPOKE TO YOU LIKE THAT. I DIDN'T RECOGNISE YOU.
AH.
SO IF I HAD BEEN SOME OTHER SLAVE, ALL WOULD HAVE BEEN WELL?
WH-WHAT? NO, I DIDN'T MEAN--
YOU SAID YOU WERE SORRY WHEN YOU SAW IT WAS ME. SO YOU CAN'T HAVE BEEN SORRY BEFORE.
THAT'S A SHAME. AND A PITY.
SLAVE OR FREEMAN, NOBODY SHOULD BE BROUGHT TO HEEL LIKE A DOG.
I FORGOT MYSELF, EENA. I SPOKE LIKE A FOOL.
OT LIKE A FOOL, KE A LORD. BUT LORD DEMINI WOULD E MADE YOU FREE- RICH TO BOOT- YOU SAID NO.
I WANT EVERYONE TO BE FREE, NOT JUST ME.
I--I'M TRYING TO CHANGE THINGS. A LITTLE AT A TIME.
A WORLD WITHOUT SLAVES! HOW WOULD THE WORK GET DONE?
BY ALL MEN AND WOMEN IN COMMON, HOLDING EQUAL DIGNITY.
HOW CAN WE BUY OR SELL WHAT THE GODDESS HAS GIVEN US FOR FREE? AND HOW CAN ANYONE OWN--
WELL AND GOOD. BUT I OWN A LITTLE OF YOU, MOTH OF THE ROOFTOPS.
AND YOU A LITTLE OF ME, DENY IT HOW YOU WILL.
EENA!
I'VE WORK TO DO!
BUT--
I'M A SLAVE-GIRL, MOTH. I'LL BE BEATEN IF I TARRY.
I FOUND HER SPEECH MORE STIRRING THAN YOURS.
BUT THEN I'M NO POLITICIAN.

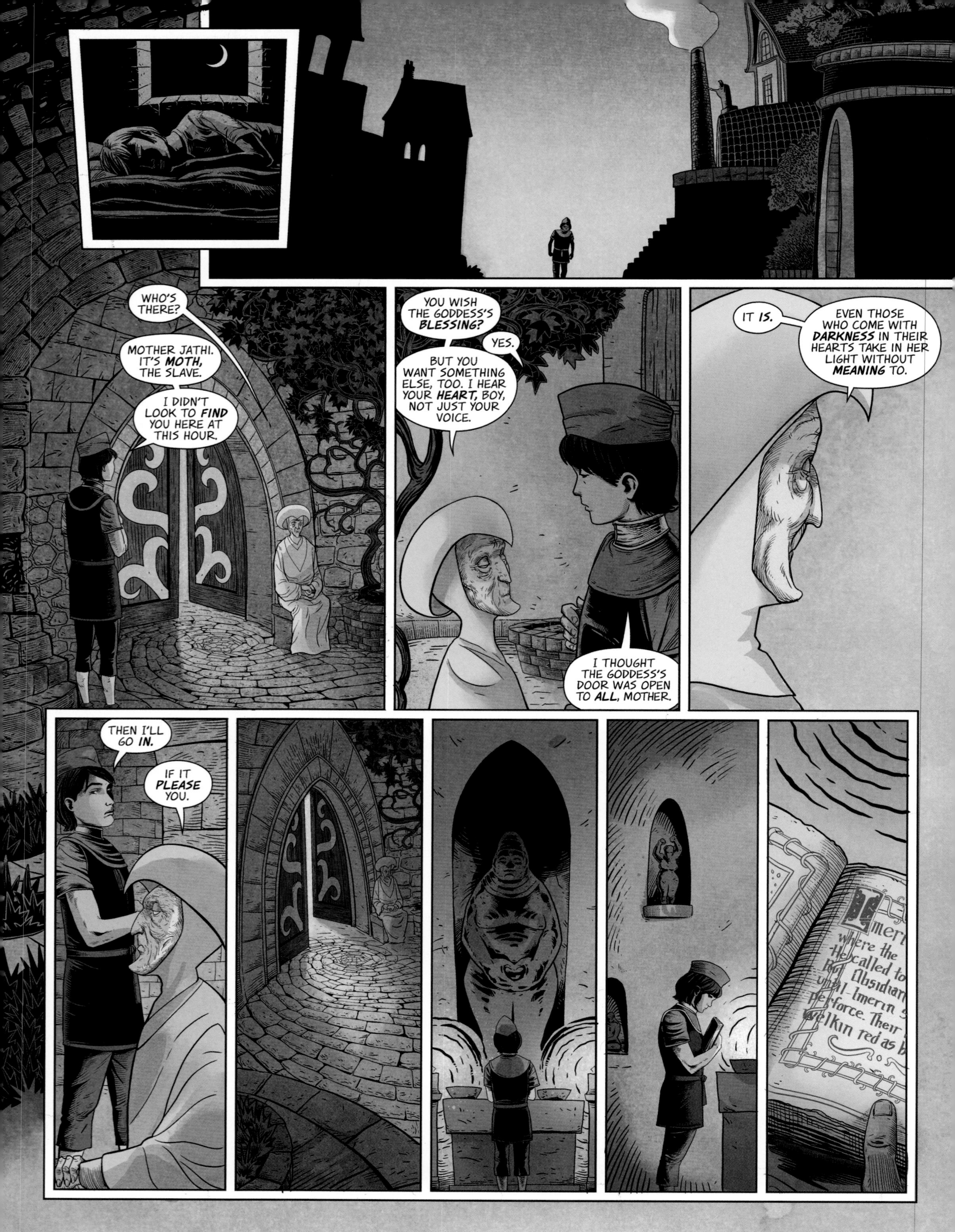
WHO'S THERE?
MOTHER JATHI. IT'S **MOTH,** THE SLAVE.
I DIDN'T LOOK TO **FIND** YOU HERE AT THIS HOUR.
YOU WISH THE GODDESS'S ***BLESSING?***
YES.
BUT YOU WANT SOMETHING ELSE, TOO. I HEAR YOUR **HEART,** BOY, NOT JUST YOUR VOICE.
I THOUGHT THE GODDESS'S DOOR WAS OPEN TO **ALL,** MOTHER.
IT ***IS.***
EVEN THOSE WHO COME WITH **DARKNESS** IN THEIR HEARTS TAKE IN HER LIGHT WITHOUT **MEANING** TO.
THEN I'LL GO ***IN.***
IF IT ***PLEASE*** YOU.

Imerin went up onto Garun Hen, where the demon Obsidian was said to dwell. He called aloud to the great beast, challenging it to do battle with him. But Obsidian was afraid and would not come, until Imerin summoned him perforce. Their fighting made the welkin red as blood, but at the last Imerin defeated and bound Obsidian in a wall of black stone. You are my vassal, he told the demon, and your power now and henceforth is in my service.

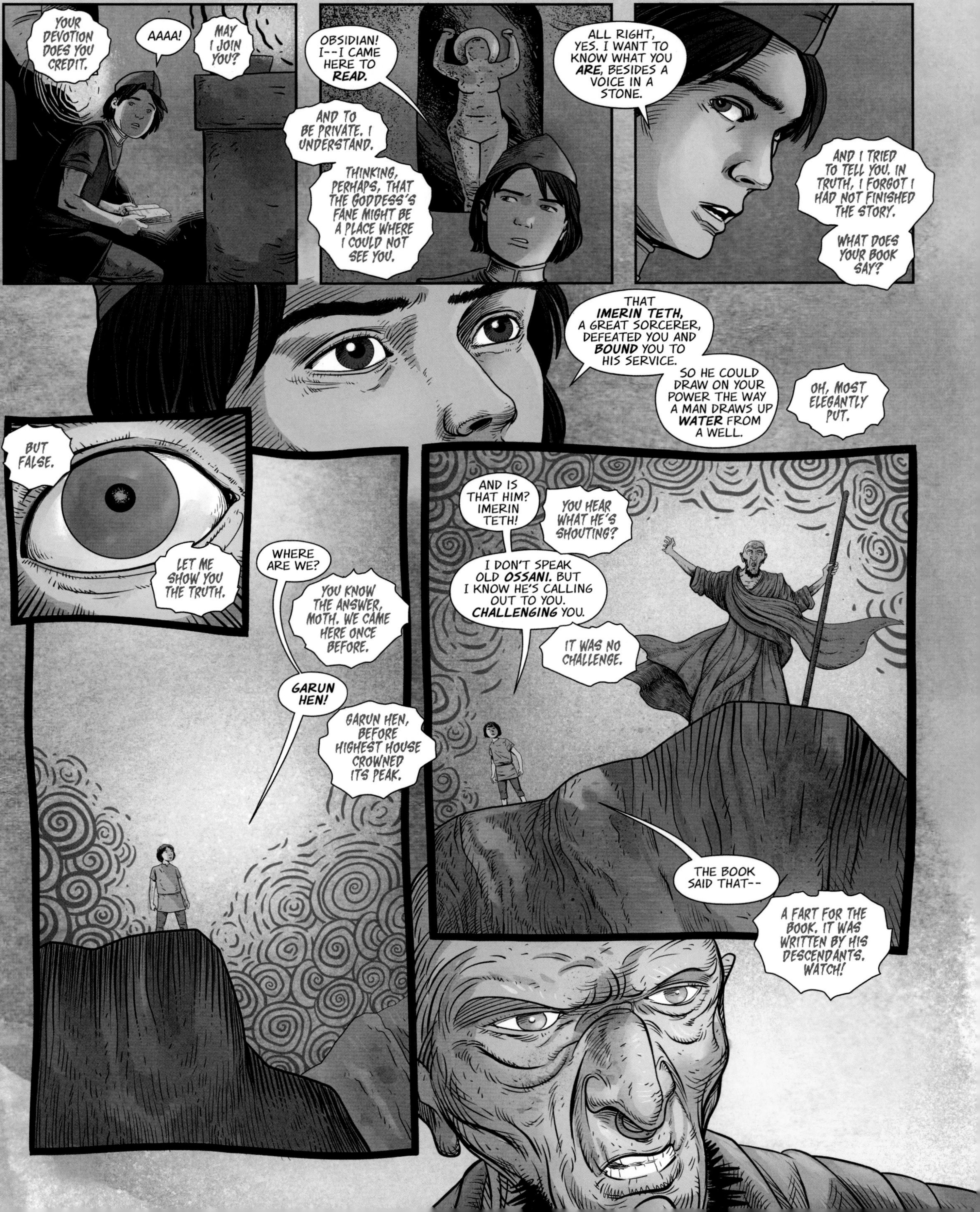
YOUR DEVOTION DOES YOU CREDIT.
AAAA!
MAY I JOIN YOU?
OBSIDIAN! I--I CAME HERE TO READ.
AND TO BE PRIVATE. I UNDERSTAND.
THINKING, PERHAPS, THAT THE GODDESS'S FANE MIGHT BE A PLACE WHERE I COULD NOT SEE YOU.
ALL RIGHT, YES. I WANT TO KNOW WHAT YOU ARE, BESIDES A VOICE IN A STONE.
AND I TRIED TO TELL YOU. IN TRUTH, I FORGOT I HAD NOT FINISHED THE STORY.
WHAT DOES YOUR BOOK SAY?
THAT IMERIN TETH, A GREAT SORCERER, DEFEATED YOU AND BOUND YOU TO HIS SERVICE.
SO HE COULD DRAW ON YOUR POWER THE WAY A MAN DRAWS UP WATER FROM A WELL.
OH, MOST ELEGANTLY PUT.
BUT FALSE.
LET ME SHOW YOU THE TRUTH.
WHERE ARE WE?
YOU KNOW THE ANSWER, MOTH. WE CAME HERE ONCE BEFORE.
GARUN HEN!
GARUN HEN, BEFORE HIGHEST HOUSE CROWNED ITS PEAK.
AND IS THAT HIM? IMERIN TETH!
YOU HEAR WHAT HE'S SHOUTING?
I DON'T SPEAK OLD OSSANI. BUT I KNOW HE'S CALLING OUT TO YOU. CHALLENGING YOU.
IT WAS NO CHALLENGE.
THE BOOK SAID THAT--
A FART FOR THE BOOK. IT WAS WRITTEN BY HIS DESCENDANTS. WATCH!

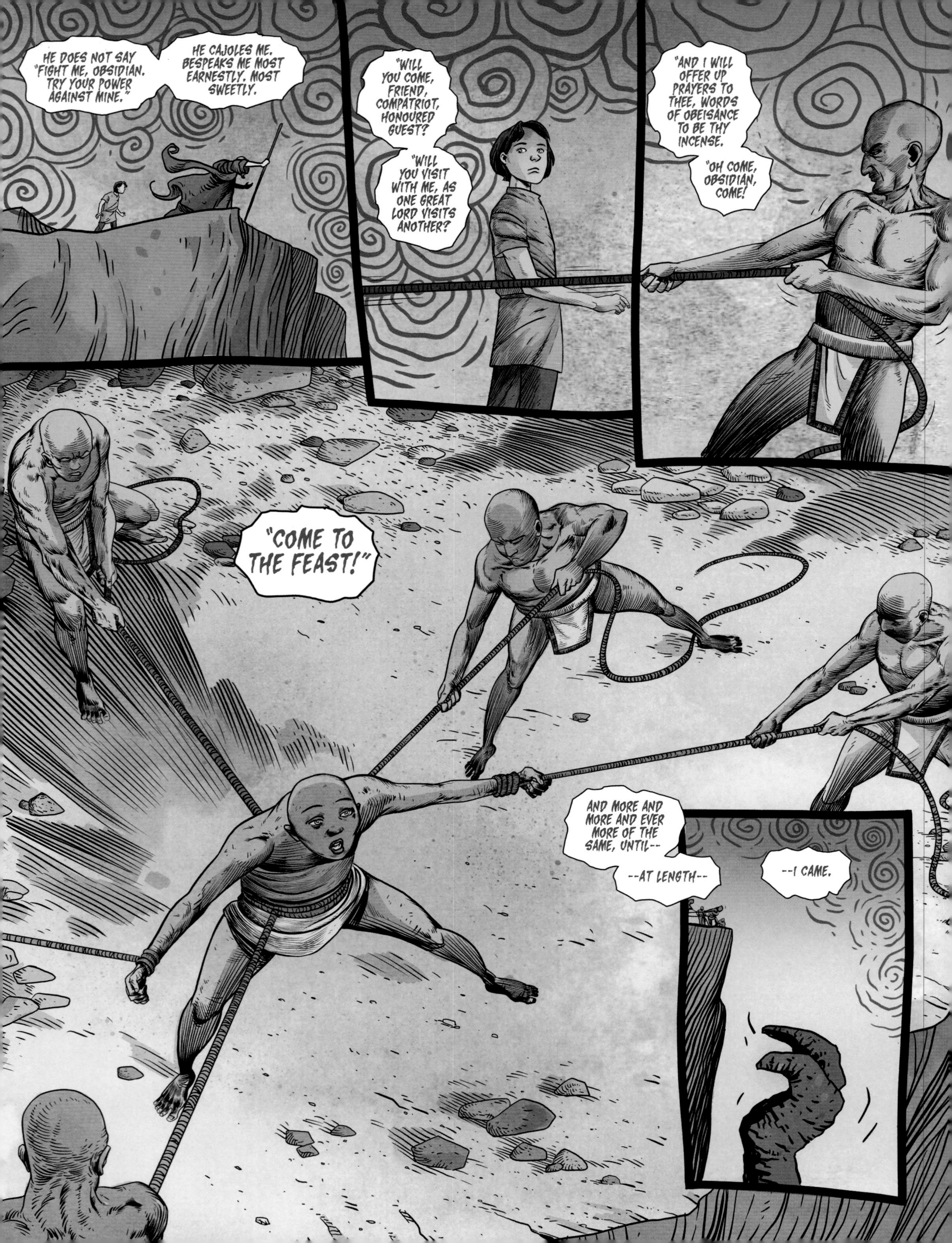
HE DOES NOT SAY "FIGHT ME, OBSIDIAN. TRY YOUR POWER AGAINST MINE."
HE CAJOLES ME. BESPEAKS ME MOST EARNESTLY. MOST SWEETLY.
"WILL YOU COME, FRIEND, COMPATRIOT, HONOURED GUEST?
"WILL YOU VISIT WITH ME, AS ONE GREAT LORD VISITS ANOTHER?
"AND I WILL OFFER UP PRAYERS TO THEE, WORDS OF OBEISANCE TO BE THY INCENSE.
"OH COME, OBSIDIAN, COME!
"COME TO THE FEAST!"
AND MORE AND MORE AND EVER MORE OF THE SAME, UNTIL--
--AT LENGTH--
--I CAME.

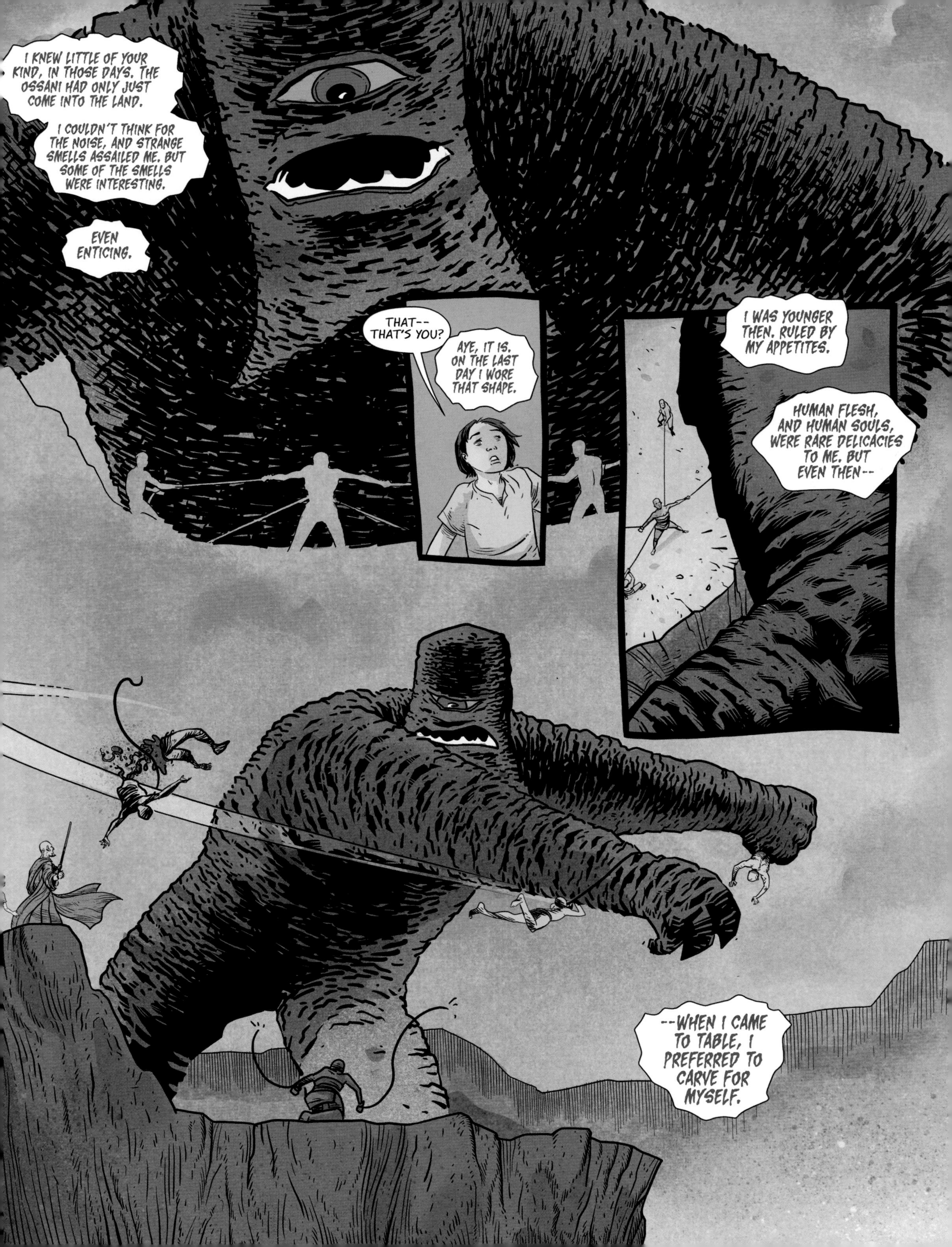
I KNEW LITTLE OF YOUR KIND, IN THOSE DAYS. THE OSSANI HAD ONLY JUST COME INTO THE LAND.
I COULDN'T THINK FOR THE NOISE, AND STRANGE SMELLS ASSAILED ME. BUT SOME OF THE SMELLS WERE INTERESTING.
EVEN ENTICING.
THAT-- THAT'S YOU?
AYE, IT IS. ON THE LAST DAY I WORE THAT SHAPE.
I WAS YOUNGER THEN. RULED BY MY APPETITES.
HUMAN FLESH, AND HUMAN SOULS, WERE RARE DELICACIES TO ME. BUT EVEN THEN--
--WHEN I CAME TO TABLE, I PREFERRED TO CARVE FOR MYSELF.

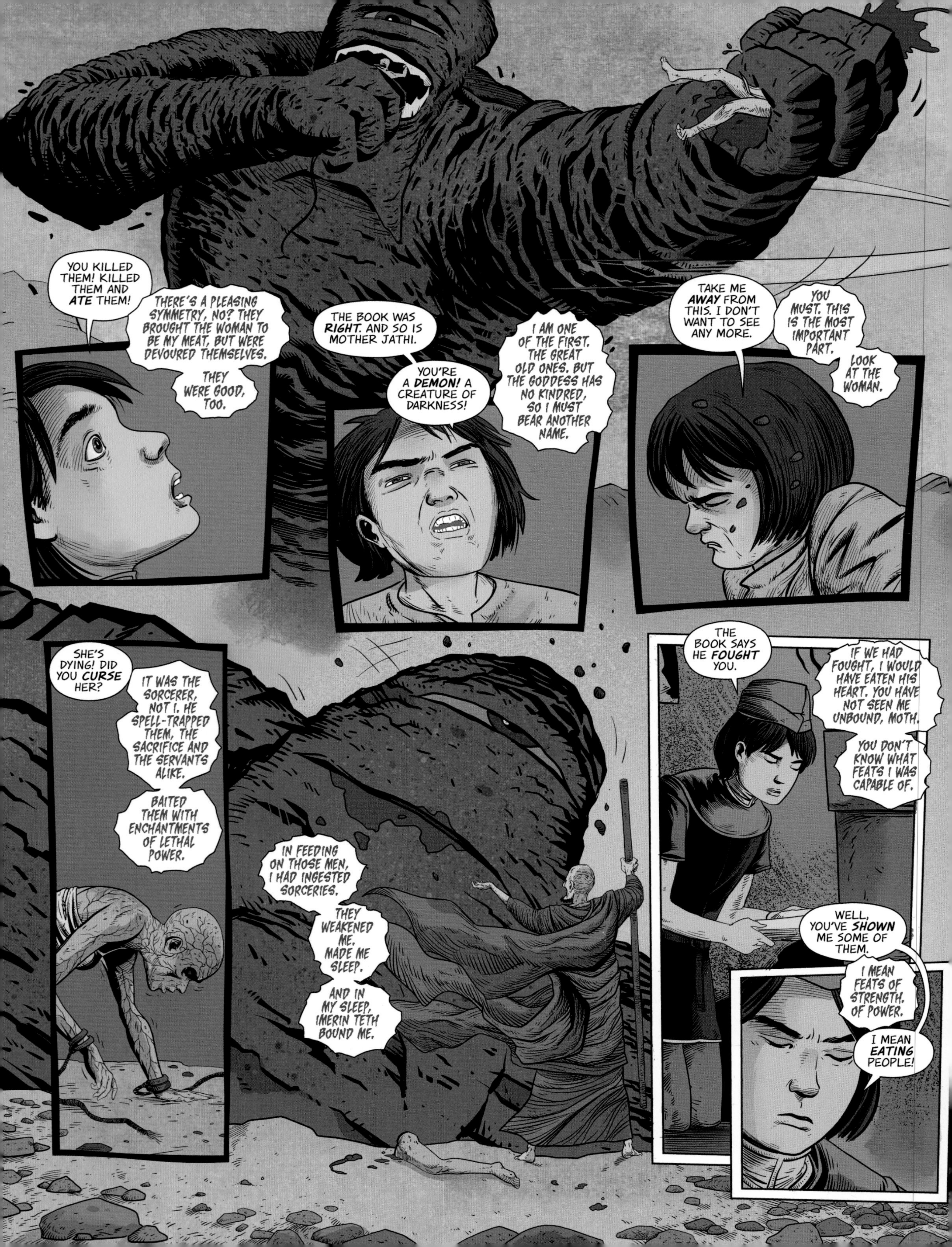

YOU KILLED THEM! KILLED THEM AND ATE THEM!
THERE'S A PLEASING SYMMETRY, NO? THEY BROUGHT THE WOMAN TO BE MY MEAT, BUT WERE DEVOURED THEMSELVES.
THEY WERE GOOD, TOO.
THE BOOK WAS RIGHT. AND SO IS MOTHER JATHI.
YOU'RE A DEMON! A CREATURE OF DARKNESS!
I AM ONE OF THE FIRST. THE GREAT OLD ONES. BUT THE GODDESS HAS NO KINDRED, SO I MUST BEAR ANOTHER NAME.
TAKE ME AWAY FROM THIS. I DON'T WANT TO SEE ANY MORE.
YOU MUST. THIS IS THE MOST IMPORTANT PART.
LOOK AT THE WOMAN.
SHE'S DYING! DID YOU CURSE HER?
IT WAS THE SORCERER, NOT I. HE SPELL-TRAPPED THEM, THE SACRIFICE AND THE SERVANTS ALIKE.
BAITED THEM WITH ENCHANTMENTS OF LETHAL POWER.
IN FEEDING ON THOSE MEN, I HAD INGESTED SORCERIES.
THEY WEAKENED ME, MADE ME SLEEP.
AND IN MY SLEEP, IMERIN TETH BOUND ME.
THE BOOK SAYS HE FOUGHT YOU.
IF WE HAD FOUGHT, I WOULD HAVE EATEN HIS HEART. YOU HAVE NOT SEEN ME UNBOUND, MOTH.
YOU DON'T KNOW WHAT FEATS I WAS CAPABLE OF.
WELL, YOU'VE SHOWN ME SOME OF THEM.
I MEAN FEATS OF STRENGTH, OF POWER.
I MEAN EATING PEOPLE!

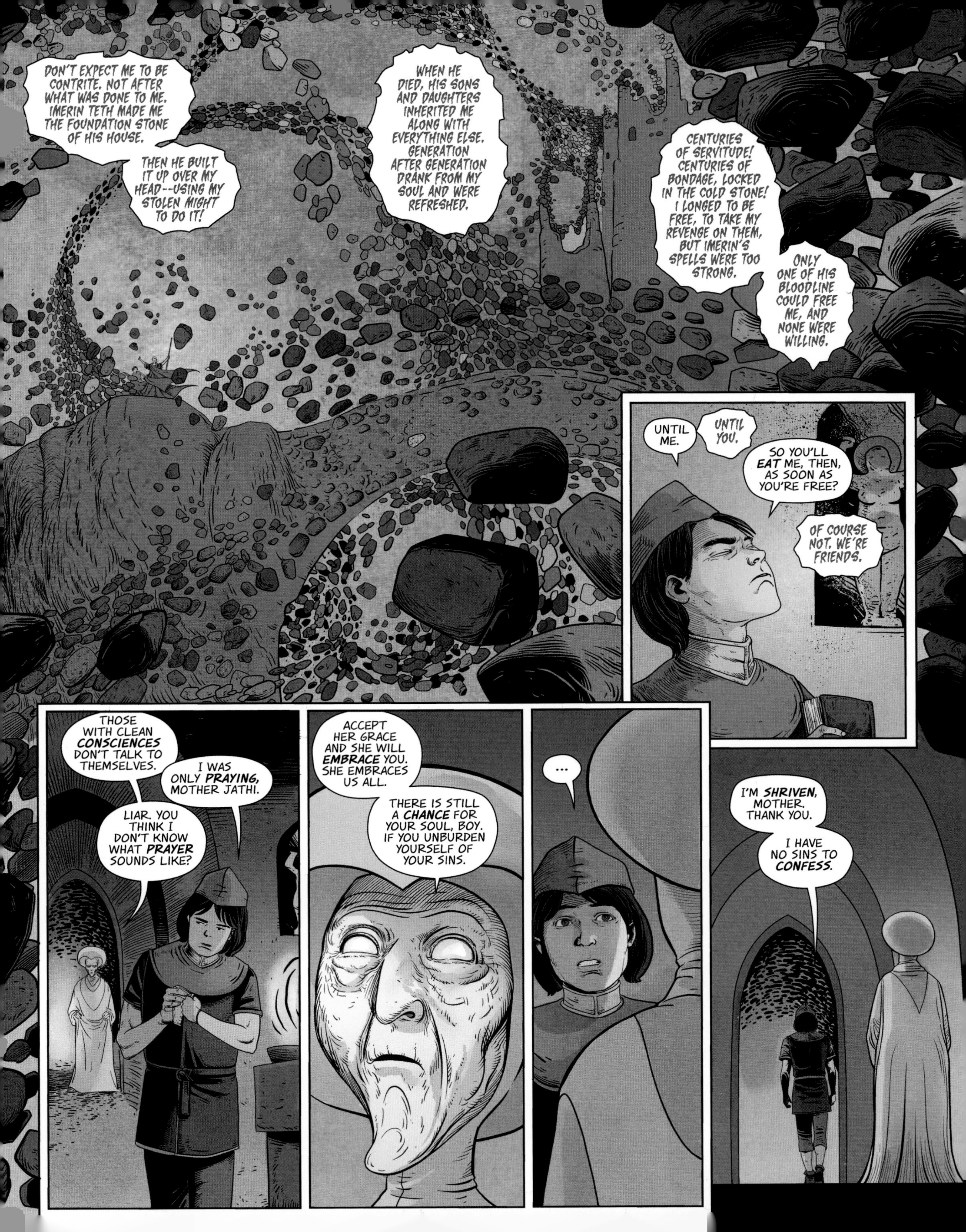
DON'T EXPECT ME TO BE CONTRITE. NOT AFTER WHAT WAS DONE TO ME. IMERIN TETH MADE ME THE FOUNDATION STONE OF HIS HOUSE.
THEN HE BUILT IT UP OVER MY HEAD--USING MY STOLEN MIGHT TO DO IT!
WHEN HE DIED, HIS SONS AND DAUGHTERS INHERITED ME ALONG WITH EVERYTHING ELSE. GENERATION AFTER GENERATION DRANK FROM MY SOUL AND WERE REFRESHED.
CENTURIES OF SERVITUDE! CENTURIES OF BONDAGE, LOCKED IN THE COLD STONE! I LONGED TO BE FREE, TO TAKE MY REVENGE ON THEM, BUT IMERIN'S SPELLS WERE TOO STRONG.
ONLY ONE OF HIS BLOODLINE COULD FREE ME, AND NONE WERE WILLING.
UNTIL ME.
UNTIL YOU.
SO YOU'LL EAT ME, THEN, AS SOON AS YOU'RE FREE?
OF COURSE NOT. WE'RE FRIENDS.
THOSE WITH CLEAN CONSCIENCES DON'T TALK TO THEMSELVES.
I WAS ONLY PRAYING, MOTHER JATHI.
LIAR. YOU THINK I DON'T KNOW WHAT PRAYER SOUNDS LIKE?
ACCEPT HER GRACE AND SHE WILL EMBRACE YOU. SHE EMBRACES US ALL.
THERE IS STILL A CHANCE FOR YOUR SOUL, BOY. IF YOU UNBURDEN YOURSELF OF YOUR SINS.
...
I'M SHRIVEN, MOTHER. THANK YOU.
I HAVE NO SINS TO CONFESS.

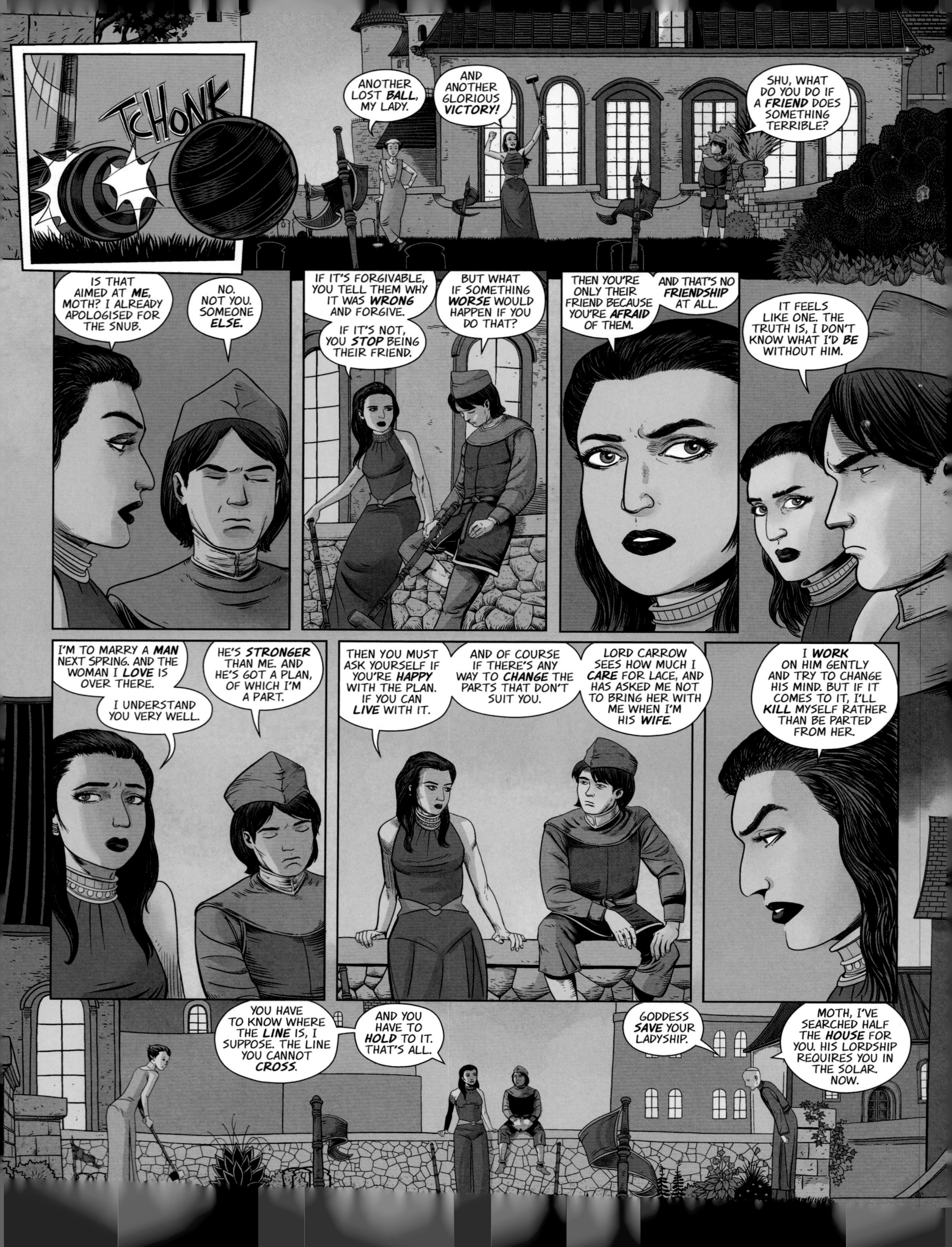
TCHONK
ANOTHER LOST BALL, MY LADY.
AND ANOTHER GLORIOUS VICTORY!
SHU, WHAT DO YOU DO IF A FRIEND DOES SOMETHING TERRIBLE?
IS THAT AIMED AT ME, MOTH? I ALREADY APOLOGISED FOR THE SNUB.
NO. NOT YOU. SOMEONE ELSE.
IF IT'S FORGIVABLE, YOU TELL THEM WHY IT WAS WRONG AND FORGIVE.
IF IT'S NOT, YOU STOP BEING THEIR FRIEND.
BUT WHAT IF SOMETHING WORSE WOULD HAPPEN IF YOU DO THAT?
THEN YOU'RE ONLY THEIR FRIEND BECAUSE YOU'RE AFRAID OF THEM.
AND THAT'S NO FRIENDSHIP AT ALL.
IT FEELS LIKE ONE. THE TRUTH IS, I DON'T KNOW WHAT I'D BE WITHOUT HIM.
I'M TO MARRY A MAN NEXT SPRING. AND THE WOMAN I LOVE IS OVER THERE.
I UNDERSTAND YOU VERY WELL.
HE'S STRONGER THAN ME. AND HE'S GOT A PLAN, OF WHICH I'M A PART.
THEN YOU MUST ASK YOURSELF IF YOU'RE HAPPY WITH THE PLAN. IF YOU CAN LIVE WITH IT.
AND OF COURSE IF THERE'S ANY WAY TO CHANGE THE PARTS THAT DON'T SUIT YOU.
LORD CARROW SEES HOW MUCH I CARE FOR LACE, AND HAS ASKED ME NOT TO BRING HER WITH ME WHEN I'M HIS WIFE.
I WORK ON HIM GENTLY AND TRY TO CHANGE HIS MIND. BUT IF IT COMES TO IT, I'LL KILL MYSELF RATHER THAN BE PARTED FROM HER.
YOU HAVE TO KNOW WHERE THE LINE IS, I SUPPOSE. THE LINE YOU CANNOT CROSS.
AND YOU HAVE TO HOLD TO IT. THAT'S ALL.
GODDESS SAVE YOUR LADYSHIP.
MOTH, I'VE SEARCHED HALF THE HOUSE FOR YOU. HIS LORDSHIP REQUIRES YOU IN THE SOLAR. NOW.

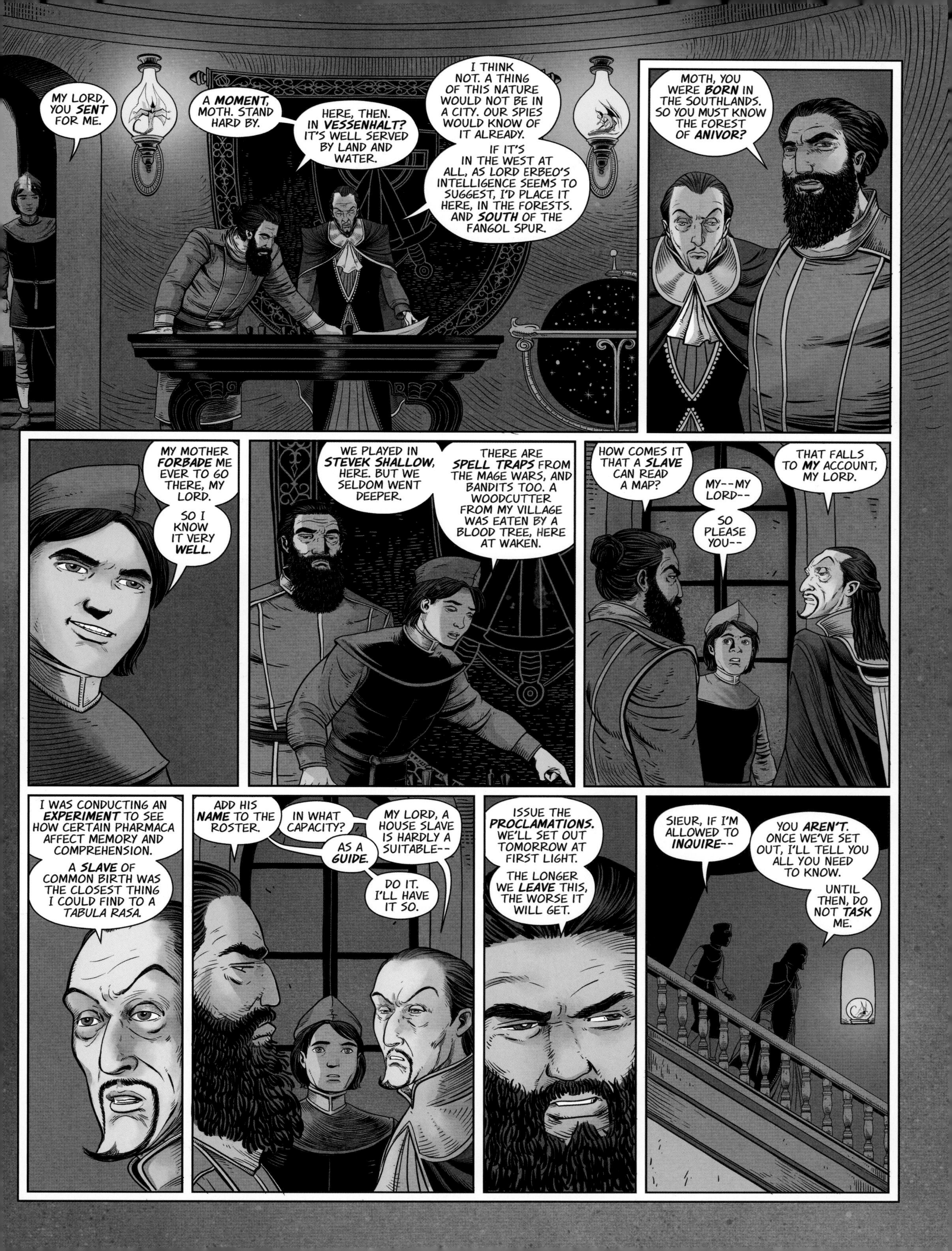
MY LORD, YOU **SENT** FOR ME.
A **MOMENT**, MOTH. STAND HARD BY.
HERE, THEN. IN **VESSENHALT?** IT'S WELL SERVED BY LAND AND WATER.
I THINK NOT. A THING OF THIS NATURE WOULD NOT BE IN A CITY. OUR SPIES WOULD KNOW OF IT ALREADY.
IF IT'S IN THE WEST AT ALL, AS LORD ERBEO'S INTELLIGENCE SEEMS TO SUGGEST, I'D PLACE IT HERE, IN THE FORESTS. AND **SOUTH** OF THE FANGOL SPUR.
MOTH, YOU WERE **BORN** IN THE SOUTHLANDS. SO YOU MUST KNOW THE FOREST OF **ANIVOR?**
MY MOTHER **FORBADE** ME EVER TO GO THERE, MY LORD.
SO I KNOW IT VERY **WELL**.
WE PLAYED IN **STEVEK SHALLOW**, HERE. BUT WE SELDOM WENT DEEPER.
THERE ARE **SPELL TRAPS** FROM THE MAGE WARS, AND BANDITS TOO. A WOODCUTTER FROM MY VILLAGE WAS EATEN BY A BLOOD TREE, HERE AT WAKEN.
HOW COMES IT THAT A **SLAVE** CAN READ A MAP?
MY--MY LORD--
SO PLEASE YOU--
THAT FALLS TO **MY** ACCOUNT, MY LORD.
I WAS CONDUCTING AN **EXPERIMENT** TO SEE HOW CERTAIN PHARMACA AFFECT MEMORY AND COMPREHENSION.
A **SLAVE** OF COMMON BIRTH WAS THE CLOSEST THING I COULD FIND TO A TABULA RASA.
ADD HIS **NAME** TO THE ROSTER.
IN WHAT CAPACITY?
AS A **GUIDE**.
MY LORD, A HOUSE SLAVE IS HARDLY A SUITABLE--
DO IT. I'LL HAVE IT SO.
ISSUE THE **PROCLAMATIONS.** WE'LL SET OUT TOMORROW AT FIRST LIGHT.
THE LONGER WE **LEAVE** THIS, THE WORSE IT WILL GET.
SIEUR, IF I'M ALLOWED TO **INQUIRE**--
YOU **AREN'T**. ONCE WE'VE SET OUT, I'LL TELL YOU ALL YOU NEED TO KNOW.
UNTIL THEN, DO NOT **TASK** ME.

Know by these presents, the houses of Aldercrest and Hask are joined in amity.

In recognition of which, Lord *Erbeo* of Hask will wed the Lady Geren Aldercrest on the eighth Mardile, the day of Lady *Shurubai's* marriage to Lord Vistin Carrow.

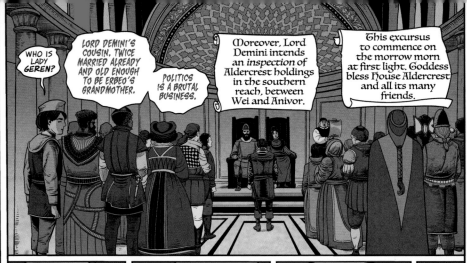

WHO IS LADY *GEREN*?

LORD DEMINI'S COUSIN. TWICE MARRIED ALREADY AND OLD ENOUGH TO BE ERBEO'S GRANDMOTHER.

POLITICS IS A BRUTAL BUSINESS.

Moreover, Lord Demini intends an *inspection* of Aldercrest holdings in the southern reach, between Wei and Anivor.

This excursus to commence on the morrow morn at first light. Goddess bless House Aldercrest and all its many friends.

DEMINI! MUST WE *LEAVE* HIGHEST HOUSE, THEN? IN MIDSUMMER?

NOT AT ALL, ESSU. I'LL UNDERTAKE THIS *JOURNEY* WITH CAEL EXTAT.

YOU AND SHURUBAI MAY KEEP YOUR HOUSEHOLDS *HERE* UNTIL MY RETURN.

THE SOUTHLANDS ARE *DANGEROUS*, MY LOVE.

AS AM *I*, MY LADY.

AND THIS "INSPECTION" WAS NOT ON YOUR *SCHEDULE* WHEN WE SPOKE YESTERNIGHT.

WHEN THERE IS DANGER A *WISE* MAN ACTS BETIMES.

WELL?

I'M WAITING FOR YOU TO TELL ME THAT I CAN'T *LEAVE* HERE.

THAT'S WHAT YOU TOLD ME *LAST* TIME.

THIS TIME IS DIFFERENT. I'M LETTING YOU LEAVE AS A MARK OF THE TRUST THAT EXISTS BETWEEN US.

BESIDES, I WISH TO FULFILL ANOTHER ASPECT OF OUR BARGAIN. LOOK DOWN AT YOUR FEET.

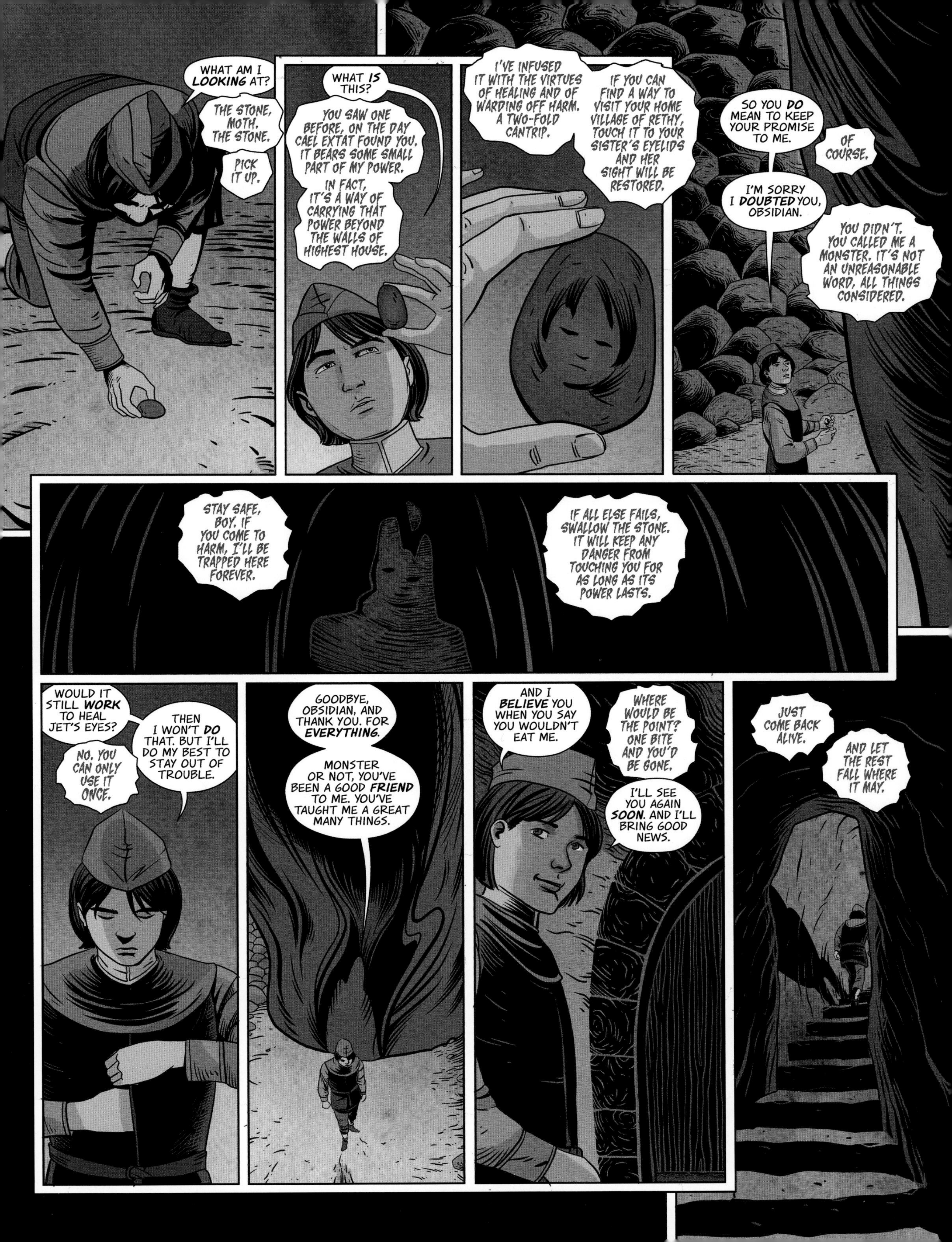
WHAT AM I LOOKING AT?
THE STONE, MOTH. THE STONE.
PICK IT UP.
WHAT IS THIS?
YOU SAW ONE BEFORE, ON THE DAY CAEL EXTAT FOUND YOU. IT BEARS SOME SMALL PART OF MY POWER.
IN FACT, IT'S A WAY OF CARRYING THAT POWER BEYOND THE WALLS OF HIGHEST HOUSE.
I'VE INFUSED IT WITH THE VIRTUES OF HEALING AND OF WARDING OFF HARM. A TWO-FOLD CANTRIP.
IF YOU CAN FIND A WAY TO VISIT YOUR HOME VILLAGE OF RETHY, TOUCH IT TO YOUR SISTER'S EYELIDS AND HER SIGHT WILL BE RESTORED.
SO YOU DO MEAN TO KEEP YOUR PROMISE TO ME.
OF COURSE.
I'M SORRY I DOUBTED YOU, OBSIDIAN.
YOU DIDN'T. YOU CALLED ME A MONSTER. IT'S NOT AN UNREASONABLE WORD, ALL THINGS CONSIDERED.
STAY SAFE, BOY. IF YOU COME TO HARM, I'LL BE TRAPPED HERE FOREVER.
IF ALL ELSE FAILS, SWALLOW THE STONE. IT WILL KEEP ANY DANGER FROM TOUCHING YOU FOR AS LONG AS ITS POWER LASTS.
WOULD IT STILL WORK TO HEAL JET'S EYES?
NO. YOU CAN ONLY USE IT ONCE.
THEN I WON'T DO THAT. BUT I'LL DO MY BEST TO STAY OUT OF TROUBLE.
GOODBYE, OBSIDIAN, AND THANK YOU. FOR EVERYTHING.
MONSTER OR NOT, YOU'VE BEEN A GOOD FRIEND TO ME. YOU'VE TAUGHT ME A GREAT MANY THINGS.
AND I BELIEVE YOU WHEN YOU SAY YOU WOULDN'T EAT ME.
WHERE WOULD BE THE POINT? ONE BITE AND YOU'D BE GONE.
I'LL SEE YOU AGAIN SOON. AND I'LL BRING GOOD NEWS.
JUST COME BACK ALIVE.
AND LET THE REST FALL WHERE IT MAY.

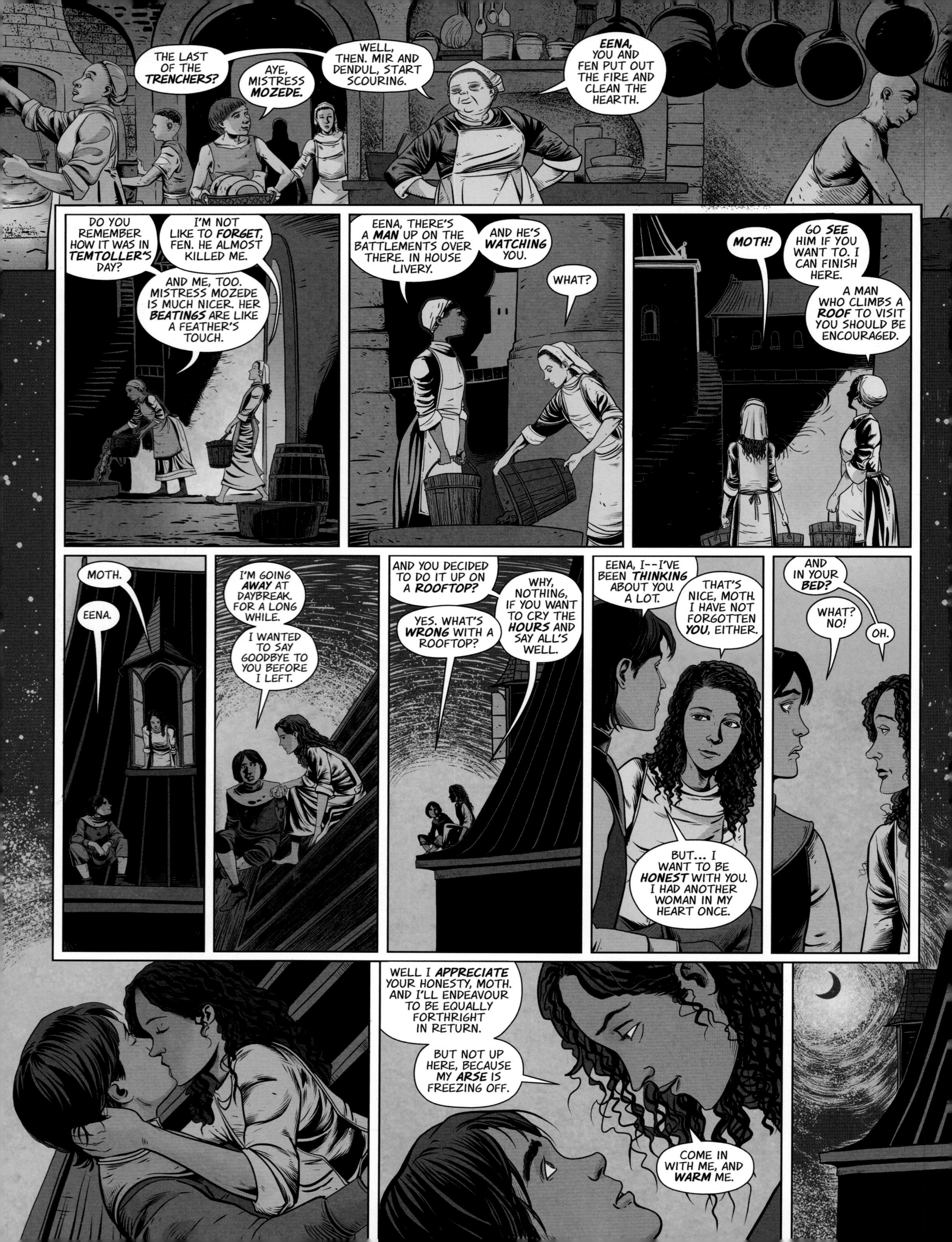
THE LAST OF THE TRENCHERS?
AYE, MISTRESS MOZEDE.
WELL, THEN. MIR AND DENDUL, START SCOURING.
EENA, YOU AND FEN PUT OUT THE FIRE AND CLEAN THE HEARTH.
DO YOU REMEMBER HOW IT WAS IN TEMTOLLER'S DAY?
I'M NOT LIKE TO FORGET, FEN. HE ALMOST KILLED ME.
AND ME, TOO. MISTRESS MOZEDE IS MUCH NICER. HER BEATINGS ARE LIKE A FEATHER'S TOUCH.
EENA, THERE'S A MAN UP ON THE BATTLEMENTS OVER THERE. IN HOUSE LIVERY.
AND HE'S WATCHING YOU.
WHAT?
MOTH!
GO SEE HIM IF YOU WANT TO. I CAN FINISH HERE.
A MAN WHO CLIMBS A ROOF TO VISIT YOU SHOULD BE ENCOURAGED.
MOTH.
EENA.
I'M GOING AWAY AT DAYBREAK. FOR A LONG WHILE.
I WANTED TO SAY GOODBYE TO YOU BEFORE I LEFT.
AND YOU DECIDED TO DO IT UP ON A ROOFTOP?
YES. WHAT'S WRONG WITH A ROOFTOP?
WHY, NOTHING, IF YOU WANT TO CRY THE HOURS AND SAY ALL'S WELL.
EENA, I--I'VE BEEN THINKING ABOUT YOU. A LOT.
THAT'S NICE, MOTH. I HAVE NOT FORGOTTEN YOU, EITHER.
BUT... I WANT TO BE HONEST WITH YOU. I HAD ANOTHER WOMAN IN MY HEART ONCE.
AND IN YOUR BED?
WHAT? NO!
OH.
WELL I APPRECIATE YOUR HONESTY, MOTH. AND I'LL ENDEAVOUR TO BE EQUALLY FORTHRIGHT IN RETURN.
BUT NOT UP HERE, BECAUSE MY ARSE IS FREEZING OFF.
COME IN WITH ME, AND WARM ME.

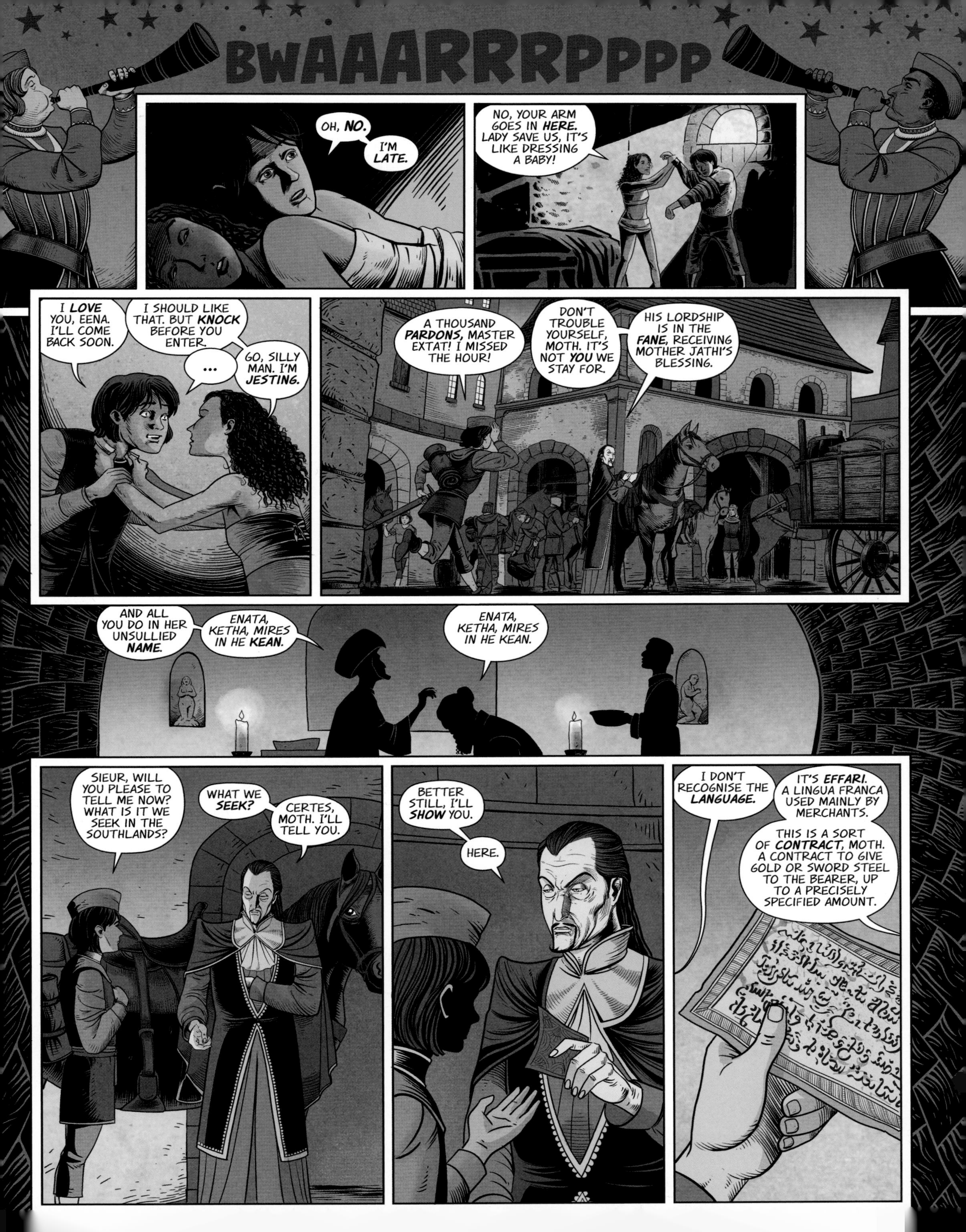
BWAAARRRPPPP
OH, NO.
I'M LATE.
NO, YOUR ARM GOES IN HERE. LADY SAVE US, IT'S LIKE DRESSING A BABY!
I LOVE YOU, EENA. I'LL COME BACK SOON.
I SHOULD LIKE THAT. BUT KNOCK BEFORE YOU ENTER.
...
GO, SILLY MAN. I'M JESTING.
A THOUSAND PARDONS, MASTER EXTAT! I MISSED THE HOUR!
DON'T TROUBLE YOURSELF, MOTH. IT'S NOT YOU WE STAY FOR.
HIS LORDSHIP IS IN THE FANE, RECEIVING MOTHER JATHI'S BLESSING.
AND ALL YOU DO IN HER UNSULLIED NAME.
ENATA, KETHA, MIRES IN HE KEAN.
ENATA, KETHA, MIRES IN HE KEAN.
SIEUR, WILL YOU PLEASE TO TELL ME NOW? WHAT IS IT WE SEEK IN THE SOUTHLANDS?
WHAT WE SEEK?
CERTES, MOTH. I'LL TELL YOU.
BETTER STILL, I'LL SHOW YOU.
HERE.
I DON'T RECOGNISE THE LANGUAGE.
IT'S EFFARI. A LINGUA FRANCA USED MAINLY BY MERCHANTS.
THIS IS A SORT OF CONTRACT, MOTH. A CONTRACT TO GIVE GOLD OR SWORD STEEL TO THE BEARER, UP TO A PRECISELY SPECIFIED AMOUNT.

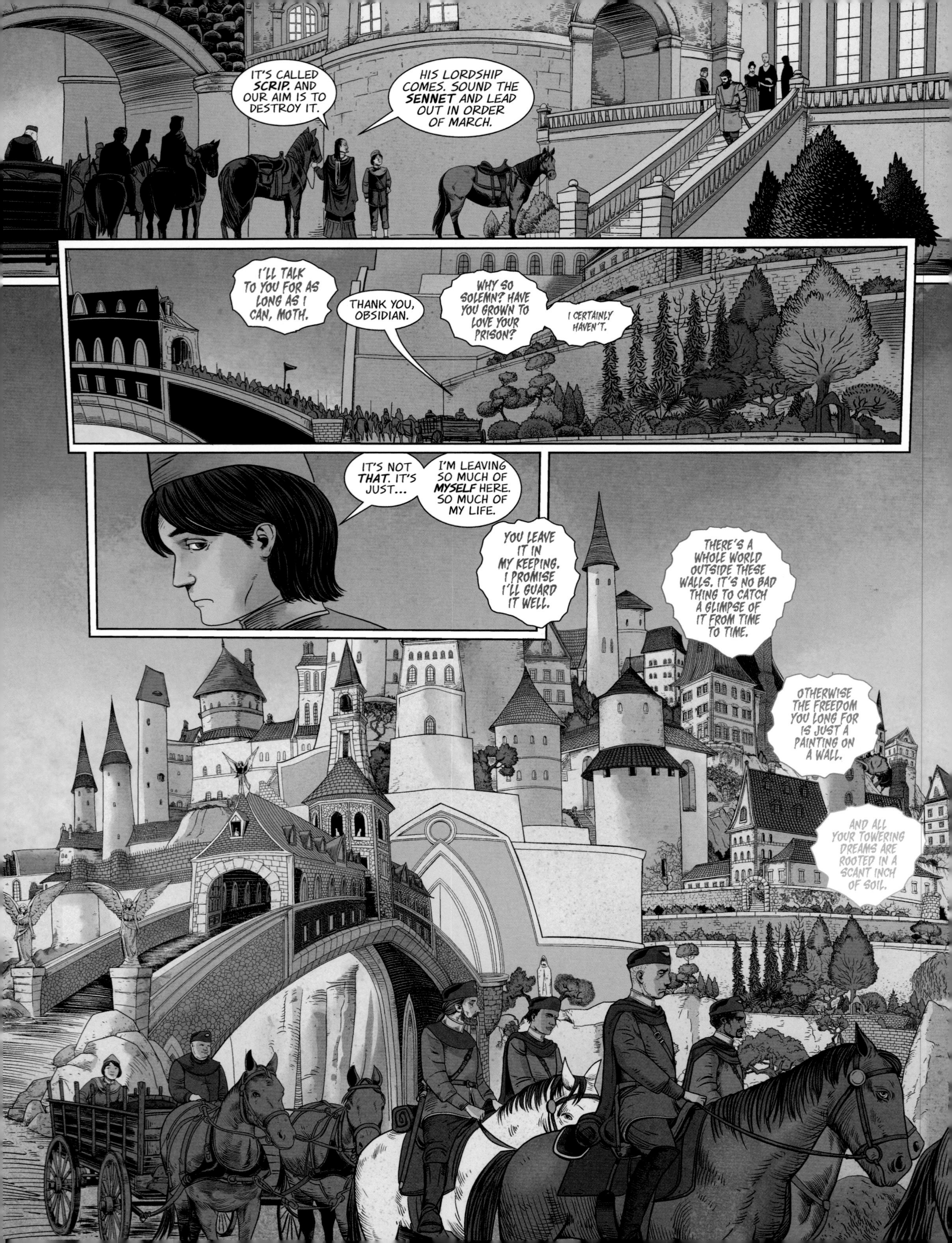
IT'S CALLED SCRIP. AND OUR AIM IS TO DESTROY IT.
HIS LORDSHIP COMES. SOUND THE SENNET AND LEAD OUT IN ORDER OF MARCH.
I'LL TALK TO YOU FOR AS LONG AS I CAN, MOTH.
THANK YOU, OBSIDIAN.
WHY SO SOLEMN? HAVE YOU GROWN TO LOVE YOUR PRISON?
I CERTAINLY HAVEN'T.
IT'S NOT THAT. IT'S JUST...
I'M LEAVING SO MUCH OF MYSELF HERE. SO MUCH OF MY LIFE.
YOU LEAVE IT IN MY KEEPING. I PROMISE I'LL GUARD IT WELL.
THERE'S A WHOLE WORLD OUTSIDE THESE WALLS. IT'S NO BAD THING TO CATCH A GLIMPSE OF IT FROM TIME TO TIME.
OTHERWISE THE FREEDOM YOU LONG FOR IS JUST A PAINTING ON A WALL.
AND ALL YOUR TOWERING DREAMS ARE ROOTED IN A SCANT INCH OF SOIL.

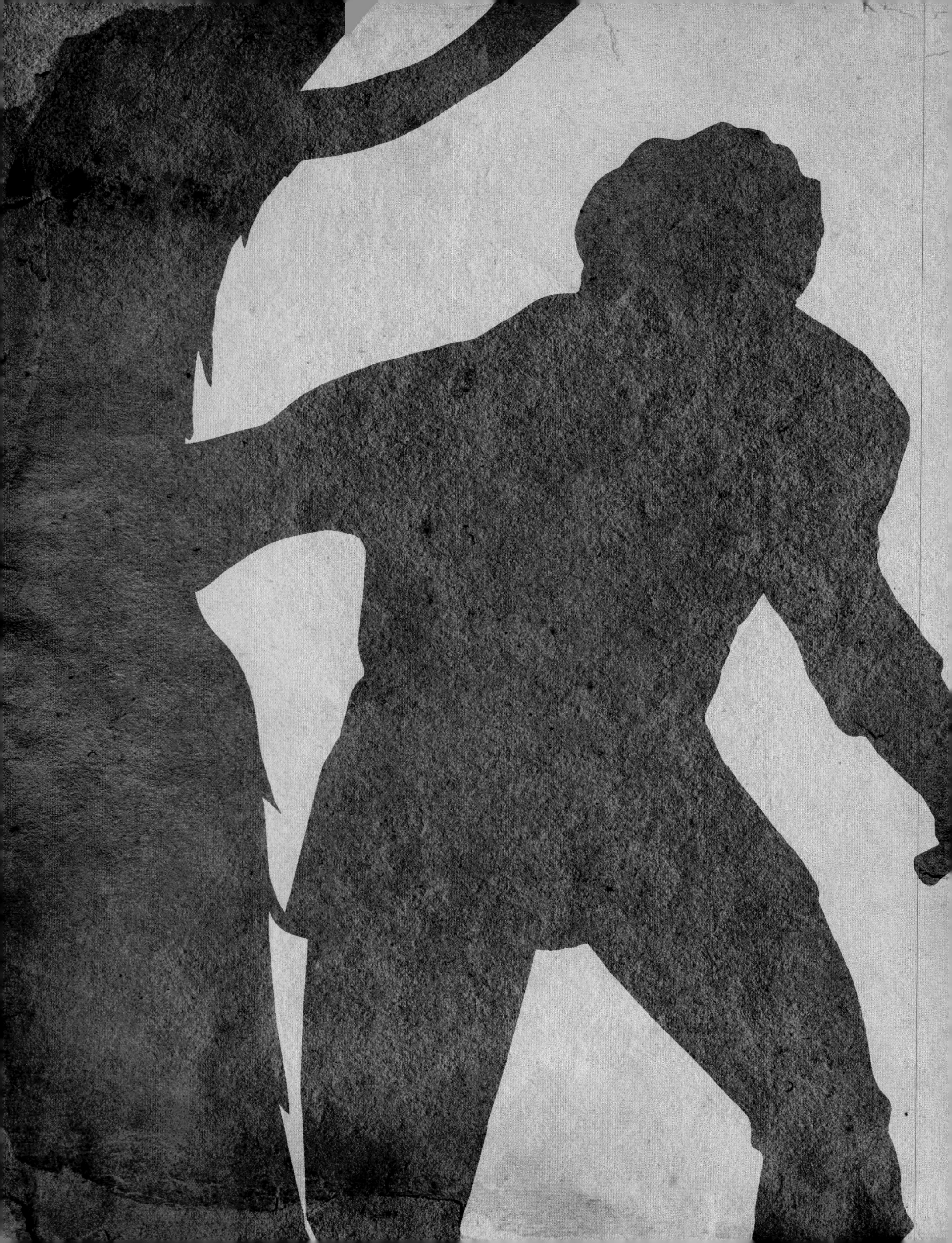

Chapter Six

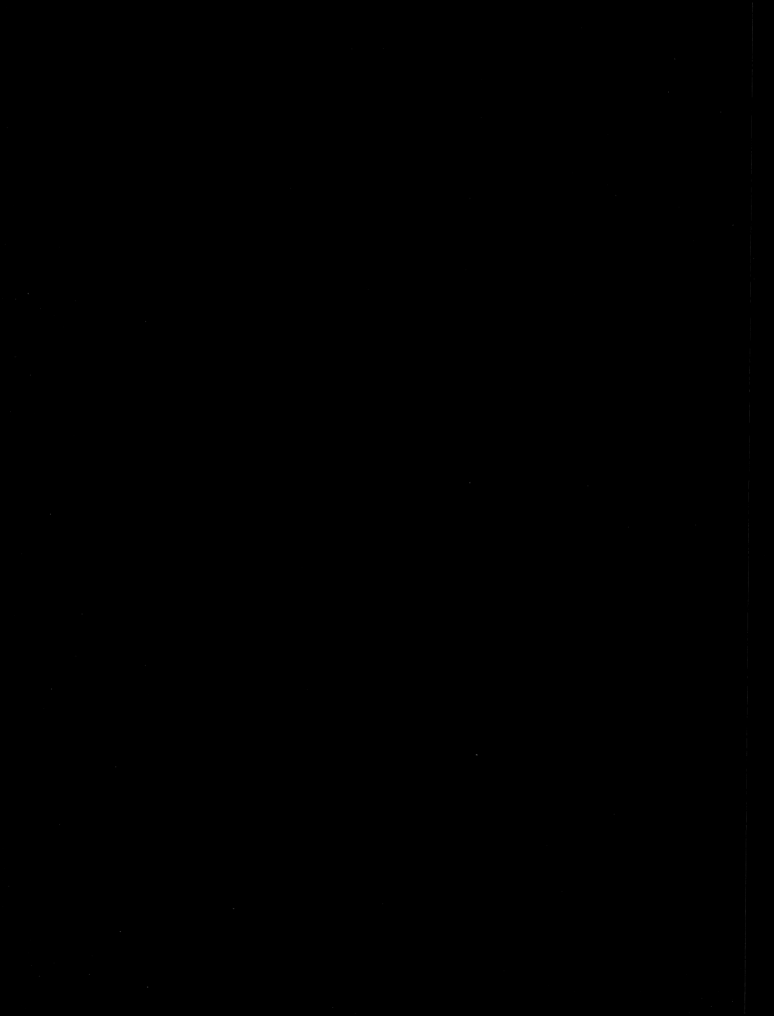

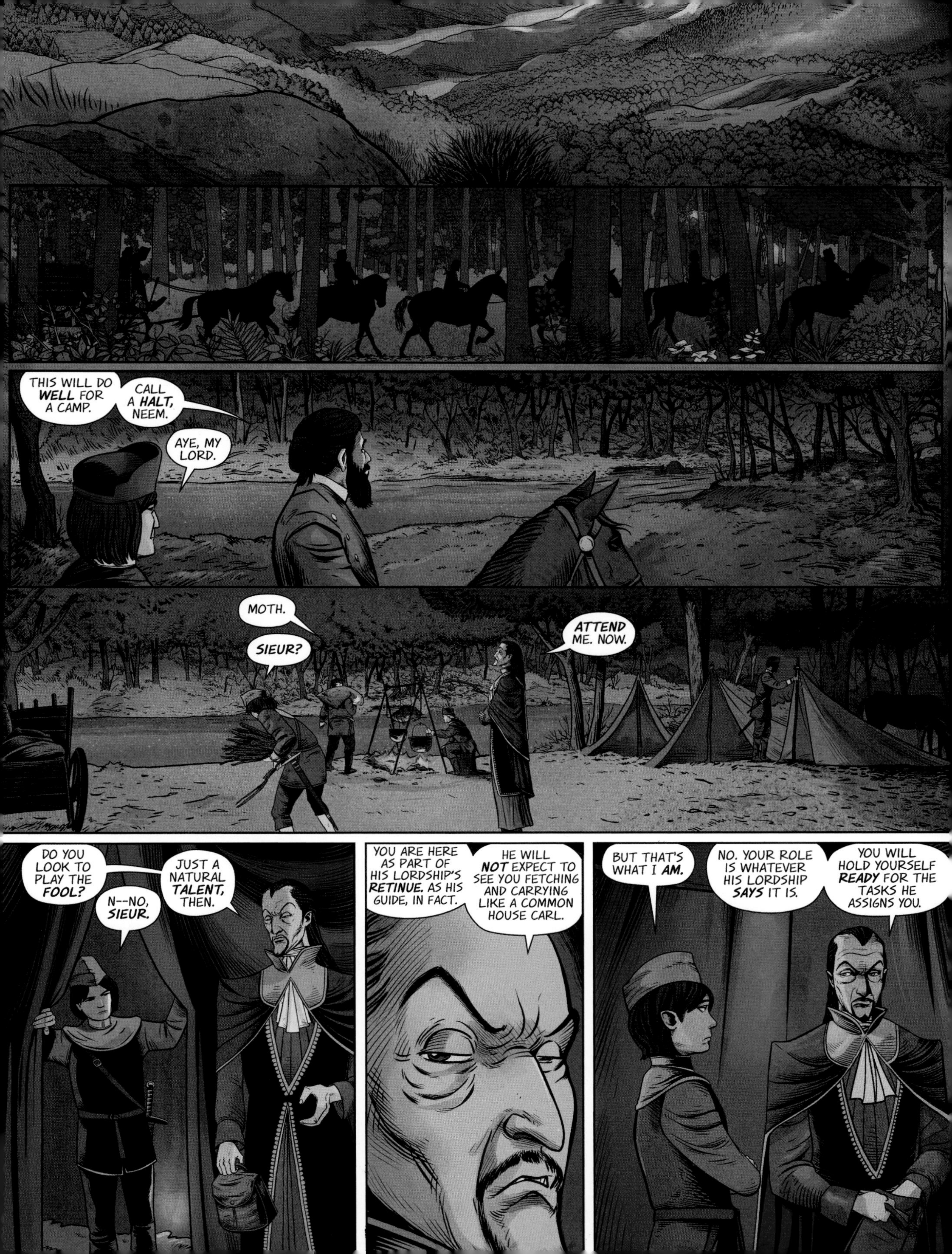
THIS WILL DO **WELL** FOR A CAMP.
CALL A **HALT,** NEEM.
AYE, MY LORD.
MOTH.
SIEUR?
ATTEND ME. NOW.
DO YOU LOOK TO PLAY THE **FOOL?**
N--NO, **SIEUR.**
JUST A NATURAL **TALENT,** THEN.
YOU ARE HERE AS PART OF HIS LORDSHIP'S **RETINUE.** AS HIS GUIDE, IN FACT.
HE WILL **NOT** EXPECT TO SEE YOU FETCHING AND CARRYING LIKE A COMMON HOUSE CARL.
BUT THAT'S WHAT I **AM.**
NO. YOUR ROLE IS WHATEVER HIS LORDSHIP **SAYS** IT IS.
YOU WILL HOLD YOURSELF **READY** FOR THE TASKS HE ASSIGNS YOU.

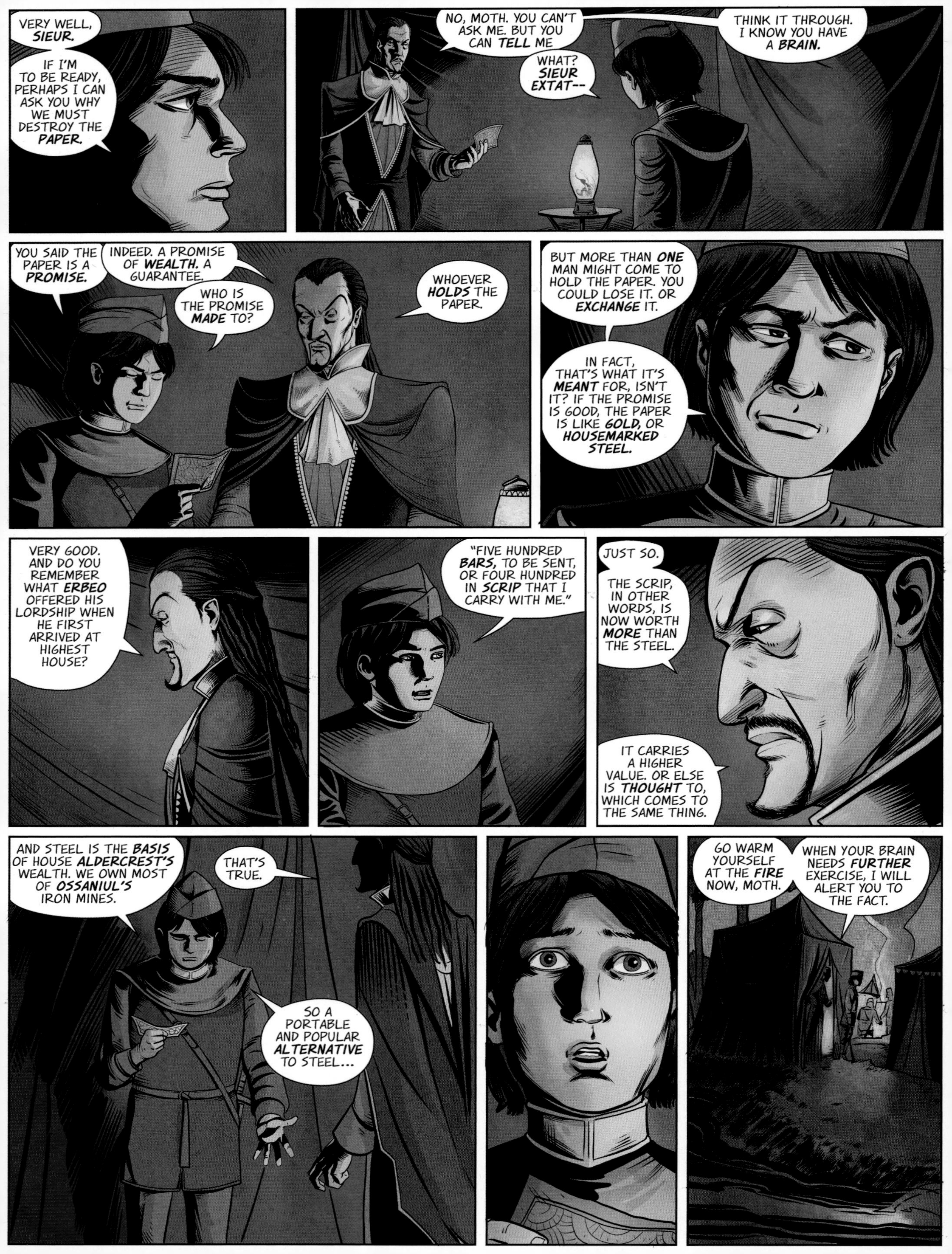
VERY WELL, SIEUR.
IF I'M TO BE READY, PERHAPS I CAN ASK YOU WHY WE MUST DESTROY THE PAPER.
NO, MOTH. YOU CAN'T ASK ME. BUT YOU CAN TELL ME
WHAT? SIEUR EXTAT--
THINK IT THROUGH. I KNOW YOU HAVE A BRAIN.
YOU SAID THE PAPER IS A PROMISE.
INDEED. A PROMISE OF WEALTH. A GUARANTEE.
WHO IS THE PROMISE MADE TO?
WHOEVER HOLDS THE PAPER.
BUT MORE THAN ONE MAN MIGHT COME TO HOLD THE PAPER. YOU COULD LOSE IT. OR EXCHANGE IT.
IN FACT, THAT'S WHAT IT'S MEANT FOR, ISN'T IT? IF THE PROMISE IS GOOD, THE PAPER IS LIKE GOLD, OR HOUSEMARKED STEEL.
VERY GOOD. AND DO YOU REMEMBER WHAT ERBEO OFFERED HIS LORDSHIP WHEN HE FIRST ARRIVED AT HIGHEST HOUSE?
"FIVE HUNDRED BARS, TO BE SENT, OR FOUR HUNDRED IN SCRIP THAT I CARRY WITH ME."
JUST SO.
THE SCRIP, IN OTHER WORDS, IS NOW WORTH MORE THAN THE STEEL.
IT CARRIES A HIGHER VALUE. OR ELSE IS THOUGHT TO, WHICH COMES TO THE SAME THING.
AND STEEL IS THE BASIS OF HOUSE ALDERCREST'S WEALTH. WE OWN MOST OF OSSANIUL'S IRON MINES.
THAT'S TRUE.
SO A PORTABLE AND POPULAR ALTERNATIVE TO STEEL...
GO WARM YOURSELF AT THE FIRE NOW, MOTH.
WHEN YOUR BRAIN NEEDS FURTHER EXERCISE, I WILL ALERT YOU TO THE FACT.

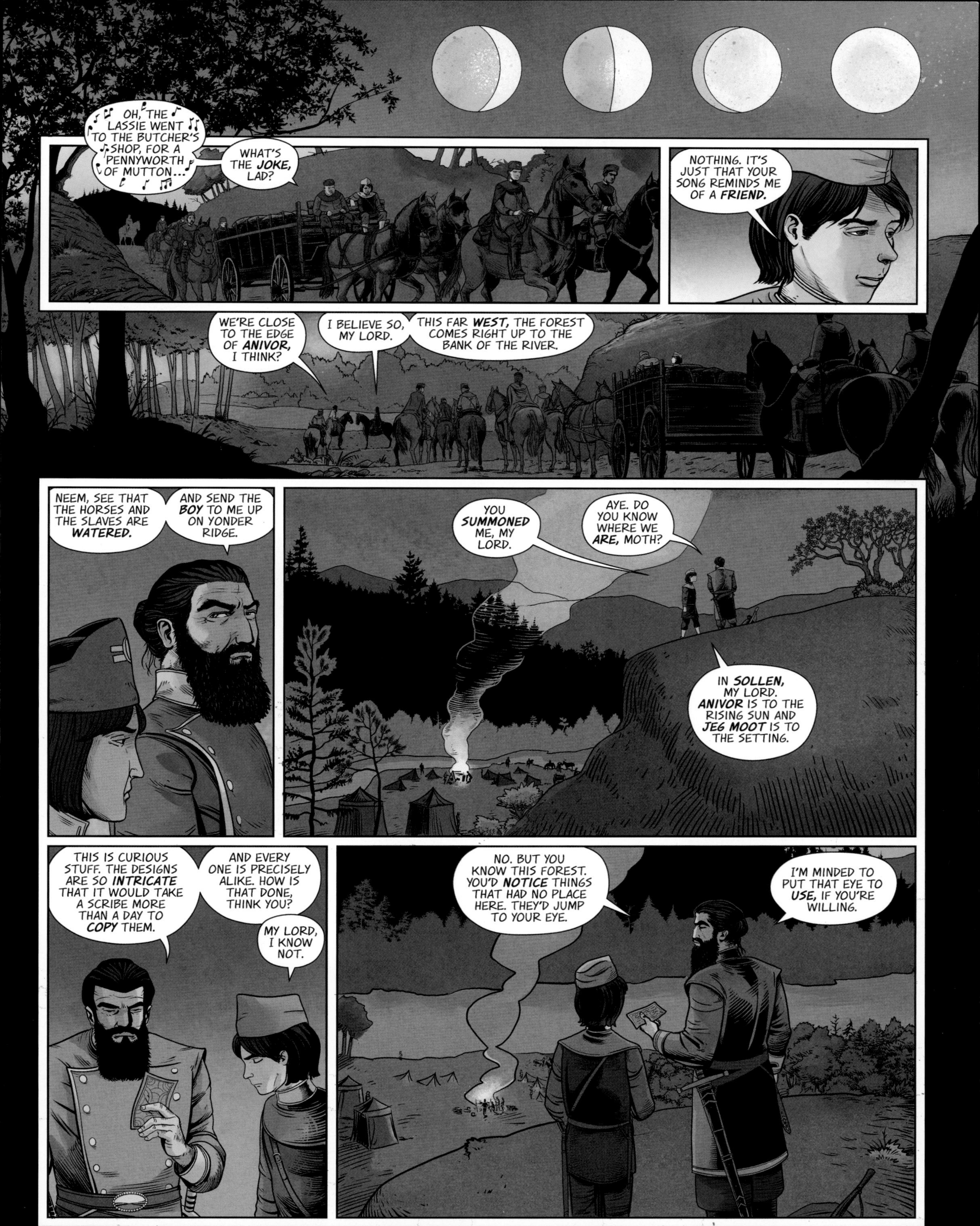

OH, THE LASSIE WENT TO THE BUTCHER'S SHOP, FOR A PENNYWORTH OF MUTTON...
WHAT'S THE JOKE, LAD?
NOTHING. IT'S JUST THAT YOUR SONG REMINDS ME OF A FRIEND.
WE'RE CLOSE TO THE EDGE OF ANIVOR, I THINK?
I BELIEVE SO, MY LORD.
THIS FAR WEST, THE FOREST COMES RIGHT UP TO THE BANK OF THE RIVER.
NEEM, SEE THAT THE HORSES AND THE SLAVES ARE WATERED.
AND SEND THE BOY TO ME UP ON YONDER RIDGE.
YOU SUMMONED ME, MY LORD.
AYE. DO YOU KNOW WHERE WE ARE, MOTH?
IN SOLLEN, MY LORD. ANIVOR IS TO THE RISING SUN AND JEG MOOT IS TO THE SETTING.
THIS IS CURIOUS STUFF. THE DESIGNS ARE SO INTRICATE THAT IT WOULD TAKE A SCRIBE MORE THAN A DAY TO COPY THEM.
AND EVERY ONE IS PRECISELY ALIKE. HOW IS THAT DONE, THINK YOU?
MY LORD, I KNOW NOT.
NO. BUT YOU KNOW THIS FOREST. YOU'D NOTICE THINGS THAT HAD NO PLACE HERE. THEY'D JUMP TO YOUR EYE.
I'M MINDED TO PUT THAT EYE TO USE, IF YOU'RE WILLING.

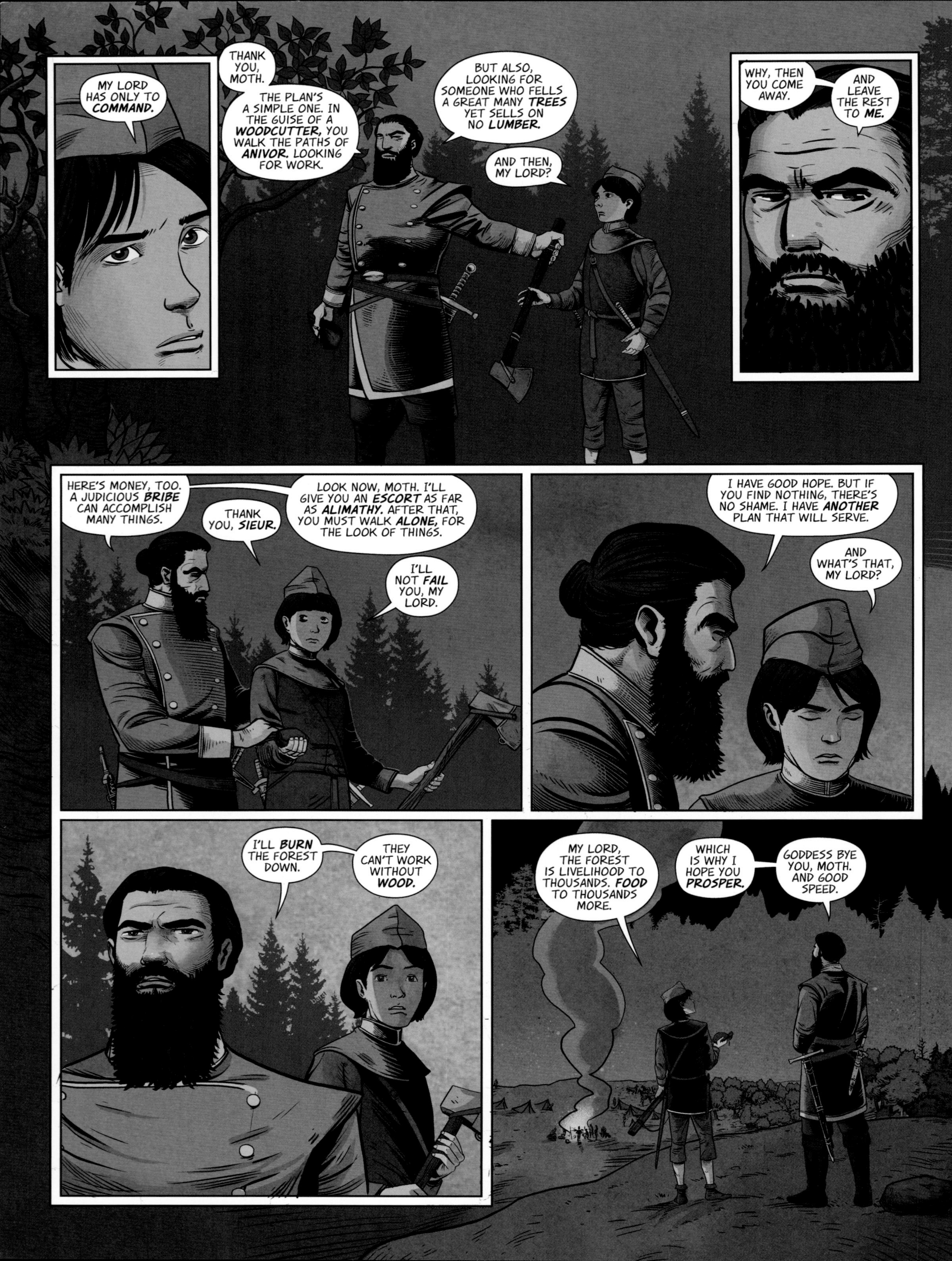
MY LORD HAS ONLY TO COMMAND.
THANK YOU, MOTH.
THE PLAN'S A SIMPLE ONE. IN THE GUISE OF A WOODCUTTER, YOU WALK THE PATHS OF ANIVOR. LOOKING FOR WORK.
BUT ALSO, LOOKING FOR SOMEONE WHO FELLS A GREAT MANY TREES YET SELLS ON NO LUMBER.
AND THEN, MY LORD?
WHY, THEN YOU COME AWAY.
AND LEAVE THE REST TO ME.
HERE'S MONEY, TOO. A JUDICIOUS BRIBE CAN ACCOMPLISH MANY THINGS.
THANK YOU, SIEUR.
LOOK NOW, MOTH. I'LL GIVE YOU AN ESCORT AS FAR AS ALIMATHY. AFTER THAT, YOU MUST WALK ALONE, FOR THE LOOK OF THINGS.
I'LL NOT FAIL YOU, MY LORD.
I HAVE GOOD HOPE. BUT IF YOU FIND NOTHING, THERE'S NO SHAME. I HAVE ANOTHER PLAN THAT WILL SERVE.
AND WHAT'S THAT, MY LORD?
I'LL BURN THE FOREST DOWN.
THEY CAN'T WORK WITHOUT WOOD.
MY LORD, THE FOREST IS LIVELIHOOD TO THOUSANDS. FOOD TO THOUSANDS MORE.
WHICH IS WHY I HOPE YOU PROSPER.
GODDESS BYE YOU, MOTH. AND GOOD SPEED.

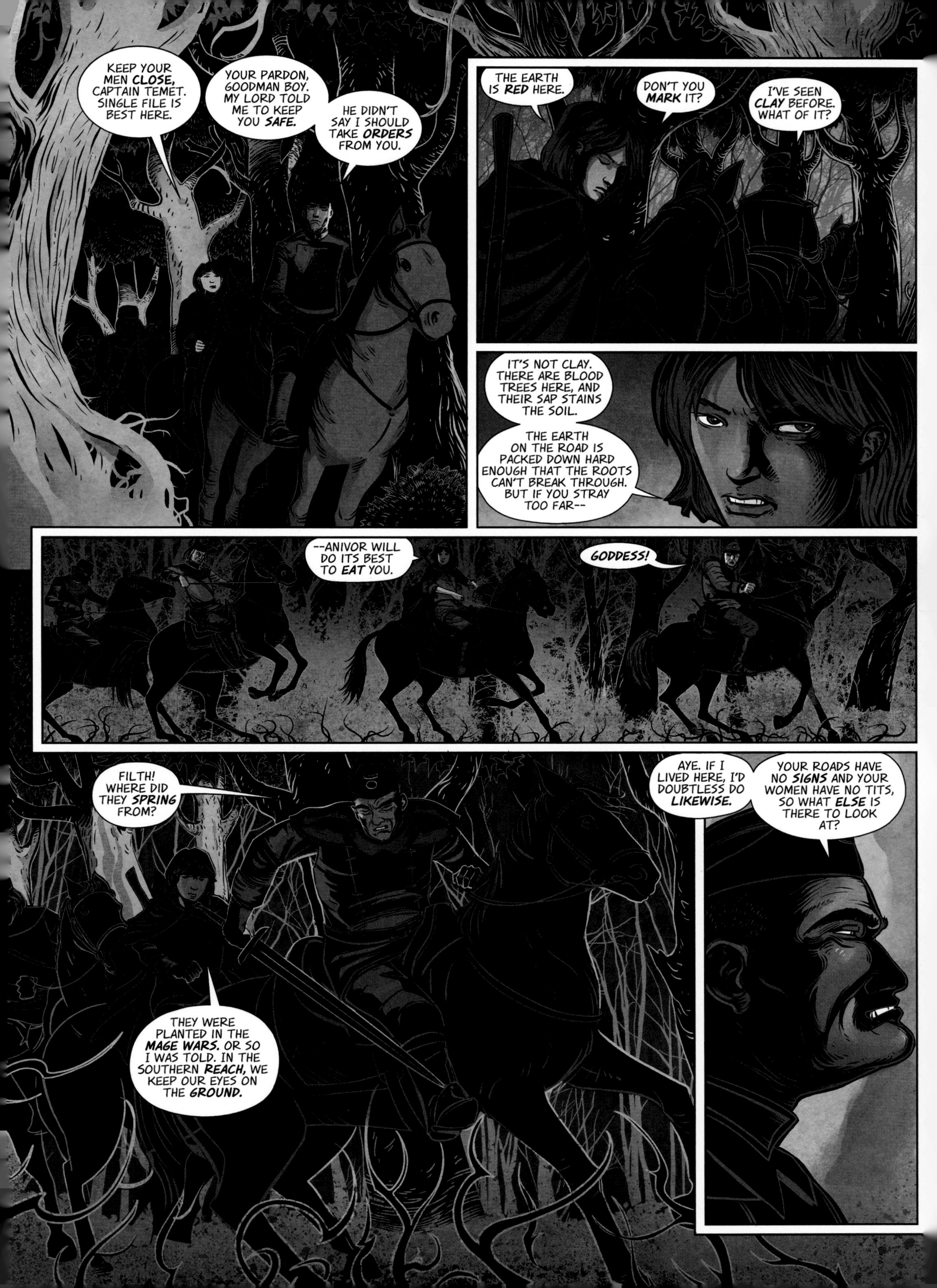
KEEP YOUR MEN CLOSE, CAPTAIN TEMET. SINGLE FILE IS BEST HERE.
YOUR PARDON, GOODMAN BOY. MY LORD TOLD ME TO KEEP YOU SAFE.
HE DIDN'T SAY I SHOULD TAKE ORDERS FROM YOU.
THE EARTH IS RED HERE.
DON'T YOU MARK IT?
I'VE SEEN CLAY BEFORE. WHAT OF IT?
IT'S NOT CLAY. THERE ARE BLOOD TREES HERE, AND THEIR SAP STAINS THE SOIL.
THE EARTH ON THE ROAD IS PACKED DOWN HARD ENOUGH THAT THE ROOTS CAN'T BREAK THROUGH. BUT IF YOU STRAY TOO FAR--
--ANIVOR WILL DO ITS BEST TO EAT YOU.
GODDESS!
FILTH! WHERE DID THEY SPRING FROM?
THEY WERE PLANTED IN THE MAGE WARS. OR SO I WAS TOLD. IN THE SOUTHERN REACH, WE KEEP OUR EYES ON THE GROUND.
AYE. IF I LIVED HERE, I'D DOUBTLESS DO LIKEWISE.
YOUR ROADS HAVE NO SIGNS AND YOUR WOMEN HAVE NO TITS, SO WHAT ELSE IS THERE TO LOOK AT?

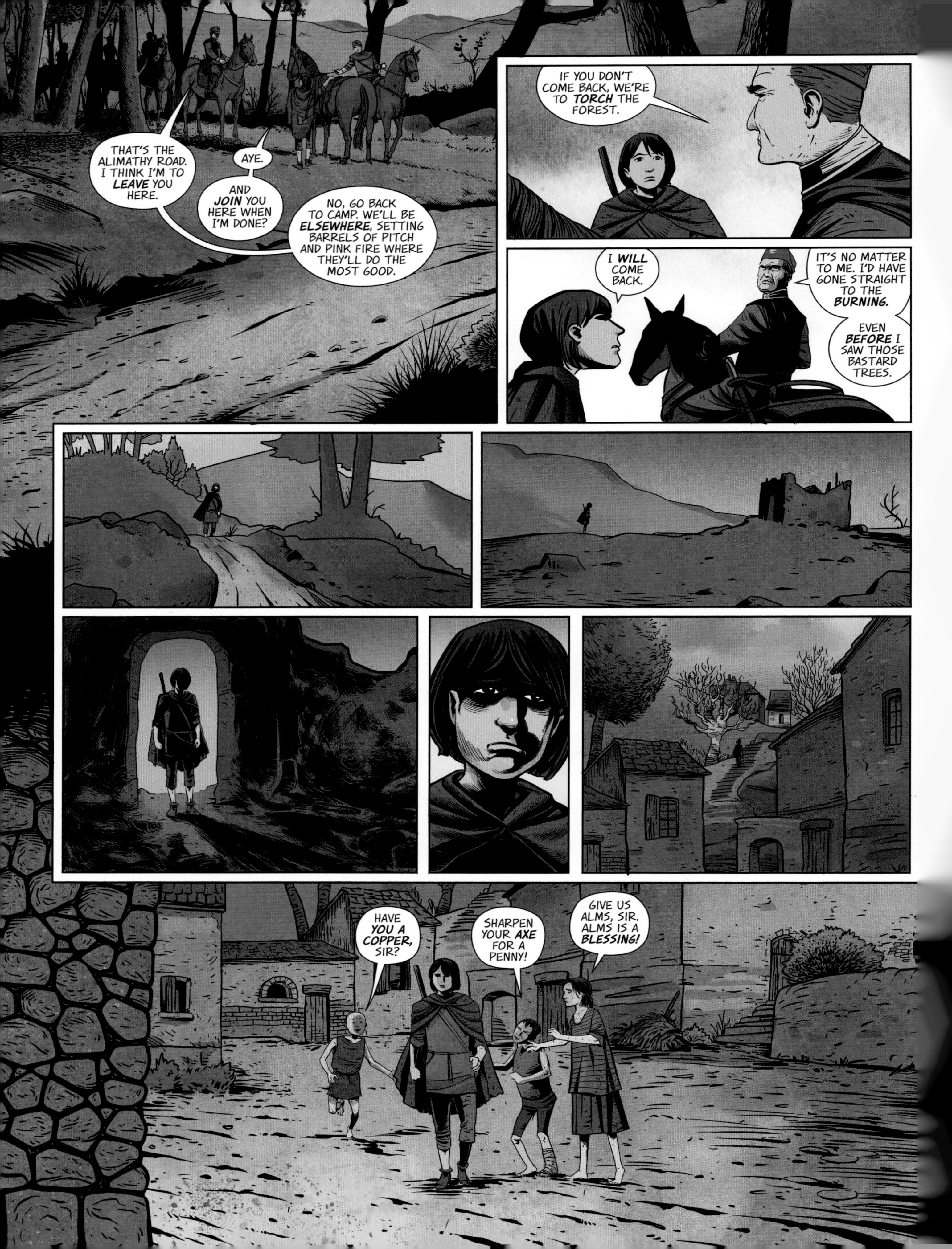

THAT'S THE ALIMATHY ROAD. I THINK I'M TO LEAVE YOU HERE.
AYE.
AND JOIN YOU HERE WHEN I'M DONE?
NO, GO BACK TO CAMP. WE'LL BE ELSEWHERE, SETTING BARRELS OF PITCH AND PINK FIRE WHERE THEY'LL DO THE MOST GOOD.
IF YOU DON'T COME BACK, WE'RE TO TORCH THE FOREST.
I WILL COME BACK.
IT'S NO MATTER TO ME. I'D HAVE GONE STRAIGHT TO THE BURNING.
EVEN BEFORE I SAW THOSE BASTARD TREES.
HAVE YOU A COPPER, SIR?
SHARPEN YOUR AXE FOR A PENNY!
GIVE US ALMS, SIR. ALMS IS A BLESSING!

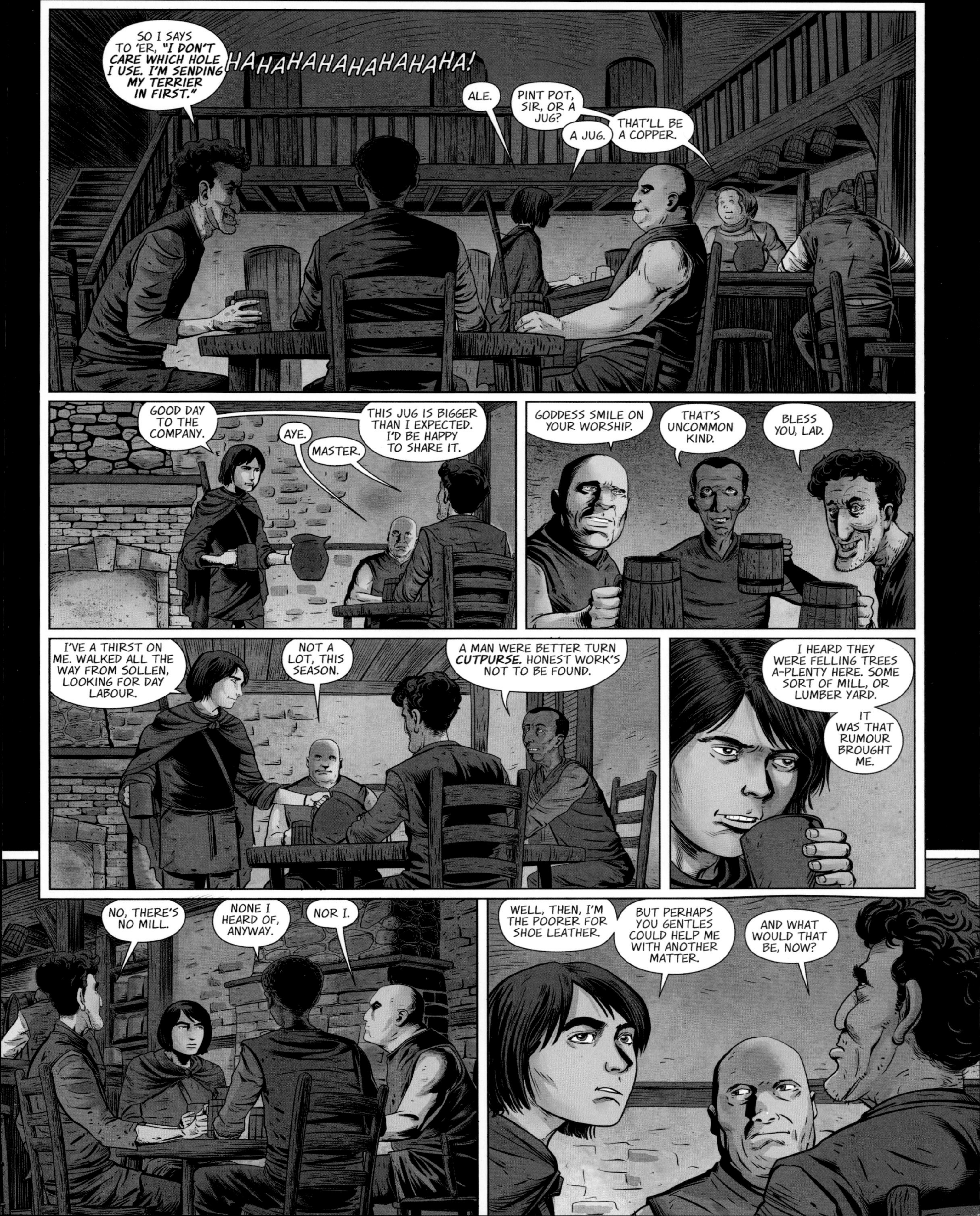
SO I SAYS TO 'ER, "I DON'T CARE WHICH HOLE I USE. I'M SENDING MY TERRIER IN FIRST."
HAHAHAHAHAHAHAHA!
ALE.
PINT POT, SIR, OR A JUG?
A JUG.
THAT'LL BE A COPPER.
GOOD DAY TO THE COMPANY.
AYE.
MASTER.
THIS JUG IS BIGGER THAN I EXPECTED. I'D BE HAPPY TO SHARE IT.
GODDESS SMILE ON YOUR WORSHIP.
THAT'S UNCOMMON KIND.
BLESS YOU, LAD.
I'VE A THIRST ON ME. WALKED ALL THE WAY FROM SOLLEN, LOOKING FOR DAY LABOUR.
NOT A LOT, THIS SEASON.
A MAN WERE BETTER TURN CUTPURSE. HONEST WORK'S NOT TO BE FOUND.
I HEARD THEY WERE FELLING TREES A-PLENTY HERE. SOME SORT OF MILL, OR LUMBER YARD.
IT WAS THAT RUMOUR BROUGHT ME.
NO, THERE'S NO MILL.
NONE I HEARD OF, ANYWAY.
NOR I.
WELL, THEN, I'M THE POORER FOR SHOE LEATHER.
BUT PERHAPS YOU GENTLES COULD HELP ME WITH ANOTHER MATTER.
AND WHAT WOULD THAT BE, NOW?

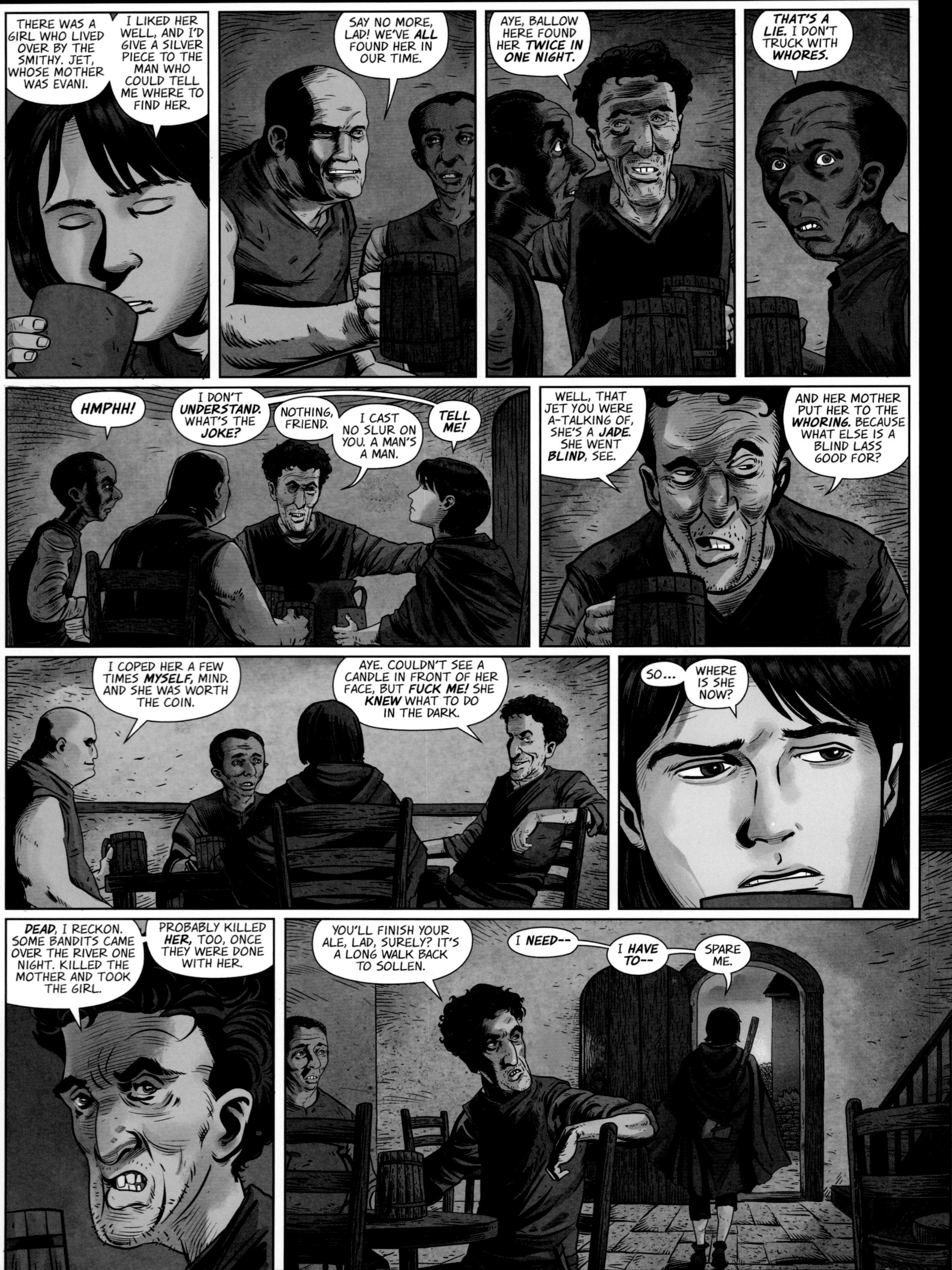

THERE WAS A GIRL WHO LIVED OVER BY THE SMITHY. JET, WHOSE MOTHER WAS EVANI.
I LIKED HER WELL, AND I'D GIVE A SILVER PIECE TO THE MAN WHO COULD TELL ME WHERE TO FIND HER.
SAY NO MORE, LAD! WE'VE ALL FOUND HER IN OUR TIME.
AYE, BALLOW HERE FOUND HER TWICE IN ONE NIGHT.
THAT'S A LIE. I DON'T TRUCK WITH WHORES.
HMPHH!
I DON'T UNDERSTAND. WHAT'S THE JOKE?
NOTHING, FRIEND.
I CAST NO SLUR ON YOU. A MAN'S A MAN.
TELL ME!
WELL, THAT JET YOU WERE A-TALKING OF, SHE'S A JADE. SHE WENT BLIND, SEE.
AND HER MOTHER PUT HER TO THE WHORING. BECAUSE WHAT ELSE IS A BLIND LASS GOOD FOR?
I COPED HER A FEW TIMES MYSELF, MIND. AND SHE WAS WORTH THE COIN.
AYE. COULDN'T SEE A CANDLE IN FRONT OF HER FACE, BUT FUCK ME! SHE KNEW WHAT TO DO IN THE DARK.
SO...
WHERE IS SHE NOW?
DEAD, I RECKON. SOME BANDITS CAME OVER THE RIVER ONE NIGHT. KILLED THE MOTHER AND TOOK THE GIRL.
PROBABLY KILLED HER, TOO, ONCE THEY WERE DONE WITH HER.
YOU'LL FINISH YOUR ALE, LAD, SURELY? IT'S A LONG WALK BACK TO SOLLEN.
I NEED--
I HAVE TO--
SPARE ME.

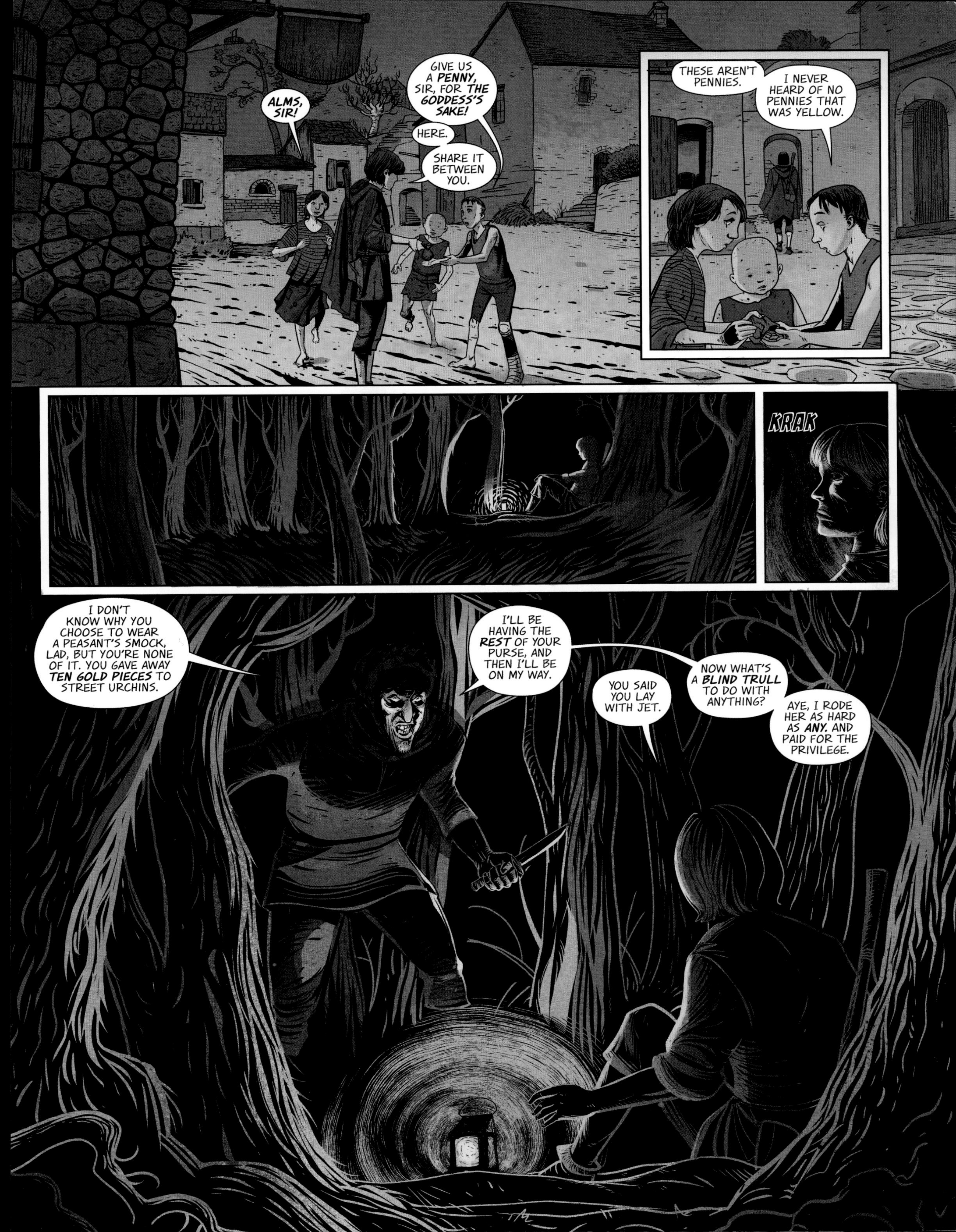
ALMS, SIR!
GIVE US A PENNY, SIR, FOR THE GODDESS'S SAKE!
HERE.
SHARE IT BETWEEN YOU.
THESE AREN'T PENNIES.
I NEVER HEARD OF NO PENNIES THAT WAS YELLOW.
KRAK
I DON'T KNOW WHY YOU CHOOSE TO WEAR A PEASANT'S SMOCK, LAD, BUT YOU'RE NONE OF IT. YOU GAVE AWAY TEN GOLD PIECES TO STREET URCHINS.
I'LL BE HAVING THE REST OF YOUR PURSE, AND THEN I'LL BE ON MY WAY.
NOW WHAT'S A BLIND TRULL TO DO WITH ANYTHING?
YOU SAID YOU LAY WITH JET.
AYE, I RODE HER AS HARD AS ANY. AND PAID FOR THE PRIVILEGE.

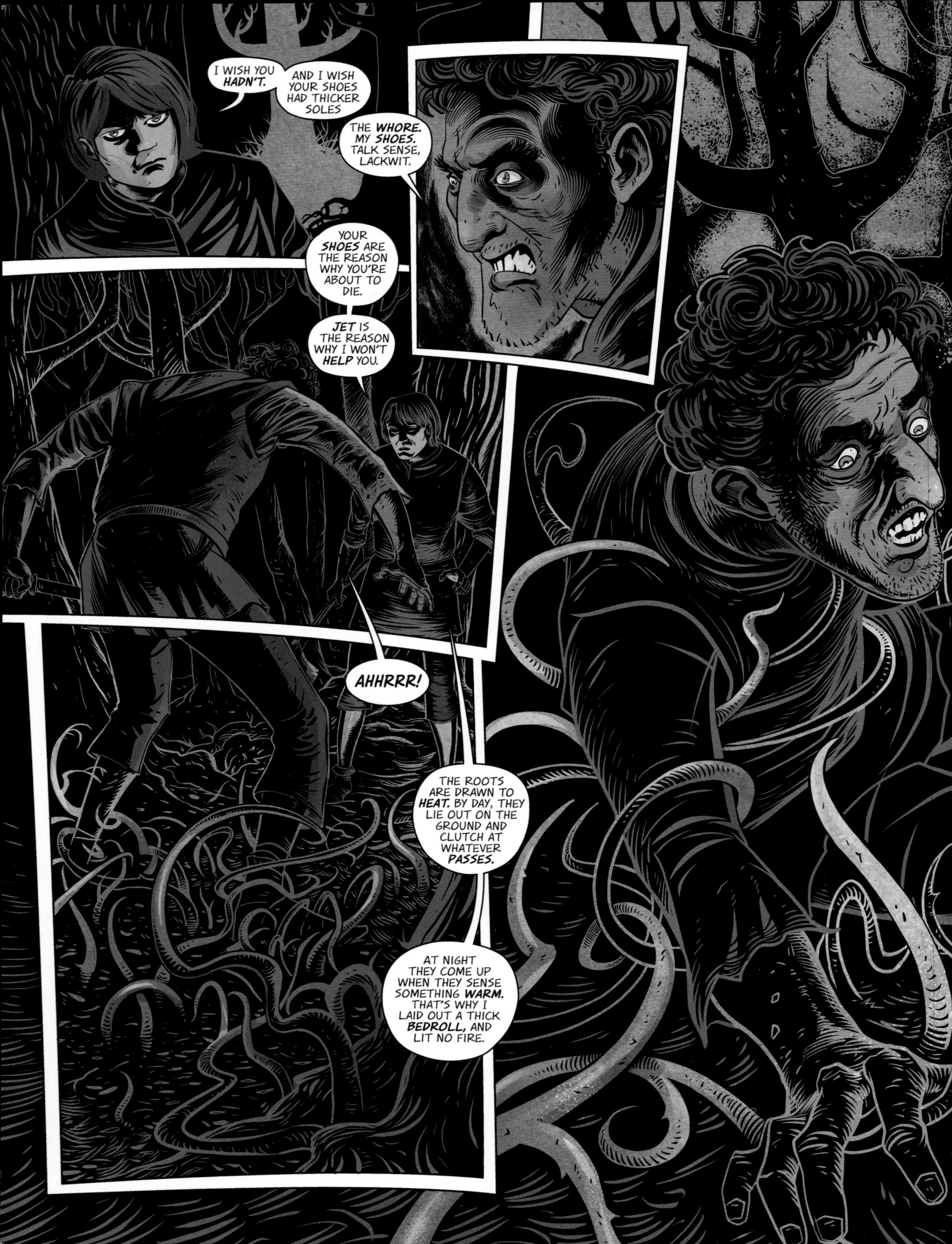
I WISH YOU **HADN'T.**
AND I WISH YOUR SHOES HAD THICKER SOLES
THE **WHORE.** MY **SHOES.** TALK SENSE, LACKWIT.
YOUR **SHOES** ARE THE REASON WHY YOU'RE ABOUT TO DIE.
JET IS THE REASON WHY I WON'T **HELP** YOU.
AHHRRR!
THE ROOTS ARE DRAWN TO **HEAT.** BY DAY, THEY LIE OUT ON THE GROUND AND CLUTCH AT WHATEVER **PASSES.**
AT NIGHT THEY COME UP WHEN THEY SENSE SOMETHING **WARM.** THAT'S WHY I LAID OUT A THICK **BEDROLL,** AND LIT NO FIRE.

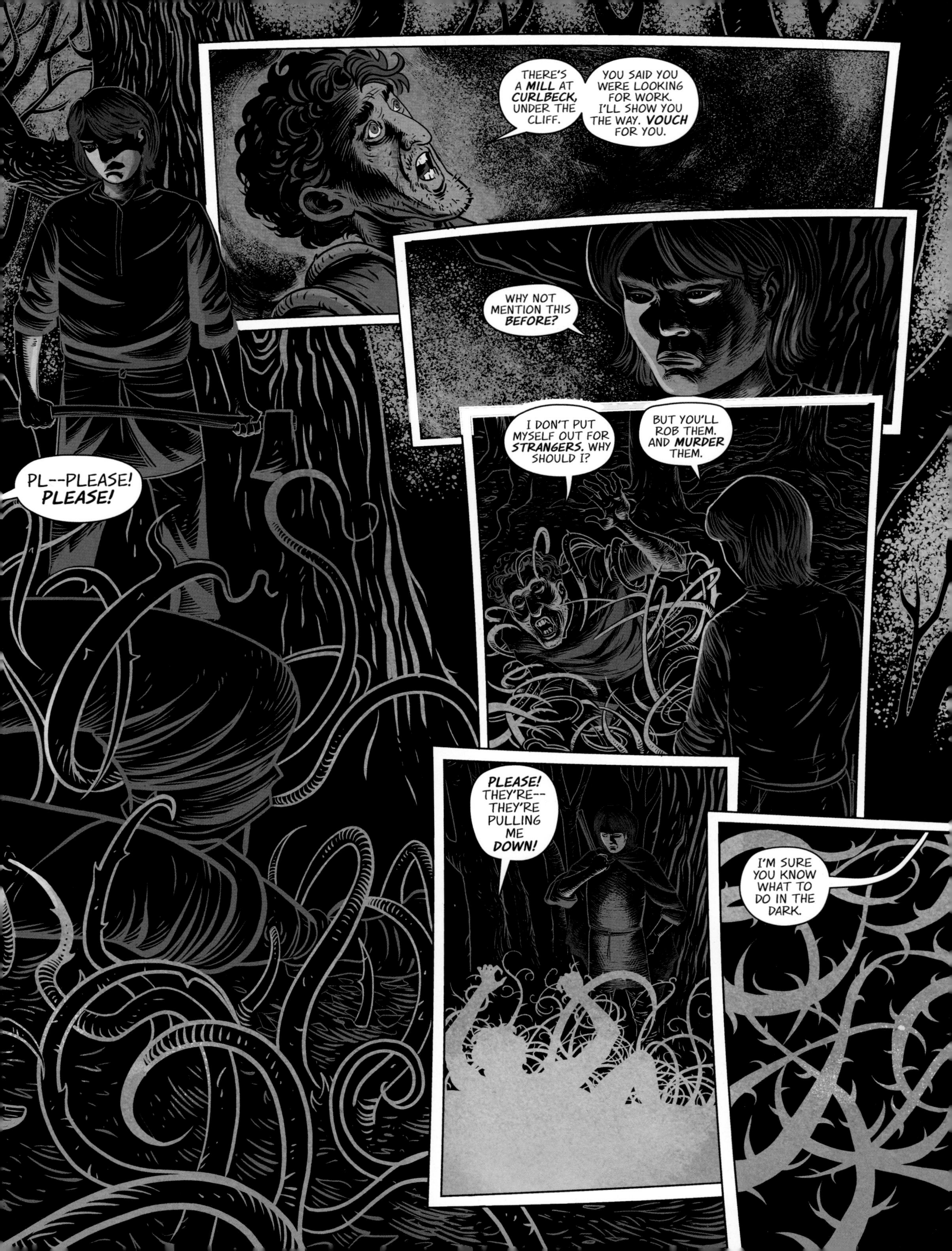
THERE'S A MILL AT CURLBECK, UNDER THE CLIFF.
YOU SAID YOU WERE LOOKING FOR WORK. I'LL SHOW YOU THE WAY. VOUCH FOR YOU.
WHY NOT MENTION THIS BEFORE?
PL--PLEASE! PLEASE!
I DON'T PUT MYSELF OUT FOR STRANGERS. WHY SHOULD I?
BUT YOU'LL ROB THEM. AND MURDER THEM.
PLEASE! THEY'RE-- THEY'RE PULLING ME DOWN!
I'M SURE YOU KNOW WHAT TO DO IN THE DARK.

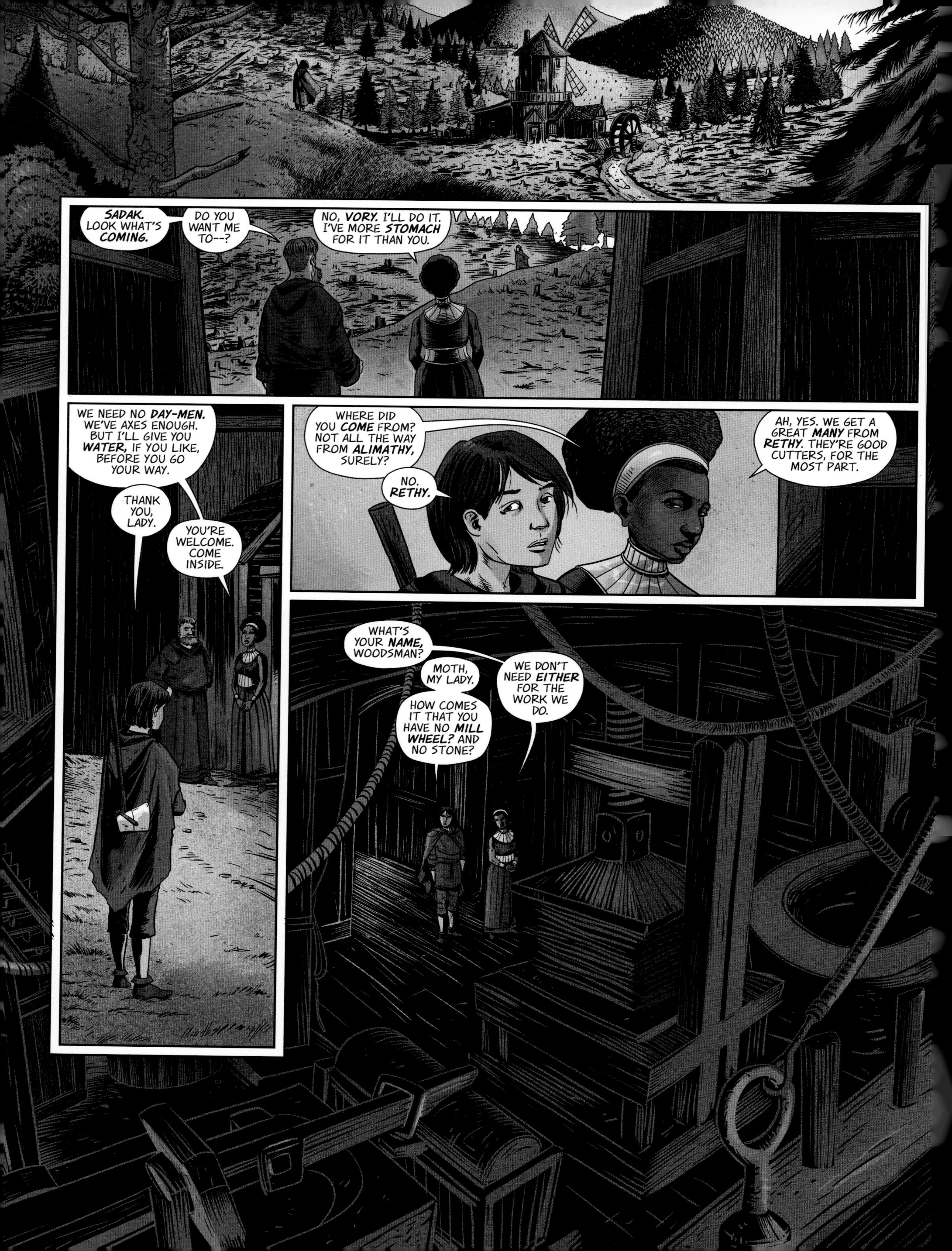
SADAK. LOOK WHAT'S COMING.
DO YOU WANT ME TO--?
NO, VORY. I'LL DO IT. I'VE MORE STOMACH FOR IT THAN YOU.
WE NEED NO DAY-MEN. WE'VE AXES ENOUGH. BUT I'LL GIVE YOU WATER, IF YOU LIKE, BEFORE YOU GO YOUR WAY.
THANK YOU, LADY.
YOU'RE WELCOME. COME INSIDE.
WHERE DID YOU COME FROM? NOT ALL THE WAY FROM ALIMATHY, SURELY?
NO. RETHY.
AH, YES. WE GET A GREAT MANY FROM RETHY. THEY'RE GOOD CUTTERS, FOR THE MOST PART.
WHAT'S YOUR NAME, WOODSMAN?
MOTH, MY LADY.
HOW COMES IT THAT YOU HAVE NO MILL WHEEL? AND NO STONE?
WE DON'T NEED EITHER FOR THE WORK WE DO.

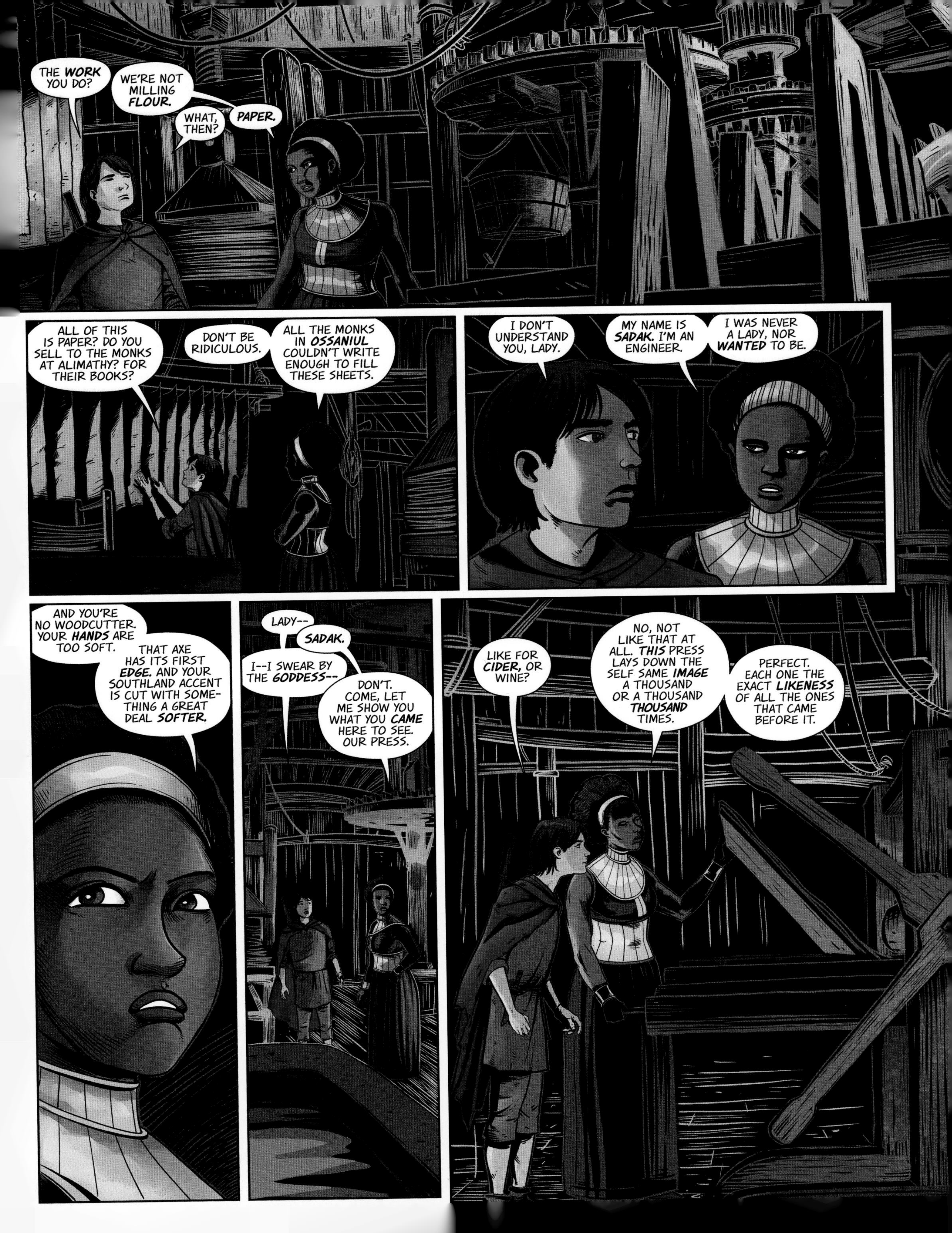
THE WORK YOU DO?
WE'RE NOT MILLING FLOUR.
WHAT, THEN?
PAPER.
ALL OF THIS IS PAPER? DO YOU SELL TO THE MONKS AT ALIMATHY? FOR THEIR BOOKS?
DON'T BE RIDICULOUS.
ALL THE MONKS IN OSSANIUL COULDN'T WRITE ENOUGH TO FILL THESE SHEETS.
I DON'T UNDERSTAND YOU, LADY.
MY NAME IS SADAK. I'M AN ENGINEER.
I WAS NEVER A LADY, NOR WANTED TO BE.
AND YOU'RE NO WOODCUTTER. YOUR HANDS ARE TOO SOFT.
THAT AXE HAS ITS FIRST EDGE. AND YOUR SOUTHLAND ACCENT IS CUT WITH SOME-THING A GREAT DEAL SOFTER.
LADY--
SADAK.
I--I SWEAR BY THE GODDESS--
DON'T. COME, LET ME SHOW YOU WHAT YOU CAME HERE TO SEE. OUR PRESS.
LIKE FOR CIDER, OR WINE?
NO, NOT LIKE THAT AT ALL. THIS PRESS LAYS DOWN THE SELF SAME IMAGE A THOUSAND OR A THOUSAND THOUSAND TIMES.
PERFECT. EACH ONE THE EXACT LIKENESS OF ALL THE ONES THAT CAME BEFORE IT.

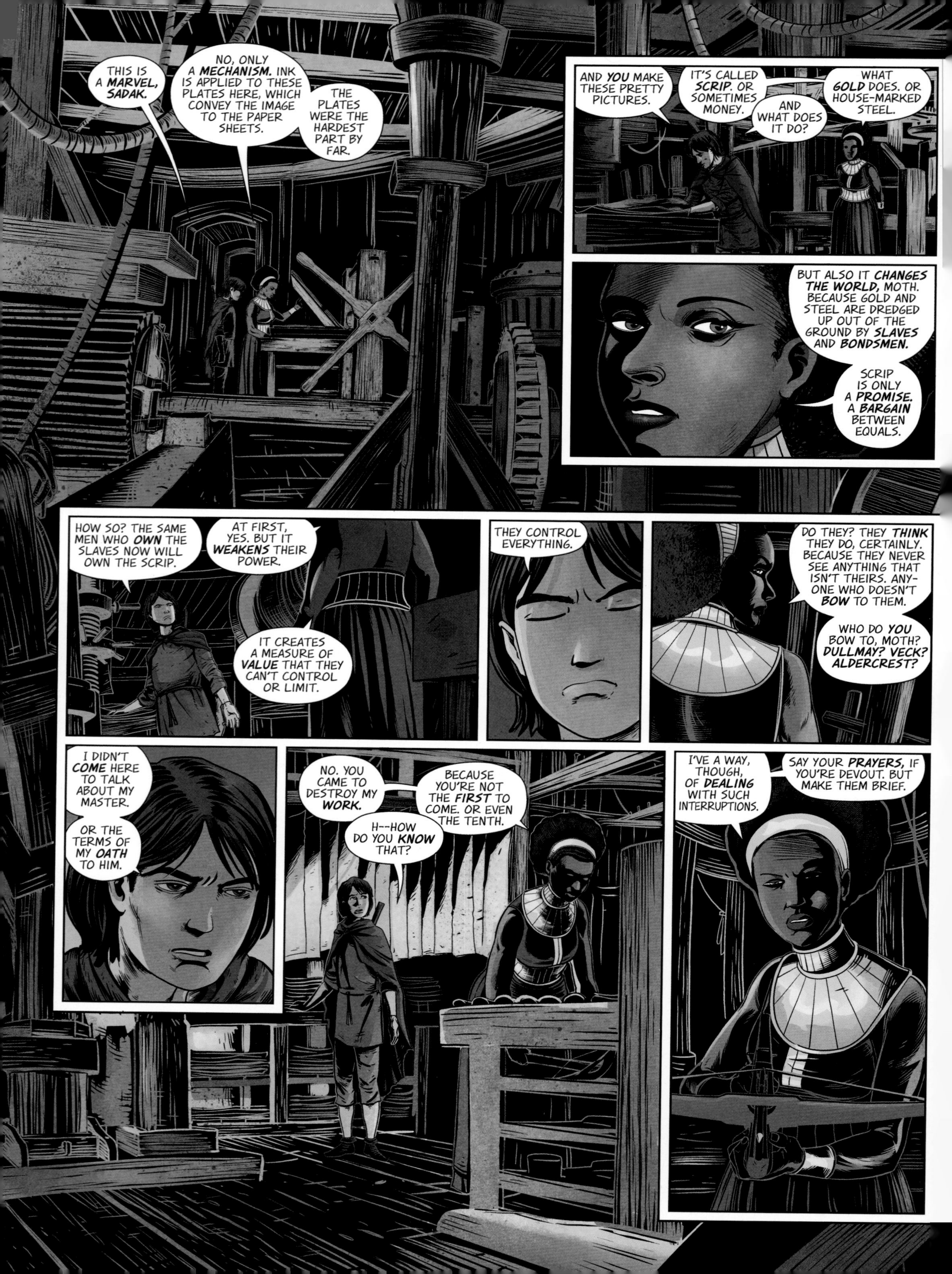

THIS IS A MARVEL, SADAK.
NO, ONLY A MECHANISM. INK IS APPLIED TO THESE PLATES HERE, WHICH CONVEY THE IMAGE TO THE PAPER SHEETS.
THE PLATES WERE THE HARDEST PART BY FAR.
AND YOU MAKE THESE PRETTY PICTURES.
IT'S CALLED SCRIP. OR SOMETIMES MONEY.
AND WHAT DOES IT DO?
WHAT GOLD DOES. OR HOUSE-MARKED STEEL.
BUT ALSO IT CHANGES THE WORLD, MOTH. BECAUSE GOLD AND STEEL ARE DREDGED UP OUT OF THE GROUND BY SLAVES AND BONDSMEN.
SCRIP IS ONLY A PROMISE. A BARGAIN BETWEEN EQUALS.
HOW SO? THE SAME MEN WHO OWN THE SLAVES NOW WILL OWN THE SCRIP.
AT FIRST, YES. BUT IT WEAKENS THEIR POWER.
IT CREATES A MEASURE OF VALUE THAT THEY CAN'T CONTROL OR LIMIT.
THEY CONTROL EVERYTHING.
DO THEY? THEY THINK THEY DO, CERTAINLY. BECAUSE THEY NEVER SEE ANYTHING THAT ISN'T THEIRS. ANY-ONE WHO DOESN'T BOW TO THEM.
WHO DO YOU BOW TO, MOTH? DULLMAY? VECK? ALDERCREST?
I DIDN'T COME HERE TO TALK ABOUT MY MASTER.
OR THE TERMS OF MY OATH TO HIM.
NO. YOU CAME TO DESTROY MY WORK.
BECAUSE YOU'RE NOT THE FIRST TO COME. OR EVEN THE TENTH.
H--HOW DO YOU KNOW THAT?
I'VE A WAY, THOUGH, OF DEALING WITH SUCH INTERRUPTIONS.
SAY YOUR PRAYERS, IF YOU'RE DEVOUT. BUT MAKE THEM BRIEF.

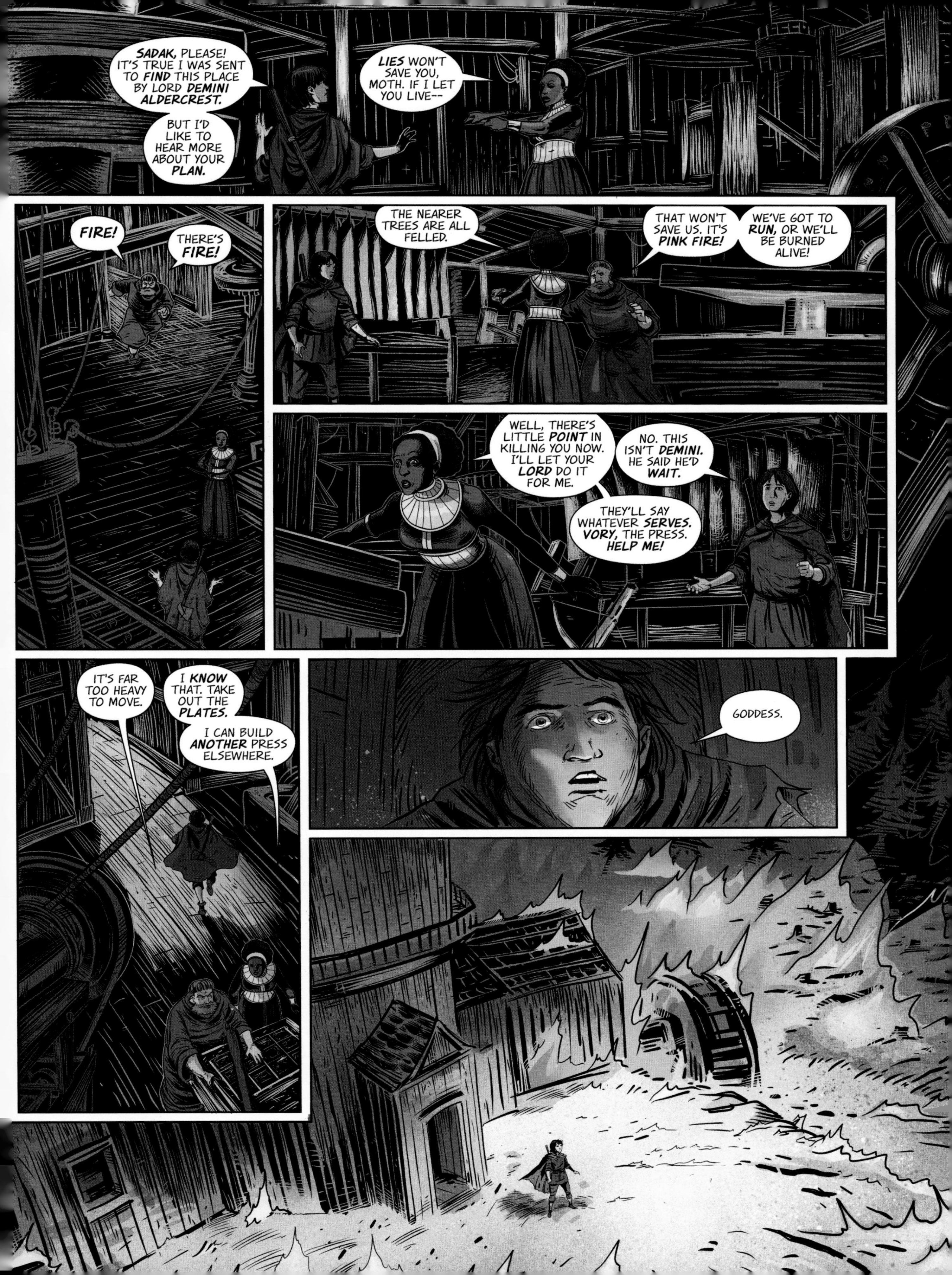
SADAK, PLEASE! IT'S TRUE I WAS SENT TO FIND THIS PLACE BY LORD DEMINI ALDERCREST.
BUT I'D LIKE TO HEAR MORE ABOUT YOUR PLAN.
LIES WON'T SAVE YOU, MOTH. IF I LET YOU LIVE--
FIRE!
THERE'S FIRE!
THE NEARER TREES ARE ALL FELLED.
THAT WON'T SAVE US. IT'S PINK FIRE!
WE'VE GOT TO RUN, OR WE'LL BE BURNED ALIVE!
WELL, THERE'S LITTLE POINT IN KILLING YOU NOW. I'LL LET YOUR LORD DO IT FOR ME.
NO. THIS ISN'T DEMINI. HE SAID HE'D WAIT.
THEY'LL SAY WHATEVER SERVES. VORY, THE PRESS. HELP ME!
IT'S FAR TOO HEAVY TO MOVE.
I KNOW THAT. TAKE OUT THE PLATES.
I CAN BUILD ANOTHER PRESS ELSEWHERE.
GODDESS.

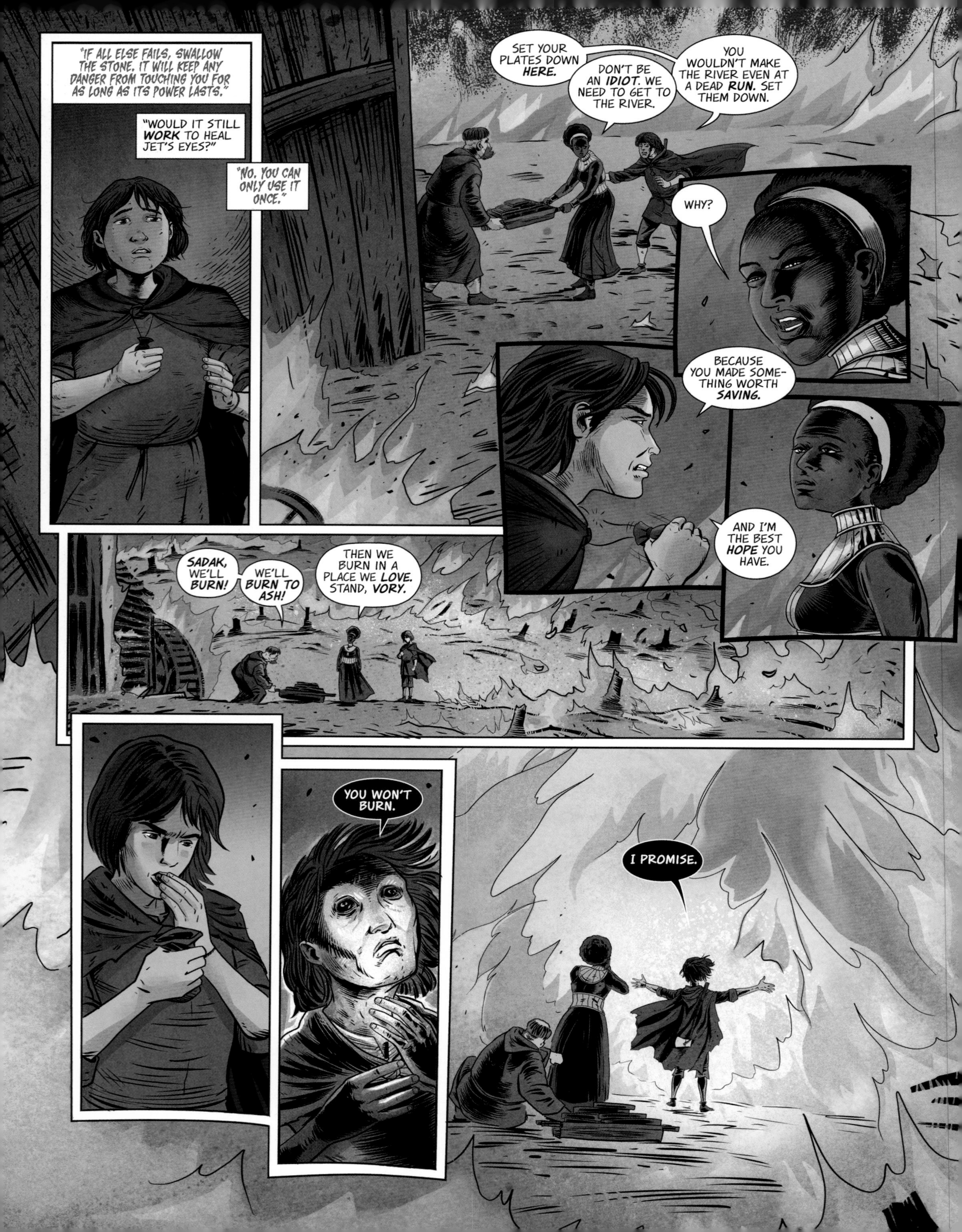

"IF ALL ELSE FAILS, SWALLOW THE STONE. IT WILL KEEP ANY DANGER FROM TOUCHING YOU FOR AS LONG AS ITS POWER LASTS."
"WOULD IT STILL WORK TO HEAL JET'S EYES?"
"NO. YOU CAN ONLY USE IT ONCE."
SET YOUR PLATES DOWN HERE.
DON'T BE AN IDIOT. WE NEED TO GET TO THE RIVER.
YOU WOULDN'T MAKE THE RIVER EVEN AT A DEAD RUN. SET THEM DOWN.
WHY?
BECAUSE YOU MADE SOME-THING WORTH SAVING.
AND I'M THE BEST HOPE YOU HAVE.
SADAK, WE'LL BURN!
WE'LL BURN TO ASH!
THEN WE BURN IN A PLACE WE LOVE. STAND, VORY.
YOU WON'T BURN.
I PROMISE.

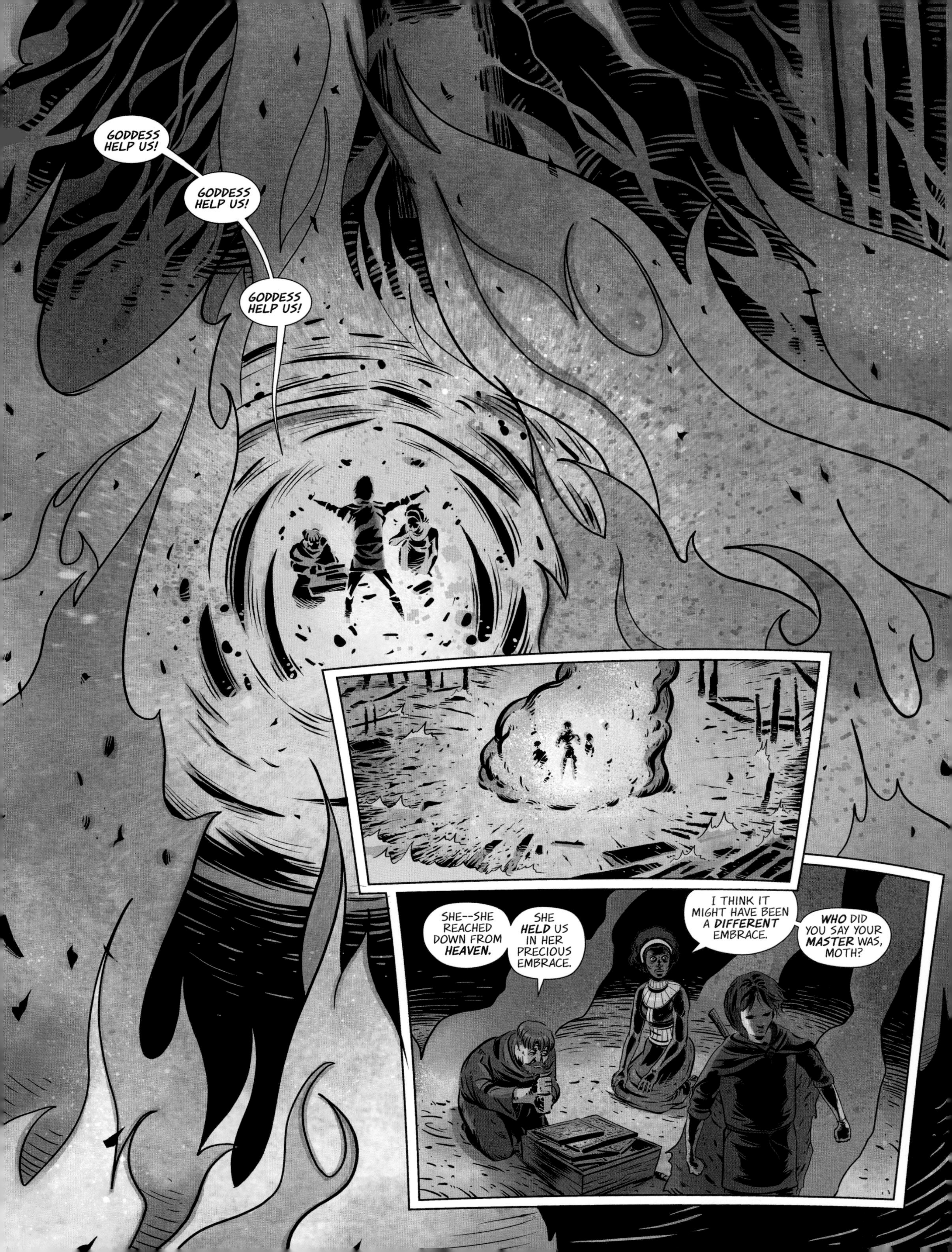
GODDESS HELP US!
GODDESS HELP US!
GODDESS HELP US!
SHE--SHE REACHED DOWN FROM **HEAVEN.**
SHE **HELD** US IN HER PRECIOUS EMBRACE.
I THINK IT MIGHT HAVE BEEN A **DIFFERENT** EMBRACE.
WHO DID YOU SAY YOUR **MASTER** WAS, MOTH?

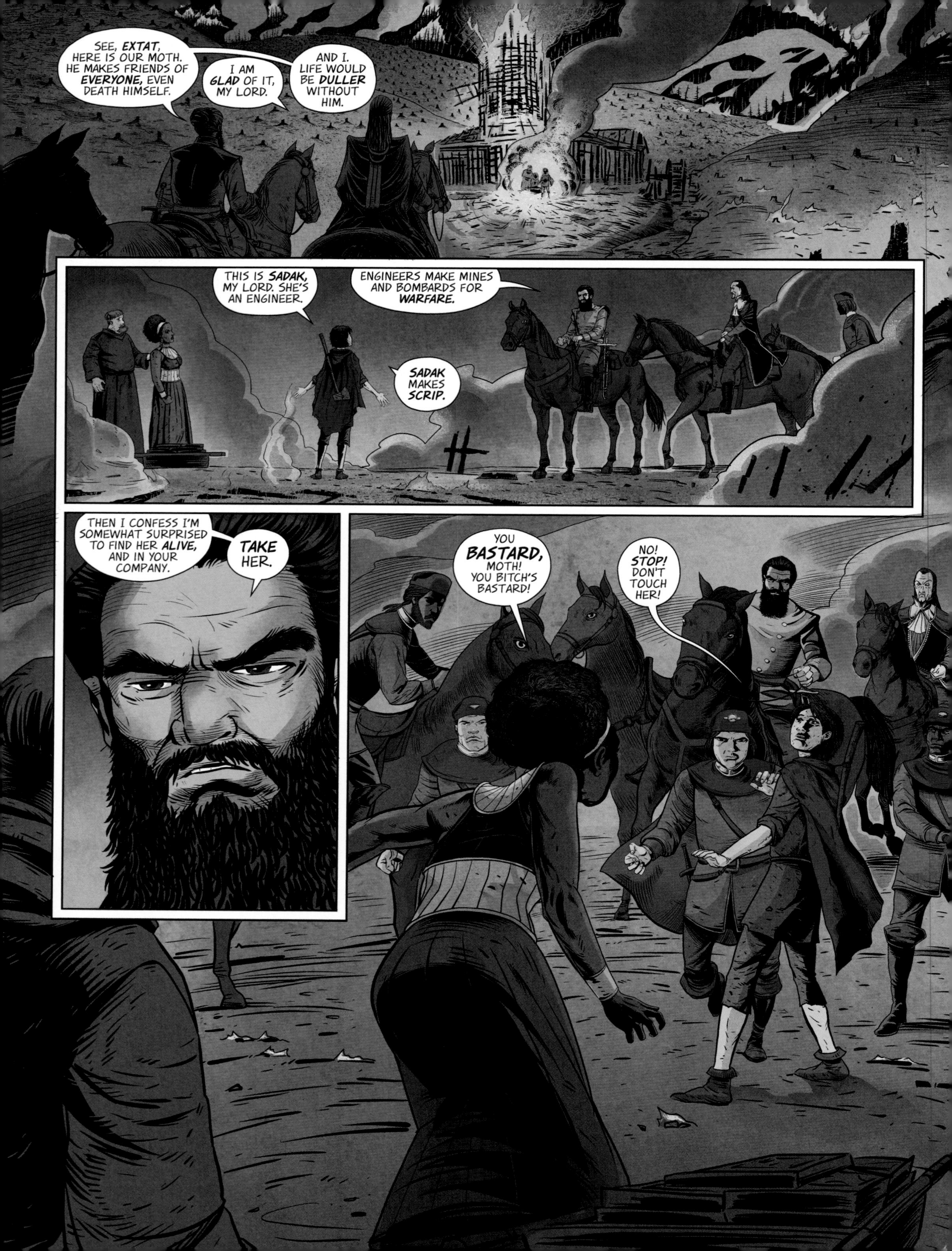
SEE, EXTAT, HERE IS OUR MOTH. HE MAKES FRIENDS OF EVERYONE, EVEN DEATH HIMSELF.
I AM GLAD OF IT, MY LORD.
AND I. LIFE WOULD BE DULLER WITHOUT HIM.
THIS IS SADAK, MY LORD. SHE'S AN ENGINEER.
ENGINEERS MAKE MINES AND BOMBARDS FOR WARFARE.
SADAK MAKES SCRIP.
THEN I CONFESS I'M SOMEWHAT SURPRISED TO FIND HER ALIVE, AND IN YOUR COMPANY.
TAKE HER.
YOU BASTARD, MOTH! YOU BITCH'S BASTARD!
NO! STOP! DON'T TOUCH HER!

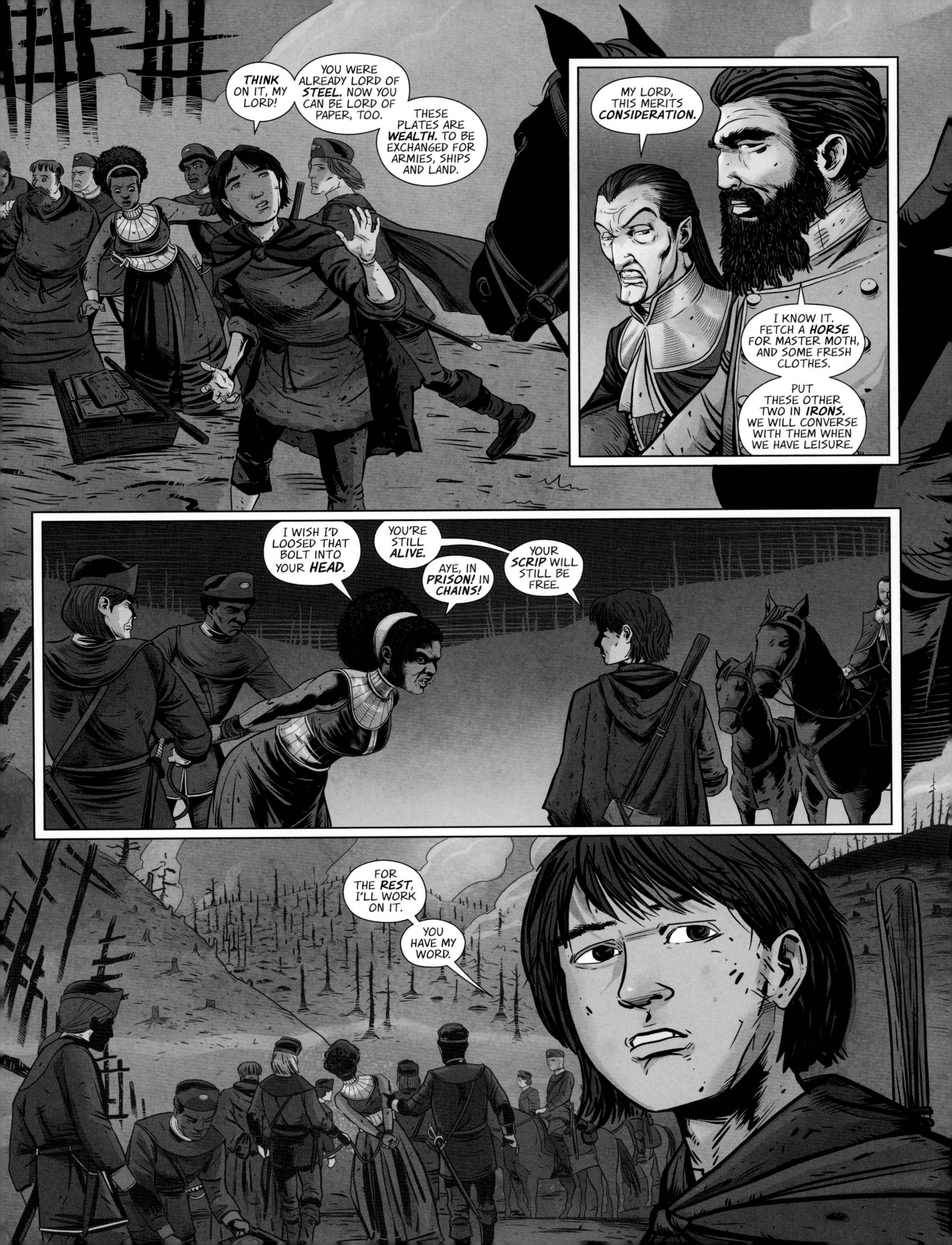
THINK ON IT, MY LORD!
YOU WERE ALREADY LORD OF STEEL. NOW YOU CAN BE LORD OF PAPER, TOO.
THESE PLATES ARE WEALTH. TO BE EXCHANGED FOR ARMIES, SHIPS AND LAND.
MY LORD, THIS MERITS CONSIDERATION.
I KNOW IT. FETCH A HORSE FOR MASTER MOTH, AND SOME FRESH CLOTHES.
PUT THESE OTHER TWO IN IRONS. WE WILL CONVERSE WITH THEM WHEN WE HAVE LEISURE.
I WISH I'D LOOSED THAT BOLT INTO YOUR HEAD.
YOU'RE STILL ALIVE.
AYE, IN PRISON! IN CHAINS!
YOUR SCRIP WILL STILL BE FREE.
FOR THE REST, I'LL WORK ON IT.
YOU HAVE MY WORD.

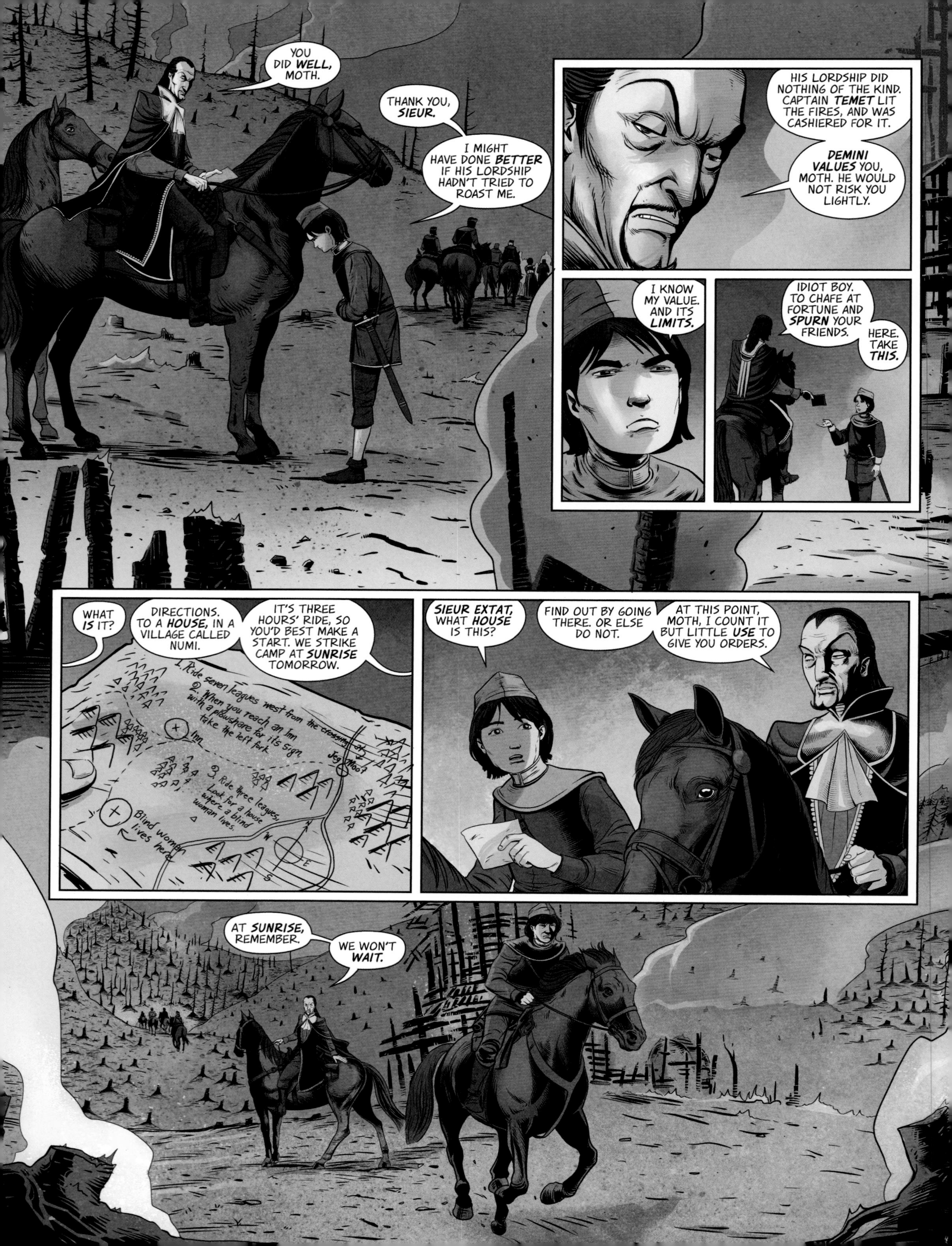
YOU DID WELL, MOTH.
THANK YOU, SIEUR.
I MIGHT HAVE DONE BETTER IF HIS LORDSHIP HADN'T TRIED TO ROAST ME.
HIS LORDSHIP DID NOTHING OF THE KIND. CAPTAIN TEMET LIT THE FIRES, AND WAS CASHIERED FOR IT.
DEMINI VALUES YOU, MOTH. HE WOULD NOT RISK YOU LIGHTLY.
I KNOW MY VALUE. AND ITS LIMITS.
IDIOT BOY. TO CHAFE AT FORTUNE AND SPURN YOUR FRIENDS.
HERE. TAKE THIS.
WHAT IS IT?
DIRECTIONS. TO A HOUSE, IN A VILLAGE CALLED NUMI.
IT'S THREE HOURS' RIDE, SO YOU'D BEST MAKE A START. WE STRIKE CAMP AT SUNRISE TOMORROW.
1. Ride seven leagues west from the crossing at
Jeg Moot
2. When you reach an Inn with a plowshare for its sign take the left fork
Inn
3 Ride three leagues. Look for a house where a blind woman lives.
Blind woman lives here
SIEUR EXTAT, WHAT HOUSE IS THIS?
FIND OUT BY GOING THERE. OR ELSE DO NOT.
AT THIS POINT, MOTH, I COUNT IT BUT LITTLE USE TO GIVE YOU ORDERS.
AT SUNRISE, REMEMBER.
WE WON'T WAIT.

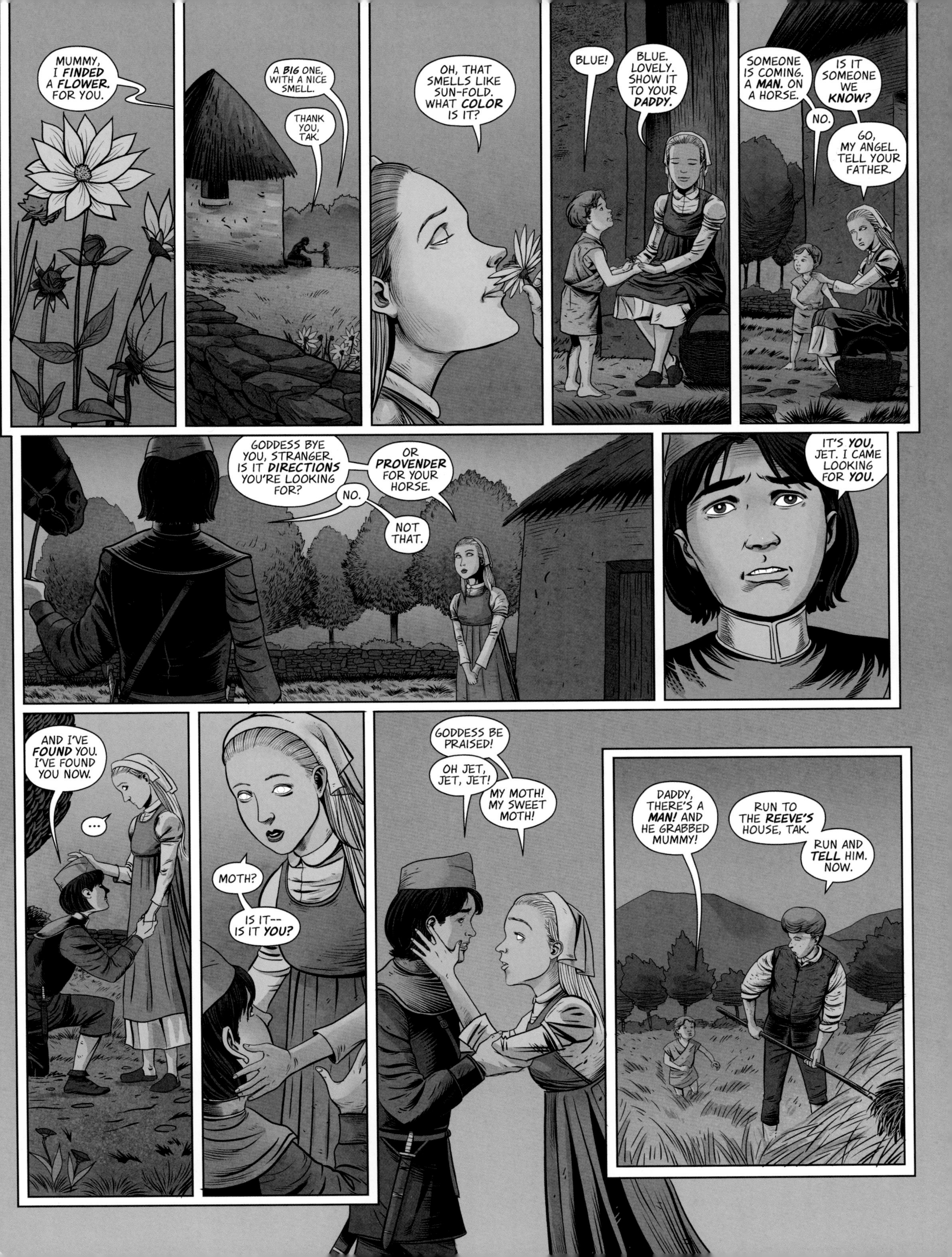
MUMMY, I FINDED A FLOWER. FOR YOU.
A BIG ONE, WITH A NICE SMELL.
THANK YOU, TAK.
OH, THAT SMELLS LIKE SUN-FOLD. WHAT COLOR IS IT?
BLUE!
BLUE. LOVELY. SHOW IT TO YOUR DADDY.
SOMEONE IS COMING. A MAN. ON A HORSE.
IS IT SOMEONE WE KNOW?
NO.
GO, MY ANGEL. TELL YOUR FATHER.
GODDESS BYE YOU, STRANGER. IS IT DIRECTIONS YOU'RE LOOKING FOR?
OR PROVENDER FOR YOUR HORSE.
NO.
NOT THAT.
IT'S YOU, JET. I CAME LOOKING FOR YOU.
AND I'VE FOUND YOU. I'VE FOUND YOU NOW.
...
MOTH?
IS IT-- IS IT YOU?
GODDESS BE PRAISED!
OH JET, JET, JET!
MY MOTH! MY SWEET MOTH!
DADDY, THERE'S A MAN! AND HE GRABBED MUMMY!
RUN TO THE REEVE'S HOUSE, TAK.
RUN AND TELL HIM. NOW.

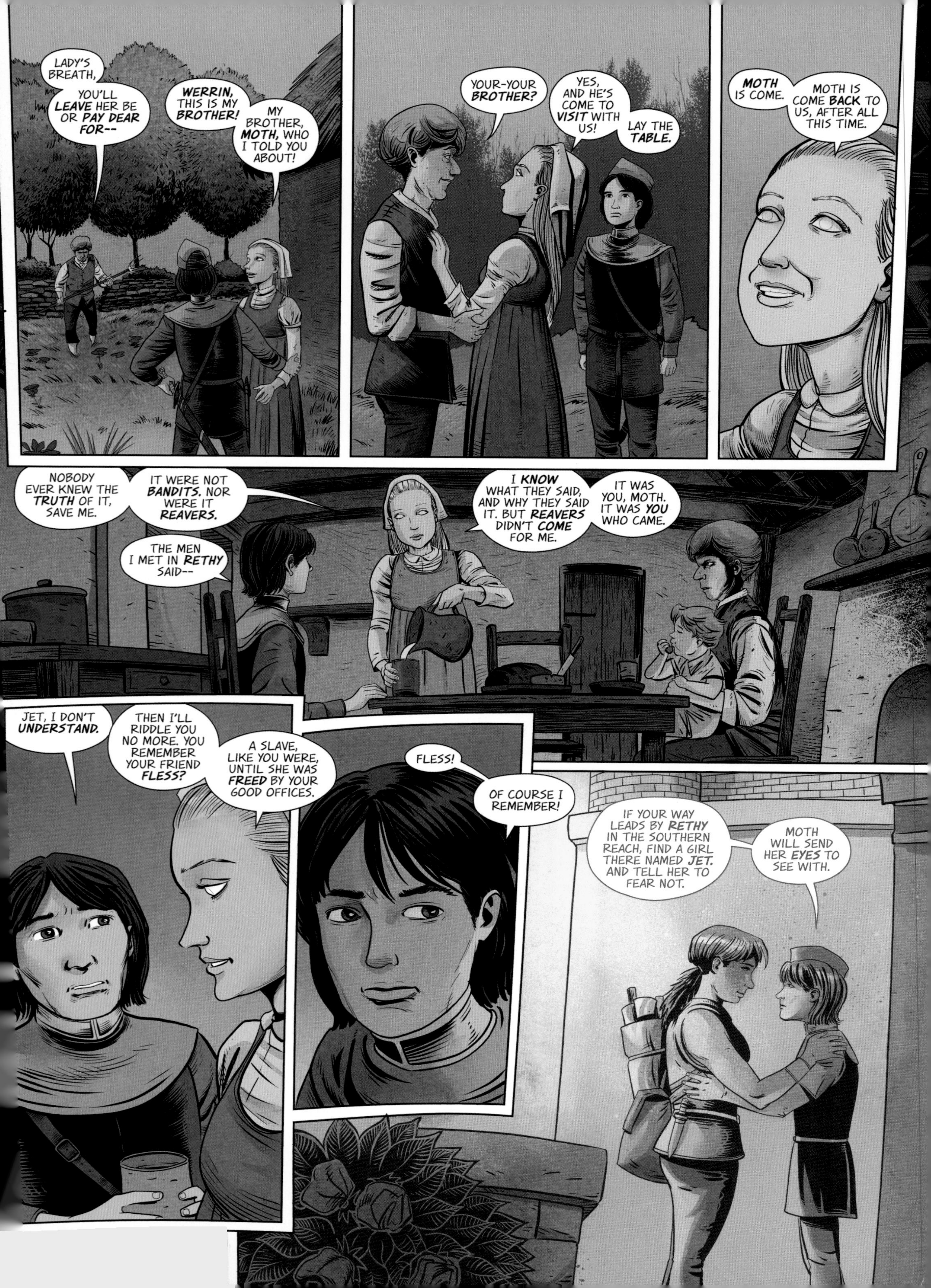

LADY'S BREATH, YOU'LL LEAVE HER BE OR PAY DEAR FOR--
WERRIN, THIS IS MY BROTHER!
MY BROTHER, MOTH, WHO I TOLD YOU ABOUT!
YOUR-YOUR BROTHER?
YES, AND HE'S COME TO VISIT WITH US!
LAY THE TABLE.
MOTH IS COME.
MOTH IS COME BACK TO US, AFTER ALL THIS TIME.
NOBODY EVER KNEW THE TRUTH OF IT, SAVE ME.
IT WERE NOT BANDITS. NOR WERE IT REAVERS.
THE MEN I MET IN RETHY SAID--
I KNOW WHAT THEY SAID, AND WHY THEY SAID IT. BUT REAVERS DIDN'T COME FOR ME.
IT WAS YOU, MOTH. IT WAS YOU WHO CAME.
JET, I DON'T UNDERSTAND.
THEN I'LL RIDDLE YOU NO MORE. YOU REMEMBER YOUR FRIEND FLESS?
A SLAVE, LIKE YOU WERE, UNTIL SHE WAS FREED BY YOUR GOOD OFFICES.
FLESS!
OF COURSE I REMEMBER!
IF YOUR WAY LEADS BY RETHY IN THE SOUTHERN REACH, FIND A GIRL THERE NAMED JET. AND TELL HER TO FEAR NOT.
MOTH WILL SEND HER EYES TO SEE WITH.

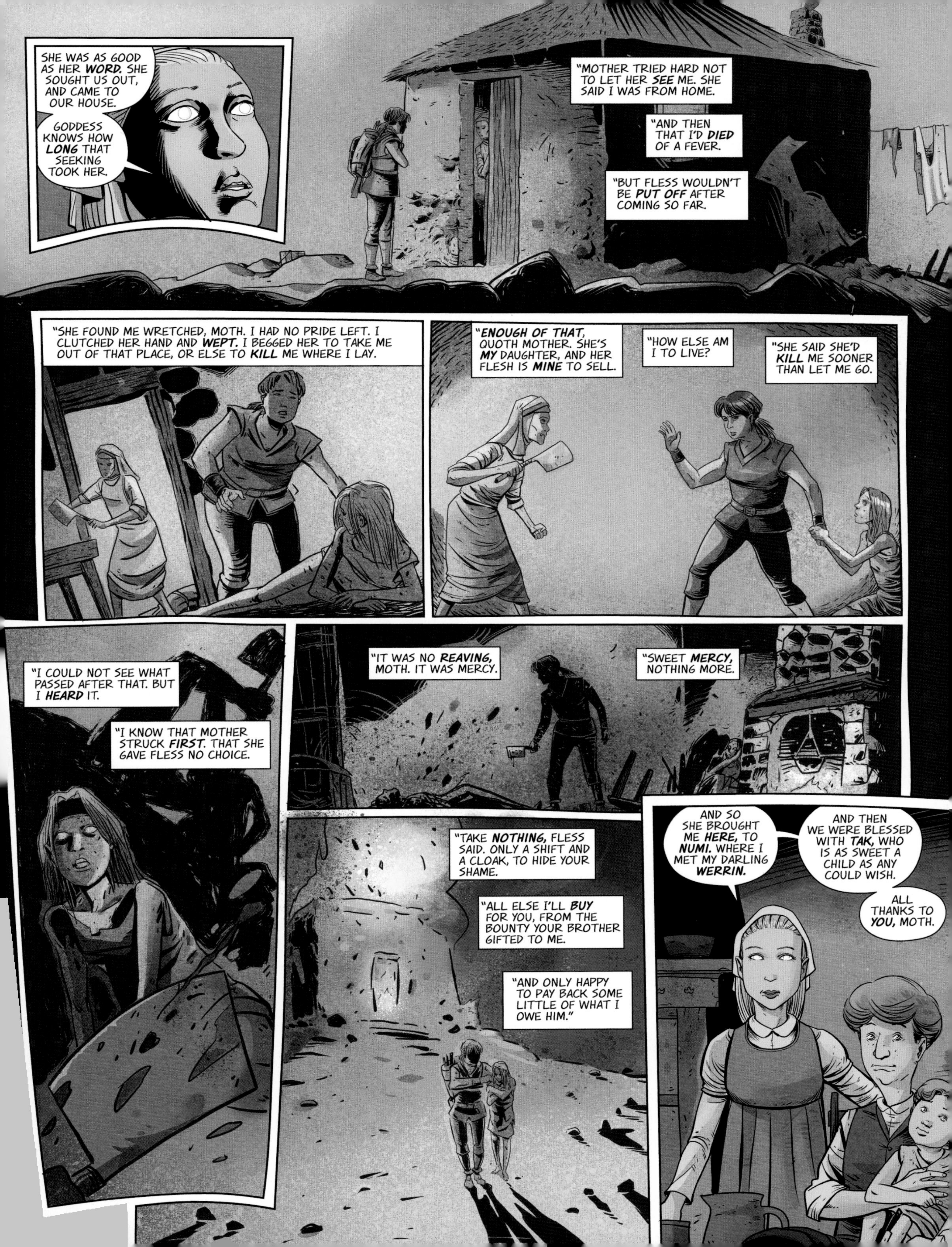
SHE WAS AS GOOD AS HER WORD. SHE SOUGHT US OUT, AND CAME TO OUR HOUSE.
GODDESS KNOWS HOW LONG THAT SEEKING TOOK HER.
"MOTHER TRIED HARD NOT TO LET HER SEE ME. SHE SAID I WAS FROM HOME.
"AND THEN THAT I'D DIED OF A FEVER.
"BUT FLESS WOULDN'T BE PUT OFF AFTER COMING SO FAR.
"SHE FOUND ME WRETCHED, MOTH. I HAD NO PRIDE LEFT. I CLUTCHED HER HAND AND WEPT. I BEGGED HER TO TAKE ME OUT OF THAT PLACE, OR ELSE TO KILL ME WHERE I LAY.
"ENOUGH OF THAT, QUOTH MOTHER. SHE'S MY DAUGHTER, AND HER FLESH IS MINE TO SELL.
"HOW ELSE AM I TO LIVE?
"SHE SAID SHE'D KILL ME SOONER THAN LET ME GO.
"I COULD NOT SEE WHAT PASSED AFTER THAT. BUT I HEARD IT.
"I KNOW THAT MOTHER STRUCK FIRST. THAT SHE GAVE FLESS NO CHOICE.
"IT WAS NO REAVING, MOTH. IT WAS MERCY.
"SWEET MERCY, NOTHING MORE.
"TAKE NOTHING, FLESS SAID. ONLY A SHIFT AND A CLOAK, TO HIDE YOUR SHAME.
"ALL ELSE I'LL BUY FOR YOU, FROM THE BOUNTY YOUR BROTHER GIFTED TO ME.
"AND ONLY HAPPY TO PAY BACK SOME LITTLE OF WHAT I OWE HIM."
AND SO SHE BROUGHT ME HERE, TO NUMI. WHERE I MET MY DARLING WERRIN.
AND THEN WE WERE BLESSED WITH TAK, WHO IS AS SWEET A CHILD AS ANY COULD WISH.
ALL THANKS TO YOU, MOTH.

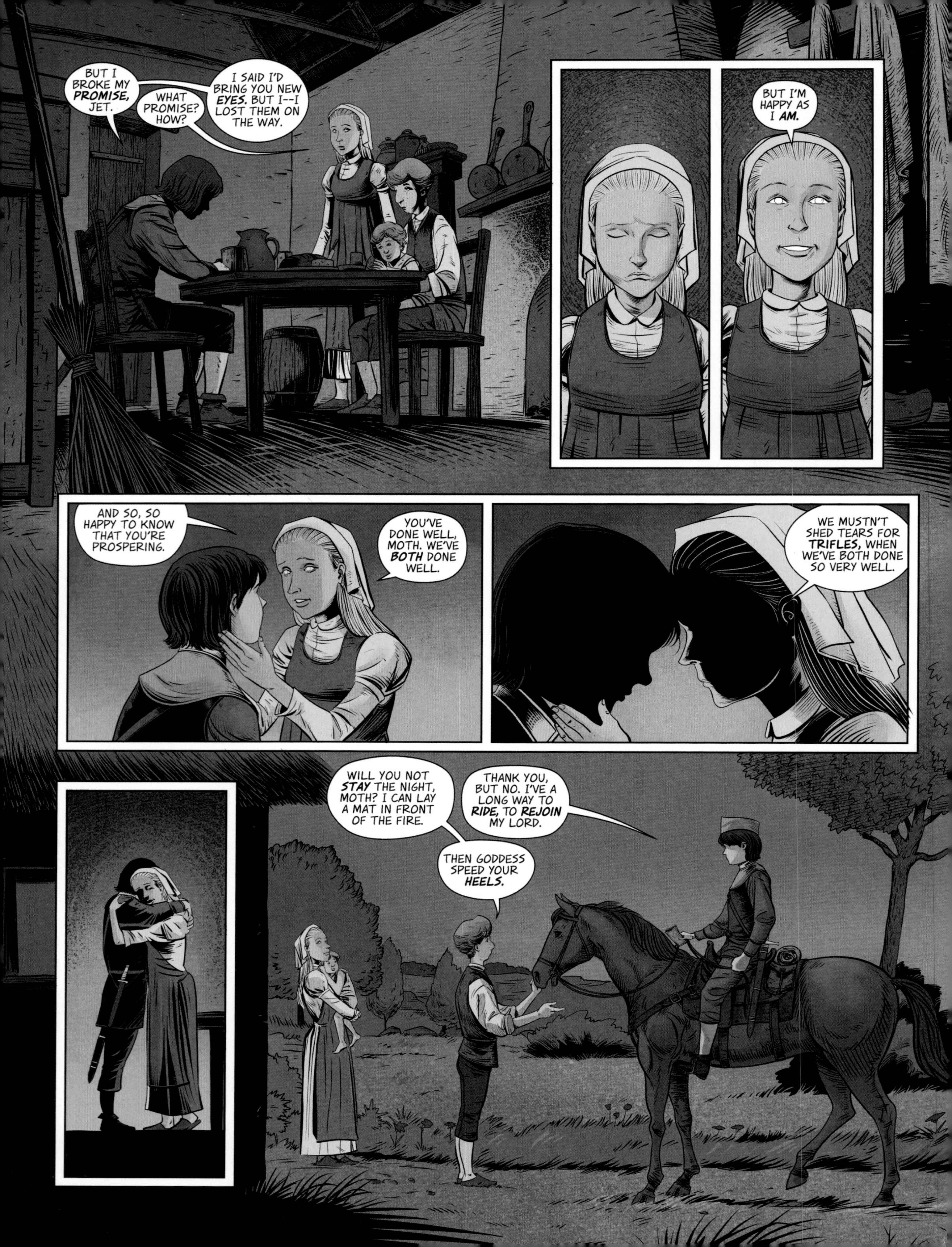
BUT I BROKE MY PROMISE, JET.
WHAT PROMISE? HOW?
I SAID I'D BRING YOU NEW EYES. BUT I--I LOST THEM ON THE WAY.
BUT I'M HAPPY AS I AM.
AND SO, SO HAPPY TO KNOW THAT YOU'RE PROSPERING.
YOU'VE DONE WELL, MOTH. WE'VE BOTH DONE WELL.
WE MUSTN'T SHED TEARS FOR TRIFLES, WHEN WE'VE BOTH DONE SO VERY WELL.
WILL YOU NOT STAY THE NIGHT, MOTH? I CAN LAY A MAT IN FRONT OF THE FIRE.
THANK YOU, BUT NO. I'VE A LONG WAY TO RIDE, TO REJOIN MY LORD.
THEN GODDESS SPEED YOUR HEELS.

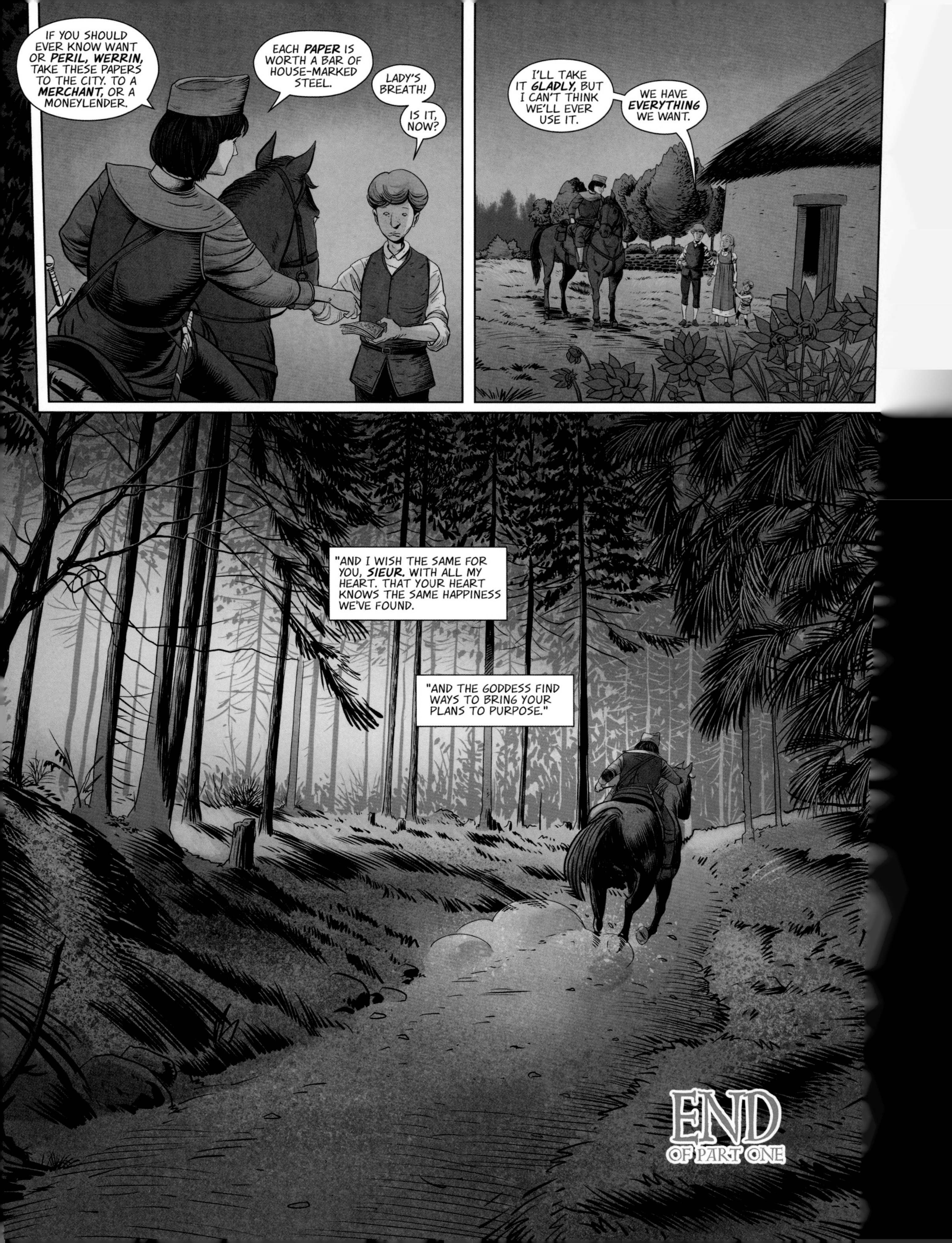
IF YOU SHOULD EVER KNOW WANT OR PERIL, WERRIN, TAKE THESE PAPERS TO THE CITY. TO A MERCHANT, OR A MONEYLENDER.
EACH PAPER IS WORTH A BAR OF HOUSE-MARKED STEEL.
LADY'S BREATH!
IS IT, NOW?
I'LL TAKE IT GLADLY, BUT I CAN'T THINK WE'LL EVER USE IT.
WE HAVE EVERYTHING WE WANT.
"AND I WISH THE SAME FOR YOU, SIEUR, WITH ALL MY HEART. THAT YOUR HEART KNOWS THE SAME HAPPINESS WE'VE FOUND.
"AND THE GODDESS FIND WAYS TO BRING YOUR PLANS TO PURPOSE."
END
OF PART ONE

Slavery in Ossaniul

From the writings of Orlin Sever, Chief Librarian of the Sisera Archive

It is hard for us, looking back from our current perspective, to understand how the institution of slavery functioned in our country before the advent of Moth. Vast social changes are wont to erase their own history. The present moment coerces and moves our memory of the past in the way the moon is said to coerce and move the oceans.

Some things, however, we can state with certainty. We know that slavery existed in Ossaniul for many centuries before the conquest. The Ossani had long depended on it to shore up their mostly rural economy, and indeed to form the backbone of their armed forces. During their period of expansion they deployed entire slave regiments, whose officers all the way up to the rank of Chiliarch were, like the lowest footsoldiers, born to servitude.

The Koviki, when they came, did nothing to disturb this order. They did, however, change the perception of it. They found a land in which there was a rigid distinction between the slave and the free man. Yet the goddess, as is universally claimed and for the most part believed, loves all alike. How could these two things be squared? If all men and women are equal in her sight, how can such extreme inequality be tolerated? How can one man own another when the goddess owns all?

It would have been possible, in the first flush of victory, to abolish the institution of slavery in its entirety. But it would not have been easy, and certainly it would not have been popular. Slavery in Ossaniul served too many purposes, intruded itself into too many relations. Parents could sell their children into servitude, for example, and husbands could sell their wives. Regional landowners and gentry, likewise, owned the populations of the towns and villages in their demesnes, and had a similar right to turn them into currency either by selling their labour for a defined period or by giving them in perpetuity to another overlord.

Bizarrely, this was not seen as a sin or even as a national shame. On the contrary, and with no sense of irony, to sell others into slavery was considered an essential liberty. To salve their consciences, the Ossani had a rich tradition of stories in which former slaves rose to high estate. In actual fact this was not something that happened often, but with history and personal experience in one scale and stories in the other, the Ossani gave most credence to the stories. They genuinely held that any slave who served his master well and did his work with diligence would, in the course of time, be elevated to the status of freedman.

These stories are fascinating in their own right. Salt-Carrier Va tells of a maiden taken as a slave in a battle between noble clans, who then rises both to freedman status and to unexpectedly high estate in her adopted clan. The historical basis of the story is hard to determine, but there was a clan leader named Va in the Teth Lineal three centuries before they built the fortress of Highest House. Mistress Blade similarly uses an example taken from war, with Blade earning her freedom by winning a series of duels against the champions of other clans. The Weaver's Daughter, by contrast, tells of a woman who is enfranchised after sewing a wedding gown for her master's new bride which allows the lady to fly and change her shape.

Leaving these tendentious examples aside, rather than unravel this tangled skein the Koviki contented themselves with clarifying the rules by which a man might become a slave, or once he was enslaved might become free again. They decreed, for example, that any slave had the right to be told by his master what his worth was in currency steel. And if he or any other produced that price, the slave's freedom could duly be puchased. Slaves could also petition their masters on saints' days and on the Feast of Innocents, with the freeing of slaves becoming a holy act of sacrifice or of contrition.

These innovations were for the most part welcomed, but they did not lead to any great social upheaval. In the first fifty years of Koviki rule in Ossaniul there were actually fewer instances of slaves becoming freedmen than there had been in the fifty years immediately before. It seems that everyone approved of the principle but very few among the slave-owning classes wished to avail themselves of the opportunity.

There are honourable exceptions, however. Demini Aldercrest, who figures so largely in the story of Moth of Highest House (perhaps the most famous of the freed slaves), was such an exception. It was not unusual for Demini to offer freedom as a reward for services rendered, to the despair of his stewards who were compelled to make frequent forays into the hinterlands to replenish the household staff. That, indeed, is how Moth came to be at Highest House to begin with—and it can fairly be said that in this respect, as in many others, his destiny could not have played out as it did anywhere else.

The Tale of
Salt-Carrier Va

She knew who she was, and so do we, although we have no inkling now of her parentage or what her name might have been. That is to say, her original name, before she became Va. Before she became the salt-carrier.

She was someone, something something, of Va Keep. Not the tallest or the strongest or the most beautiful, but still a child of that place. She lived in Va's halls, slept in a chamber in one of Va's towers. Or, as it might have been, a stable in its yards. A hut against its wall. A pallet in its cellars. We do not know. What we know is that she lived there.

Then the Teth came, with men of war and horses and fire and great spells, and they levelled Va to the ground. They killed the men of the keep, and they killed the women. The women wore the same armour as the men, fought in the same lines, so who could tell? The children, if they fled, were mostly ignored, but if they stayed the Teth soldiers killed them too, so as not to have to hear the weeping of children. The weeping of children casts a man down and keeps him from peace with himself.

Lord Tollu of the Teth came upon a man who was twisting a spear into the side of a child, and the sight made him unhappy. "Forbear," he said. The warrior withdrew his spear and stood back. He was startled at the order, whose purport he could not understand, but he was loyal to his lord and so obeyed.

"Do you live still?" Tollu asked the child. She was a girl, of perhaps ten years. Her name, as I told you, is long since lost. It was not the only

thing lost that day. She had seen her kin cut down, her lord's head mounted on the end of a pike, her home brought to the ground so that stone did not stand upon stone. She was, at that moment, almost nothing.

But there is immensity, sometimes, in an almost.

"I live," the little girl told the great lord. "It's not so great a wound."

Lord Tollu nodded. "Then walk with me," he said. And he passed on into the keep.

The girl found her feet, somehow. Blood ran freely from the gash in her side but she found her feet and followed the lord. The soldier who had wounded her watched her go with a heart that was somewhat troubled. If she died what he had done was nothing, one of a thousand bloody acts on a bloody day. If she lived—and especially if she lived in Lord Tollu's favour—it might be different.

Tollu walked across the great courtyard. The killing was mostly done now. The men of the Teth were leading out the horses from the stables of the keep, carrying the gold and silver and cloth from the family rooms, heaping up the weapons from the armouries. Already it was obvious that this was a rich prize and all would benefit from it.

The little girl followed Tollu. Blood from her wound ran down her side, down her legs. The courtyard was floored with rushes and the rushes stuck to the bloodied soles of her feet. She

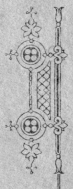

stumbled many times and once she almost fell, but she reached out and steadied herself against the flank of a horse that stood patient, waiting to be led away. The horse was white. The girl left a red handprint upon its shoulder.

Lord Tollu reached his own mount, and climbed up into its saddle. He watched the girl coming along behind him, more slowly. He waited until she reached him. All his men waited too, watching. The girl was the last living inhabitant of Va Keep, not counting the animals. They waited to see what the Lord would do with her.

Tollu looked down at her where she stood, swaying a little, beside his great black charger. Perhaps he read an omen in her stare, in her being alive at all when her house and kin were gone. Still, she was only alive because he had intervened. It was most likely that she was no omen at all, but only a child. That was all she looked like.

"What is your name?" he asked her. And his hand was resting on the hilt of his sword as he spoke.

"Va," the girl said.

The answer startled Tollu, and vexed him. "Va is the name of this place," he said. "Va is fallen. Choose another name."

The girl said nothing.

"Choose another name," Tollu commanded her again. And still she did not speak.

The Lord was aware that if he commanded her a third time and received no answer he would have to cut her down. Perhaps, he thought, that would even be for the best. But he had become entwined in her life when he told the warrior to spare her. If he were to go back on that decision now, his earlier mercy might be read as weakness. And in some measure the girl

touched his heart, standing there robed in her own blood.

These, or some other thoughts, ran through his mind. He did not ask a third time. He reached down and she took his hand. He lifted her into the saddle behind him, and together they rode from that dead place. Lord Tollu knew that his warriors would set aside for him the share of what they had won that was rightfully his. Perhaps they would count the girl as part of his share, perhaps not. It was common enough to take slaves from among the conquered, but the Teth at that time were not wont to do so. They would take a noble prisoner sometimes, for ransom, but even that was rare. They slew their enemies and took their enemies' cattle. They knew the difference.

Highest House was not yet built. Ik Imil was the stronghold of the Teth and Lord Tollu's house, and to Ik Imil he returned now that the campaign was over. He gave the girl to the leeches to be healed. He told them who she was, but not the name she had given herself. He just said she was a girl of Va Keep who he had decided should live. He was the Lord, so none of the men spoke against his decision.

His wife and daughters did.

His wife, the Lady Stone, said it was bad luck to bring a wounded child, a child of the enemy, within Ik Imil's walls. The ghost dogs, who follow the scent of blood, might even now be sniffing out her trail. If the Teth's luck changed for the worse they would know that it was their Lord's reckless act that had brought the ghost dogs to them.

His daughters said that bringing the girl into Ik Imil might be read as a reproach to them—as though he were saying that a foreign child had found better favour with him than his own.

Tollu told them to be quiet and say no more.

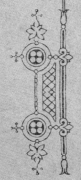

And to confound them, for his nature like many men's nature worked by contraries, he gave the child when she was well again the task of carrying salt to his table.

This was a great honour. The hall at Ik Imil was a hundred strides across and a dozen families ate there. Lord Tollu sat at the highest table with the fire at his back and his wife and daughters at his side. To carry salt to him, Va had to walk past all the other tables, all the lesser families. She carried the salt bowl, which was of beaten brass, and the salt paddle which was of poured silver. She placed these precious things before the Lord, then when he had taken she placed them before his lady, and so on down the ranks of his daughters to Shia Alia, the youngest. Lord Tollu had no sons.

There was great surprise and great remark among the Teth at what their Lord had done, bestowing such a favour on a foreign girl who by rights he should have killed. Those who had kept silent before, about the sparing of her life, complained now at her being raised over slaves with ten or twenty or thirty years of service on their backs.

The soldier who had almost slain her, whose name was Bekt, spoke loudest of all. He said he wondered if his Lord was mad, that he came between a man and his kill without a reason and then set the carrion up in robe and boots to serve him salt.

Lord Tollu came to Bekt in the great hall after meat and mead. He stood before him with his hand on his hilt. "You think me mad?" he asked.

"Only what you did," Bekt said, fearful of Tollu's anger. "Not you."

"And who does mad things but only a madman?" Tollu said.

Bekt saw his death in his Lord's eyes, and did not fight it. He knelt and bared his neck. Tollu took head from shoulders, cleanly, and no man spoke against Va after that. Even the Lady Stone and those lesser ladies who had sprung from her loins kept their counsel. They were not afraid, except of diminishing Tollu in the eyes of his liegemen. Out of love for him they stayed silent, though they had not changed their minds.

Years went by in this wise. The girl Va grew to womanhood. The Lord Tollu grew old.

Every night the girl Va, and then the woman Va, carried salt to him at his table. Every night she picked up the bowl and the paddle from where it stood in the kitchen and carried it along the corridor that led from the kitchen into the hall. The walls of the corridor were rough stone. Nine paces were all it took to walk it from one end to the other.

Every night the girl Va, and then the woman Va, scraped the edge of the salt paddle against the wall. Not for all nine paces. With the first step she could still be seen from the kitchen. With the last step she could be seen from the hall. But for the remaining seven paces she was visible to nobody. So she set the paddle to the stone for those seven paces.

Seven paces were not enough for her to test the sharpness of the edge. She could not stop or slow, or lower her other hand which held the bowl. All she could do was to strop the paddle against the stone, one short stroke every night.

"The girl Va is a woman," Lady Stone said to her husband. "It's not meet that a woman serve salt to you. She might have lain with a man, and the sin of it steal the savour of the salt."

"She has not lain with a man," Lord Tollu said, and he spoke truly. No man of the Teth would lie with her.

"The girl Va is a woman," his daughters said. "You should marry her away to the Luma or the Kashete. Or else make a gift of her."

"I will not marry her away," Lord Tollu said. "Or make a gift of her." And he spoke sense. No man of the Luma or Kashete would take as gift or bride a woman with no kindred.

Time for that girl had stopped when she was spared. Though Tollu had prevented her death, he had not given her life. He knew that now. He should have let her die, or adopted her as his daughter. Either of those things would have been good. But he had held her in between, and now must hold her still.

Years went by in this wise, until one night Va came into the hall, a woman old enough to have daughters and sons of her own. One step she took, then seven steps, then one more. And this night she did not strop the paddle, but instead tested its edge against the skin of her leg. It was sharper than any sword: it laid her flesh open, though she barely pressed at all.

She went on into the hall. She stood before Lord Tollu, and she set down the bowl. But she did not set down the paddle.

At the last moment the Lady Stone saw the blood trickling down Va's leg and guessed she had a weapon. She rose from her place but she was too slow. The paddle was at Lord Tollu's throat and it had broken the skin there though she barely pressed at all. The Lord's arms were at his sides. He could not move before Va slew him, nor no man or woman there could come between.

"You killed my kindred," Va said to the Lord.

"In the way of such things," Tollu answered her. He could not nod. Even in speaking he widened the little wound she had made.

"And now I will kill you," Va said.

"In the way of such things," he answered her. "But let me speak first."

"I will let you speak a dozen words," Va told him. "No more."

Tollu said "I name this girl my daughter. No man or woman harm her."

Then Va drew the paddle across his throat, and Tollu died where he sat.

The warriors in the hall drew their swords and would have slain Va. But the Lady Stone with tears flowing down her cheeks bade them let her be. "My husband was your Lord until he died," she said. "And he gave you a command before he died, which you and I and all of us must obey."

So Va became a woman of the Teth, and when they were done hating her for slaying their Lord they honoured her for her courage and her loyalty to her clan. If she was as loyal to the Teth as she had been to the Va, they said, she would do well enough.

Lord Tollu, as I have said, had no sons. Lady Stone led the Teth for seven years before she died of a fever in the Black Winter.

Then Va led them. She led them well for forty turns of the sun, and they grew mighty under her. Their deeds in war were great and bloody. They won lands in the south that were rich in metal, and a mountain fastness in the north where Highest House now stands.

And she is counted in the lineage of Lord Tollu. And so are her children, and the children they bore.

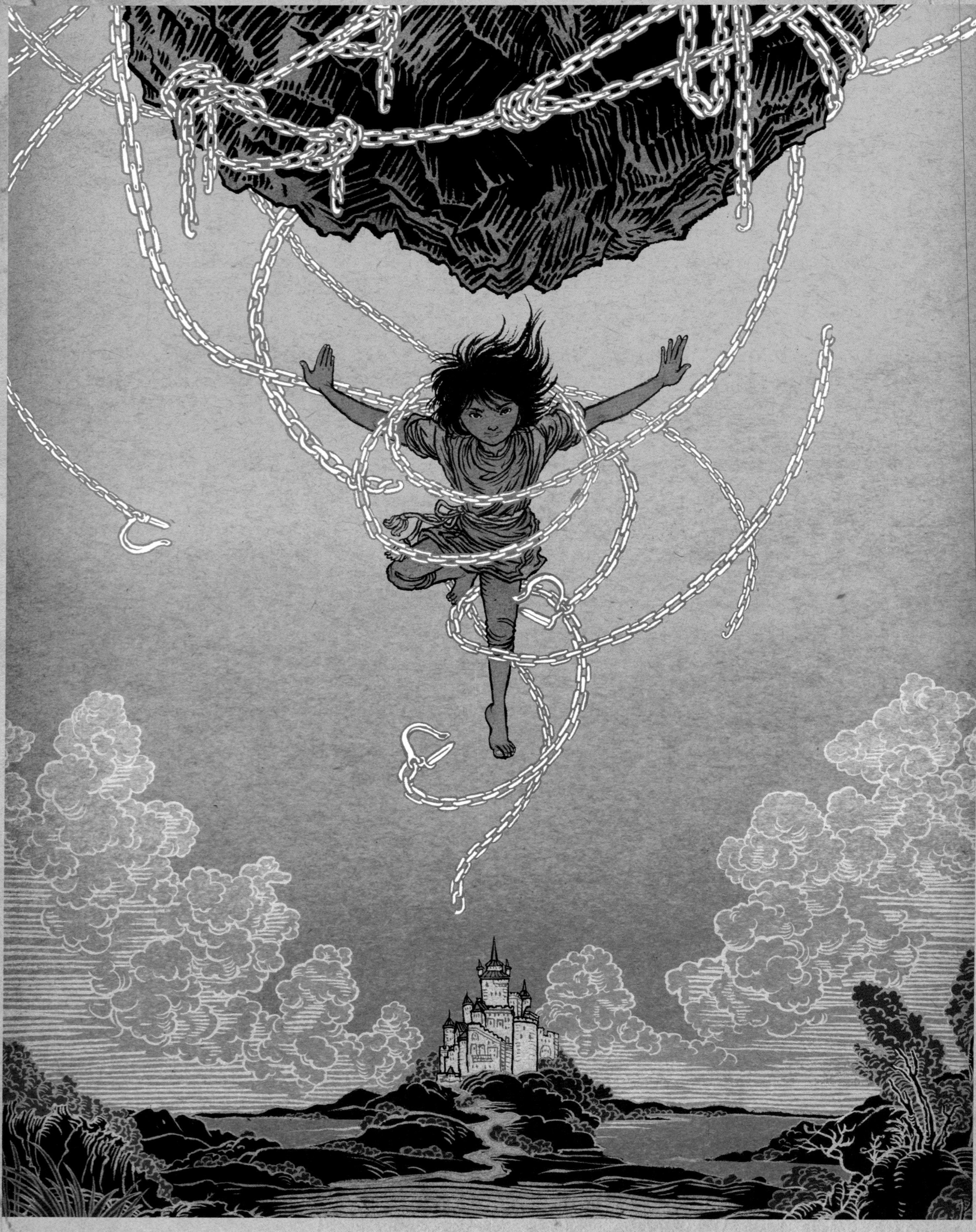

art by YUKO SHIMIZU

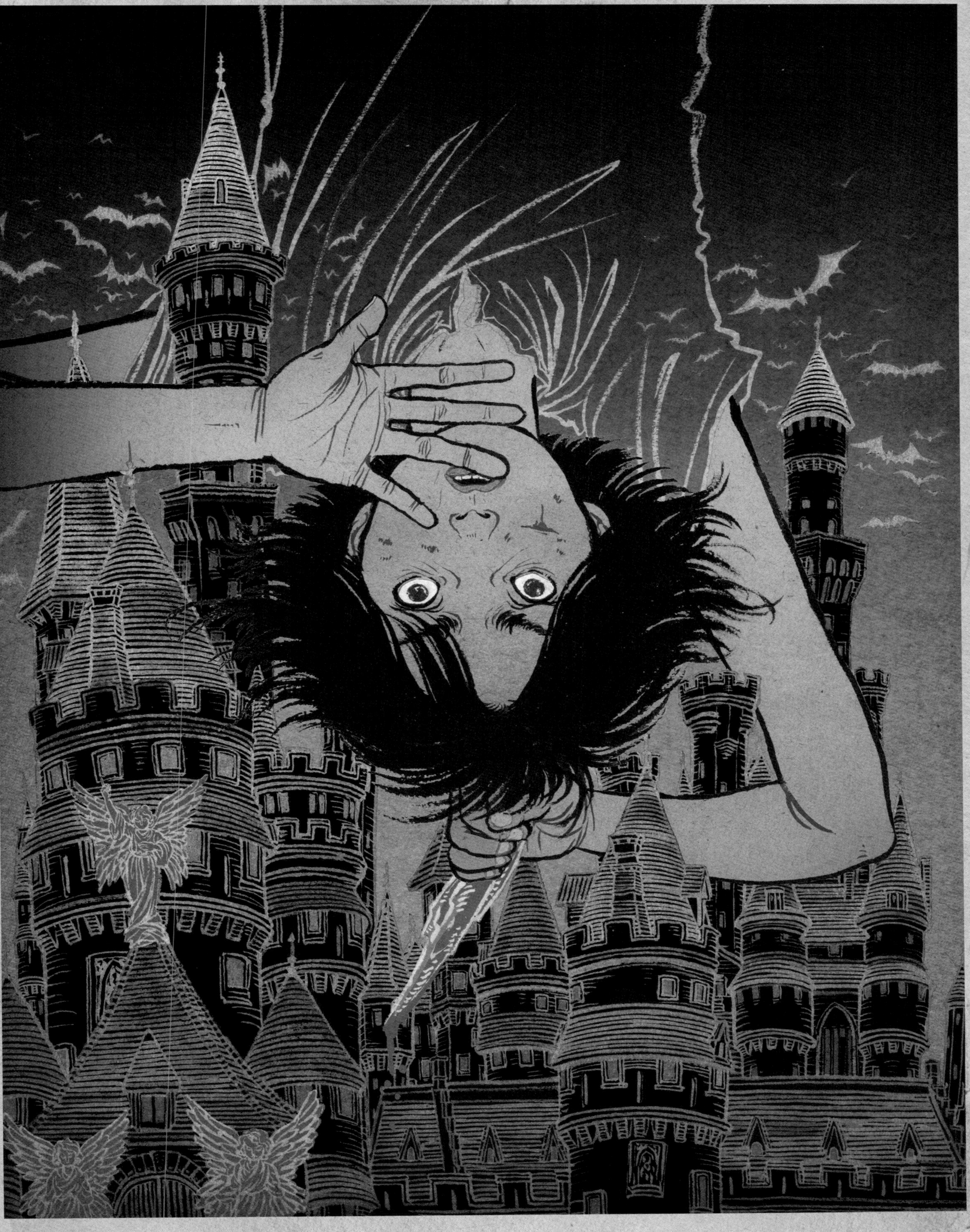

art by YUKO SHIMIZU

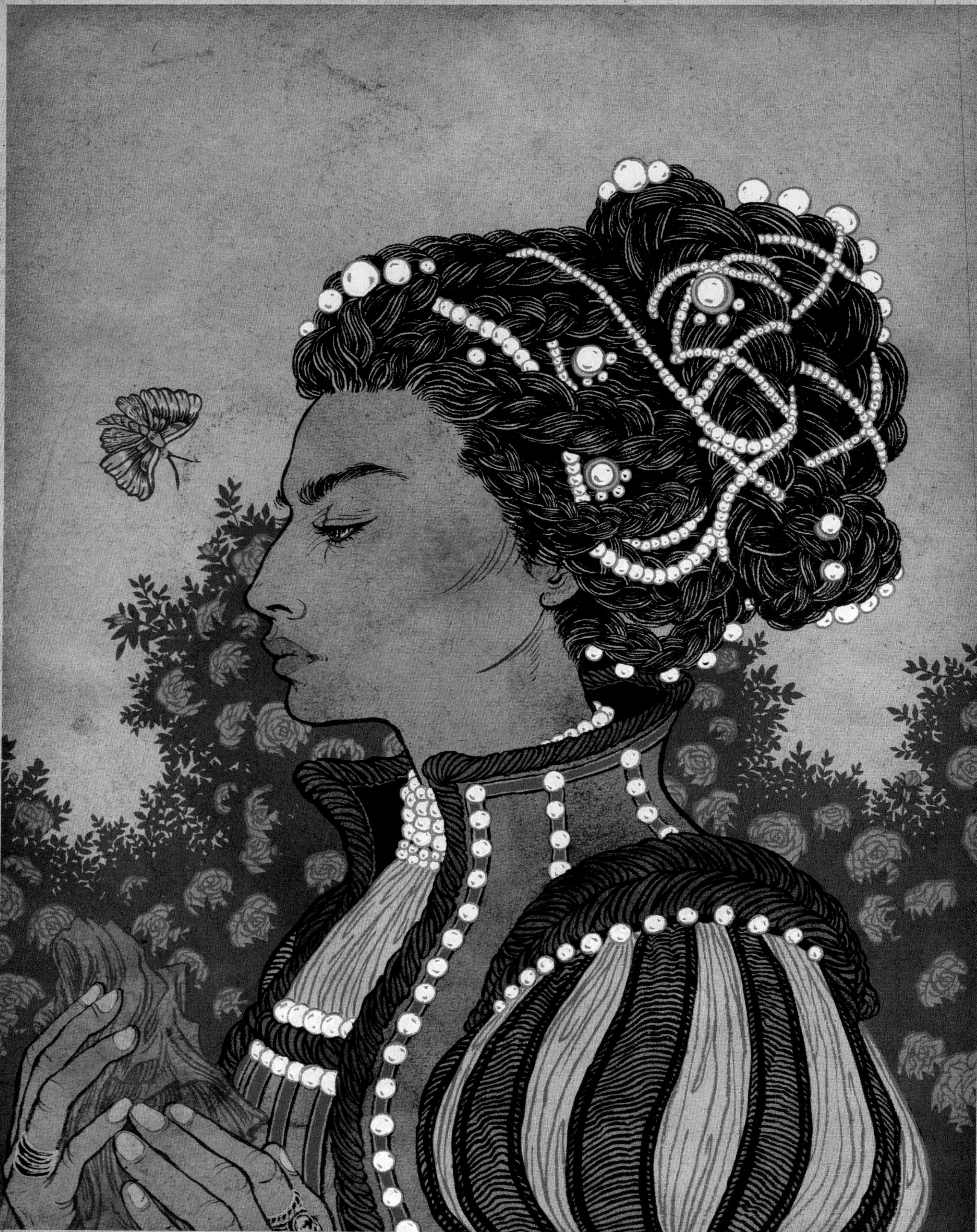

art by YUKO SHIMIZU

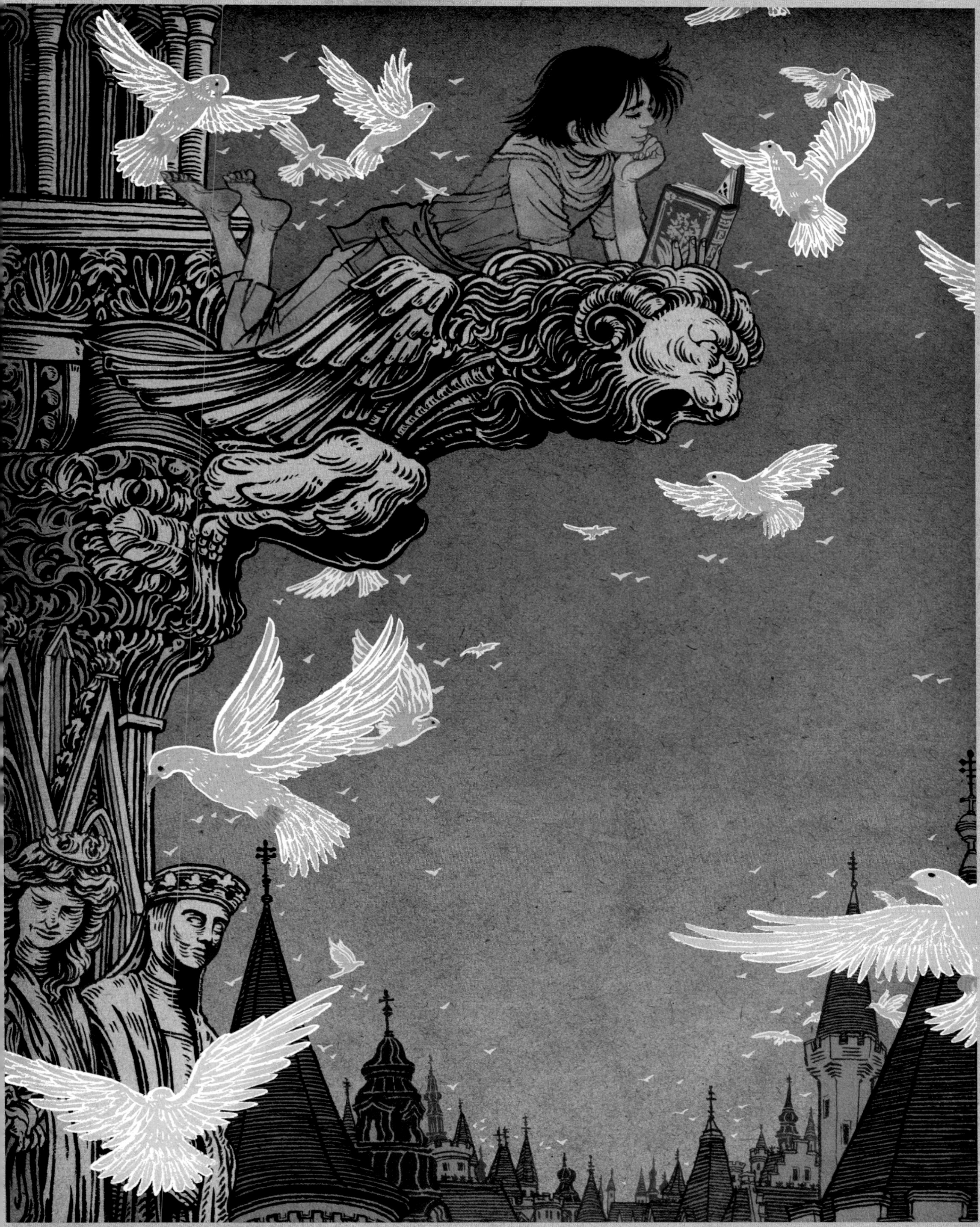

art by YUKO SHIMIZU

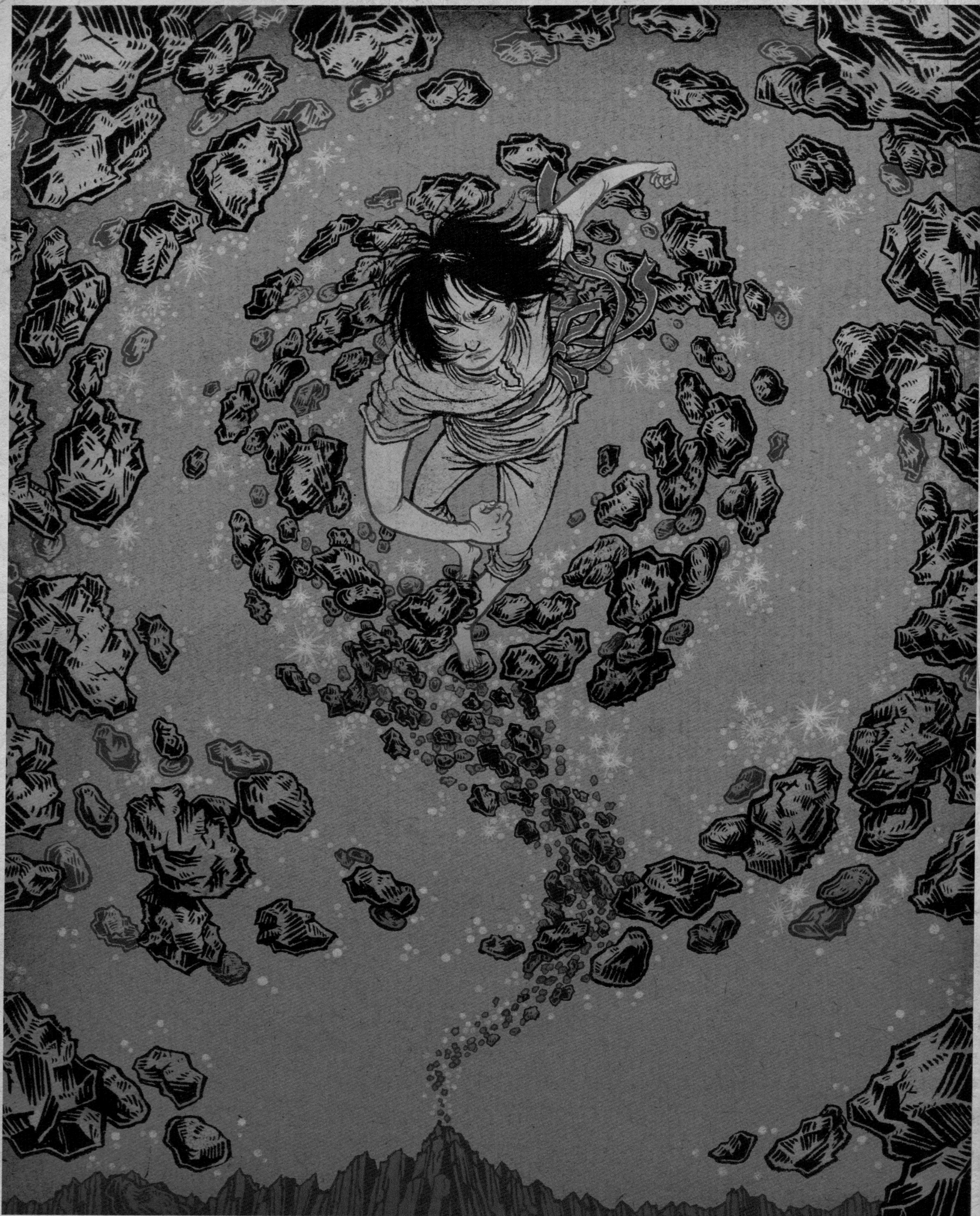

art by YUKO SHIMIZU

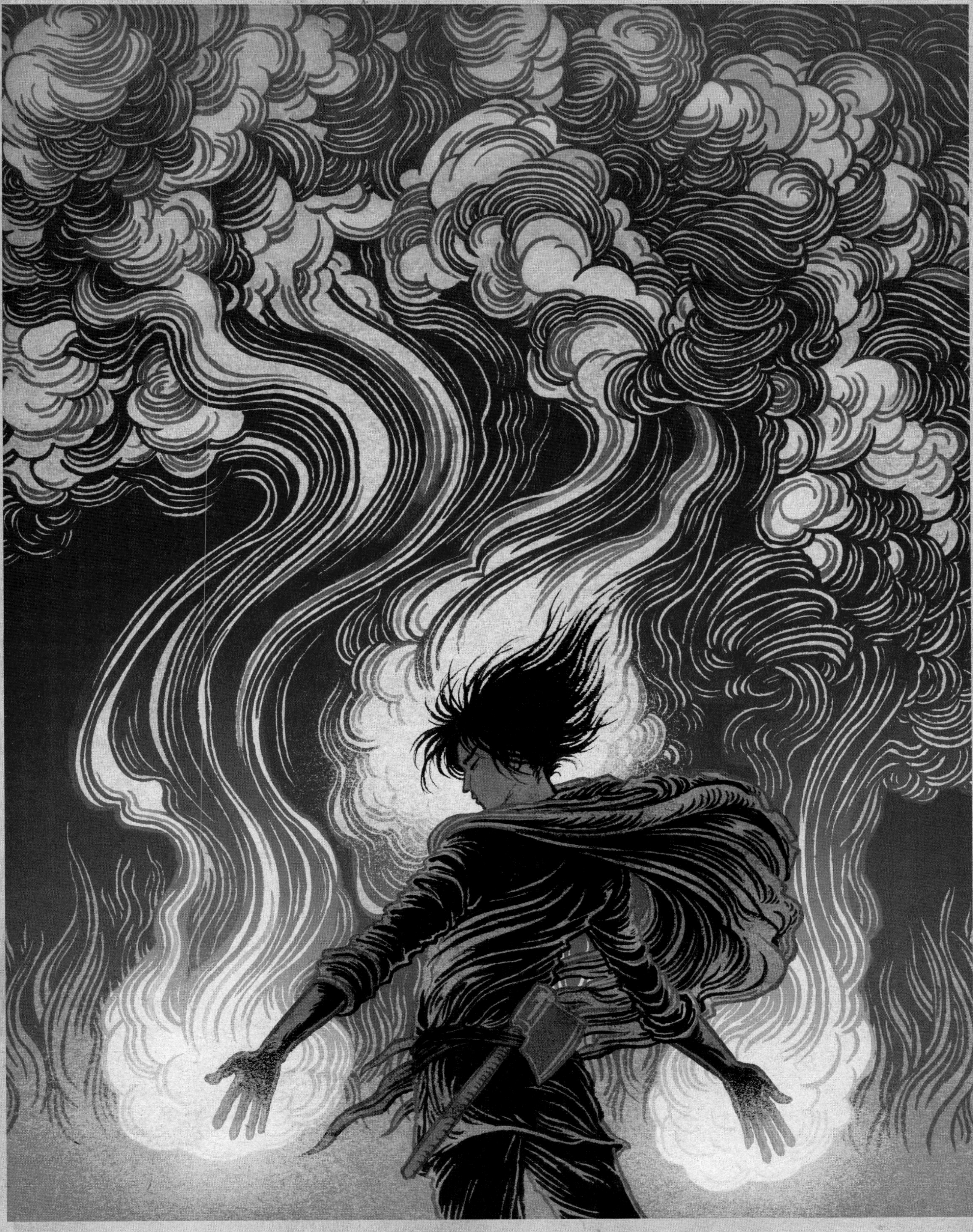

art by YUKO SHIMIZU

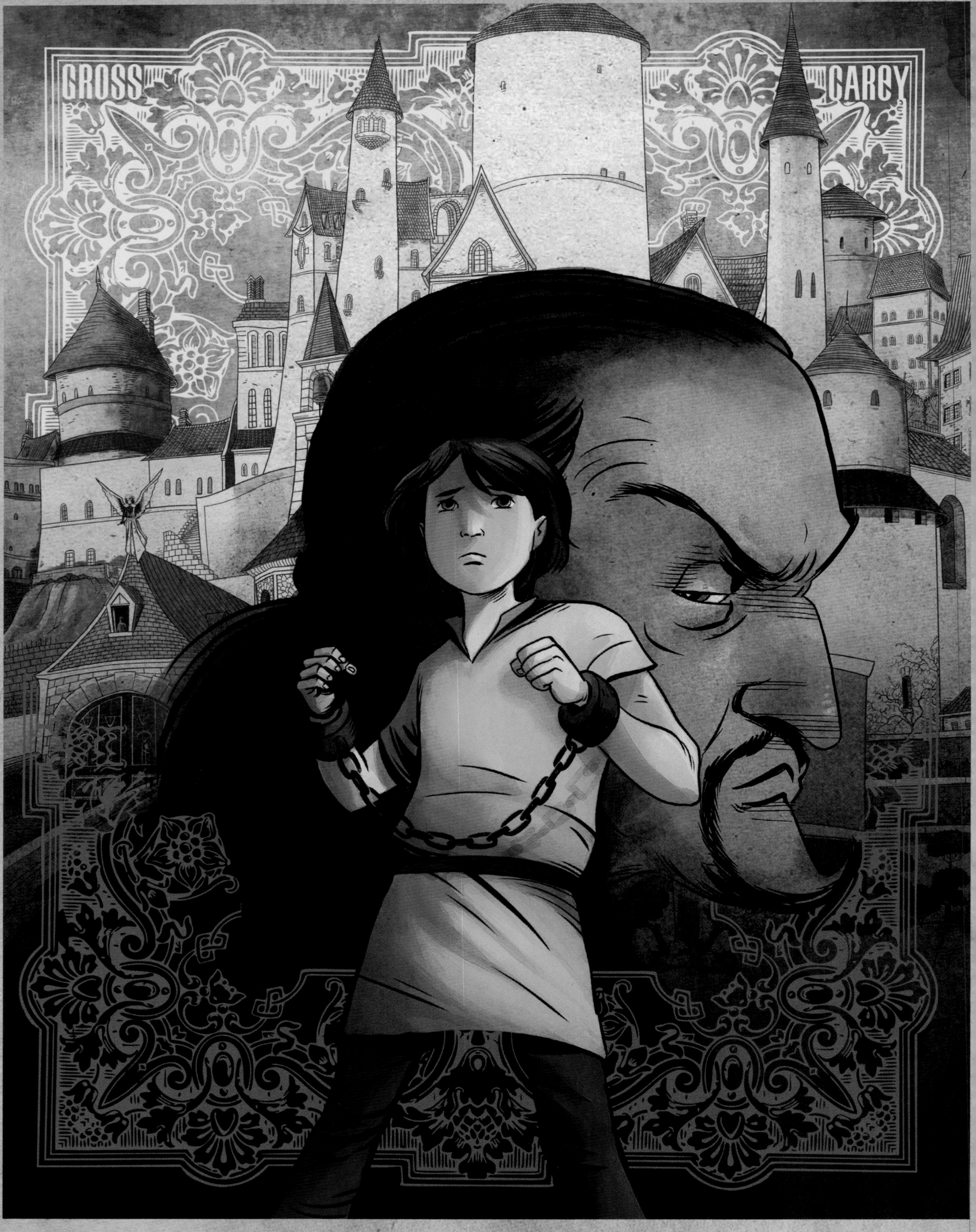
GROSS
CAREY

art by PETER GROSS

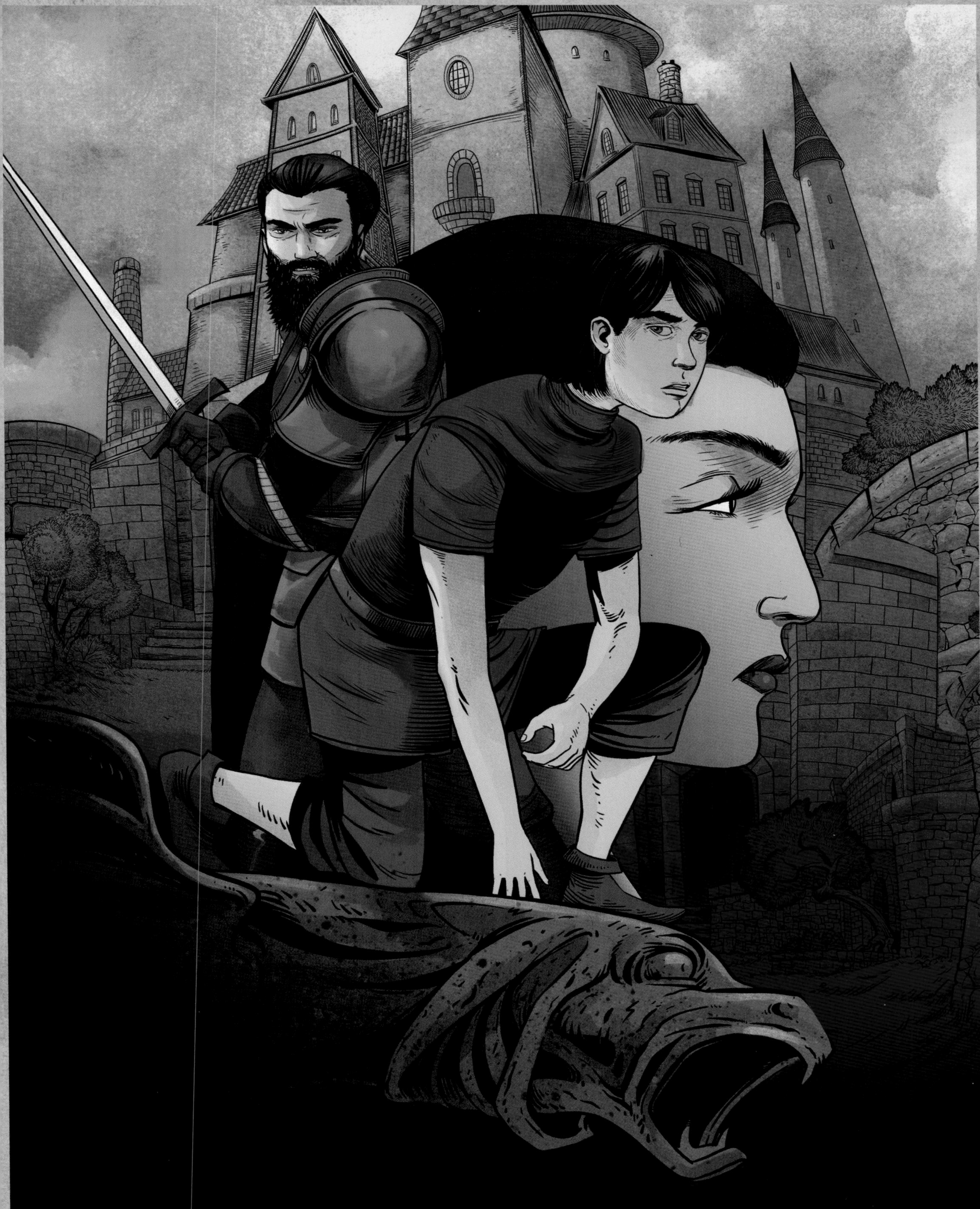

art by PETER GROSS

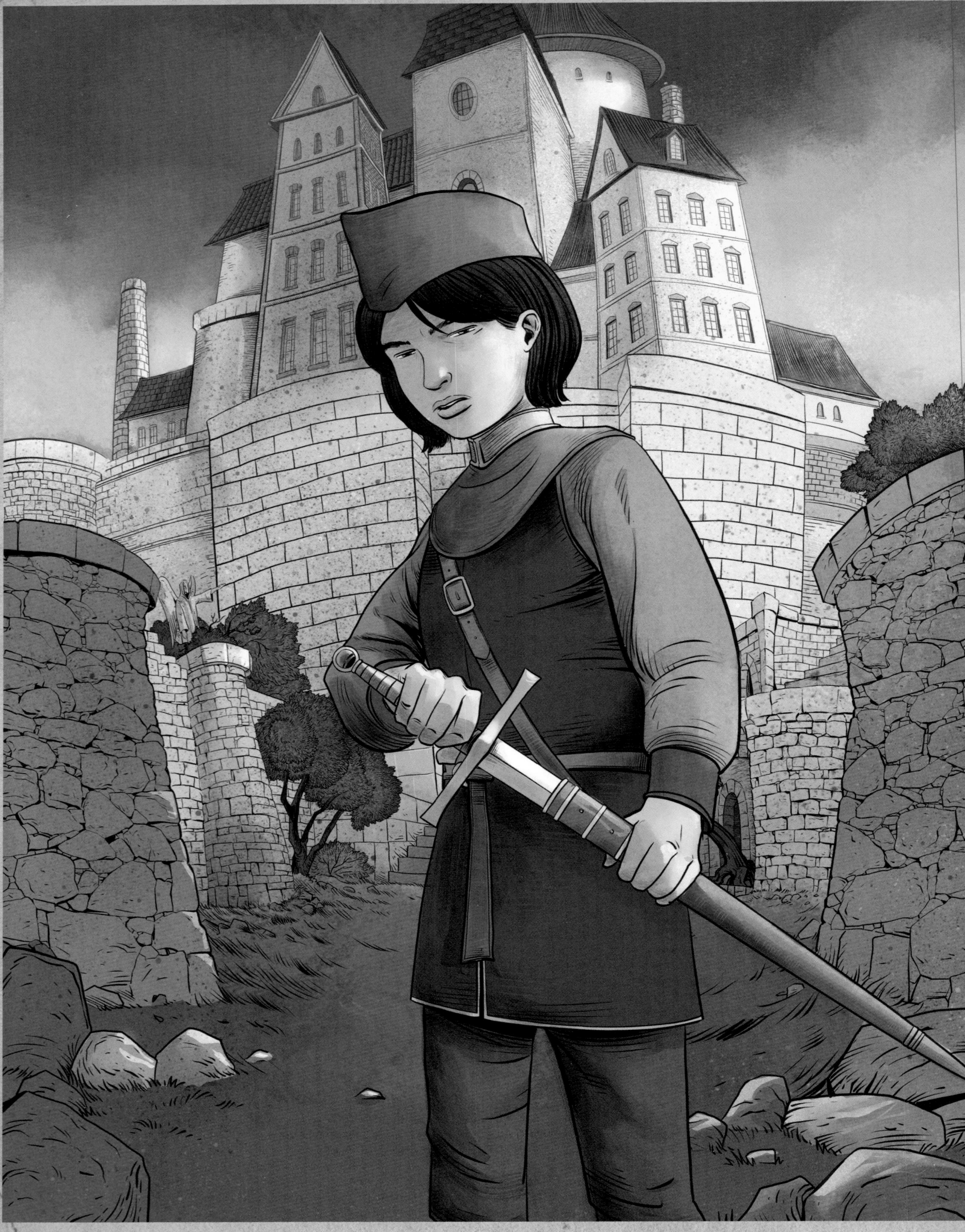

art by PETER GROSS